WRITTEN ON GLASS

It is 1946 and the Temperleys and the Chancellors are old neighbours, living on the south coast of England. Marius Temperley has recently left the army and is struggling to fit into civilian life. His quick-tempered and passionate sister, Julia, has been running the family business since her father's death. When seventeen-year-old Topaz Brooke visits her cousins, Jack and Will Chancellor, for the first time since the outbreak of war, she finds that a great deal has changed. Both brothers are in love with Julia Temperley. As the years go by, family secrets are revealed, and the Temperleys and the Chancellors learn that passion can be both destructive and redemptive.

Books by Judith Lennox
Published by The House of Ulverscroft:

SOME OLD LOVER'S GHOST
THE DARK-EYED GIRLS

Judith Lennox was born in Salisbury, Wiltshire. She read English at Lancaster University and now lives in Cambridgeshire with her husband and three sons. She is the author of six highly praised and topselling novels.

JUDITH LENNOX

WRITTEN ON GLASS

Complete and Unabridged

CHARNWOOD
Leicester

First published in Great Britain in 2002 by
Macmillan
London

First Charnwood Edition
published 2002
by arrangement with
Macmillan Publishers Limited
London

MvB 01/03 .

British Library CIP Data

Lennox, Judith
   Written on glass.—Large print ed.—
Charnwood library series
   1. Domestic fiction
   2. Large type books
   I. Title
   823.9′14 [F]

ISBN 0–7089–9427–X

Published by
F. A. Thorpe (Publishing)
Anstey, Leicestershire

Set by Words & Graphics Ltd.
Anstey, Leicestershire
Printed and bound in Great Britain by
T. J. International Ltd., Padstow, Cornwall

This book is printed on acid-free paper

To my brothers
Christopher and David

Part One

Homecoming

August 1946

1

'Oh, *Topaz*. Your *hat*. It'll be covered in smuts.'

Topaz drew back into the railway carriage. She did not sit down, though, but remained standing, her forearms resting on top of the open window as she looked out at the passing countryside. The whistles and hoots of the engine provided a chorus to the unfolding of the Dorset landscape, with its rolling hills and narrow streams, and fleeting, tantalizing glimpses of a bright, shifting sea.

Some of what she saw was familiar, but a great deal was not. She wondered whether it had changed or whether she had forgotten; after all, it was seven years since she had visited her Chancellor cousins. She had been ten when she had last said goodbye to Jack and Will in 1939. A *baby*.

The war, of course, had left its mark. Ancient meadows had been ploughed up to grow wheat or potatoes and the houses, with their peeling paint and missing rooftiles, had a faded, neglected air. Anti-aircraft posts stood grey against the golden stubble of corn fields and concrete tank traps loomed like hulking giants beside winding country roads.

Her mother spoke again. 'And do close that window. The *dust*.' Veronica Brooke flicked a speck from her pale lilac linen jacket and checked her beautiful face in her compact mirror. 'And tidy your hair.'

Topaz drew up the window and glanced in the mirror. It seemed to her that her hair was as it always was, a longish dark-red clump, but to oblige her mother she pulled off her beret and yanked at the tangles with her comb. There was a sort of fizzing feeling in her stomach, a mixture of excitement and happiness that made it hard to sit quietly as her mother would have preferred. Before the war she had visited her Chancellor cousins every year, staying with them for a fortnight each summer. Those visits stood out in her memory, like pearls on a wooden-bead necklace.

The train slowed as it approached the station. In the distance Topaz glimpsed in the hollow of the valley the grey roof of Missencourt, surrounded by trees. Then she saw the motor car making its way along the narrow road that ran parallel to the railway line. She shrieked and dashed into the corridor, and hurled open a window.

'Will!' she screamed. 'Will!'

From the driver's seat of the car, Will Chancellor waved back. As the engine slowed, Topaz ran along the corridor of the train, jumping over suitcases and holdalls, weaving between standing passengers, darting around pushchairs and dogs as she kept pace with the car.

Her mother's voice followed her as she hurtled through the carriages. 'Oh, *Topaz*.'

The train drew up at the station. As soon as it stopped, Topaz flung open the door and threw herself into Will's arms.

'You've grown,' he said, beaming at her, but the words contained none of the disappointment and criticism that the phrase so often conveyed these days.

At twenty-two, Will was the younger of her two cousins. He, too, had changed: Topaz's memory of Will as a voluble schoolboy, all teeth and glasses and gangling limbs, was replaced by this tall, fair young man, whose features seemed to have hardened and cohered in a way that her own round face had not. Topaz thought that she would remember this moment for ever: after such a long absence, the bliss of being in the place she liked best, with the people she liked best.

The porter had taken Mrs Brooke's luggage. 'Hello, Aunt Veronica,' said Will. 'How lovely to see you.' He kissed her cheek. 'I hope the journey wasn't too frightful.'

'Only one first-class carriage.' Veronica wrinkled her nose in distaste.

Will loaded the luggage into the Austin Seven. Mrs Brooke sat in the front passenger seat, and Topaz climbed into the back behind Will. 'How's Auntie Prudence?' she asked as Will drove away from the station. 'And Uncle John? And the boys — are the boys still awful?'

'Mum's fine. And so's Dad. And the boys are still awful of course; that's what they're for, being awful.' Will's father was a housemaster at a boys' school.

'And Jack? Is he home yet?' Will's elder brother, Jack, was in the army.

'Next week. We had a telegram.'

'I bet Aunt Prudence is thrilled. He's been abroad for ages, hasn't he?'

'Four years. Mum's planning a party to celebrate. She's inviting all the relatives.' Will rolled his eyes.

Topaz remembered Will and Jack as boys, sun and moon, fair, fragile Will, and the older, darker, quieter Jack. Though Will had scrawled a few letters to her during her exile in the Lake District (boy's letters, blotted and brief), she had not heard from Jack, who had sailed with the Royal Engineers to North Africa in the spring of 1942 and had not been back to England since. But then, she told herself, Jack had always been Julia's particular friend.

They had reached the School House. The front door was ajar; catching sight of Prudence Chancellor, Topaz waved and blew kisses.

* * *

After lunch Topaz and Will walked from the School House to Missencourt, the Temperleys' home. Marius and Julia Temperley were Jack and Will's closest friends. All Topaz's best memories of Dorset included the Temperleys.

They talked, filling in a seven-year parting.

'Did you mind, Will?' asked Topaz. 'Did you mind not being in the Forces?'

Will shrugged and pushed his glasses back on to the bridge of his nose. 'It reminded me of games lessons at school — hanging around on the boundary, watching the others, never being in the thick of things. And, of course, with both Jack and Marius in the army, I suppose I felt rather left out.'

Topaz and her mother had spent the war years in an hotel in the Lake District. The hotel had been cold and uncomfortable, and had seemed to exist in a separate world from the one described in the news bulletins on the wireless.

'And teaching . . . ' Will went on. 'Hardly *heroic*.' Will had spent the last three years teaching Latin and science at his father's school, filling in for masters who had been called up.

'Did you hate it?'

He grinned. 'I used to count the days till the end of term. Just like when I went to school there.'

'Will you stay?'

'Not likely. I'm not much good at it, to be honest. They only put up with me because of Dad and because they couldn't get anyone better. Jack was always the brainy one, wasn't he? And, anyway, most of the other masters are back now. And even if I didn't loathe teaching, I wouldn't want to stay *there*. At my father's school, living with my parents. I want to do something more . . . more . . . '

'What?'

'I need to show them I can do something on my own, don't I?'

There were still violet smudges, Topaz noticed, in the

hollows beneath Will's eyes. She asked curiously, 'Does your heart really murmur?'

An attack of rheumatic fever at the age of five had damaged Will's heart. 'I don't know,' he said. 'I've never listened to it.'

'Can I?'

Will paused, and Topaz pressed the side of her head against his chest, listening. Then she drew away. 'I don't know what hearts are supposed to sound like.'

They stood on the verge as a car rattled past. 'Nineteen-thirty-four Riley MPH,' said Will admiringly, watching it disappear round the bend. 'A beauty. Only twenty of them ever made. Terrific acceleration.' Topaz had a sudden memory of a much younger Will, ink blots on his fingers, proudly showing her his list of car numberplates.

She threaded her arm through his as they walked on. 'In the war I used to think about you,' she said. 'You and Jack and Julia and Marius. When I was fed up, I used to imagine this walk from the School House to Missencourt. And here I am, aren't I?' She craned her neck, trying to see the Temperleys' house through the trees. 'And when Jack comes home next week', she went on, 'everything will be just the same as it was before, won't it?'

'Do you think so?'

'Don't you?'

'Well, we were kids then, weren't we? Lots of things have changed.'

'But people still *feel* the same, don't they?' Will didn't reply. 'You must have missed Jack awfully,' Topaz added. Yet she had a sudden, clear memory of an incident from years ago: Jack and Will tossing a coin to see who should ride pillion on horseback behind Julia; the flare of triumph in Will's cornflower blue eyes when he won and the anger in Jack's.

'There's Julia,' said Will, smiling.

7

A bicycle was hurtling towards them. At the foot of the hill, Julia jumped off. 'You're late! I thought you were never coming.' She flung her arms around Topaz. 'I got fed up waiting so I came to meet you.' She stood back, staring at Topaz.

'Go on, say it,' said Topaz resignedly. 'I've grown.'

'Well, you have, haven't you? You've got *bosoms*.'

'*Julia* — ' said Will, embarrassed.

'She has. Much more bosom than me.' Julia was wearing a white cotton shirt and tan-coloured slacks, and her long brown hair was caught back in an untidy ponytail. She was tall and slender, all attenuated limbs and hollowed, patrician features, and large, deep-set grey eyes. It always seemed to Topaz that the way Julia looked didn't go with the way Julia was. That Julia's uncommon beauty gave no warning of Julia's short temper or fatal tendency to act on the spur of the moment.

'Bosoms are an awful nuisance, actually,' said Topaz. 'They get in the way of everything. And when I run, they wobble.'

They turned the corner and there was Missencourt. The elegant, rectangular building fitted perfectly into the backdrop of woodland and valley, its pale Purbeck stone curtained by Virginia creeper. At the back of the house French windows opened on to a paved terrace, which gave on to a wide, sweeping lawn. The tall cypresses that marked the boundaries of the garden cast dark shadows on the grass. In the centre of the lawn was a circular pond. Water lilies floated on its surface. Topaz recalled the carp that swam in the pond, threads of gold in the dark green depths.

And yet even Missencourt had changed. Though the house seemed unaltered by the passing of time, the lawn had been dug up and planted with vegetables, so that grey-green brassicas and the feathery tops of carrots grew in place of the velvety grass of Topaz's memory.

'Mum's out,' explained Julia, 'but Marius is in the study. Go and say hello to him, Topaz. He's longing to see you.'

★ ★ ★

Through the half-open door, Topaz saw Marius Temperley sitting at his desk. He looked up.

'Good Lord. *Topaz*,' he said, rising. 'You look marvellous.'

A welcome change, she thought, from, *you've grown*. And she still had to stand on tiptoes to kiss him. Tall and broad-shouldered, he was brown-haired and light-eyed like all the Temperleys, though in Marius's case, his eyes were not grey, but a faded blue, and the Temperley Roman nose was no longer quite straight, a souvenir of a fight at school many years before.

'I didn't mean to interrupt you.' She indicated the heaps of paper on the desk.

'No, no.' He smiled at her. 'I'd be glad of an excuse to stop, to tell the truth.'

'Are you frightfully busy?' There were stacks of files on top of the cabinets and on the floor.

'There's some sorting out to do. Not', Marius added hastily, 'that Julia didn't do a brilliant job.'

The Temperleys owned a radio-manufacturing business. The offices and workshop were in the nearby village of Great Missen, housed in a disused chapel that had once been the home of an obscure and gloomily self-denying religious sect. When Francis Temperley, Julia and Marius's father, had died during the war, Julia, in Marius's absence, had taken over the running of the business. Will had once tried to explain to Topaz how wirelesses worked, but when he had begun to talk about radio waves her mind had seemed to freeze, clutched by a confused image of the grey, stormy surf at

9

Hernscombe beach somehow sloshing through the skies.

'How are you, Topaz?' Marius asked. 'How was your sojourn in the Lakes? A mixture, I suppose, of boredom and beauty.'

'Yes,' she said, thinking of her seven years' exile. 'Boredom and beauty. That was just about it. It was all right, really. Nice walks. The hotel was awful, though. Silver service for an omelette of dried eggs and a few tinned peas. And I was afraid Mummy might marry one of the colonels.'

'Colonels?'

'There were hordes of them staying at the hotel. They had red faces and handlebar moustaches. They called Mummy the memsahib.'

Marius grinned. 'And now? You're back in London, I assume.'

'Since March.'

'Will you go back to school?'

'No, thank goodness.' She shuddered. 'It would be awful, starting at a new one.'

'So what next?'

'Mummy hopes I'll get married.'

'Anyone in mind?'

She shook her head. 'Sweet seventeen and never been kissed,' she said flippantly. 'Although . . . '

''Although'?' he repeated, brows raised.

'One of the colonels at the hotel once offered me a bar of chocolate in exchange for a kiss.'

'Topaz.'

She said, only slightly ashamed, 'You have no idea how desperate I was for chocolate. And it wasn't so bad, really. His moustache was a bit prickly, though.' She looked at him. 'What about you? Are you glad to be home?'

'Do you know, I think you are the first person to ask me that.'

10

She thought that there was a weariness in his eyes. 'I suppose', she said thoughtfully, 'in some ways being in the army might be . . . *simpler*.'

'In some ways,' agreed Marius. 'But yes, of course I'm glad to be home. It's just . . . different. With Dad gone, especially.'

'Yes, of course. I'm so sorry, Marius.'

'How's your mother?'

'Mummy's very well. Though she was fed up about the flat. You know our old flat was bombed in the war. It's taken ages to find a new one.'

As she talked, she remembered that one of the things she had always liked most about Marius Temperley was that, even when she was a little girl and he was quite grown up, he had always listened properly to her. He hadn't half-listened, as so many people did, while doing something else, or pausing with barely disguised impatience before moving on to someone more important.

'Anyway,' she finished, 'we'd just moved in, and then something went wrong with the boiler. So we came here.'

'Well,' he said, 'I'm delighted that you did.' And she felt her heart lift and soar.

★　★　★

The train stopped at every station from Paddington. All the seats were taken, so Jack Chancellor stood in the corridor, his kitbag propped up beside him. He had been demobilized from the army a week earlier than he had originally expected; now his confidence about surprising his family and not forewarning them of his early release seeped away as he neared his destination. He wished he had phoned, he wished he had sent a telegram. He wished the whole business of coming home was over and that he could go from being away to

11

being back without the messy middle bit of tears and greetings.

Wedged in the corridor between a sailor sleeping off the ill effects of the previous night and a chap smoking a foul-smelling pipe, Jack acknowledged to himself that at the heart of his doubts lay Julia. If Julia still cared for him then he would be happy; if she did not, then he might as well have remained in Italy.

At Yeovil he left the London train and took the little branch line that plunged south through the hills to Longridge Halt. Settling into a corner seat, his thoughts returned to Julia. They had known each other from infancy. Their mothers' friendship had meant that they, too, were destined to be friends. Then, at nineteen, Jack had joined up. He had been posted to a training camp in the north of England. In 1941, returning home for a fortnight's leave, he had seen Julia through different eyes. She seemed to have grown up in his absence — or was it he who had changed, altered and toughened by army life, in the course of which he had acquired a tentative sexual confidence? He had seen her for what she was, a startlingly beautiful and desirable young woman.

The miracle (even now he still thought it miraculous) was that she had felt the same way about him. Jack never expected things to be easy, always anticipated difficulty. Walking Julia home from the School House to Missencourt, he had kissed her for the first time. Touching her finely grained skin, her full mouth, had been another homecoming. Though he had been cautious at first, afraid of rejection, she had responded to him. A few days later, in the privacy of the woods behind Great Missen, he had stroked her breasts and had run his fingertips down the flat, soft musculature of her stomach.

They had been late back to Missencourt that day. Julia's father — clever, charming Francis Temperley

12

— had been standing at the end of the drive, waiting for them. 'Thought you'd got lost,' was all he had said, but something in his eyes had made the skin on the back of Jack's neck crawl, sensing danger. And afterwards there never seemed to be the opportunity to spend time alone with Julia.

Afterwards he had ached for her. Before being posted abroad, he had been given a brief twenty-four hours' leave and had headed for Missencourt. In the room that had once been Julia and Marius's playroom, with its curling maps of the world and yellowing reproductions of old masters, they had clung to each other. Her hair had drifted against his face as he had drawn her to him, his hands tracing the contours of her body, his mouth hungry, searching. She had said, her voice shaking, *I don't want you to go, Jack, I don't want you to go*, and he had opened his eyes and focused on the pinkish shape of Africa pinned to the wall behind her, aware of a mixture of happiness and desperation. He had told her that he loved her and, through the approaching footsteps in the corridor, he had believed that he had heard her whisper in return that she loved him.

They had sprung apart just before her parents came into the room. The remainder of the evening had been a torment. Jack had stumbled in his replies to Adele Temperley's kind enquiries about his future and he had gabbled nonsensical responses to Francis Temperley's words of advice. When he had taken his leave after half an hour, there had been a hundred things he had wanted to say to her. But, 'You'll write, won't you?' was all he had managed as Julia stood on the doorstep, flanked by her parents. Then he had walked away down the drive and Missencourt's front door had slammed shut before he could turn around for a last glimpse of her. The following day he had left for Plymouth, to embark on the long voyage to North Africa.

Julia had written long, cheerful letters to him that

made fun both of wartime austerities and of her own attempts to fill her absent elder brother Marius's place in her father's business. In Egypt, in Sicily, and in Italy, Julia's mocking voice had echoed as Jack had turned the pages of her letters, and her grey, teasing eyes had gazed down at him. 'Oh, for Heaven's sake, smile, Jack,' he had imagined her saying. 'Always so serious.' And he had managed, most of the time, a grin.

The only time her cheerfulness had failed her had been when Francis Temperley had died. *The most terrible thing, Jack. Daddy has died of a heart attack. I don't know how I shall bear it.* And then a long gap, six months during which she had not written. At that time Jack had been working his way up the battered spine of Italy, shoring up bridges, detonating those which could not be saved, laying pontoons. He had written to Julia, but he had never been much good at saying what he felt, and his words had stared back at him, failing to convey the depths of his sympathy. *When I come home,* he had promised himself, *when I come home I will make it up to her.*

Throughout the war years he had looked forward to the moment of their reunion. And yet, returning to England, his optimism had begun to falter. The country had changed for the worse in his absence. London, with its heaps of rubble and ruined streets and squares, had taken him by surprise in its unwelcoming dreariness. He had been shocked by the uniform drabness of his fellow countrymen's appearance, and by their complaints and pushiness. After he had left the demob centre, a greasy little fellow had sneaked out of the shadows and offered him a tenner for his army-issue suit. Jack had sent him away with a flea in his ear. Later, climbing on to the train at Paddington, a middle-aged man had elbowed in front of him and plonked his fat behind on the last vacant seat. A fellow soldier had caught Jack's eye and shrugged, a small, eloquent raising of the shoulders that said, *civvies*.

The long, slow, train journey had given ample time for all his doubts to multiply. Julia, after all, had been only seventeen when he had left England in 1942. Still a schoolgirl. Far too young to know her own mind. And even if she had once felt something for him, she might no longer do so now. She might have forgotten or regretted the fleeting intimacies they had shared.

The train was slowing for Longridge Halt. Jack gathered up his kitbag and overcoat. With a final screech and hiss of steam, the engine drew to a halt.

He was the only passenger to alight at the station. As the train drew away, he began to walk, not to the School House, but towards Missencourt. He'd see Julia first, he decided, and then he'd go home. It wasn't as though his parents were expecting him today.

After the stuffy train journey it was a pleasure to breathe fresh air. The walk calmed him and the cloudless sky raised his spirits, lessening his exhaustion and unease. The fields in the lower part of the valley bristled with golden corn stubble and on the higher slopes sheep grazed, little puff-ball blobs. Soon, Jack promised himself, soon he would go and see Carrie and Sixfields. The narrow road curved through the woodland that surrounded Missencourt. The trees soared overhead, blotting out the sky. Jack thought of all the things he was going to say to Julia. This time he wouldn't let anything stop him.

He left the road, taking the path through the trees that led to the perimeter of the Temperleys' garden. The sound of a distant ripple of laughter made his heart leap. Jack gazed over the lawn to the terrace and saw her. She was sitting in a deckchair. She was wearing a shirt and trousers: the boyish clothes and the different, older Julia, jolted him.

There was someone with her. A man, sitting beside

her. Jack did not immediately recognize him. Fair-haired, slight . . . *Will*, he realized. And as he watched, Julia reached out and ruffled Will's hair in a gesture that spoke to Jack of both intimacy and affection.

Once, in Italy, Jack had been shinning along the struts beneath a bridge, checking its roadworthiness for an oncoming convoy, when he had caught sight of the black, lumpy shape of a grenade, hidden in the V between the metal girders. A careless movement, or his weight placed on the wrong part of the crumbling structure, and the grenade might have gone off. In an instant, a day that had previously been bright and unthreatening had altered, menacing his entire future. He remembered that moment now.

He must have made some sort of sound because Julia rose to her feet, staring at him, her eyes wide, her lips parted. She didn't, he thought grimly, look exactly pleased to see him. He crossed the garden to the terrace.

★ ★ ★

She couldn't believe it was him at first. She looked up and saw the man standing in the shadow of the trees, and thought for one mad, mind-twisting moment that it was her father. Her heart lurched and she began to shake. By the time she was able to stand, by the time elation had begun to take over from shock, Jack had reached the terrace, and was saying in a cold, drawling voice, 'Thought I'd drop by for a few minutes on my way home. But you seem to be busy.'

She flung her arms around him and kissed him. He did not respond, did not hug or kiss her in return. Feeling bewildered and foolish and suddenly frightened, she stood back. Jack shook hands with Will. Her voice trembling slightly, she offered Jack a drink, but he refused, saying, 'Better not. Things to do.' Will asked

16

him questions about his journey and about Italy, questions that Jack answered curtly and uninformatively, and which she herself hardly heard for the panic welling up inside her. Jack didn't smile, and there was a hardness and distance about him that went with his altered appearance: the thickened outline of his shoulders, the layers of sunburn that stained his skin brown. He had become, Julia thought, her shock returning, a stranger.

After Jack and Will and Topaz had gone, knowing that she must be alone because she was going to explode, Julia went to the kitchen with the excuse of preparing the dinner. There she took one of the plainest plates from the dresser and hurled it against the wall, where it smashed into a great many little pieces. Then she sat down at the table, put her head in her hands and wept. After a while, she blew her nose on a tea towel and scrubbed her eyes, and tried to calm down. One of Julia's paddies, her father would have said affectionately.

But thinking of her father didn't help, so she lit a cigarette and began to clear up the broken bits of plate. She felt both exhausted and restless at the same time. Since she had heard of Jack's imminent demobilization, she had been able to think of little else. The years had fallen away and, for the first time since her father's death, she had recalled the possibility of happiness. It was as though, with Jack's return, things could begin to come right again.

She had always loved Jack. She couldn't remember a time without Jack. When they were children, she and Jack had been inseparable. Will had often been unwell and because Marius had always moved on to the next stage (prep school, big school, work) before the rest of them, the four had often been reduced to two. Julia and Jack had climbed trees together, ridden together, sailed together. He had matched her recklessness with a

17

carelessness and confidence that she had secretly envied.

The army had changed Jack. He had looked at her differently, treated her differently. Encountering this older, altered Jack, she had felt an answering excitement. When he had kissed her, one kind of love had metamorphosed into another. The intensity of her pleasure in his touch had taken her by surprise, though it had not surprised her that it was Jack who had made her feel this way because Jack had always been hers.

Then he had gone away, posted abroad with his regiment. After Julia had left school, she had helped her father at the radio workshop. From early 1941, Temperley's had been in operation twelve hours a day, six days a week, making radios for military use. Julia, who was bored by both the domestic and the academic, had discovered that the demands of the job helped to fill the gaps left by the absence of Marius and Jack. She had been secretly relieved that her work had spared her the obligation of joining one of the women's Services: the WAAFs or the Wrens would have meant leaving home and sleeping in a dormitory with lots of other women, which she would have loathed.

She hadn't thought much about what she and Jack would do when the war ended. Sometimes, when all the news seemed to be bad, it had felt to her as if it would never end. And when at last the tide turned she remained superstitiously afraid that if she dared to make plans, then she would lose him.

But it wasn't Jack who was taken from her, but her father. Tragedy had come unexpectedly, while she was off guard. She remembered every detail of that terrible day. It had been a wet Sunday in October and her father had taken the dogs out for a walk. He'd asked her to go with him, but she hadn't because she'd been riding and was drenched. She remembered her father saying, *A bit more rain won't make any difference then, will it, darling?* but she had shaken her head and dashed upstairs to find a towel. A small decision, but one she had since regretted a thousand times. An hour later, while she was playing the piano, there had been a knock at the door. Her mother had answered it. She could not make out the words, but the tenor of the voices had given her a first inkling of disaster, and she had lifted her hands from the piano keys and waited, fear uncoiling in her stomach. *Jack,* she'd thought, *Jack.*

But it wasn't Jack. One of her father's employees had found him curled up beside a stile, almost as though he'd settled down for a nap. Sally, the old labrador, had been crouched beside him. They hadn't let her go to him; she had hated them for that. She had spent the afternoon searching for Rob the puppy, who had bolted. She had walked for miles, eventually discovering the dog soaked and shivering, its lead tangled in a blackthorn bush.

That day had changed her life in many ways. It wasn't simply the grief that had seemed always to fill her head, wearing her out with its constant proximity. Almost equally shocking was the abrupt realization that bad things could happen to her, to Julia Temperley. Whatever catastrophes the past few years had brought to others, they had not touched her. She was intelligent enough to know that the war had given her opportunities she would not otherwise have had. If it had not been for the outbreak of hostilities, then Marius would have been working for the family business, not she. She had no idea what she would have done in peacetime; she had never been able to imagine herself doing any of the sorts of job women did.

But when her father had died she had understood the precariousness of happiness. She hadn't written to Jack for months afterwards because she had been unable to find anything in her desolate soul worth sharing. When she had begun to write again, it had been an effort to disguise the changes in her, to pretend she was still Jack's old, familiar Julia. She viewed her former self with contempt: spoilt, naive, childish Julia, who had thought her happy, safe little world would go on for ever.

After her father's death her relationship with her mother, never close, worsened. Adele's obvious grief angered her. Julia had hated it that her mother had taken to wearing blacks and greys and to refusing social invitations, gestures which seemed to Julia to be born of exhibitionism, of a desire to parade her feelings, and demand sympathy. A small part of Julia had known this to be unreasonable, but she had pushed the knowledge away, refusing to let herself cry in public, missing work only to attend the funeral. She knew that a great many people assumed that with Francis Temperley dead and his son in northern France, Temperley's Radios must fold. She had refused to let that happen: her father had created Temperley's, and she would keep it alive for him. Fuelled by a mixture of rage and obstinacy, she forced herself to step into her father's shoes. By then Temperley's was manufacturing the basic civilian receivers specified by the Ministry of Supply. At first she made mistakes, took bad decisions, and for a while Temperley's lurched dangerously close to disaster. That they survived was, she knew, due far more to the experience and loyalty of the foreman and technicians than to her own bumbling efforts. But by the beginning of 1945, they had caught up with the backlog of orders and the War Ministry was no longer breathing down their necks with accusations of inefficiency.

Throughout this dark time she had longed for Jack. When Jack came home, she had told herself, everything would be all right again. But Jack remained in Italy and, even after the war in Europe ended in May 1945, the long process of demobilization seemed agonizingly slow.

In Jack's absence Julia spent much of her spare time

with his younger brother, Will. Never a patient person, bereavement had hardened her, robbing her of what little forbearance she had. She was short-tempered with her old friends and hadn't the energy or enthusiasm to make new ones. She hated people for mentioning her father, seeing their expressions of sympathy as motivated only by duty, yet she also hated them for not mentioning him — how could they fail to understand that he was constantly on her mind? She knew that she was touchy and impossible, but could not seem to change herself. Only Will, whom she had known all her life, seemed to understand — and forgive — her sharp tongue, her moodiness. In the early days, during that first bleak Christmas without her father, Will accompanied her on long walks through the frosty countryside as she tried to wear herself out enough to be able to sleep at night. He tried to cheer her up, taking her to the cinema, sitting with her through an excruciating pantomime at the village hall. He taught her to drive: lessons which, because of petrol rationing, took place mostly in the garage and courtyard of the School House, with Julia operating the pedals and gearstick, and Will describing to her imaginary traffic. He brought her gifts: a novel he had found in a secondhand bookshop, a wooden pencil box he had made for her, a bunch of violets gathered from the copse. He listened when she needed to talk and put up with her silences, was good-humoured when she was snappish, reassuring when she was despairing. Above all, he was *fun*. Sometimes, with Will, she found herself forgetting her grief and laughing.

Though they never spoke of it, Julia guessed how much Will minded being declared unfit for military service. She thought that they both had in common that they had been left behind to carry out unglamorous, necessary tasks. You didn't get a medal, she had once said wryly, for working through the night to fulfil a War

21

Ministry order. You didn't get medals, Will had responded, for putting up with the Third Form.

It had been in front of Will that she had, at last, cried. They had taken a rare day off and had cycled to the coast. Halfway there, skirting the land that belonged to Will's mad Cousin Carrie, they had paused at the top of a hill to catch their breath. The early spring sunshine, with its promise of warmer days to come, had washed over the fields and the distant sea. Julia had thought how much her father would have loved it, and had howled and howled for *hours*. Most men, she had thought afterwards, would have run a mile, faced with an hysterical woman, but Will had just held her and mopped her tears and hadn't even looked embarrassed. Then, when he had seen she was ready for distraction, he had told her about his favourite cars and about his plan to run a garage when the war was over.

That had been the first time it had crossed her mind to wonder whether Will was attracted to her. She had dismissed the idea almost immediately: Will had been nice to her because he was, simply, *nice*. Yet the question had remained, somewhere at the back of her mind, reassuring and comforting. Will's company was enjoyable and easy. He never argued with her, was never critical of her. Now, faced with the memory of the cold judgement in Jack Chancellor's eyes, Julia found herself wondering furiously whether she had wasted the past few years hankering after the wrong brother.

★ ★ ★

At the School House Prudence Chancellor had escaped Veronica by going out into the garden to bring in the washing. She unpegged the rows of garments slowly and carefully, folding each one neatly, placing it in the basket. There were two long lines of washing and she thought that perhaps by the end of the second one her

22

normally even temper would have recovered. Tomorrow, slipping over to Missencourt for a cup of tea with Adele Temperley, she'd be able to laugh. 'One of the boys dropped a glass of water on the floor while I was dishing out the supper,' she'd tell Adele. 'And Veronica just *sat there*. Didn't go and get the dustpan and brush to sweep up the glass, or mop up the water with a napkin, or offer to take over serving while I cleared up. Just sat there looking disapproving, as though she was waiting for some non-existent servants to sort everything out.'

Prudence sighed and moved on to the second line of washing. She really must make an effort, she thought. Talk to Veronica about the things that interested her — though it sometimes seemed to Prudence that her sister-in-law really wasn't interested in anything but herself — and make sure the boys didn't bother her.

Glancing back into the house, she saw, through the long tunnel of corridor, that the front door had opened. Will had come into the house. There was someone with him. Prudence thought at first that it was Marius, and then, looking again, she knew that it was not. She had to put down the washing basket because her fingers suddenly seemed to have lost their strength. She stood, staring through the intervening layers of window and door, at her elder son, whom she had not seen for four years.

She had always imagined that when — if — Jack came home, she would run to him, take him in her arms. But, overwhelmed by the intensity of her emotions, she could not for a moment move. She stood alone in the garden, knowing that no one, not even Jack himself, should see her like this. Then, when she was able to bear such happiness, she wiped her eyes with a clean duster from the basket and went indoors to greet her son.

2

Carrie Chancellor never opened Sixfields' heavy front door (Jack had always assumed it was glued to the jamb by a paste of damp and cobwebs), so he walked to the back of the house. The dogs began to bark as he crossed the stone flags, but he clicked his fingers and they ran to him, nuzzling their noses at his outstretched hand. The scullery door was open, so he went indoors and stood at the foot of the stairs and called out Carrie's name. From above, he heard the uneven tread of her feet and the click of her stick on wooden floors.

The house was just as Jack remembered it, something between a treasure cave and a junk shop. Sixfields farmhouse was a large, rambling building, begun in medieval times and added to throughout the centuries. From the outside the different levels of roofline and the many walls out of true gave a pleasing impression; indoors, ceilings lowered suddenly, cracking the heads of the tall and unwary, and narrow passageways snaked between a multitude of irregularly shaped rooms. The small, dusty windows and Carrie's aversion to electricity contributed to the confusing nature of the house by ensuring that it was permanently plunged into a greyish gloom.

Carrie's aversion to throwing things away added to the difficulty in negotiating the building. Every shelf and cupboard was overflowing, and the floors were scattered with a treacherous mixture of threadbare rugs and yellowing newspapers. Jack wondered whether, if he glanced closely at the newspapers, he would glimpse a headline about the Great Exhibition or the opening of the Suez Canal. Odd little Victorian knick-knacks — an elephant's foot umbrella stand, a nest of occasional tables — clustered in darkened corners. On the walls, faded eighteenth-century engravings mingled with creased photographs and lists of stock prices at Dorchester Fair. Every item of furniture, every niche and shelf was heaped with books and papers and boxes, covered with a liberal felting of dust. Looking around, Jack glimpsed an old parasol with an ivory handle lying discarded on top of a bookcase and a cracked pair of gaiters peeping from beneath an armchair. He wondered whether some long-dead Chancellor had discarded them decades ago and they had simply never been tidied up.

A voice said, 'Jack,' and he looked up, and saw Carrie standing at the top of the stairs.

He knew better than to offer to help her down, so he smiled and said, 'I hope it's not an inconvenient time to call, Cousin Carrie. Only I've just got home.'

'I heard.' She hobbled downstairs and paused, drawing level with him.

Carrie was twice Jack's age and more than a head shorter. An attack of polio twenty-eight years before had left her with a withered left leg and one shoulder higher than the other. There was, nevertheless, something imposing about her. Now, under the gaze of her sharp blue eyes, Jack had to force himself not to turn away.

Eventually she said, 'You'd like some cider, I suppose,' and he concluded that he had passed some sort of test.

When they were sitting in the parlour, he said, 'I see you've ploughed up the Great Meadow.'

'Had to. Ted Pritchard insisted, the interfering so-and-so. For the war effort, he said.' Carrie snorted derisively. 'Told him that field was all thorn and flint, but he wouldn't listen. He said that if I didn't plough, some busybody committee would take over the farm. I'd have liked to have seen them try *that*.'

Jack imagined Carrie holed up in Sixfields' attic,

taking potshots at the War Agricultural Committee. She went on, 'I reminded him that his grandfather was my grandfather's plough-boy. And I told him I'd set the dogs on him if he brought anyone nosing around, causing trouble. So he backed down, of course.' Carrie sneered. 'Never could stomach a coward. Anyway, I ploughed up the field so that I didn't have to see the fool again.' She knotted her callused fingers around her glass. 'It was war this, war that, for years, you know, Jack. They even tried to park some evacuees on me.' Carrie cackled. 'Didn't last the week. Didn't like the house. Even the land girl sleeps in the cottage.'

'Land girl?'

'There were four to begin with. Just the one now. No staying power, these modern girls.'

Jack felt a momentary sympathy for the unknown, unfortunate land girls. He looked at Carrie.

'It can't have been easy running the place on your own.'

Carrie raised a crooked shoulder. 'I'm used to it. I don't complain. Busy time of year, though. You're lucky to catch me in, Jack. Mark Crabtree still works for me, and his sons now that they're back. And they're sending me prisoners of war to help bring in the harvest.'

'I'll give you a hand, if you like,' he said. 'As soon as all the fuss is over.'

'Will you, Jack? Good. Four in the morning sharp, mind. Don't be late.'

He remembered his errand. 'My mother said to tell you that we're having a little get-together — '

'The return of the hero?'

He muttered, 'Something like that. This afternoon.'

'And you've brought me an invitation? How thoughtful,' said Carrie sarcastically. 'You know I don't attend family parties.'

He thought, *But if you hadn't been invited, you'd*

26

never have let us hear the end of it. 'I'll tell Mum no, then,' he said.

There was a silence. Carrie was frowning, as though thinking hard about something. Eventually she said, 'But I'm glad that you're home,' and he blinked, surprised.

'Don't gawp, Jack. You'll catch flies.'

He recalled the rest of his instructions. 'And Mum said may we borrow the big plates?'

'If you look after them.' Carrie hauled herself out of her chair. 'No chips or scratches, mind.'

Jack followed her along a passageway to Sixfields's cavernous kitchen. The three vast dressers were crowded with crockery. Scattered among cracked cups and plates that looked as though they belonged in a jumble sale, Jack glimpsed lovely old gilded platters and pieces of blue and white porcelain, centuries old.

'Fetch them down for me, won't you, Jack?' Carrie pointed with her stick to the topmost shelf of the dresser.

The plates were cream coloured and decorated in russet-brown, and on the borders were entwined the initials of some long-dead Chancellor. Carrie offered a length of twine and newspaper from a yellowing heap, and Jack wrapped the plates up carefully. When he had finished, he said, 'Do you mind if I have a look round the place before I go?'

'As you wish.' With a wave of her hand he was dismissed.

★ ★ ★

Carrie Chancellor wasn't Jack's true cousin. Carrie's father had been John Chancellor's father's eldest brother, which made Carrie, Jack supposed, either his second cousin or his first cousin once removed, he had never bothered to work out which. Carrie's father,

Archibald Chancellor, had prospered; Jack's father, John Chancellor, had not. To the already substantial Sixfields estate, Archibald Chancellor had added more acres. Family rumour said that Archibald had put away a fortune in the bank and in stocks and shares, which his only daughter, Caroline, had inherited on his death. Carrie's parsimoniousness had enabled her to survive the difficult years of agricultural depression between the wars. She had never married, had never named an heir. The disposition of Cousin Carrie's will was a subject of frequent, muttered interest at Chancellor family reunions.

Now, leaving the house, Jack walked fast through the fields that lay behind it. He had always loved Sixfields. Though for Will childhood duty visits to the farm had been a torment, Jack had enjoyed them. Unlike Will, Jack had never been afraid of Carrie. It had not occurred to him to be afraid of her. To him, Carrie Chancellor was a part of her cluttered, dusty, fascinating house and her beautiful, sweeping estates. Carrie, who despised the timid, had recognized Jack's lack of fear and had tolerated him, speaking to him with passable civility when he had visited, allowing him to explore the house and grounds. In turn, Jack had respected her need for privacy, a need which he understood. A solitary, unhappy adolescent, Sixfields had been a refuge for him.

He followed the tall hedgerows in the direction of the sea. Poppies nodded on the verges and a wren darted through a thicket of hazels. Jack wished that he, like Carrie, could escape this afternoon's party. Hordes of relatives he hadn't seen in years would be squashed into the School House. The thought depressed him; he wasn't sure why. Because he didn't even *like* many of his relatives, perhaps, or because he had become unused to family occasions. He walked faster, brushing aside the long grass. If it hadn't been for Julia he might have felt differently about the party. It was hard to celebrate when the woman you loved no longer cared for you.

Climbing a stile, he paused, looking around. Sixfields' land fell away to either side of him. He was surrounded by meadow and woodland, caught within the great blue arc of the sky. Behind him sunlight glinted on the undulating roof of the house. In the distance was the sea, its colours shifting as the sun dipped behind a cloud. Jack took a deep breath and felt a little of his anger and disappointment slip away. Everything else might have changed, but Sixfields, at least, had not. The solidity of it, its security and history, soothed him. He felt a sudden pang of envy for Carrie Chancellor, who had never had to decide where she was going to live or what she was going to do. Who had been born with both land and money, enough to survive Depression and war: no, not just survive, to remain *unchanged* by Depression and war. The lives of almost everyone else he knew — including his own — had been shaped by the turbulent events of the century. You had to be as rich as Carrie Chancellor for these things not to touch you.

His thoughts drifted back once more to Julia. In the moment that he had glimpsed Julia and Will together on the terrace at Missencourt, all the old resentments and jealousies, which time and parting had softened and blurred, had tumbled back. It had always seemed to Jack that everyone preferred Will. His parents had expected little, forgiven much in their delicate younger son. Even the ranks of dreadful Chancellor aunts and uncles and cousins had seemed to soften for Will. No one shared Jack's ambivalence. He would, if asked, have said that he loved his younger brother. He would not, of course, admit to anyone that he sometimes also hated him. Hated him for his sunny nature and for his ability to win affection. Life must be, Jack had often thought, so much *easier* for Will.

He had come first with only two people: Julia and Carrie. Yesterday, seeing Julia and Will together on the terrace, it had occurred to Jack that during his long absence Julia's allegiance might have altered. Why should someone as lovely as Julia wait years for *him*? He had felt foolish and humiliated. The shock had exaggerated the already difficult emotions of his homecoming, and his sense of detachment and alienation had persisted throughout the remainder of the day.

Now Jack closed his eyes, and breathed in the warm summer air. He wondered whether he might just have leaped to conclusions, might just have added two and two together and made five. The peace of the ancient landscape seemed to reach inside him, healing him. Jack welcomed the sudden feeling of release, and then he slid off the stile and walked on.

★ ★ ★

Topaz spent that morning helping Prudence with the preparations for the party. '*Salmon*,' she said longingly when Prudence unearthed the tins from the back of the larder.

'I'm afraid I've been hoarding. Since before Jack went away. I've been waiting for a suitable occasion. Something to celebrate.' Prudence stared at the tins of salmon. 'I suppose . . . sandwiches . . . or salad . . . '

'I could make vol-au-vents, if you like,' offered Topaz. There had been a cookery book at the Lake District hotel which she had read from cover to cover.

'Could you?' Prudence looked relieved. 'How marvellous. I loathe that sort of cooking, I'm afraid. Too fiddly. I haven't the patience.'

'Though they need loads and loads of butter — '

'Don't worry about that. Carrie let us have some. And I asked Maurice, I'm afraid, for extra flour.'

Maurice was a Chancellor cousin. He owned a draper's shop in the nearby town of Hernscombe, where he was prominent in the local tradesmen's association. 'It must be black market,' Prudence added guiltily. 'I didn't ask. Maurice really is the most dreadful crook. But needs must.'

Adele and Julia arrived at one o'clock. By that time the vol-au-vents were cooked, so Topaz and Julia were sent to the dining room to polish the cutlery. As she sloshed Silvo on to a duster, Julia muttered, 'I didn't want to come, you know.'

'Why not?'

Julia rubbed at a serving spoon. 'Having to be polite to awful people.'

'But lots of lovely food,' Topaz reminded her. She felt ravenous just thinking about the salmon vol-au-vents. She longed for lovely food. Dreamed about it sometimes. 'And it's so nice that we're all together again, isn't it?'

Julia did not reply. Looking at her set expression, Topaz said tentatively, 'You are pleased that Jack's home, aren't you?'

There was a silence, and then Julia wailed, 'It's just that he was so — so *different*! So cross — so *unfriendly*!' The serving spoon fell with a clang to the floor.

'Perhaps', said Topaz, 'he was tired.'

'And I'd been looking forward to him coming home for so long! And then it was awful!'

'The journey — '

'There was so much I meant to say to him, and I didn't say any of it because it all went wrong and I don't know why!'

'Such a long way . . . he must have been exhausted.'

Julia paused, looking at Topaz, sudden hope in her eyes. 'Do you think so?'

'He went to bed early. And he didn't say much.

31

Perhaps now he's had a rest . . . '

Julia looked away. Then she said, 'You see, I thought he was cross with me. I thought he didn't like me any more.'

Topaz stared at her. It was, she thought without rancour, one of life's great unfairnesses that Julia, dressed in an old pleated skirt and a white blouse that looked suspiciously like a leftover from her school uniform, with her eyes red from crying and her hair anyhow, should still look beautiful. Whereas, clad in a magenta satin dress cut down from a French evening gown of her mother's and after enduring a night with her hair in curlers, she herself looked, Topaz concluded, like an overripe *plum*.

'How could Jack not like you best?' she said gently. 'And Will too. They've always liked you best.'

Some of the tension seemed to slip from Julia's taut frame. 'Oh, *Will*,' she said dismissively.

The front doorbell rang. 'Oh Lord,' said Julia, grimacing. 'Party time.'

* * *

Later that afternoon, finding herself trapped by one of Jack and Will's uncles, who was telling a very dull anecdote — something to do with a tractor and a policeman — Julia tried not to yawn. Out of the corner of her eye, she caught sight of Jack. Head down, scowling, he was crossing the lawn to her, hardly bothering to reply to the adoring relatives who waylaid him to congratulate him on his safe return.

She smiled brightly as he approached. 'Are you enjoying your party, Jack?'

'Not immensely. Can we talk?'

'Of course.' Her voice was light and careless. She wasn't going to forgive him *that* easily. 'Leonard was telling me the most amusing story.'

'I meant', he said, 'that I'd like to talk to you alone.' He glowered at the other men and they melted back into the crowds. She could feel the intensity of his gaze. It seemed to heat the surface of her skin. Her anger deepened: anger with Jack for expecting her to obey as soon as he snapped his fingers, anger with herself for responding to him so easily.

He took her elbow in a proprietorial way, guiding her through the throng. *Hateful, hateful man*, she thought. How dare he assume he could just turn up and order her around — as though she *belonged* to him?

They went into his father's study. When he started to speak, she interrupted him. 'All this must be rather *dull* for you, Jack.' She was pleased to see that she had caught him off balance.

'Dull?'

'Family parties in Dorset. So different from what you must be used to. After Italy,' she went on vaguely. She was wandering around the room, fiddling with the fringes on a cushion and the inkstand on Jack's father's desk. 'And Egypt. So much more . . . *exotic*. I mean . . . bazaars . . . and camels . . .'

'And harems,' he said sarcastically. 'And pharaohs and pyramids and dancing girls. It wasn't like that, Julia.'

'How disappointing. Just like home, then.'

'Not at all like home. Dust and flies and heat and noise.'

There was a silence. Part of her wanted to go to him, to close her eyes and rest her head against his shoulder, but she did not allow herself to do so, afraid that if she let go after so many months of self-control she might dissolve, or fragment into little pieces.

And besides, lying awake for most of the previous night, an obvious explanation for Jack's changed attitude had occurred to her. Now she said lightly, 'You must have met lots of interesting people when you were away.'

'Some, I suppose.'

'We must all seem rather mundane in comparison.'

'Julia, I — '

'You must miss all that,' she continued relentlessly. 'The company — '

'I missed *you*,' he said, suddenly, roughly.

Her mouth went dry. 'Did you, Jack?'

'Yes, I did.' His face was slightly flushed. 'All the time.'

'Then why — '

'And you, Julia? Did you miss me?'

'Yes.'

'Is that all? 'Yes'?'

She forced herself to meet his gaze. 'What more do you expect?'

'Nothing,' he muttered. 'I expect — nothing.'

She felt suddenly unendurably weary, the accumulation of years of hard work and deprivation and loneliness. Tiredness swamped her, so that she couldn't be bothered teasing him any more, and something in her seemed to give way at last and she said quietly, 'I don't seem to have felt anything much at all for a very long time. Since Daddy died, actually. I'm sorry, Jack, but there it is.'

She thought that he might walk out, leave her to stew. But instead he came to stand beside her.

'That was what I wanted to say. About your father. I know I wrote, but that's not the same, is it? I just wanted to say that I'm so sorry. You must still miss him so much.'

When she closed her eyes, she felt his fingers brush against hers. Her defences crumbled, and she heard herself murmur, 'Oh Jack — '

And then the door burst open, and a strapping young girl, who seemed to Julia to be bursting out of her navy

34

blue gymslip, stared at them with interested eyes and said loudly, 'Aunt Prudence has been looking for you everywhere, Jack. You have to cut the cake.'

★ ★ ★

Julia found Will in the garage, crouching by the wheel arches of his father's old 1928 Aston Martin.

'What are you doing?'

'There's a bit of rust . . . I'm just sanding it down.'

'They're cutting the cake.' She perched on an old footstool which had lost its stuffing, watching him.

Thinking over her conversation with Jack, she felt muddled and confused. One moment she had detested him and the next she had wanted him to take her in his arms. It gave her a headache just to think about it. Surely it wasn't possible to love and hate someone at the same time? Love should be in one compartment, hatred in another.

'Talk to me, Will,' she said.

'What about?'

'Anything. Anything at all.'

So he talked to her — something to do with his Cousin Maurice and a garage — and she watched him, noticing how his hair fell over his face as he bent over the car, so that he had constantly to flick it back with an oily hand, and seeing how his eyes shone with enthusiasm as he spoke. And she thought how easy he was, and how pleasant and soothing it was to be with him, and she sat back on the stool, her arms wrapped around her knees, and began, for the first time that day, to feel better.

★ ★ ★

There were a great many Chancellors and they all ate and drank an enormous amount. The more they drank,

35

the noisier and more argumentative they became. Topaz ran back and forth, handing round plates of food. In the kitchen, Prudence and Adele made huge pots of tea and Mrs Sykes, Prudence's help, washed glasses and complained about her bunions. Topaz's feet, squashed into a pair of her mother's old evening shoes, ached too.

Every now and then one of the guests would ask her who she was and she'd tell them that she was Jack and Will's Cousin Topaz, and they'd look blank, and then she'd explain that she was Aunt Prudence's brother's daughter, and then they'd lose interest. It was as though, she thought exasperatedly, if you weren't a Chancellor you didn't count.

When most of the food had been wolfed down and most of the bottles of gin were empty, she was given charge of two small boys, Teddy and Billy, whose mother was expecting again and needed a break. Billy was quite sweet, but Teddy stuck out his tongue and said rude words to try to shock her. So she crossed her eyes and said the rather choice words she'd learned from the gardener at the Lake District hotel, and Teddy roared with laughter. Then they dragged her out to the pond to see the frogs and roared with laughter again when she tripped over the wretched too-small shoes and ended up to her knees in pond water.

Heading back through the house in search of the bathroom, a small boy pulling at each arm, she caught sight first of Angela Chancellor (fourteen years old and ferociously bossy) coming out of Uncle John's study, and then a few moments later, Julia and Jack. She was about to call out to Julia, to ask her where on earth she'd been all afternoon, when she saw Jack reach out a hand and with one finger carefully tuck a tendril of stray hair back into Julia's straggling ponytail. The intimacy and possessiveness of that small act startled her and she felt ashamed, as though she had been eavesdropping, so as quietly as possible she hurried both little boys back the way they had come.

She was threading through the crowds in the drawing room, when she heard, over the din, her mother's voice. 'Of course, Topaz simply doesn't have any talents.' She felt her face go hot and would have crept out of the room had not Teddy Chancellor chosen that moment to leap out from behind the sofa and pull her hair. She stumbled against a side table, knocking over a bottle of gin, which broke with a loud scatter of glass on the parquet floor. There was a sudden silence, and everyone stared at her. Then they all started to talk at once.

'Oh, *Topaz*.' (Her mother, wearily.)

'Ooh, butterfingers — '

'The children — they'll cut their feet — '

'The rug — ruined — '

'Don't *run*, Billy — '

Then a quieter, calmer voice said, 'It might be an idea if you all went into the garden while we cleared up. Angela, perhaps you'd fetch the dustpan and brush. Mrs Brooke, I'm sure that someone will find a chair for you on the terrace. As for you — ' and Marius drew Teddy Chancellor to him and whispered something in his ear. Topaz saw Teddy's eyes open very wide.

They all trooped out into the garden, leaving Marius and Topaz in the drawing room. There was a treacherous stinging feeling behind Topaz's eyes, but she thought that if she blinked very hard it might go away. When the floor was swept and she was able to trust herself to speak, she said, 'So stupid of me, ruining the party.'

'Nonsense. Do them good to go outside, get some fresh air. Calm them down a bit.' Marius took her hand. 'Come on. Time to escape, I think.'

They went to the garden of the adjoining boys' school. Because it was the summer holidays they had it to themselves. Standing by the goldfish pond, breathing in the scent of the lilies, Topaz's face cooled a little.

37

'It's not a disaster,' Marius said gently. 'Only a bottle of gin.'

Topaz simply doesn't have any talents. She blurted out, 'It's just that Julia is so beautiful *and* she knows about wirelesses and things, and Will knows all about cars, and Jack is good at *everything*, and I — ' and she looked despairingly down at herself ' — well, just *look* at me!'

'You look perfectly fine to me.'

'*Marius*. It's very sweet of you, but I have seen my reflection in the looking glass, you know.'

'That shade . . . what is it? Red . . . mauve — '

'Magenta.'

'It may not', he said tentatively, 'be your colour.'

'And my shoes — '

'What's wrong with them?'

'Apart from the fact that they're two sizes too small, they're wet.'

'Wet . . . ?'

'I was trying to catch frogs.'

'With your *shoes*?'

She smiled weakly and he said, 'That's better.'

After a while she sighed, and said, 'What Mummy said — ' she couldn't bear to repeat it, especially to him, but she suspected that she would also never be able to forget it ' — it's true, though, isn't it?'

'Of course it isn't.' He sounded angry. 'You have plenty of talents, Topaz. You're a pretty handy cook, by all accounts, Prudence said so. And you put up with those horrendous little tykes — I'd have throttled them after five minutes.'

She giggled. 'What did you say to Teddy?'

'That if I ever catch him pulling a lady's hair again, I shall put the very large black spider I brought back with me from France into his bed one night.' He offered her his cigarette case. Topaz took one, flattered that Marius, who was about ten years older than her, should think

38

her grown up enough to smoke.

'And — ' he said ' — as for you, another thing. Everyone likes to be with you.'

'*Marius* — '

'It's true. They do. They like to talk to you. You have an air of serenity, Topaz. That's a rare gift. You couldn't describe any of the rest of us as serene, could you? Not Jack or Will. Certainly not Julia.' He lit her cigarette for her. 'Tell you what, how about going to the flicks with me tomorrow night? I have to go to London in the morning, but there's a film on in Bridport I've been wanting to see for ages. Would you like that?'

'Oh yes,' she said. 'Yes, Marius, *please*.'

★　★　★

The following morning Topaz was given the task of taking the big plates back to Sixfields. Opening the front gate, she waved to the land girl, who was heaving boxes of apples on to the back of a cart. The land girl called out, 'Don't bother knocking, she never answers. Go round the back and give her a shout.'

The back yard was a wide expanse of cobbles and mud, with stables to one side and a barn to the other. A very old and dirty Bentley was parked by the barn. Four dogs dashed towards her, barking loudly. She knocked on the back door, but there was no reply, so she went indoors and found herself in a scullery full of dusty gallon jars and blue and brown medicine bottles.

'Miss Chancellor?' she called out. Her voice echoed in the cobwebby darkness. 'Miss Chancellor?'

Corridors branched off in all directions and narrow staircases wound away into nothingness. Through the dim light, she saw a face and she jumped, though she held on to the plates, thank goodness.

'Miss Chancellor?'

'And who else would I be?' Carrie Chancellor limped

39

down the corridor towards her. 'Who are you?'

'Topaz Brooke,' she said, flustered.

'*Topaz.* What sort of a name is that?'

'My father chose it.'

'Hardly a *Christian* name.' Carrie Chancellor headed off down a fork in the corridor; Topaz followed after her.

'Prudence's niece,' said Carrie suddenly. 'You're Prudence's niece, aren't you?'

'Yes. Aunt Prudence's brother Thomas was — '

'I'm not interested in your life story, girl. Hurry up.'

Carrie Chancellor was small and thin and wiry, and her cropped brown hair had begun to grey. She was wearing a sludgy-coloured tweed skirt and jacket and a bottle-green jersey. Her small-featured, oval face might once have been agreeable, but had become reddened and polished by exposure to wind and rain, and etched with deep lines around the eyes and mouth.

'Seen enough, have you?' Carrie's sharp voice made Topaz jump again. 'Fetch that chair and you can put the plates back on the dresser.' Carrie found a knife to cut the string that bound the wrappings. 'And how were the jollifications yesterday?' she asked, with sarcastic emphasis.

'The party? Oh, it was lovely.' Though it hadn't been, at all, until the end.

'All one big happy family?'

'Well, we — '

'Jack doesn't like parties,' added Carrie maliciously.

'I'm sure he enjoyed himself — all his friends were there — Marius and Julia and — '

'Jack's like me. Doesn't like fuss.' Carrie's knife snapped through the twine. 'Julia?' Her brows twitched together. 'There's no Julia in the family.'

'Julia Temperley. She's not family, she's a friend.' Topaz dragged the chair over to the dresser and climbed on to it. It wobbled precariously on the uneven brick floor. In her mind's eye she saw Jack's fingertips touch Julia's hair. Carefully, she placed the plates on the topmost shelf. 'Aunt Prudence thinks Julia and Jack might get married. They're awfully fond of each other. I think — '

'You can go now.' Carrie's voice cut into the stream of words.

Topaz stared at her. 'Pardon?'

'I said, you can go. I can't spend the whole day chatting, you know. I've a farm to run.'

As she walked back through the front garden, the land girl called out, 'Not in one of her welcoming moods, then?'

Topaz wheeled her bike down the path. 'She seemed a bit cross.'

'I wouldn't feel bad about it.' The girl was leaning on a spade, smoking a cigarette. 'Just don't come expecting a friendly chat with her tonight, that's my advice.'

'Why not?'

'Because I'm giving my notice. My Mum's got me a job in Timothy White's.'

She looked pleased with herself, so Topaz said, 'How marvellous. Congratulations.'

'Can't wait. You won't see me for dust, I can tell you. But madam's not going to be happy.' The land girl nodded to the house. 'Just her and the Crabtrees to run this place — I don't know how they'll manage. Still, not my problem.' She spat on her hands and picked up the spade again. 'Keep out of her way tonight, that's all I'm saying. She's not going to be in the best of tempers.'

Topaz almost said, *Well, actually, Marius Temperley is taking me to the cinema in Bridport tonight*, but just managed to confine herself to a quick goodbye. Cycling the three miles back to the School House, she sang to herself while she tried to decide what she would wear. Her pleated grey skirt, perhaps, though she was afraid it made her bottom look enormous. Or her tartan dress that had been her uniform in the top form at school. Definitely not the magenta satin.

But as she entered the hallway of the School House, the telephone rang. She answered it.

'Topaz?' Marius's voice.

'Hello, Marius.'

'I'm terribly sorry, Topaz, but I'm not going to be able to make it tonight.'

'Oh,' she said, and was aware of a diminishing of the day, as though it had somehow shrunk.

'I'm afraid I have to stay in London. Something unexpected has turned up and I'm going to be here for a while.' He was speaking fast and his voice sounded odd. 'I'll explain everything when I get back. And Topaz — could I ask you whether you'd be so kind as to do something for me? Would you tell my mother that I'll be home on Thursday afternoon?' He put the phone down.

Topaz went into the drawing room. Her mother was standing at the window, smoking. 'They all seem to have gone out,' said Veronica peevishly. 'And I can't find where Prudence keeps the gin.'

'I know,' said Topaz. She made her mother a drink.

Veronica sipped appreciatively. 'You mix a good martini, Topaz.' Topaz's black mood lifted a little at the compliment.

'I've telephoned the plumbers', Veronica went on, 'and they told me that they've almost finished.' Her smile was conspiratorial. 'So we can go home. It'll be nice to have a place of our own again, won't it, Topaz?'

★ ★ ★

On the train to London that morning, Marius put away his copy of *The Times* after gazing at it blankly for ten minutes. Then he stared out of the window, thinking.

He was travelling to London in the hopes of seeing Suzanne Miller. He had met Suzanne during the war, in the spring of 1944; their affair had been brief, breathtaking, unforgettable. They had been stationed in Northumberland, in a cold and draughty army camp, waiting to be entrained south in preparation for the D-Day invasion of France. It wasn't, he had thought even at the time, that she was exceptionally beautiful. Small, curvy, dark-haired and dark-eyed, you would not, glimpsing her in a photograph with the rest of her unit, pick her out as prettier than half a dozen others. But she had a quality that no photograph could completely capture, an energy, a zest for life that set her apart from the rest. In the mixture of tension and boredom that had characterized the first half of 1944, he had been drawn to her enthusiasm and her capacity for pleasure, finding in her, perhaps, something that he himself lacked.

God knows what she had seen in him. But the first night they met, walking her home from the pub (the memory aroused him even now) they had hardly been able to wait long enough to seek shelter in the forests that lined the road between the village and the camp. The first time they had made love, they had lain on a bed of pine needles and had glimpsed a ceiling of stars through the branches overhead. Now, closing his eyes, he could still recall the scent of resin and the scent of her skin.

Their affair had lasted for only six weeks, the most intense and heady six weeks of his life. Then he had been posted south with his regiment. In June he had set sail for France. Though he had written to Suzanne, he had received no reply to his letters. Returning to England earlier in the year, he had tried to trace her. At first he had been motivated partly by resentment, by a need to let her know how much her lack of communication had hurt and angered him. Then curiosity had taken over. No one seemed to know where she was. He discovered that she had left the Services not

43

long after he had been posted to France, and in doing so had severed contact with all her old friends. Though part of him knew that his quest was futile, that she had not written to him because she had not cared enough to write to him, that she must have long ago forgotten him and made a new life for herself, he continued doggedly to try to trace her through her former colleagues and through service organizations.

Two days before, he had received a letter from Evelyn Thomas, a friend of Suzanne's. At first, the ominous tone of Evelyn's letter had jolted him. '*It's taken me a long time to answer your letter*', she had written, '*because I wasn't sure what to do. Things have been difficult for Suzanne, Marius. A great deal has changed for her since you knew her, and I'm not sure that trying to get in touch with her is an awfully good idea. It's been a long time, after all.*' Now, as the train approached London, threading through red-brick suburbs, he considered Evelyn's words. *A great deal has changed for her . . .* Well, a great deal had changed for all of them, hadn't it? Suzanne might not have adjusted easily to life after the Services. She might be struggling to make ends meet in a badly paid job, perhaps, or, in the acute housing shortage that was the legacy of the war, have found herself trapped in some leaky slum. The address Evelyn had given him was an Islington one, in an area which had been grim before the war and heavily bombed during it.

There could, of course, be an obvious explanation for the warning tone he had detected in Evelyn Thomas's letter. Suzanne might have married. If so, he would congratulate her, take his leave, and never see her again. His mind drifted, asking uncomfortable questions. Why had he, on returning to England, decided to look Suzanne up? Why was he neglecting his responsibilities to travel to London today? He had no hope, after all, of starting up their affair again. Her failure to reply to his

44

letters from France had told him all he had needed to know of his importance to her. He wasn't fool enough to concoct improbable rationales for her failure to communicate, or explanations to brush aside a silence of more than two years.

What did he really know about her? That she liked to drive too fast, that she was proud and independent. And that, in bed, she was hungry, uninhibited, generous. They had had little in common then; after such a long separation they would have even less now. When they had talked, he and Suzanne had usually argued. Their backgrounds and beliefs had been separated by a vast gulf. She had mocked his minor-public-school education, his middle-class code of conduct. There had been things that she had done or said which had jarred him. He had not liked himself for minding that she sometimes swore, nor had he liked himself for noticing that she blew on her tea to cool it down and always dunked her biscuits. But he had noticed, nevertheless. Worse, she had seen that he minded her small transgressions of good taste: *Lord, Marius,* she had said once, *you couldn't take me home to your parents, could you?* Her voice had been mocking, her gaze judging him, perceiving his shallowness. Perhaps that was why Evelyn was warning him off. Perhaps Evelyn was at heart the oldfashioned sort, who believed that, the war ended, the classes should return to their former rigid separation.

As the train swung into Paddington, he confronted his motives for undertaking this journey. He needed to see Suzanne again because she had made him feel alive, as no woman had done before or since. He needed to know whether he was still capable of such intensity of feeling. Since his return to England several months ago, he had felt oddly distanced from both work and family. Though he had tried to pick up the traces of his former existence, they drifted from his hands, insubstantial and

45

uninvolving. It frightened him to think that the numbness he had felt since his homecoming might be permanent.

She was, he thought, his last hope.

★ ★ ★

Sissons Street, where Suzanne lived, branched off to the north of Tufnell Park Road. The tall, four-storeyed houses might once have been elegant, but now showed signs of long neglect. Most had been divided into flats: rows of names were scrawled on cards beside the front doors. Areas of waste ground where buildings had once stood were littered with weeds and rubble. Many of the surviving houses bore evidence of bomb damage: missing tiles, boarded-up windows and broken pilasters. Paint peeled from doors and window frames, and the chunks of stucco fallen from the fascias gave oddly indecent glimpses of bare brick beneath. An air of apathy hovered fog-like around the broken buildings, as though no one could face the effort of bringing them back up to scratch.

Outside Number 14, Marius paused for a moment, looking up. The house was, if anything, in a worse state than its neighbours. The wrought-iron porch had fallen away and lay in a tangle of rusted metal in the dank front garden, and the steps that led up to the door were cracked and chipped. He scanned the cards pinned to the jamb and found Miller. Which answered one question: she had not married. He was about to press the bell when the door opened and an elderly woman came out. He held the door ajar for her and slipped inside as she left the house.

Suzanne's room was on the top floor. Climbing the stairs, treading over scraps of damp carpet and discarded cardboard boxes, Marius thought that she might be out, that he should have written, that she

46

would have forgotten him. He hadn't a clue what he was going to say to her. He could not see any way of passing this off as a casual, unplanned visit. He had been a fool to come here, he thought suddenly, savagely. There was the impulse to turn on his heel and walk away, so, reaching the top landing, he rapped on her door before he had time for any more second thoughts.

He heard footsteps. The door opened. He saw her eyes widen, her jaw drop.

'*Marius.*'

'Suzanne.'

There was a long moment when neither of them spoke. Then she said, 'You'd better come in.'

He followed her into the room. It was, if anything, worse than he had expected. There was black mould beneath the windows and strips of tape held shattered windowpanes in place. A clothes horse draped with damp washing stood in front of a one-bar electric fire. In the far corner of the room were a gas ring and a washing-up bowl, heaped with dishes. Tins and packets of food were crammed on to a rickety shelf above the makeshift kitchen. A door led to an adjoining room: the bedroom, he assumed. The furniture was sparse and ugly — a cheap sofa that had gone shiny with age, a painted table and a couple of chairs. One of the table legs was shorter than the others and was supported by a pile of books.

'It's not the Ritz, is it?' she said, and he knew by the defensiveness in her voice that she had read his thoughts.

'It's . . . nice and bright,' he said. The south-facing room was uncomfortably warm.

'The window won't open — the sash has stuck and I can't budge it. And I have to have the fire on to dry the clothes.'

He said, 'The washing line . . . ?' and she shook her head.

'It's a communal garden. People take the good things.'

'Oh.' How depressing, he thought, to live somewhere where people stole clothes from the washing line. 'Shall I have a go at the window?' he offered.

'If you like.'

Heaving at the recalcitrant sash gave him time to gather his thoughts. She had changed; it was hard to pinpoint precisely how she had changed, but she had. Her dark hair was perhaps a little longer than he remembered and she had lost weight, but there was something more than that. It was as though her features had blurred, robbing her of some of her former clarity and brightness. Her eyes were wary, untrusting. But her low, husky voice still had the power to make him shiver, to remember what they had once shared.

He managed to open the window an inch or two. Cooler air flooded into the room. 'Thank you, Marius,' she said. 'Now we can breathe.' Her eyes narrowed. 'How did you find me?'

'Evelyn Thomas gave me your address.'

She looked angry. 'The silly little cow.'

He made a gesture of appeasement. 'I had no other way of getting in touch with you.'

Suzanne stripped towels from the drying rack, folding them with a quick flick of the wrist. He said, 'I don't understand why you didn't answer my letters.'

'What would have been the point?'

Before he could stop himself, he said, 'Common courtesy, for one thing — '

She laughed. 'Oh Marius. I'd forgotten what a stuffed shirt you are.'

He struggled to swallow down his anger. 'It would have meant something to me, that's all.'

'Which was why', she said softly, 'I didn't want to write to you.'

He had to turn away. 'Is there someone else?'

48

For the first time, she smiled. 'In a manner of speaking.'

'Ah.' He saw what a fool he had been, coming here. 'I'll go, then.'

He was halfway to the door when she said, 'I'm sorry, Marius. I'm being a bitch, aren't I?' She took a deep breath. 'There isn't another man, if that's what you mean. There hasn't been anyone since you, and that's the truth. It's just that — well, all that — the war, you and me — seems so long ago.' She managed a crooked smile. 'You haven't a ciggie, have you? I'm dying for one. I've run out and I haven't been able to get to the shops.'

He offered her his cigarettes. 'Evelyn said things had been difficult for you.'

She gave a croak of laughter. 'You could say that.' She looked at him sharply. 'What else did she tell you?'

'Nothing much.' He lit her cigarette. 'Only that you'd left the ATS early.'

'Not long after you went to France.'

'Why? I would have thought — '

'You know I was never one for taking orders, Marius.'

Something in her tone warned him not to ask more. He wondered whether she had left in disgrace, been court-martialled, perhaps. He found it hard to imagine: she was intelligent and resourceful, not the sort of woman the army would have wanted to lose.

'Have you found a job?'

'I do a bit of sewing.' She gestured to the old Singer on the table.

He said hesitantly, 'I've some friends in the City. I could make enquiries, if you like, see if they need anyone.'

'I'm fine, really.'

'It'd probably be office work, but — '

'I said, I'm fine.' That warning note once more. Then

49

she smiled again. 'It's been lovely to see you, Marius, but I've things to do.'

'I thought perhaps we could go somewhere for lunch — ' He broke off, hearing a sound from the adjacent room. A thin, high-pitched wail. He stared at her, speechless, his thoughts suddenly frozen.

'My cat,' she said. 'Marius, I don't think lunch would be a good idea.'

Another cry. His mind seemed to unlock and, in the peeling of a second, to understand everything. 'That's no *cat* — ' he muttered, and went to open the bedroom door.

'Marius — ' She moved in front of him, but he pushed past her and flung open the door. And found himself face to face with the infant standing in her cot. Catching sight of him, she began to cry with renewed vigour.

★   ★   ★

He said again, 'When was she born?'

Suzanne was holding the baby in her arms, murmuring gently to her. 'I told you, Marius, it's none of your business.'

But it had occurred to him that it could be very much his business. He didn't know much about babies, but he guessed the child was around eighteen months old.

He said roughly, 'I can go and check at Somerset House, you know.'

She looked furious, but she muttered, 'The winter before last.'

'I mean — *exactly* when was she born?'

She pressed her lips gently to the infant's tousled dark hair. Then she glared at him, her eyes defiant. 'December the twenty-sixth, nineteen forty-four. Boxing Day. My little Christmas present.'

Nine months back from 26 December took him to

50

the end of March. He had first met Suzanne in late March. *There hasn't been anyone since you, Marius,* she had said, not ten minutes ago. He had to pause for a moment, trying to absorb the implications. Then he said, 'She's mine, isn't she?'

Her back was to him, the baby propped against her shoulder. He said again, 'She's mine, isn't she, Suzanne?' and after what seemed like an age she nodded.

He sat down on the threadbare sofa, aware of a mixture of emotions: shock and anger and shame. He understood so much now. Why she had left the ATS, why Evelyn had written, *A great deal has changed for Suzanne.*

'Why didn't you tell me?' he whispered, and she shook her head, but did not reply. The baby was playing with the beads Suzanne wore around her neck, touching them with her finger so that they rolled along the string.

'Did you think I wouldn't stand by you?'

Her cool gaze met his. 'I didn't see why you should have to pay for a month's pleasure.'

'Six weeks,' he said irritably. 'We knew each other for six weeks.'

'A month, six weeks — what does it matter? It doesn't make any difference.'

'We have a child. That makes all the difference.'

'*I* have a child. She's mine. Just mine.' At the edge of her voice, he detected fear.

'She's my daughter.' Yet he did not even know her name. He went to the window, trying to think clearly. Thoughts rushed through his head. He had fathered a child. Suzanne — proud, independent Suzanne — had lived in poverty while he had lacked for nothing at Missencourt. His difficulties in fitting back into civilian life now seemed a shameful luxury, the spoilt grumbles of one who had always had it easy.

It was already clear to him what he must do: that he

51

felt reluctance only intensified his guilt. 'We'd better get married,' he said.

She looked startled. 'Don't be ridiculous. You can't possibly marry me, Marius.'

'Why not?'

'You just can't, that's all.'

'She needs a father. Children need fathers. She's my child, my responsibility.'

'Such an oversized sense of duty . . . *marriage* — dear God.' Her voice shook.

'Why not?' he said again.

'Because — ' she stared at him ' — because my father works on the railways. Because I left school at fourteen. Because we would fight like cat and dog.'

He disregarded her last objection, and said, 'Those things don't matter.'

'*Don't matter!*' she repeated scornfully. 'Which world have you been living in? Listen to me, Marius, just listen. What on earth do you think your family would say if you brought me — and my daughter — home with you? Do you think they'd welcome us with open arms?'

'My father's dead,' he said. 'There's only my mother and sister.' Crushing down his doubts, he added with a conviction he did not feel, 'They'd adore you both, I know they would.'

'Like hell they would.'

He felt removed from reality, dazed by shock, unable clearly to consider anything other than what he must do, had to do. 'She's my child,' he said stubbornly.

'You don't know what you're saying — '

Oh, but he did. He was proposing to marry a woman he did not love, to father a child he did not know. Yet he did not see that he had any alternative. They must marry as quickly as possible, he decided. Put things right. He could allow himself no time for second thoughts.

He glanced around the room, unable, this time, to keep the disgust from his voice. 'You can't bring up a child here. Look at it, Suzanne. For God's sake.'

'It's all right.'

'You can't put the washing out because people steal it . . . and how the hell do you get her pram up and downstairs? And there's damp in here, I can smell it. Is this what you want for her? Is it?'

He thought that, were the child not in her arms, she would have hit him. But then, suddenly, her defences seemed to fall, and she shook her head slowly.

'No. No, it's not.' She looked exhausted.

There was a long silence and then he said more gently, 'You'd love Missencourt, Suzanne. Everyone does. The baby would be able to have her own bedroom and there'd be a huge garden for her to play in as she gets older. And the sea's only five miles away.'

She murmured, 'The countryside . . . I'm used to towns . . . '

'She could learn to swim and to sail. Julia could teach her to ride.' He pulled at the collar of his shirt: in spite of the open window, the room still seemed over-warm. 'We'd be able to afford to send her to a decent school,' he pointed out. 'She could have ballet lessons, music lessons, whatever she wanted. On your own, you can't give her any of that, can you, Suzanne?'

There were tears in her eyes. She whispered, 'Marius, there's something I must tell you — ' but he interrupted her.

'Later. I have to see about the licence.'

And he had to escape the cramped, claustrophobic flat. Had to have time to think, to become used to this new reality. He said a hurried goodbye and left the room.

3

On Tuesday mornings Julia always took Salem for a ride. As she came out of the copse into the sunlight, she caught sight of Jack cycling towards her. Salem, who had a thing about bicycles, rolled his eyes and tossed his head.

Jack propped the bike against the hedgerow and crossed the road to her. 'Yours?' He ran his hand down the horse's velvety neck.

Julia shook her head. 'Penny Craven's.' Penny was a friend of Julia's; she owned a riding stables. 'Wish he was mine.'

The stallion showed the whites of his eyes as a pheasant broke cover from the hedge. 'Nervy, though,' said Jack, holding the bridle.

'He took the five-barred gate on Chalk Meadow just like that. Didn't hesitate.'

He glanced up at her. 'You should wear a hat.'

'You know I hate them, Jack.'

He still looked disapproving, but he said, 'Thanks for coming on Sunday.'

'I enjoyed it. We never have family parties. Not enough of us, I suppose.'

'Frankly, there are far too many of us. All vying for position, trying to prove we're better than our neighbour.'

She laughed. 'Not you, Jack.' Though he had his hungry, competitive side, she thought.

'My cousin Maurice lent us some records,' he explained, 'so I'm nipping over to Hernscombe to give them back. Like to come? We could take a boat out — or walk the cliff path.'

'I can't.' He looked away, but she caught the

expression in his eyes, and added quickly, 'I mean it, Jack, I'd love to, but I can't. I promised to help Penny at the stables. She lets me ride the horses in return. Though if you wouldn't mind waiting for me — '

'Yes?' He picked up his bicycle.

'An hour, then.'

They cycled the five miles to the coast. Julia was glad of the physical exertion, which distracted her from the doubts that gnawed at her. Whether she and Jack were friends again. Whether they were anything more than friends.

They dropped the records off at Maurice Chancellor's draper's shop. After a while Julia went outside to stand in the sunshine, leaving Jack talking to Maurice.

Jack emerged ten minutes later, glowering. 'Poisonous little toad.' Heading through narrow lanes to the harbour, he explained, 'He offered me a job.'

'Maurice? You won't take it, will you?'

'I'd rather shoot myself.' His lip curled. 'After I've polished off Maurice first, obviously.'

Jack swung off his bike as they reached the harbour. They walked side by side along the breakwater. She thought what a ridiculously handsome man he was, with his strong profile, dark, slightly curling hair, and navy blue eyes.

Now, those eyes were bleak. 'Maurice owns the shop,' Jack said slowly, 'and he has part ownership of a chain of garages, and he lives in a big house and runs a car that he somehow manages to find petrol for. His wife wears a fur coat and his kids go to private schools. I haven't quite managed any of that, have I?'

'Something will turn up,' she said comfortingly.

'Will it? I'm twenty-six, and I'm living with my parents, and I'm just another demobbed soldier without a job, and this — ' the flat of his hand struck the crossbar of the bicycle ' — is how I get about.'

Waves crashed against stone piers and fishing boats

bobbed in the water. Julia threaded her hand through Jack's arm, snuggling up to him, and he seemed to relax because he turned to her and said, 'Shall we go to the beach? If you're up to the climb.'

★   ★   ★

Hernscombe Cove was a narrow sandy inlet to the north of the town, which could be reached only by a precipitous descent from the cliff top fifty feet above. During the war both cliff and beach had been fenced off with tangles of barbed wire and concrete defences. Rusting knots of wire still coiled among the gorse and sea pinks.

Jack led the way down to the beach, finding footholds in the sandy soil, steadying himself by holding on to clumps of marram grass. Halfway down he paused and stood upright. Then, with a loud whoop, he began to run, gathering speed with his descent before collapsing on to the soft, pale sand below.

'Idiot!' shouted Julia, from halfway down the cliff. Jack sprang to his feet and held his arms outstretched.

'Come on!'

'I can't — ' But she did, of course, hurtling down the path, exhilarated by speed, loving the feeling that at any moment she might lose control, tumble downwards, unable to halt her plunge.

He caught her in his arms. She clutched him, gasping for breath and laughing at the same time. Then he kissed her. Short, gentle kisses at first, which allowed her to catch her breath between them. His hands threaded through her hair and there was sand in her shoes. She closed her eyes and felt the roughness of his chin against her face, the warmth of his body against hers. As he drew her to him, his caresses became more demanding. It was as though she was standing on the cliff again, about to hurtle downwards. His hands

56

kneaded the bare skin beneath her blouse and the sound of the sea mingled with the pounding of her heart.

Then, suddenly, he pulled away. She heard him groan.

'Jack . . . ?' she whispered.

He did not reply, but walked out to where the sea lapped the shore. She felt bereft and rather foolish.

She ran to him. 'What is it?'

'I'm sorry,' he said. 'I didn't mean to do that.'

'I *liked* you doing that.'

He made an impatient gesture. There was an unpleasant, sinking feeling inside her. She kicked off her sandals and began to wade out to sea, stumbling slightly on the curved ribs of the impacted sand.

Jack called out to her. 'Where on earth are you going?'

'To the rock.' A tiny islet in the middle of the bay jutted out of the water. They had dived from the rock when they had been children.

'That's crazy. You'll get soaked.'

She glanced back at him. 'Did I do something wrong?'

'Of course not.' He sounded angry.

'Then why did you stop?'

'For God's sake, Julia.'

'*Tell me.*'

He clenched his fists. 'If you must know, I stopped because I was on the verge of fucking you. Here. Now. On this beach.'

His language, and his tone of voice, halted her. Then she said, 'I wouldn't have minded.'

'But *I* would.' He scowled. 'It wouldn't be right, Julia. Not with you.'

'But — ' she felt utterly miserable ' — you've done it with other women.'

'Yes,' he said evenly.

'Then why not me?'

'Because you matter. And they didn't.'

She waded back to shore, feeling the press of the water against her legs and the sharp edges of the shells against the soles of her feet. His hands settled in the hollows of her waist.

'You're soaked.'

'I am rather.'

Sheltered by the lee of the cliff, the sand was soft and dry and warm. She lay beside him, her head cradled on his shoulder, his arm decorously around her. The sun beat down and after a while she said, 'What are we going to do?'

He had closed his eyes. 'Well, if you mean just now, then I think I'm going to go to sleep. And if you mean our future, then we'll talk about that later.'

Our future. She lay still, treasuring the moment, remembering all the times they had come to Hernscombe Cove when they had been children. The four of them and their mothers, clambering down the cliff path, laden with buckets and spades and towels and swimming costumes and picnic hampers. They had swum from April to October, turning blue in the icy water, the sand scraping against their goose-pimpled skin. Their mothers had sat on the beach, knitting or sewing or dividing up cakes and sandwiches, and talking, always talking. It had always surprised Julia that grown-up women, who seemed to lead such dull lives, should find so much to talk about.

Now she imagined coming here with her own children. She and Jack would hold their hands while they paddled. Later they would teach them to swim. Julia, too, closed her eyes, listening to the gentle hiss and rush of the sea and to Jack's breathing as he slept.

★　★　★

Carrie Chancellor woke in the early hours of the morning. Though she tried to empty her mind and drift back to sleep, all her anxieties crowded in, multiplied by the events of the last few days. The few hours' sleep had done nothing to relieve her exhaustion and the dragging tiredness made her feel chilled in spite of the warm weather.

Jack's homecoming, the red-haired girl's visit (she couldn't remember her name — something to do with jewels — Pearl? Ruby?), the land girl giving her notice. Too many shocks and surprises. Carrie preferred her days to be uneventful, shaped by the seasonal patterns of the farm. Strangers, unexpected visits, unanticipated conversations, upset her. On top of everything else, Mr Smallbone, her solicitor, had called that afternoon. *I was just passing by*, he had said, before broaching his usual topic of conversation, her failure to make a will. She had got rid of him quickly, sending him scuttling out of the yard with the dogs at his heels. Yet her elation in that temporary victory had quickly faded. Phrases had echoed in her mind for the remainder of the day. *If you die intestate, Miss Chancellor, then your estate may be divided on your demise.* Now, sitting up in bed, alone in the great old house of her forebears, death seemed neither improbable nor distant. Her health had been poor since the attack of polio she had suffered at the age of nineteen. She was prone to bronchitis and had twice almost died of pneumonia. Today, working in the fields, her aching limbs and painful joints had reminded her constantly of her frail physique and increasing years.

If she had had an heir . . . But she hadn't, no use dwelling on that one. Who would have wanted to marry a cripple, even for Sixfields? A shy young girl, her illness had ruthlessly stripped from her what little confidence she had had in her appearance, so that she had

59

afterwards avoided people, protecting herself with a hostile carapace.

Dear Lord, but she ached tonight. The long day in the fields, she supposed — harvest was always exhausting. How much longer . . . she whispered, and tried to push the frightening thought away. It seemed to her that she had aged recently, that her body, never an ally, was becoming even less forgiving. Looking down at her hands, she saw how the skin stretched over the bones, without a scrap of flesh to cover them. She was drying out, she thought, desiccating. She hadn't had the curse for six months: odd that she, who was not a maternal woman, should mind.

If you die intestate . . . Sixfields must go to a Chancellor, yet she despised her closest relatives, the ones who fawned around her, pretending concern when she could see in their eyes only greed. She imagined the estate sold off, split up, all that history gone. Now the house creaked and rustled, and in her mind's eye she pictured all the countless, empty rooms, filled with furniture and books and knick-knacks, slowly disappearing beneath a blanket of dust. No footsteps echoed in Sixfields' silent corridors; no voices ever called for her in the night. She was aware of a loneliness so intense that it seemed to crush her, pressing the air out of her lungs as her illness had done all those years ago.

She climbed out of bed and went to the window. Pulling back the curtain, she looked out. The fields and meadows spread out before her, lit by the full moon. She knew every stream, every tree. She knew where the pale hellebores pushed their flower heads through the beechmast, she knew the carpet of thyme and rockrose and orchid in the ancient hay meadows. When they cut the hay, the scent was intoxicating.

They had begun to plough the Hundred Acre field. Carrie could see in the moonlight the converging lines of ridged soil. After Jack had visited on Sunday, she had

60

climbed the stairs and watched him from this window. He had crossed the fields and then paused at the stile. Then he had circled slowly round, gazing at all four corners of the land. Watching him, she had wished she possessed a fraction of his tense, coiled energy. And she had known that he felt for Sixfields as she did, loved it as she did.

Jack, she thought, and gripped the sill to steady herself. He didn't irritate her as much as most of her relatives. And she needed — Sixfields needed — his youth, his strength. And how greatly she would enjoy putting the others' noses out of joint! Why not Jack?

She thought of him: a tall, handsome boy. She remembered how, years ago, he had always loved to explore the house, how his dark blue eyes had flicked around the rooms, settling on object after object. She had glimpsed avarice there, an avarice that ran like a dark vein through so many of the Chancellors. She had neither youth nor beauty with which to bind him to her, but she had something else that might hook him: money and land, and the power that came with both.

Carrie smiled. And as for the other thing, the thing that had rattled her so much — well, there were scores to be settled, weren't there?

★   ★   ★

Jack spent Wednesday helping to mow the last of Sixfields' hay meadows. In the evening, when he was sluicing the dust from his hands and face at the tap in the yard, he opened his eyes to see Carrie watching him from the back door.

She said abruptly, 'There's something I wanted to say to you, Jack.'

He shrugged on his shirt. 'Go on.'

'Not here. In the parlour.'

He followed her indoors. As she limped down the

61

corridor, she said angrily, 'I'm not getting any younger, you know. And that wretched land girl's upped and gone. Not that she was much use.'

He opened the parlour door for her. 'I'll help out till you find someone else, if you like.'

She shot a glance at him. 'You enjoy the work, don't you, Jack?'

'It suits me.'

Carrie took a bottle of sherry from the sideboard. The shoulders of the bottle were grey with dust. She said, 'I wondered whether you'd like to work here permanently, Jack.'

He felt a mixture of surprise and pleasure. Yet his cautious nature and his knowledge of Carrie's legendary meanness made him hesitate. He wouldn't have her treat him as she had treated the land girl. He needed to know exactly what she was offering.

'As what?' he asked. 'As a labourer . . . ? Or your land manager . . . ?'

'Neither. I've decided to make my will, you see.' Carrie poured out two small measures of sherry. 'I've decided to leave Sixfields to you, Jack.'

I've decided to leave Sixfields to you, Jack. At first, he couldn't take it in. He could almost hear his heart pounding. There was sweat on his brow and his shirt clung to his back. He wanted to ask her to say it again, so that he could be sure he hadn't dreamed it. *I've decided to leave Sixfields to you, Jack.* Years later he thought how strange it was that a few words could alter the course of a life.

'The farm . . . ?' he whispered. 'To *me* . . . ?'

'And there's money in the bank, of course. I've always been careful with money. Never frittered it away like some.'

In his mind's eye he seemed to look down upon the estate, and see the house and the lands that surrounded it. *His . . .*

'I don't suppose you'll have to wait all that long,' Carrie added brusquely, as she hobbled back to her chair. 'My health's never been good. It'll be yours before you know it.'

'Carrie — '

'Do you want it, Jack?'

'Yes,' he said. He wanted Sixfields so much. He hadn't known how much till this marvellous, unanticipated moment. 'Yes, I do.'

'Then that's settled. I'll write to my solicitor.'

'I never thought . . . I'd always assumed . . . '

'What?'

'One of my cousins or uncles . . . they're closer to you . . . '

She said dismissively, 'They're a useless bunch. You're the best of the lot, Jack. And you love the place, don't you? I've seen it in your eyes.'

Slowly, he nodded. He heard her say, 'There's one thing, though. I would expect you to live on the farm.'

'Of course. I'd be pleased to.'

'You could have the cottage.' She was watching him. 'You haven't other plans, have you, Jack?'

'Other plans . . . ?'

'There've been a lot of weddings recently. Soldiers coming home to their sweethearts. I thought the church bells might wear out. You haven't any thoughts in that direction, have you, Jack?'

In his mind's eye, he saw Julia running down the cliff towards him. 'Well, I — '

'You see, I don't believe in early marriages.'

He sensed that he stood on a knife edge. Carrie was difficult and capricious. Now that such an extraordinary gift had been offered to him, he must be careful not to jeopardize it.

'A little bird mentioned to me', said Carrie, 'that you'd been seen once or twice with the Temperley girl.'

'Julia?' He glanced sharply at her.

She made a small gesture. 'As I said, I don't believe in early marriages. They are almost always a mistake. And I've heard that the Temperley girl is . . . flighty.'

'Flighty?' he echoed, and he remembered Julia at his home-coming party, surrounded by men, enjoying the admiration in their eyes. And Julia sitting on the terrace with Will, her fingers ruffling his hair.

'Just gossip,' said Carrie carelessly. 'One hears gossip.' She handed him a glass. 'What do you say?'

When he stared at her blankly, she whispered, 'Sixfields, Jack.'

'Yes, Carrie,' he said. It was hard to speak and the room was airless and constricting. 'Oh yes.'

'Then let's drink to it.' She raised her glass. 'To Sixfields.'

'To Sixfields.' Jack drank. The sherry was sickly sweet, and seemed to stick in his throat like glue.

★   ★   ★

He cycled to the top of the hill and dismounted, propping the bike against a five-barred gate, looking back at the house.

His. All this — the house, the acres that surrounded it, the money in the bank — could be his. Jack wondered how many weeks or months it would be before that thought did not shock him, did not speed his heart and send the blood rushing through his veins. He knew that Carrie's bequest had the power to change his life. In the meantime he would have a place of his own, and a purpose to his days. And when he came into his inheritance —

Thirteen years ago, after his father had lost his savings in the Depression, the Chancellors had left their graceful, spacious home to the north of Bridport, and had moved to the School House. Jack had never forgotten the humiliation. His old, familiar bedroom had been exchanged for a smaller one, decorated in institutional greens and creams; sometimes, when there had been more than the usual number of boarders, he had been obliged to share a room with Will. His fellow pupils had known, of course, that his tuition was free, dependent on his father's post as housemaster. *Teacher's pet*, they had whispered. *Your people short of a bob or two, are they, Chancellor?* He had learned to silence his tormentors in his own way, with his fists, but he had never forgotten. Money might not buy you happiness, but he had known since the age of thirteen that life could be damned miserable without it.

Now he fumbled for his cigarettes as he recalled his conversation with Carrie. *I've decided to leave Sixfields to you, Jack.* His hands shook as he flicked the lighter. Half a dozen uncles and cousins, more closely related to Carrie, had a greater claim to Sixfields than he. Suddenly he was seized by doubt, convinced that she would change her mind and leave the estate to someone else. That she would never write the promised letter to her solicitor. That she was playing with him, dangling everything he wanted in front of his envious gaze, only to snatch it away.

He closed his eyes, drawing on his cigarette, trying to calm himself. *Steady, Jack*, he thought. No reason, provided he was careful, for Carrie to change her mind. He just had to play his cards right.

I don't believe in early marriages, Jack. Yesterday, drifting off to sleep on the sand, he had thought of asking Julia to marry him. Now his earlier doubts returned. *I've heard the Temperley girl is flighty.* He had sensed a passion in Julia that had matched his own. She had offered herself to him and it had been damned difficult to do the right thing. Her ardour had taken him by surprise and had sat oddly with her distant, untouchable beauty. She had changed, she was no longer the innocent schoolgirl he had left behind in 1942.

He wondered whether someone had taught her to respond like that. Had she known other men during his long absence? The worm of suspicion coiled and uncoiled in his heart as Jack recalled fragments from the letters his fellow soldiers had received in North Africa and Italy. Letters from faithless wives: *I don't know how to tell you this, Bert, but I've been seeing someone . . .* Letters from neighbours whose protestations of disinterested helpfulness sat ill at ease with the gleam of avid prurience that clung to every ungrammatical phrase: *I seen your Annie down the Bull last night with a soldier . . .* Once more, Jack pictured Julia's closed eyes and parted lips. The thought came unbidden into his mind that she would have been easy. *Easy.*

Jack crushed the cigarette end into the dry grass, making certain it was extinguished. He needed time to think. Time for Carrie's extraordinary offer to sink in. A little of the tension fell from him. He had only to wait, he told himself. Wait, and make sure no one else was sniffing around Julia. Wait, and keep the old lady happy. Carrie must be pushing fifty, he reminded himself, and, as she herself had pointed out, her health was feeble. She wasn't the sort to make old bones. If he waited, if he was careful, then he could have both Julia and Sixfields.

★　★　★

The hot weather persisted. Julia, who had a sneaking preference for winter and a sentimental attachment to log fires and to Christmas, couldn't settle to anything. After a rather half-hearted argument with her mother, and yet another failed attempt to telephone Jack, she was reduced to wandering around the house, trying to find shelter from the sun.

If Marius hadn't so unaccountably disappeared, she thought peevishly, as she paused in the drawing room, tuning the dial of the radio, passing an ivory chessman from hand to hand. So exasperating of him to have gone away just when she needed someone to talk to. For the twentieth time she wondered what on earth he was doing. Topaz had recited a garbled message about Marius telephoning from London, but since then they had heard nothing. Julia felt a flicker of curiosity. It wasn't like Marius to be so secretive. Privately, she hoped he was doing something exciting — arranging a trip to the theatre, perhaps, or a holiday. It was so long since they'd had a holiday.

Yet again she thought back to Tuesday. It had been such a lovely day: Jack had kissed her and she had been certain that he loved her. But now, standing at the window of the playroom, pleating and unpleating the folds of curtain, it occurred to her that he hadn't actually *said* he loved her. He had told her that he wanted to make love to her, but then he had made love to other women and he hadn't been in love with them.

But he had said 'our future', she reminded herself. Lying in his arms on the sand, she had assumed he meant marriage. Half an hour later, a family of day-trippers had invaded their beach, shrieking as they lurched on wedge heels down the steep path. They had woken Jack up and afterwards he had seemed tired and disoriented. He had been late for an appointment and they had hurried back home without saying a great deal more.

She had expected him to call the following day, but he had not. *He's helping at Sixfields*, Prudence Chancellor had explained each time Julia had telephoned. In the forty-eight hours since she had parted from Jack, Julia's certainty had diminished. Now doubts haunted her. Should she have let Jack kiss her?

67

Should she have told him how much she wanted him? Looking back, she felt both uneasy and embarrassed. Had she thrown herself at him? Had she cheapened herself? Did he think less of her — had he lost his respect for her?

She wished she could think of something other than Jack. The trouble was that everyone but herself seemed to have something important to do. Marius had his mysterious business in London and Jack was working on the farm. Even Will was busy — something to do with a garage, she recalled vaguely. There was Topaz, of course, but Topaz would be gone in a day or two, and then she, Julia, would be aimless again.

For the first time, she admitted to herself the truth. She missed her job. She hadn't thought she would, but she did. Working at Temperley's had given a shape to her day and had made her feel part of the world. As Julia Temperley, manageress of Temperley's Radios during her brother's absence, she had *mattered*. Peoples' livelihoods — even the war effort — had depended on her. Often that dependency had frightened her, often she had longed for Marius to return so that she could pass over the reins of the company to him and slough off the responsibilities that kept her awake at night. Often she had longed for time to catch up on her old pastimes: riding, walking the dogs, seeing friends.

But there was a limit to how much time you could spend walking and riding, and some of her friends had moved away and others she had alienated during the months of depression that had followed her father's death. Most of those who remained had jobs of their own, or had married and had children, and so had little time for her. For weeks now she had felt that she was drifting, empty and aimless. She missed the company that work had provided and the sense that she was doing something useful. She missed the mental exercise, and the challenge and excitement.

She hadn't said a word to Marius, of course. She knew that she mustn't let him suspect that she had been anything other than delighted to hand him back his job at Temperley's. It couldn't have been easy taking up the reins again after five years in the army and she would not add to his difficulties by making him feel guilty for reclaiming what was his. And besides, she had Jack, didn't she? Jack's homecoming would fill the gap. If only he would telephone . . .

The sound of a car heading down the gravel drive cut into Julia's thoughts and she looked up. When she caught sight of Marius, sitting in the front seat of the taxi, she smiled, relieved. She was about to run out to greet him when she saw him go to the back door and open it. A young woman climbed out of the car. She was holding a small child. Even from the playroom, Julia could hear the child's screams.

She couldn't think why Marius had brought a strange woman and child home with him. And without warning them. She must be an old friend, perhaps, whom he had met on the train, and had invited to tea . . .

Adele had gone outside to meet the new arrivals. Julia ran out to join them.

The sun beat down on the gravel courtyard. The child bawled. Marius looked grim.

Then he said, 'Mother. Julia. I'd like you to meet my wife, Suzanne. And my daughter, Tara.'

★   ★   ★

They sat in the drawing room, drinking tea. Or, rather, with cups of tea in front of them. Marius hadn't touched his tea and Adele's hands trembled, making the cup rattle against the saucer. And the child was arching her back, red-faced and screaming in her mother's arms, so no takers *there*, thought Julia, who didn't trust herself to pick up her cup because she was afraid she might throw it at someone: Marius, probably.

Adele repeated, 'A special licence . . . ' and Marius said again, 'It seemed the best way. Sort everything out quickly.'

There was a long silence. Adele took a deep breath. 'I didn't know . . . If you'd said . . . ' She made a visible effort to gather her thoughts. Then she said quietly to Marius, 'You were married today? In London?' He nodded. 'And the child? Why hadn't you told me about the child?'

He started to speak, but Suzanne interrupted him. 'It was my fault, Mrs Temperley. Marius didn't know about Tara.' Through the child's yells, Julia caught traces of Suzanne's Cockney accent. 'He only found out on Monday. I hadn't told him. It was my fault. There, love, there.' She joggled the little girl up and down. Tara's face was bright red and streaked with dirt. Two long trails of snot hung from her nose. There was a damp patch, Julia noticed, on her bottom.

Suzanne said to Marius, 'If I could take her somewhere and change her it might calm her down a bit. And you could talk properly.'

'Let me take her.' Adele crossed the room to Suzanne and held out her arms.

'Mrs Temperley — '

'You must be exhausted, Suzanne. And I am her grandmother, after all.' Adele's voice trembled. Silently, Suzanne passed her the baby. Adele drew the grubby, bawling little thing to her as she walked out of the room, not seeming to care, thought Julia with revulsion, about the snot and the damp patch.

'I'd better — ' Marius's sentence hung unfinished in the air, then he dashed out after his mother.

Which left Julia and Suzanne together. What tactful little phrase, wondered Julia savagely, would salvage *this* social situation?

Suzanne spoke first. 'Blimey, I don't half need this.' She managed a smile as she picked up the cup of tea. 'What a day.'

'Really?' said Julia coldly.

'Such a fuss. Weddings.' She swallowed a mouthful of tea. Julia saw her make a little grimace.

'Sugar?'

'Thanks.' Suzanne was about to help herself to sugar using the teaspoon from her saucer; pointedly, Julia offered her the sugar spoon. Suzanne's small, vivid face, which was pale already, went a little paler.

Some of the tea had slopped into the saucer. When Suzanne raised the cup, drips trailed to the Indian rug. She glanced across. 'A serviette . . . ?'

'Napkin,' said Julia automatically, handing her one.

Suzanne bit her lip. She dabbed at the rug. Then she looked Julia squarely in the eye.

'I know what you're thinking. I daresay I should be thinking much the same in your place. I don't suppose you'd have chosen someone like me for a sister-in-law, would you? But I am your sister-in-law whether you like it or not, so you may as well get used to it. And if we're to share a house, then for Marius's sake we may as well be civil to each other, don't you think?'

For the first time Julia understood the full implications of Marius's appalling alliance. She stood up.

'Share a house? Share *my* home? With you? Never.' She was shaking. 'Never.' She ran out of the room.

★ ★ ★

If Jack wouldn't come to her, then she must find him. Fury lending her speed, Julia cycled through the copse, along the lane.

When, twenty minutes later, Jack answered the door of the School House, Julia flung herself into his arms.

71

'*Jack*,' she said, and burst into tears.

In the drawing room, he gave her his handkerchief and she managed, between sobs and blowings of her nose, to explain about Marius and his awful wife and revolting baby.

'And she's going to live at Missencourt, Jack! At *my* house!'

'Adele's house,' said Jack.

She knew that, strictly speaking, he was correct, but she said obstinately, 'It's *my* home. I've always lived there.' Then, when he did not reply, she cried out, 'And where have you *been*, Jack? I've been waiting for you!'

'Helping out at Sixfields,' he muttered. He seemed preoccupied, his full attention on something other than her. Suddenly he said, 'Something extraordinary's happened. Something marvellous. I haven't told anyone yet. My cousin Carrie's going to leave Sixfields to me. The house, the farm, the money — the lot. She wants me to work for her, help run the place.' Jack's voice was taut with excitement. 'It's everything I've ever wanted, Julia: work I'll enjoy, and I'll be able to live at the cottage. It'll solve all my problems.'

It would solve both their problems, she realized. Some of her misery slipped away. 'I'll come with you, Jack,' she said. 'We can get married, can't we? Then we can both live at Sixfields and I won't have to stay at Missencourt with that awful woman.'

When he did not reply immediately, she added quickly, 'I don't mind if it's only a little place. I don't mind where I live so long as I'm with you. And Missencourt would be unbearable, with *her* there.'

He said, 'Julia, I can't possibly marry you now,' and her mind seemed to go blank, frozen. 'I mean — ' he began, as she whispered, 'Not marry me?' Yet she had always assumed that one day she and Jack would marry. Always.

'Not now.' He made a vague gesture with his hands.

There was an odd feeling in the pit of her stomach. It reminded her of how you felt when you stood at the shoreline and the sea sucked the sand from beneath your feet. She was off balance, all her old assumptions knocked away.

She gasped, 'Oh,' and he said quickly, 'Carrie doesn't approve of early marriages. And I don't want to ruffle her feathers. We just need to wait a while, that's all.'

She hardly heard him. She remembered the beach and how she had, quite literally, flung herself at him. She said, 'It doesn't matter. It was a silly idea.' She caught sight of his expression. The embarrassment and guilt she recognized in his eyes added to her humiliation.

'Julia.' He reached out a hand, coaxing her. 'I only meant that we can't get married just yet. That's not unreasonable, is it?'

That's not unreasonable . . . She flung off his hand. 'So we should wait till it's convenient for you?'

He flushed. 'I didn't mean that.'

'Didn't you?' Suddenly, she wanted to hurt him. 'I don't need you, Jack. I can manage without you.' Yet she had no idea where she would go, unable to remain at Missencourt, unable to marry Jack. She only knew that she must at all costs claw back her pride. 'Plenty of other fish in the sea,' she said viciously and was pleased to see him flinch.

'What do you mean?'

'You seem to believe that I'll go on waiting for ever.'

'Was there someone else?' he said, suddenly. 'While I was away?'

'What if there was? What's it to you?' Julia grabbed her sunglasses from the table.

'Who?'

'Oh, for God's sake — ' She made to leave the room.

'One of the airmen at the base? Someone from town?'

She said disgustedly, 'What I did or didn't do while

73

you were away is none of your business now, is it?'

Jack's eyes had hardened. '*Will*,' he said softly.

The single word halted her, halfway to the door. She swung round. 'What did you say?'

'That perhaps you're not too fussy.' His voice was like ice, his gaze contemptuous. 'That one brother might do as well as another.'

She raised her hand to slap his face, but he caught her wrist. She cried, 'Will's ten times nicer than you, Jack! Ten times nicer to *me*!' and had the satisfaction of seeing that, beneath the tan, his face had paled.

She pulled away from him. She said coldly, clearly, 'Go and live at Sixfields if that's what you want. I hope you hate it. I hope it makes you miserable. You deserve it. I hope it makes you lonely and miserable and mad like your Cousin Carrie.'

★ ★ ★

Julia was halfway between the School House and Missencourt when she slid off the bike and sat down on the verge, her knees bent up to her face. This time she did not weep, but fumbled in her pocket for her cigarettes and matches. There was one cigarette, but no matches, which seemed, just then, the last straw. She let her head fall forward on to her folded arms and she closed her eyes. She longed to shut out the expression on Jack's face and the recollection of the things that she and he had said. She felt sick with shock and her head throbbed.

She did not know how long she had been sitting there when she heard a car draw up and a familiar voice call out, 'Julia?'

She looked up, and saw the Chancellors' old Aston Martin.

'Hello, Will.'

'Are you all right?'

'Bit of a headache.'

'Can I give you a lift anywhere? Are you going to Missencourt?'

She shook her head. Then she rose to her feet and climbed into the car beside him. She could see the concern in his eyes, but could not yet face explanations, answers.

'I'll put the bike in the back,' he said.

She sat in the passenger seat, the unlit cigarette dangling between her fingers as he lifted her bicycle into the back of the car. He climbed in beside her.

'Have you a light, Will?'

He flicked a lighter. 'This is my last one,' she said. 'But we can share.' She passed him the cigarette. 'Marius has got married,' she told him. 'And he has a baby.' She felt peculiarly flat, drained of emotion.

Will coughed and handed her back the cigarette. 'Marius? *Married? When?*'

'Today. In London.' She gave a crooked smile. 'Turn-up for the books, don't you think?'

Will's eyes were wide. 'You've met her?'

'Met *them*. Just now. I was awfully rude to her, actually.'

'He never said anything — '

'He didn't, did he?'

'Did you know about her? Had he mentioned her?'

'Not a dicky bird,' she said lightly.

'*God*. What's she like?'

'Pretty, in a common sort of way. Not Marius's type, I would have thought.'

'And a *baby*?'

'A daughter. *Tara*.' Julia made a face. 'She could at least have given it a proper name. It yelled all the time. Got on my nerves.'

'Poor Julia,' he said sympathetically and she felt tears sting at the back of her eyes. She didn't want Will to be kind because if he was kind to her then she would begin to feel again, and she couldn't face that, not just yet. It was so much easier just to sit here smoking, saying horrid, bitchy things about Marius and his new wife and daughter.

'Shall I drive you somewhere?' he asked and she nodded, biting her lip.

'I thought I'd give her a run,' he explained as he put the car into gear. 'Not far, I'm afraid — she gobbles petrol.'

The Aston Martin purred along the narrow country road. After a while he said, 'Bit of a shock for you all.'

She gave a croak of laughter. 'You could say that.' She whispered, 'The thing is, I've nothing left now.' The thought terrified her.

He darted a glance at her. 'Julia, you know that's not true.'

'But it is. I haven't got Missencourt and I haven't got Temperley's.' Her voice was low and scratchy, and she felt exhausted. 'I miss my work, you see, Will. I mean, really miss it. I didn't expect to feel like that, but I do. And I don't want to share Missencourt with Suzanne. I know that's not very nice of me, but there it is.'

'It might not be so bad,' he said comfortingly. 'It's just the shock, I expect. You might get to like her.'

Tall trees rose to either side of them, blocking the sun. She noticed that the leaves of the horse chestnuts were already turning yellow in expectation of autumn. She said very quietly, 'It's not only Marius, you see, Will. It's Jack. I've just been with Jack.'

'And . . . ?'

'And I asked him to marry me.'

He braked so sharply she had to reach out to the dashboard to steady herself. The car drew to a halt in the shade of the trees.

'And he said . . . ?'

'No. He said no.' She cried out, 'What am I going to do, Will? What am I going to do?'

'Well.' A pause. 'You could marry *me*.'

She laughed. 'Will — '

He shot her a glance. 'Why not? It'd be fun.'

'*Silly.*'

He turned away, looking out into the woodland. Julia sat and smoked. After a while, when the silence had gone on too long to be companionable, she glanced at him.

The hurt in his eyes shocked her. 'Will,' she said, 'I didn't mean . . . ' Her voice trailed away. 'I didn't think you were serious.'

'I didn't think you'd say yes,' he said. 'But I didn't think you'd *laugh*.'

She felt dreadful. 'I wasn't laughing at you, Will. It was just a surprise, that's all.' When he did not answer, she touched his shoulder. 'A nice surprise.'

He looked round at her. 'Really?'

'Of course.' And she was, she found, immeasurably touched. 'It's very sweet of you,' she said gently, 'but you don't have to worry about me. I'll be all right, really I will. You don't have to feel sorry for me.'

'I don't feel sorry for you. That wasn't why I asked you to marry me.' His hand gripped the steering wheel so hard his knuckles whitened. 'I asked you because I love you.' Her disbelief must have showed in her face, because he said, 'Is that so hard to believe?'

'Will — '

'I thought *you* were different,' he interrupted angrily. 'It's bad enough with Mum and Dad. They still seem to think I'm a kid. God, I'm sick of it. Sick of being poor old Will, who can't manage by himself, who needs looking after. I didn't think *you* were like that.'

She put her hand over his. 'Dear Will,' she said gently.

He said, 'It was always you and Jack, wasn't it? I was always looking on, always on the outside. And then Jack went away and it was different. You seemed to notice me.' He studied her face. 'Or were you just making do?

Putting up with me till Jack came home?'

It was Julia's turn to feel annoyed. 'How can you think that of me?'

He shrugged and repeated, 'It was always you and Jack.'

'That doesn't mean I don't care about you, too.'

Momentarily, he brightened. Then he slumped back into the seat. 'As . . . a sort of brother . . . or a friend . . . someone to pass the time with . . . You don't feel the same way about me as you do about Jack.'

Over the last few days, her feelings for Jack had veered wildly between elation and misery. At Hernscombe Cove she had offered herself to Jack. When she remembered that, she felt hot with shame.

She stared out at the trees. 'Most of the time I seem to feel angry or upset with him. It can't be *love*, can it, to feel like that?'

'*I* love you, Julia,' Will said fiercely. 'I adore you.'

Once more, tears smarted behind her eyes. Tears of relief, this time. That someone loved her, cared about her, put her first.

He coaxed her, 'We've had fun, haven't we?'

She remembered how he had tried to cheer her up, after her father had died. She smiled. 'Lots of fun.'

'That time we went to that awful pantomime — '

'The scenery fell down — '

'When we got lost, coming back from our picnic, because they'd taken away the signposts — '

Her laughter threatened to slide of out control. He said, 'I've missed you this past week.' He put his arm around her shoulders, drawing her towards him. How nice it was to be with Will, she thought. How easy and fun and uncomplicated.

'Marry me,' he whispered. His lips brushed against her cheek.

Much later she thought that she married him because she was too tired to argue. Because in the course of an afternoon all her old convictions were flung up into the air and scattered in disarray, like spillikins. Jack, Marius, Will: nothing had been quite as she thought it was.

Which was more important, she wondered, to love or to be loved? She needed to be loved. She had lost her father, she had lost both Missencourt and Jack. When Will whispered, 'Please, Julia, it would be such fun,' she gave him her answer.

★   ★   ★

The following morning Prudence drove Veronica and Topaz to the railway station. 'I'm sorry it's been so — so *hectic*,' she said apologetically. 'All those *scenes*. I do loathe *scenes*.'

Since the news of Marius's marriage and Julia's engagement had broken, both the School House and Missencourt had resounded with tears and upraised voices and slammed doors.

Veronica said, 'I suppose we shall see you next at the wedding. I don't suppose it'll be a grand affair, will it, Prudence?'

Prudence changed gear rather noisily. 'They plan to be married as soon as the banns are read.'

'Ah,' said Veronica, with a small smile.

'Not that there's any reason to rush.' Prudence was pink.

At the station Prudence kissed them goodbye before heading back to the School House. Topaz waved until the car was out of sight. The good weather had broken, and the grey skies spat rain. She did not yet join her mother in the Ladies' Room, but remained outside, sitting on a bench, her hands dug into the pockets of her mackintosh.

After a few minutes she caught sight of a car. When it drew up beside the station Marius climbed out.

'Thank goodness I've caught you. I wanted to say

goodbye. I brought you this.' He handed her a package. 'To make up for the cinema.'

'What is it?'

'You can open it on the train.'

She slid the parcel into her pocket. Then she said, 'I haven't had the chance to congratulate you, Marius. On your marriage and your daughter.' She reached up and kissed his cheek. 'Tara. Such a lovely name.'

'It's something to do with a film. Suzanne's favourite film.'

'*Gone with the Wind.*' Topaz had seen it five times. 'It's the name of Scarlett O'Hara's home.'

'Oh.' He looked bewildered; she felt suddenly sorry for him. She said gently, 'It'll be all right, Marius, I know that it will. You'll be so happy.'

'It's just that I don't *know* them — ' he began, and then he broke off, and smiled ruefully. 'I'll be glad when the dust settles, that's all. My poor mother.'

'I suppose,' she said, 'with both of you getting married . . .'

His face clouded. 'I've tried to speak to Julia, to stop her rushing into things, but she won't listen to me. My mother tried too, but that just seemed to make her more determined.'

'Doesn't your mother want Julia to marry Will?'

'No.' He shook his head. 'No, she doesn't.'

'Why not?'

The rain was thickening; puddles had begun to form at the sides of the road. 'Because she doesn't love him,' said Marius. His face was grim. 'And why not start with love, if you have the chance?'

The train was coming down the line. Marius helped them with their luggage. Topaz flung her arms around him and hugged him. Then she climbed into the carriage.

The train was crowded, but someone offered Veronica a window seat, while Topaz squeezed between a portly gentleman in a bowler hat and a very fat lady cradling a Pekinese on her lap.

Leaving her cousins, she had always felt sad, but this time the sadness had a different edge to it. There was an unpleasant, empty sensation in the pit of her stomach. She felt as though the world had moved on without her, leaving her behind. The place she had thought she had known, the people she had thought she loved most in the world, were no longer the same. They had become almost unrecognizable, almost strangers.

Her elbows pinned to her sides by her fellow passengers, she unwrapped the parcel Marius had given her. There were three bars of chocolate and a note attached to them, saying, 'So you don't have to kiss any more colonels. Love, Marius.'

She put the chocolate and the note back in her pocket. With a lurch and a great puff of smoke, the train pulled out of the station. Topaz rose to her feet. She heard her mother sigh, 'Oh, *Topaz*,' as she opened the door of the compartment. And then she began to run back along the corridor, her gaze darting through window after window.

But Marius had already driven away, and Missencourt was lost among the trees and the rain, and her bosoms joggled up and down as she ran, reminding her of her grown-up, cumbersome body. So after a while she slowed and went to stand by a window, staring out at the retreating countryside.

Her breath misted the pane. With the tip of her finger she wrote her name on the clouded glass. She paused, her finger outstretched, and then she wrote another name. Then, in a single sudden movement, she drew the flat of her hand quickly down, wiping the glass clean, and walked back through the train to her compartment.

Part Two

The Ice Palace

1946–1949

4

The Brookes' first-floor flat was in Bayswater, in Cleveland Close, a quiet, semi-circular road ten minutes' walk from Kensington Gardens. Topaz's bedroom window looked out on to a small crescent of grass and trees. In the autumn the leaves drifted from the white poplars, covering the lawn with a soft blanket.

The new flat was smaller than the one in which they had lived before the war. Their belongings, reclaimed out of storage, seemed out of place in the pale Georgian rooms. The heavy cedarwood chests and carved occasional tables, remnants of Veronica Brooke's girlhood in India, looked dark and overbearing beneath the delicate arabesques and curlicues of the plaster ceiling bosses and cornices. Veronica seemed disappointed in the flat, but then Veronica, thought Topaz, seemed disappointed about most things: men, and life, and her daughter.

Topaz hauled the furniture around the rooms, trying to make it fit in better, while her mother sat on the sofa and smoked. One by one their old acquaintances of pre-war days reappeared, Veronica's friends greyer and shabbier, Topaz's unrecognizable, their plaits and scuffed knees replaced by sausage curls and face powder.

Veronica's friends sympathized with her about the cramped rooms. 'Yet so much easier, in some ways,' they reminded her, 'with domestic help so hard to come by.'

Dorothy Blanchard had known Veronica before the war. She had a daughter called Joyce, who was much the same age as Topaz. Joyce Blanchard was supposed to be Topaz's friend. While Veronica and Dorothy drank gin and lemon and played cards, Topaz and Joyce were sent out for walks.

'It's so they can talk about sex,' explained Joyce one cold autumn afternoon.

'How do you know?' They were skirting the Round Pond; the sharp breeze whipped up jagged little waves on the surface of the water.

'I listened at the door.'

Joyce Blanchard had flat, marmalade-coloured hair and smooth, freckled skin. Her pale eyes, which were of no particular colour, were reduced by the lenses of her glasses. She had a furtiveness, a natural impulse towards disloyalty that made Topaz wary of her.

Nevertheless, she was curious. 'What did they say?'

'They were talking about your daily help. Mrs Hemmings. Only she's not Mrs Hemmings really.'

Topaz stared at Joyce. 'You mean she's called something else?'

'No, silly,' said Joyce rudely. 'I mean, she's *Miss* Hemmings.'

It was on the tip of Topaz's tongue to point out that Mrs Hemmings must be Mrs Hemmings because she had a little boy, but she realized just in time what scorn she would heap on herself. Suzanne, after all, had been unmarried when she had had Tara.

'She had a love affair in the war', continued Joyce, her voice lowered as though disapproving listeners lurked in the rose bushes, 'with an American soldier. A *black* American soldier.' She glared triumphantly at Topaz. 'That's why she has to be a cleaning lady. She's lucky to get that, Mummy says. Awful, isn't it?'

Topaz nodded. 'All that vacuuming. I always seem to suck up the things I shouldn't, like buttons and sixpences, and miss the dust.'

'I meant', said Joyce heavily, 'how awful to have a baby without being married.'

'I suppose so.' Topaz dug her hands into her pockets,

and wondered if it was teatime and they could go home yet. Joyce fixed her once more with her colourless glare.

'You do know about the birds and the bees, don't you, Topaz?'

'Course,' she said airily.

There was a silence. Then Joyce said, 'A girl at school told me that you have to do it for an *hour*.' Her tone had altered, and she looked both disgusted and alarmed and began to walk very fast across the grass back to the Porchester Terrace gate.

★   ★   ★

The truth was, Topaz reflected as she queued in the butcher's shop the following day, that her knowledge of the birds and the bees was rather sketchy. Her mother had never talked to her about such things and, though the gardener's boy at the Lake District hotel had given her a brief and monosyllabic description of what men and women did on their wedding night, she suspected that his knowledge was, like hers, only theoretical. She wondered whether she should talk to Julia, who was, after all, now a married woman.

The queue shuffled slowly forward. Checking her ration book to make sure she had enough coupons to buy lamb cutlets, Topaz tried once more to pinpoint why Julia's wedding day had been such a strangely joyless occasion. It couldn't have been just that bread was still rationed or that the wedding cake's royal icing was, in fact, cardboard painted white, or that the champagne, acquired by Maurice Chancellor from who knows where, was flat — it was as though they had all been trying so hard to be happy and cheerful that the effort had exhausted them, making them as flat as the champagne. Jack's absence hadn't, of course, helped — though his presence, Topaz felt, might have made things even worse.

The butcher ran out of lamb cutlets just before Topaz was served, so she bought scrag end instead. Walking home, she had just turned into Cleveland Close when she caught sight of a familiar figure heading towards her. Recognizing Marius, her heart lifted, and she smiled and waved and ran to meet him.

'You didn't tell me you were coming!'

'I had to see someone at the Ministry of Supply. I wasn't sure how long it would take.' He kissed her cheek.

In a nearby cafe Marius ordered cakes and tea.

'How's Tara?' asked Topaz.

'She's very well.' He offered Topaz the sugar bowl. Then he frowned and said suddenly, 'She screams if I come near her. She'll let my mother pick her up, but not me. I had no idea it would be like this.'

'I suppose she's just not used to men.'

'But I'm her *father*,' he said angrily. 'I don't mind if she cries when she sees the butcher, the baker or the candlestick maker. But I do mind if she screams every time she sees me.'

'It must be . . . hurtful.'

He didn't reply. She asked, 'And Suzanne? How is she?'

'Fine. Just fine.'

She waited for him to say more, but he didn't, so after a while she went on, 'And Julia and Will?'

'They're still looking for somewhere to live.'

'It must be rather squashed at the School House.'

'Though with Jack gone . . . ' Marius shrugged. 'Julia and Will could stay at Missencourt, you know. We've plenty of room.'

'Yes, of course.'

'It's all rather a mess, I'm afraid,' he said quietly and then seemed mentally to shake himself. 'Anyway, what about you, Topaz? How are you? Enjoying London? What are you doing with yourself?'

'Standing in queues, mostly. Our daily help can only come for a couple of hours each day, so I do the shopping while she cleans the flat and does the washing.'

'It doesn't sound a lot of fun.'

'Oh, I don't mind. Though it'll be nice when there's real things instead of pretend things.'

'What do you mean?'

'Well, like Julia's wedding cake. Cardboard instead of icing. And this marzipan. Semolina instead of almonds.' Topaz peeled the marzipan from her Battenberg slice, and rolled it into a ball. 'And I go to parties,' she told him. 'They are so awful, Marius. There's always a buffet where people stare at you if you drop things on the floor, which I always do. And there's dancing and no one ever asks me to dance. And then there's games . . . ' she rolled her eyes ' . . . I mean, *really*. Can you imagine me, playing sardines, having to squash into a wardrobe. I'm seventeen, for heaven's sake.' She sighed. 'It must be nice to be properly grownup, not to have to do boring things any more.'

'You have to do other boring things. Like paying taxes and going to work.'

'I suppose so.' Privately she thought that she might rather like to go to work; at least then she would have some money of her own.

Marius enquired after her mother. 'Mummy's very well,' she said.

'Picking up the threads?'

'Mmm. All her old admirers are coming out of the woodwork. I must say, Marius, that it's a good thing I know you and Will and Jack. Mummy's admirers aren't much of an advertisement for your sex. Still — ' she helped herself to another cake ' — boys come to the parties. Eligible young men. So you never know, do you? I might meet the love of my life, mightn't I?'

★ ★ ★

She didn't meet the love of her life, but at a party in St John's Wood she met Francesca Lovatt. After the buffet one of the mothers clapped her hands together and suggested charades, so Topaz, with the excuse of powdering her nose, made her way out through the back of the house.

The garden was long and narrow and walled. Topaz walked past a half-hearted vegetable plot and the rusting remains of an Anderson shelter. At the end of the garden there was a compost heap and a ramshackle greenhouse. The sky was clear and speckled with stars; shivering in her puff-sleeved velvet frock, she jumped up and down a few times, rubbing her bare arms. Then she became aware that there was a girl sitting inside the greenhouse, smoking a cigarette and watching her. Feeling rather foolish, she opened the glass door.

'Is it warmer in here?'

'A bit. Close the door quickly if you're coming in.'

Inside the greenhouse was airless and musty. The soil floor was scattered with dirty straw. The girl's eyes narrowed. 'You're Joyce Blanchard's friend.'

'Acquaintance,' said Topaz firmly. 'Joyce is my acquaintance. My name's Topaz Brooke.'

'Francesca Lovatt.' Francesca blew out a thin stream of blue smoke.

'What are you doing in here?'

'Smoking, obviously.' She offered Topaz a packet. 'Want one?'

Topaz took a cigarette and sat down beside Francesca on a heap of sacks. Francesca's lighter flared.

Topaz shivered again. 'It's freezing.'

'It's better', said Francesca, 'than charades.'

'We could light a fire.'

'With what?'

'Well — ' Topaz glanced round ' — those sticks,

90

perhaps.' In one corner of the greenhouse was a heap of twigs, some supporting dry, brown tomato plants.

They snapped the twigs in half and lit the bonfire with Francesca's lighter. Francesca put out her hands, warming them over the fire. Her fingers, like the rest of her, were long and thin. She had a long, thin, intelligent face, and long, fine, light brown hair. There were odd little crinkles around her eyelids, so that her grey-green eyes looked older than the rest of her.

'I always thought', said Topaz, 'that I was the only person who hated parties.'

'Plenty of people hate parties.'

'Pretty girls like them, I suppose, because everyone wants to dance with them.'

Francesca stared at her. 'It wouldn't help, though, would it?' she said scornfully. 'You wouldn't want to *marry* any of those boys, would you? And that's what these parties are for.'

'Don't you want to get married?'

'My sisters are married and it's rather put me off.'

'How many sisters have you got?'

'Three.'

Topaz was envious. 'Lucky thing.' She put the last of the twigs on the fire. 'If you don't want to get married, what will you do?'

'I'm going to get a job. It would be nice to work in a theatre, don't you think?'

The fire was dying down, the greenhouse chilling again. Topaz gathered up great clumps of matted straw from the floor and flung them on the embers. There was a whoosh and a roar, and flames shot up to the glass ceiling. Sparks settled on the greenhouse's wooden struts and the dried leaves of the tomato plants charred and disintegrated.

Francesca beat out the flames with a sack. 'I was going — ' she said, stamping on the fragments of glowing straw ' — to get a newspaper.' She was slightly breathless. 'We could look in the advertisements, couldn't we?'

Topaz smiled. Blackened fragments of straw floated through the cold air. 'Yes. Yes, we could.'

★　★　★

Marius thought that if he had been asked to choose one word to describe his marriage, then that word would have been *polite*. He and Suzanne were unendingly polite to each other. Their constant mutual enquiries after each other's day and each other's health were, he suspected, as wearing to Suzanne as to him.

He did not try to break through the barrier of politeness because he was afraid of what might lie behind it. If he had looked her in the eye and insisted she say what she felt, then she might have told him what she thought of a marriage that neither of them had wanted. As it was, he had only to grit his teeth, to say the right things, to forget the closeness of minds that he had once, remembering his father and mother, believed to be a natural part of marriage.

Only in bed did they find any intimacy. There he could remember why six months earlier he had searched for her. Only when there was no need for words did they communicate. Matching her response and her recklessness left him exhausted and elated, his mind emptied of its nagging anxieties and concerns.

But afterwards, all passion spent, she would turn aside and stare up at the ceiling, and he'd hear himself say, 'Was it all right for you, darling?' in the stilted, unnatural tones of a bad film actor. And she'd make some anodyne reply and close her eyes, telling him that she was tired. Yet he knew that sometimes she lay awake for an hour or more, not sleeping. Both of them lying awake, not speaking, trying not to disturb the other.

Often he thought how changed she was from the

young woman he had known in Northumberland. The energy and zest for life that had first attracted him had been replaced by wariness, as though she was holding something back, deliberately suppressing a part of herself. He put the changes in her down to her experiences of the last few years. He managed to piece together a little of what had happened to her. After she had left the ATS, her family had refused to take her in. To survive, she had rented furnished rooms and taken what work she could find. He could not begin to imagine what it must have been like to give birth to her child, alone and unsupported. He wondered whether she had considered giving Tara up for adoption, but felt it intrusive to ask. He guessed that responsibility and social censure had worn her down, robbing her of the spontaneity and enthusiasm that had first entranced him. He told himself that in time things would get better, yet after three months of marriage he saw no evidence of improvement. Sometimes he'd catch sight of her walking round the garden, her arms wrapped around herself, darting glances at the trees and hedges as if they caged her; as if, in taking her to Missencourt, he had imprisoned her.

She seemed ill at ease, unfamiliar with much of their day-to-day life. Though she tried to help Adele with the garden, she couldn't tell a weed from a seedling and seemed surprised at the length of time it took to coax plants from the soil. That there was a bus to Dorchester only twice a day and that the nearest bus stop was a mile from Missencourt also shocked her. That Missencourt itself depended on a private generator for its electricity, had no mains gas and used a septic tank horrified her.

The first time Marius suggested a Sunday walk she said, 'Where to?', and when he vaguely sketched out a route through the fields and lanes, said again, 'But where to, Marius?' That one might walk with no particular destination in mind bewildered her. Though she went with him, stepping cautiously around cowpats and skirting mud and puddles, he was not sure whether she enjoyed it. Only at the coast did her surroundings seem to touch her, to move her. Standing on the cliff top, gazing out to the Channel, he saw to his surprise that there were tears in her eyes. The wind, she said, blinking, brushing them away, but he was not sure whether he believed her. Then she began to ask him about the D-Day landings. Whether the planes of the invasion force had flown over this cliff. Where he had sailed from, where he had landed. What it had been like. He had found himself answering questions he had previously evaded, talking more freely than he had done to anyone else. He didn't tell her everything, of course, because there was a limit to what you could expect people to hear. Walking back to Missencourt, he had sensed the beginnings of a closeness between them.

The mood was broken as soon as they reached the house. Tara had woken from her afternoon nap, loudly upset, and after she had soothed her Suzanne had been withdrawn and preoccupied. Though Tara's existence had led to their hasty marriage, she seemed to come between them instead of drawing them closer. After three months Tara still had not accepted Marius, still seemed to regard him as an intrusive and terrifying stranger. Her howls disrupted the tranquillity of Missencourt. Her repeated rejection of him wore at him, hurt him, undermined him. In the army he had encountered recalcitrant subordinates and autocratic superiors; at Temperley's he dealt with difficult customers and demanding bureaucrats. None had Tara's knack of getting beneath his skin and rubbing his emotions raw. Though Suzanne assured him that it was just a matter of time, Marius sensed that even she was beginning to despair. Though the months in the countryside had taken the pallor from Suzanne's cheeks, Tara's constant demands tired her. She rarely had an uninterrupted night's sleep. Her exhaustion showed itself in the shadows around her eyes and the occasional sharpness of her tongue.

Tara, thank God, had taken to Adele. Or was it, Marius wondered, that Adele had the knack of knowing what to do with Tara? Which he, most definitely, did not. In his gloomiest, most introspective moments, he wondered whether Tara's lack of acceptance pointed to some fundamental failing in him, some huge, previously unacknowledged character flaw. That Tara alone perceived, and told, the truth about him.

Suzanne and Tara's sudden appearance had at first been a severe shock and a disappointment to Adele. Yet, oddly, after the initial dust had settled, Adele seemed happier than she had been for months. There was a spring in her step, a contentment in her eye. When he plucked up courage to ask her opinion of Suzanne, Adele said, 'She seems a thoughtful girl.' As thoughtfulness was the quality his mother prized above all others, he was both relieved and delighted.

Adele's approval went some way towards making up for Julia's unrelenting animosity. Since her marriage, Julia's visits to Missencourt had been infrequent and brief. Sometimes, enduring Suzanne's silences, Tara's tears and Julia's hostility, Marius was aware of a deep, dark anger, an emotion which he felt ashamed of, but could not erase.

★　★　★

Topaz found a part-time job working for an historian called Rupert de Courcy, who lived in Russell Square. Rupert de Courcy did not live up to his dashing name: balding and grey, he wore baggy tweed suits and had a disconcerting habit of breaking off in mid-sentence and staring into the distance while tapping the nail of his forefinger against his front teeth.

She worked during the afternoon so that she could still do the shopping in the morning. Her tasks for Mr de Courcy were menial: filing, the mailing of letters, typing. Her typing was two-fingered and laborious, and after a month she had failed to fathom the mysteries of the filing system. 'Cross-reference, Miss Brooke, cross-reference,' Mr de Courcy told her, rather irritably. So she scribbled pencilled reminders and stuffed them into files; sometimes, opening the bulging folders, they floated to the floor, a grey and white blizzard.

There was also the problem of the Bequest. Mr de Courcy was responsible for the administration of an educational charity called the Mallingham Bequest, another romantic-sounding soubriquet that failed to live up to its promise. The Mallingham Bequest doled out a pittance each year to the various poor urban scholars who satisfied its requirements, one of which was to study history at university. Bank statements and letters detailing the amounts paid out to them arrived with worrying regularity. Topaz was supposed to record the sums and balance them at the end of each month. The difficulty was that she had no idea in which columns to put the figures, and, besides, she could not understand how numbers should balance. It wasn't a thing, she thought despairingly, that numbers *did*. After several blotted, scratched-out attempts, she took to hiding the correspondence relating to the Bequest at the back of the bookshelf, behind *The History of Northampton-shire*. For years afterwards the merest mention of Northants would make her conscience twinge.

Most evenings Topaz met Francesca in a cafe after work. The cafe was in Leicester Square. They met there in the hope that some of the glamour of the surrounding theatres might rub off on them. So far it hadn't. Every now and then beautiful, elegantly dressed creatures would flit into the cafe and then disappear back into the night, trailing clouds of perfume and unobtainable mystique, leaving Topaz and Francesca sick with envy and longing.

Topaz confided in Francesca about the Bequest.

Francesca sniggered. 'Students are starving in garrets because of you, I expect, Topaz.'

'Oh dear.' She imagined them, hollow-eyed and tubercular. She sighed. 'You are lucky, Francesca, working for a theatrical agency.'

Francesca stirred her tea. 'Margaret Lockwood phoned this morning.'

Topaz was impressed. 'Did you speak to her?'

Francesca looked mournful. 'They don't let *me* speak to famous people. I just do the filing and make the tea.'

Topaz, too, made tea. For Mr de Courcy himself and for Miss Black, his typist, who arrived once a week to collect the latest hand-written instalment of Mr de Courcy's biography of Edward VI. Topaz liked Miss Black, who told her about her salad days after the First World War. 'Such a scream, my dear. The most marvellous parties.' Now, Miss Black looked after a widowed mother in Twickenham.

Miss Black also told fortunes. After Topaz had drunk her tea, Miss Black would seize her cup, give the tea leaves a swirl and peer short-sightedly.

'Your luck's going to change soon, dear. I see a tall, dark stranger.' Her large eyes gleamed. 'He's a passionate man with deep feelings and he's going to sweep you off your feet.'

Mr de Courcy's younger brother, Peter, sometimes called at the Russell Square house. He wore a voluminous black coat and a ragged red scarf. He seemed to irritate Mr de Courcy; Topaz herself found him slightly nerve-racking. At first he ignored her, then, one day, he came to stand behind her while she was writing out her cross-references.

'Backward-sloping hand. Sign of a repressed personality,' he said.

She asked Miss Black about Peter de Courcy. 'He's an artist,' breathed Miss Black.

'Is he famous?'

'In certain circles, yes.' Miss Black lowered her voice. 'Some of his work is considered rather *shocking*.'

Topaz reported this conversation to Francesca in the cafe. Francesca said, 'That means he paints nudes. Maybe he'll want to paint you, Topaz.'

Topaz imagined herself reclining on a sofa like the fat odalisques in the National Gallery. She giggled and, after a few moments, Francesca's eyes crinkled up around the corners and she, too, began to laugh.

★　★　★

In mid-December, on a cold, blowy evening that whipped the dead leaves from the gutters, the de Courcy brothers argued in the room adjacent to Topaz's. Topaz put her hands over her ears so as not to hear.

Peter de Courcy came out of Rupert's study, slamming the door behind him. It was six o'clock: packing her bag, shrugging on her coat, Topaz tiptoed, trying not to disturb him.

She was knotting her scarf, when he said, 'Where are you going?'

'Home.'

'How about a drink?'

She stared at him. 'You and me?'

He made a great show of peering under the desk and behind the curtains. 'I can't see anyone else.' He glanced at her. 'And do your face, or they won't let you in. You look so *young*.'

She put on lipstick, dabbed powder. Her hand shook. She had been asked for a date, she thought. Her first date. Well, last summer Marius had asked her to the cinema, but they hadn't gone because he had married Suzanne instead, and besides it hadn't really been a date because Marius had never thought of her like *that*. She was unsure whether Peter de Courcy thought of her like that, either. Perhaps he just wanted company, didn't like drinking by himself.

He took her to a pub in Soho. The private bar was small and dark and smoky, with worn brown plush seats. He asked her what she'd like to drink, so she said a gin and lemon because it was what her mother always drank. She had never been in a pub before.

The gin and lemon tasted horrible. She must have shown her disgust because he smiled and said, 'Not used to drinking?' She shook her head. 'I suppose you don't smoke, either?'

She had practised with Francesca. 'Of course I do.'

His cigarettes were pungent and untipped. He lit hers and then held up the match. 'Blow it out.' She blew. 'What's your name?'

She was slightly shocked that he had asked her to the pub without taking the trouble to find out her name beforehand. She told him.

'Topaz . . . ' he said, slowly. He looked at her in a way that made her blush. 'It suits you.' His gaze drifted downwards. 'You'd be quite passable if you didn't wear those frightful clothes.'

She glanced down at her winter coat, box-pleated skirt and jersey. 'What's wrong with them?'

'Tweed and cashmere . . . A refugee from the dyed-in-the-wool upper-middle classes. Literally.'

She wasn't quite sure what he meant, but she persevered because she wanted to know. 'What should I wear, then?'

His eyes, which were hooded and weary-looking, narrowed. 'Rich colours and fabrics. Russets and emeralds. Silks and velvets.'

She imagined shops full of such glorious things, instead of the dreary utility garments that still filled the rails. She said, 'I didn't think men knew about clothes.'

'Didn't you, Topaz?' He crushed his cigarette stub into an ashtray. 'Then what a narrow little world you must live in.'

★ ★ ★

Her uncertainty about Peter de Courcy persisted. Though she went with him to the Soho pub twice more the following week, she remained half-convinced that he only asked her because she was there. She wasn't even sure whether he liked her. Often he laughed at her. Her tastes, her appearance, her comments were frequently the object of his amusement or contempt.

Mostly he talked about himself. He lived in Fitzrovia and he was on the verge of great success, he told her. Until now his career had been restrained by society's shackles of repression and prudery. The time had come to break through those bounds, he said, to push them to their limits.

He rarely asked her about herself. She didn't mind: her life had been so dull compared with his. Before the war he had travelled to France, Italy and North Africa. Hungry for new experiences, even at second-hand, she asked him about the people he had met, the places he had seen, but his answers were disappointingly vague. Though he recalled the approbation his exhibition had met with in Provence, or the paintings he had sold in Oran, he could not describe to her what Provence or Oran had looked like. He was an artist, she reminded herself. Words were not his medium.

They were standing outside the entrance to Tottenham Court Road tube station the first time he kissed her. It was seven o'clock and the streets and pavements were busy. They were about to say goodbye, always an awkward business, because saying 'See you soon' or 'See you next week' assumed things she didn't dare assume. So she offered her hand to him and said, 'Well, goodbye then,' and he flung his head back and gave a peal of laughter.

'What is it?'

'Oh *Topaz* ... ' He wiped his eyes. 'How about saying goodbye *properly*?' He pulled her towards him and kissed her. He hadn't a moustache, so at least he didn't scratch.

He said, 'Your first kiss ... What did you think of that?'

She knew that it would be tactless to tell him about the colonel. 'It was very nice.'

'*Very nice* ... ' He began to laugh again. He was still laughing as he melted into the crowds.

★ ★ ★

Marius had to go to London on business. He asked Suzanne whether she would like to go with him.

'You must have shopping to do, with Christmas so near. Or perhaps there are people you'd like to see. And you must miss London — '

'*Miss* it!' They were at breakfast; she pushed aside her teacup and went to the window and stood, her back to him, her arms wrapped around herself.

He remembered how she had walked around the garden, as if trying to push back its boundaries. 'I know you've found it hard to settle.'

'There's nothing to settle *to*.' The words burst out of her as if pent up for too long. 'It's all so *empty*. So ... so *nothing*. I find myself longing for someone just to walk down the drive. The postman ... anyone at all. Just so that things *change*.'

'Of course they change,' he protested. 'And there's

Bridport and Dorchester only a bus ride away. And all the people we know.'

'*You* know. They don't know *me*. They're not the slightest bit interested in *me*.'

'That's nonsense — ' he began, but she interrupted him.

'You know that it's true, Marius. There was some initial curiosity and then they retreated back into their safe little shells.'

'Surely the boot's on the other foot. We've had invitations, but you've turned them down.'

Her eyes flashed. 'That simply isn't true. We went to that cocktail party.'

'We left early,' he reminded her. 'You insisted.'

She shrugged. 'It was awful.'

He began to feel angry. 'And the Barringtons. We left early then, too — '

'Dull people, dull conversation. And that horrible dog kept nuzzling me.'

'You have to make an effort.' He knew he sounded pompous.

Her gaze was cool and clear. 'Why, Marius?'

'Because they're our neighbours.'

'I don't share their political views,' she said. 'I don't share their tastes or their background. The fact that we live near to each other — well, that's just an accident of fate, isn't it? Hardly a basis for friendship.'

Or for marriage, he almost said, but managed to stop himself. He took a deep breath. 'It's just that I'm concerned that you'll be lonely.'

'I'm lonelier in the company of those people,' she said scornfully. 'And I can't believe that you, Marius, really have all that much in common with them.' Her voice softened a little, though her dark eyes still challenged him. 'I won't come with you to London because I think I'm going down with Tara's cold. But it would be marvellous if you could pick up a few things for me.'

In Selfridge's that afternoon he handed Suzanne's list to the salesgirl in the haberdashery department and wandered around, looking for Christmas presents. Emerging from the shop, he found a phone box and called the Brookes' flat. Topaz was out, Veronica Brooke told him, she had an office job. Afternoons only, so inconvenient when she was needed to make up a bridge four. The office was in Bloomsbury; she finished work at six.

The cold had intensified and a yellowish fog clung to the streetlamps and to the branches of the trees. Marius put up the collar of his coat and dug his hands into his pockets. As he turned into Russell Square, he glimpsed Topaz coming out of a tall brick building near the corner of Bedford Place. The man with her was thirty-five, fortyish, perhaps. He was wearing a black coat, a wide-brimmed hat and a long red scarf. Topaz was clutching to her breast a heavy-looking bag. The palm of her companion's hand brushed against her back, then her bottom, as they headed down the stone steps.

'Marius!' cried Topaz, catching sight of him.

'I was in town, so I thought I'd look you up.' He glanced at her companion. 'Aren't you going to introduce me, Topaz?'

'Of course.' She seemed flustered. 'Marius, this is Peter de Courcy. Peter, this is Marius Temperley, an old friend of mine.'

They shook hands. Marius noticed that the cuffs of Peter de Courcy's coat were frayed and that he stank of alcohol and French cigarettes.

'I was wondering whether you'd have supper with me,' said Marius.

'*Oh*. But Peter and I — '

'You don't mind, do you, old chap?' He gave Peter de Courcy the look he had perfected in his army days for incompetent subordinates. Peter de Courcy muttered

103

something and disappeared into the fog.

When he was out of earshot, Topaz said, 'Marius. That was very *tyrannical* of you.'

He took her shopping bag from her. 'Does your mother know about him?'

In the dim light of the street lamp, he couldn't tell whether she had reddened. She said, 'No. Why should she?'

'You seemed very close.'

'We're just friends.'

'Rubbish.' He began to walk down Montague Street, Topaz trotting beside him.

'Marius — '

'He's far too old for you.'

She stopped suddenly. 'If you're just going to tell me off, Marius, then I don't want to have supper with you.'

'Sorry,' he muttered.

In a cafe in a side street off Tottenham Court Road, they peeled off coats and scarves and gloves and hats. Condensation trailed down the insides of the windows and there was a smell of wet wool and steak and kidney pie.

The waitress took their order. Marius explained why he was in London. 'Business. And shopping, for Suzanne.'

'How is she?'

'Fine,' he said. 'Fine.'

'You always say that.'

'Actually, we almost quarrelled.'

'*Almost* quarrelled?'

'We're very good', he admitted with a fleeting smile, 'at almost quarrelling.'

A silence. Then she said, 'Peter's very nice, you know, Marius. He's an artist.'

He thought, *Of course he bloody is*, recalling the shabby clothes, the overlong hair, the pouches and shadows of Topaz's friend's dissolute face.

'He's going to be famous.' She beamed. 'He wants to paint me.'

The waitress served the food. He said, 'You won't let him, will you?'

'Why not?'

There were many tactful replies to that, but he managed none of them. Instead, he said bluntly, 'Because it's not *painting* you that he's interested in.'

First she looked blank, then she went scarlet. Then she dug her knife into her steak and kidney pie, tearing the pastry shell apart. 'I suppose you find that surprising.' Her voice was low and taut.

'I didn't mean that.' He didn't make much of an attempt to hide his cynicism. 'Don't let yourself get attached to him, that's all I'm saying. Men like that aren't interested in anything that lasts.'

'He'll love me and leave me, you mean?'

'That's about it.'

Her eyes glittered. 'Perhaps I don't mind. Perhaps I don't care. Perhaps it's better than nothing.'

He said unkindly, 'I thought you had better taste, Topaz.'

She put down her knife and fork, and stood up.

'Where are you going?'

'Home.' She was putting her coat back on.

'Topaz — ' He felt suddenly ashamed; he reached out a hand to her. 'Please. I didn't mean to offend you. I just don't want you to get hurt.'

But she walked out of the cafe, leaving him sitting alone. After a while, he looked down at the two plates of steak and kidney pie and discovered that he wasn't hungry at all. So he tossed a couple of coins on to the table and then he, too, left the cafe.

★   ★   ★

During the long, slow journey home, Marius had plenty of time to think how badly he had handled the situation.

105

Damn it, he had even forgotten to give Topaz the Christmas present he had bought her in Selfridge's.

He had always appreciated her originality, her sense of adventure and lack of conformity. The thought of her being seduced by an ageing roué depressed him. There were things he should have said, things that might have prevented her throwing herself away on that lecherous cliché of an artist. He had always seen that she conspicuously lacked a protector. Conspicuously lacked *love*. Which was why, of course, she had fallen for the first man to take an interest in her.

He thought fleetingly, pointlessly, of telephoning her mother and immediately dismissed the idea. He dozed intermittently during his journey, his dreams punctuated by the discomfort of the cold, jolting train, and by the greater discomfort of his own thoughts. It was almost midnight by the time the train reached Longridge Halt. The fog had settled in the valleys, so that, walking home, he could see clearly only a few yards in front of him and had to search for the familiar landmarks that defined his path.

The porch light was on at the house, welcoming him home. Marius let himself indoors and climbed the stairs. As he tiptoed past the nursery, he heard Tara begin to stir, to make the small, snuffling moans that were the familiar prelude to her full-throated howls. In the bedroom he said Suzanne's name, but she remained curled up in the blankets, deeply asleep. He noticed the bottle of aspirin on the bedside table.

Tara's cries were becoming louder. Marius went back to the nursery. Tara was standing in her cot, clutching the rail, her face red and wet with tears. Seeing him, her howls intensified and he felt an impotent rage.

Then he noticed the despair in her eyes and his anger died as suddenly as it had been born. Lifting her out of the cot, he said gently, 'You and I are going to have to come to some sort of understanding, my love.'

Wrapping a blanket around her, he carried her downstairs, out of earshot of the bedrooms.

In the drawing room, she howled, throwing her head back, clenching her fists. He wiped her eyes and nose and cradled her against his shoulder, murmuring to her as he paced around the room, patting her back. If he had found it hard to adapt to the changes in his life, how much worse, he thought, must it have been for her. How incomprehensible the world must seem to her. Her misery was born of the changes in her short life, the different places in which she had lived, the poverty she had been born into. He had a long absence to make up for.

As he walked and rocked and murmured, he saw that outside the mist was swirling around the lawns and terrace, so that the trees rose from it unrooted and ghostly, already silvered by frost. Above the surface of the pond, the fog moved and swelled. The peacefulness of the scene reached inside the room and after a while it seemed to Marius that Tara's cries were becoming less furious. Half-hearted, almost. He continued to walk and to pat, and eventually he felt her head slip slowly forward until it was resting against his shoulder. Her silky black curls brushed against his face. She shuddered as she drew breath, but her small body had relaxed. She seemed to become heavier. Marius slowed, his voice now no more than a whisper. He knew that something miraculous had happened. Very carefully, he sat down on the sofa.

Afraid that his gaze might provoke her once more to fury and fear, it was a few moments before he dared look at the plump curve of her cheek, the long black lashes still dewed with tears, and the violet tinge of her closed eyelids. He bent and kissed her.

For the first time since he had returned to England, he seemed to see things clearly. He suspected that his own uncertainty and lack of confidence had kept him apart from his daughter. He had seen Tara as a responsibility, a burden, and not as the gift that she was. She was his hope for the future, his way through the mist.

As for Topaz, he'd phone her tomorrow and apologize. He would start again, Marius promised his daughter silently. And he would do better.

★　★　★

Topaz had not seen Peter de Courcy since the evening Marius had visited. The day before that he had taken her to his studio, shown her his paintings and asked her to pose for him. Though she had been both flattered and excited, she had also had misgivings. What if he wanted to paint her without her clothes on? Undressing for bed that night, she had looked at herself in the mirror. So much white flesh, marked by the pink indentations left by brassiere, girdle and suspenders. *It's not painting you he's interested in.* Marius had only given voice to her own doubts.

As she arrived at work on the afternoon before Christmas Eve, Miss Black whispered to her, 'Mr Peter's here. They're having the most frightful row.'

This time Topaz didn't put her fingers in her ears. The raised voices echoed through the walls. They were arguing about money. She had unwound her scarf and hung her coat on the peg, when Peter came out of his brother's study, slamming the door behind him. He paused, seeing Topaz.

'The *bugger*,' he said. 'The tight-fisted, penny-pinching *bugger*.' The words were slightly slurred.

He headed down the stairs. She ran after him. 'Peter!' she called, and he paused and turned.

'I wondered when I was going to see you.'

He looked away. 'I hadn't planned . . . ' He climbed a few steps towards her. His eyes were bloodshot and puffy. *I thought you had better taste, Topaz.*

'You see', he said, enunciating his words carefully, 'I don't fancy that hefty-looking chap's fist in my face.'

'Marius?'

He smiled. 'I don't think he took to me. Sorry, sweetheart.' He started down the stairs again.

'But I thought you wanted to paint me!'

He said, 'I doubt if my wife would approve.' Then he walked out of the front door.

She went back upstairs. Rupert de Courcy was standing beside her desk. Around him, the floor was covered with sheets of paper. He was holding in his hands the third volume of *The History of Northamptonshire*. With a sense of gloomy inevitability, Topaz recognized on the scattered papers the letterhead of the Mallingham Bequest.

As she walked out of the building, she thought, *Not bad, Topaz Brooke, not bad, to lose both job and man within ten minutes of each other.* And it wasn't as though she had ever really got the hang of either.

When she arrived home, her mother was pacing up and down the drawing room. 'That *frightful* woman,' said Veronica. She looked furious.

'Who?' Topaz unwound her scarf.

'Dorothy Blanchard. She *cheats*. I hadn't won for *weeks.*' Veronica's nostrils flared. 'We only play for sixpences, of course, but it's the *principle*!' Her brow furrowed. 'I'm happy never to see the wretched woman again, but it leaves us one short.'

'I won't be working for Mr de Courcy any more,' Topaz unbuttoned her coat, 'so I could fill in, if you like, Mummy.'

'Could you, darling?'

Veronica dispensed endearments parsimoniously, as if drawn from a depleted source. Touched by the unaccustomed affection, Topaz whispered, 'Course, Mummy.'

Veronica stared at her daughter. 'We really must buy you some new clothes. I hadn't realized how much you'd grown. We shall go and see Kitty.' Kitty was Veronica's dressmaker. Veronica smiled. 'That'll be fun, won't it, Topaz?'

5

When Jack had gone abroad in 1942, a weight had lifted from Will. The need to compare himself continually with his strong, clever, handsome, older brother had gone. In Marius's and Jack's absence, he and Julia had fallen naturally into each other's company. And as Julia was both captivating and beautiful, he had equally naturally fallen in love with her. Because it was obvious to him that Julia did not reciprocate his feelings, he had kept them to himself. He knew that she wrote to Jack, but did not know whether her letters were those of a friend or a lover. His attempts at courtship — his gifts and posies — were accepted by her coolly and pleasantly, but brought her no closer to him.

During the war years Will's physical intimacies had not been with Julia, but with a waitress who worked in a cafe in Hernscombe and a land girl at a farm near Bridport. Both were sensible girls who let him go so far and no further. The pleasures and frustrations that characterized his hurried, rumpled encounters with Hester and Sadie had nothing in common with the mixture of anguish and elation that Julia inspired in him. Will had concluded that he desired Hester and Sadie, but loved Julia. There remained something untouchable about Julia, so that even in Jack's absence she seemed distant from him. He had grown accustomed to that distance, occasionally letting off steam by drinking too much or, on the rare occasions petrol rationing permitted it, driving too fast. When Julia had accepted his proposal of marriage, it had been as though the Venus de Milo had nodded her marbled head or the Mona Lisa had cracked a grin.

For weeks afterwards it made the hairs on the back of

111

Will's neck stand upright to remember the evening they had announced their engagement. They had driven back to the School House (Will had wanted to tell everyone *immediately*) and, finding no one there but Mrs Sykes, had headed for Missencourt. There, Julia had marched into the drawing room and told the Temperleys and Prudence that she was going to marry Will. There had been a stunned silence, and then Adele Temperley had said angrily, 'Oh, don't be so *silly*, Julia!'

That it had been Adele — mild, gentle Adele — who had spoken so had jolted Will. That had been when he had begun to realize that though others might share his shock that Julia had agreed to marry him, they might not also share his jubilation.

Then Jack had come into the room and Julia, rather white-faced, had repeated her announcement. Will had seen in books the phrase 'the colour drained out of his face', but had until then assumed it to be a figure of speech. Just before Jack turned on his heel and walked out of the house, Will had caught a glimpse of the expression in his brother's eyes. Another realization: just how deeply Jack was hurt, followed by a flurry of guilt, self-justification (after all, Jack had had his chance), and triumph. He had been rather ashamed of feeling triumphant, and had made to go after Jack, but his mother had placed a warning hand on his arm, staying him. *Not now*, she had whispered. *Give him time.*

Yet time had done nothing to alter or to soften events. Both the School House and Missencourt had seethed with argument, discussion, dissent. The two marriages — Marius and Suzanne's, Julia and Will's — had caused seismic cracks in the landscape of the Chancellors' and Temperleys' lives.

Will disliked quarrels and upsets. It was in his nature to please rather than to provoke. It had always been Jack who had been at the centre of storms and tempests, not him. To be the focus of disapproval or opprobrium upset him, making him anxious and nervous. There was still a part of him that needed Jack's approval. So, a couple of weeks before the wedding, Will had visited Jack at Sixfields.

The visit had gone wrong from the beginning. Geese and dogs hurled themselves at him as he entered the yard. He slipped in the mud, almost fell flat on his face. Through the open barn door, he caught sight of Jack repairing the little grey lend-lease tractor.

Will was conciliatory, reasonable, patient. Jack ignored him, and the clank and clatter of tools almost drowned Will's words. After a while, his carefully composed phrases trailed into silence. Then, unable to stop himself, he said, 'You shouldn't be using the pipe wrench. You should use a spanner.'

The muscles of Jack's hands, gripping the wrench, tautened. Then he straightened, and, looking Will in the face for the first time, he said, 'She doesn't love you, you know. She really doesn't love you.' Breathless, a pain in his diaphragm as though Jack had hit him, Will walked out of the barn. 'Well, damn *you*,' he muttered out loud, all thoughts of reconciliation abandoned.

After their marriage, he and Julia went to live at the School House. Though the newspapers had been full of headlines about the housing shortage, Will hadn't realized how bad things were until he began to look for somewhere to live. He had discovered that whole families were living in single rooms; that wives and children were lodged with in-laws, divided from husbands who worked elsewhere; that hundreds of families were squatting in disused army camps, so that cabbages and carrots now sprouted between the rows of Nissen huts, and children played on tarmac squares that had once echoed to the rhythm of marching boots.

The trouble was that, living with his parents, Will didn't *feel* married. It was as though he and Julia were still friends, who happened to be sharing the same room. He supposed this was why the physical side of marriage was a bit of a disaster. Though Julia said that she enjoyed it, he sensed that she didn't much. Will himself was not at ease, making love to her in his parents' house. He could not rid himself of the conviction that his mother and father could hear every creak of the bed, every gasp of breath. And there was the utterly irrational fear that Jack was somewhere within earshot, watching, contemptuous of his fumbling performance. So he and Julia had let things slide; though they hugged and kissed a lot, weeks passed in which they did not make love. Will was uncomfortably aware that this was not how young married couples were supposed to be. So he gave Julia presents to try to cheer her up: flowers and trinkets, a pair of nylons and expensive soap, bought under the counter from Cousin Maurice.

Meanwhile, he had started up the garage he was renting from Maurice. The garage had not been the immediate success Will had hoped it would be; sited on an isolated stretch of moorland road, what little passing trade there was hurled itself past as if impatient to reach the balmier coast. And, though he enjoyed the practical side of running a garage, he struggled with the paperwork. After a while he began to avert his eyes from the forms and invoices heaped up on his desk. When, one evening, he forced himself to go through everything, he found, to his horror, that the garage was losing money. Just a small amount each week, but a debt had accumulated. Things would soon pick up, he told himself as he struggled not to panic. Petrol rationing must soon come to an end and, when it did, people would return to the prewar habit of motoring for pleasure.

At the turn of the year one of Will's customers at the garage told him about a house for rent. Perched at the top of a hill, accessible only by a rutted green lane

114

leading off from the road, the house was a mile and a half from the nearest neighbour or shop. Though the name, Hidcote Cottage, conjured up whitewash and thatch and old rooms of crooked charm, the two-up, two-down had been built between the wars, and the grey pebbledashed walls and slate roof had a sombre bleakness that seemed to blend into the dark little copse enclosing it. Inside the floors were quarry-tiled or covered in greyish-brown lino and the walls painted institutional creams and greens. The cottage had been requisitioned during the war and used by officers from a nearby RAF base. A gas mask hung from a peg in the hallway, a khaki water bottle lay discarded on a sill.

Will agreed to take the house on the spot, afraid that if he hesitated, some other homeless couple would snap it up. He tried to ignore his misgivings, telling himself that they'd transform the grim little house into something light and airy and homely. The following day, taking Julia to see Hidcote Cottage for the first time, he watched her anxiously, trying to read her expression as she wandered around the cramped rooms. She was wearing an old fur coat that was much too big for her and her long, delicate face was framed by its vast, gingery collar.

He said hesitantly, 'What do you think, darling?'

'But it's so *small*. And so *cold* — '

'We can do it up. Paint the walls. Get some rugs.'

'Yes,' she said faintly.

His stomach churned nervously. 'It'll mean we don't have to live with Mum and Dad any more.'

'Yes,' she said again. Her shoulders hunched. Then she seemed to make an effort, because she smiled at him and said, 'It'll be fine, Will. It'll be marvellous, won't it, having a place of our own?' and he felt a great wave of relief.

★ ★ ★

115

The cottage was awful, poky and isolated and desperately cold, but at least it was theirs. A *cave*, Julia thought, would have been preferable to continuing to share the School House with Will's parents and a dozen schoolboys.

They moved in one weekend at the beginning of January. Julia started unpacking on Monday morning, after Will had left for the garage. You couldn't sit in the front room because of the packing cases and boxes. The heat from the kitchen did not seem to touch the rest of the house. Julia worked wearing gloves, a scarf and the moth-eaten fox-fur coat that had once belonged to her grandmother.

They seemed, she thought, as she went through the boxes, to have an unbelievable amount of *stuff*. Will's model aeroplane collection jostled against a shoebox full of rosettes and certificates Julia had won at gymkhanas and a glass thing for serving punch that one of Will's odder aunts had given them as a wedding present. Very few of the wedding presents had been *useful*. Prudence had (thank goodness) given them sheets and towels. Marius and Suzanne had given glasses, lovely smoky-coloured antique glasses — Marius must have chosen them, Suzanne couldn't have possibly. Adele had given them china, and Will's Cousin Carrie, who was supposed to be very rich, had given them a wardrobe so ugly and so huge that it would not fit through the narrow doors of Hidcote Cottage, and remained marooned in the outhouse with the coal and the mangle. Jack hadn't given them anything at all and neither had he come to the wedding. But she would not think about Jack.

Except for the budgerigar which had been Topaz's gift, the remainder of the wedding presents were either hideous (garishly embroidered dressing-table sets) or dull (tea towels). Julia hid the dressing-table sets in a drawer and fed the budgie millet. All the drawers and cupboards seemed to be full, but there were still a great many unpacked boxes.

By six o'clock she felt grubby and cobwebby, so she decided to have a bath. There wasn't a proper bathroom, only a sink in the outhouse and a lavatory which, though joined on to the rest of the building, you entered from outside — quite the worst thing about the house. Julia dragged the tin bath into the kitchen and filled it with hot water boiled on the stove. She hadn't thought about dinner yet, but they could have toast; she was sure Will wouldn't mind. And besides, if Will came home and found her in the bath, that might help, mightn't it? To herself, Julia called it the Bed Thing, and she knew that when it didn't work, Will was miserable. She wasn't sure why it wasn't working. There was no one she could talk to about things like that.

On their wedding night, Will had been rather drunk and, though he had tried to make love to her, nothing much had happened. He had been terribly apologetic and embarrassed, but privately Julia had been relieved because she had had the most awful headache. During their brief honeymoon in South Wales, she had had the curse, and then they had returned to Dorset. Their marriage had finally been consummated in the School House, with Will burying his face in her shoulder to stop himself crying out as he climaxed, and Julia mortified by every creak and squeak of the old iron-framed bed.

It took an age to fill the bath and the six inches of water cooled very quickly, so she had a good scrub and didn't stay in long. It didn't seem worth getting dressed again properly, so after she had dried herself, Julia put on her pyjamas with the fur coat over the top. Will was late, so she had to empty the bath herself, baling the water into the outside drain. By the time she had finished, she was more fagged out than before she had started.

117

She leaned against the front-door jamb, catching her breath, looking out to the copse and the path. High up in the branches of an elm tree, an owl hooted. A rabbit darted through the undergrowth, the light from the open door momentarily catching its jewelled, startled eyes. The stillness, the mystery of it, entranced her. Pulling her coat around her, staring out into the darkness, she smiled, treasuring the moment.

Then she saw the small light of Will's torch, bobbing through the darkness. She waved and called out to him.

He kissed her. 'What are you doing?'

'Looking at the stars. I think I can see the Seven Sisters.'

'If you look just to the side, you'll be able to see them more clearly.'

She did so, and the faint, shifting pattern became a scattering of bright stars. Will kissed her again. 'You smell nice.'

'Bath salts.'

He slid his hands beneath the heavy folds of the fur coat, and frowned. 'What are you wearing?'

'My pyjamas.'

'You'll catch your death.' He took her hand, leading her into the house, closing the door behind them. In the bedroom he kissed her again as he undid the buttons of her pyjamas. Muffled by coat, blankets and eiderdown as his hands explored her body, she thought, *It's all right, it's going to be all right, I knew that it was going to be all right.*

★　★　★

There didn't seem to be much point in unpacking boxes when there was nothing to unpack them into, so the following day Julia hauled them up to the landing and stacked them against the wall. There was just room to get round if you breathed in.

The dirtiest rooms in the house were the kitchen, outhouse, and lavatory. Thick grey hanks of cobweb gathered in dusty corners and around grimy window-panes, and the red quarry tiles were blackened by dirt. Julia thought she'd whizz through all three rooms in a day, but by the end of the week she hadn't even finished the kitchen. On Friday the stove wasn't working properly and the water was only luke-warm. And she had forgotten to bring in the washing from the previous day, and there had been a frost overnight, so the sheets and towels clung stiff and frozen to the line.

She decided to tackle the kitchen floor, which was, quite honestly, disgusting. But she had run out of household soap and had to cycle to the shop a mile away; returning to the cottage, the bike skidded on the icy ruts of the path and she ended up on the verge, her knuckles skinned, her bottom bruised and her dignity severely dented.

Coming home that evening, Will shouted out cheerful greetings.

'You've a smut on your nose, darling.' He kissed her.

'Have I?' She rubbed at it with a tea towel. She felt tired and unexpectedly close to tears.

He peered into the saucepan on the hob, and, finding it empty, said, 'What's for supper?'

'Supper?'

'It's — ' he glanced at his watch ' — half past six.'

'I hadn't realized,' she said sarcastically. 'How time flies when you're enjoying yourself.'

'I'll give you a hand, if you like.' He began to open cupboards, the *wrong* cupboards, Julia noticed: he didn't seem to know where the food should be kept.

'There isn't anything,' she said. 'There isn't any food.'

'Oh.' He seemed nonplussed, as though this was not a possibility he had imagined. 'Didn't you go to the shops?'

'I did go to the shops, but I forgot to buy food.'

'Well.' He scratched his head. 'We'd better go to Mum and Dad's, hadn't we, darling? Cadge some supper there.'

She said huffily, 'I'm not telling your mother that I forgot to buy supper.'

'Mum won't mind. She always cooks loads.'

'Will.' It was an effort to keep her voice level. 'We're not going to your mother's because I'm not having her thinking I'm the sort of idiot who can't run a house properly.'

'We have to eat *something*.' He sounded bewildered.

Julia found a few wizened vegetables. 'I'll make soup,' she muttered furiously as she flung them into the sink. She began to peel the potatoes, but had to stop because her eyes had filled with tears.

Will put his arm around her. 'What's wrong?'

'It's just that it's so *cold*!' she wailed. 'And everything seems to take ten times longer than I think it will! And I fell off my bicycle!'

He was immediately concerned. 'Did you hurt yourself?'

'Only a little,' she sniffed. 'Knuckles and knees.'

'I'll kiss them better.' He slid the knife out of her fingers, took her wet hands in his, and kissed her bruised knuckles, one by one. And, kneeling on the kitchen floor, kissed her toes and her knees as well.

Then Will remembered the Christmas cake. They dined on cake and a bottle of sweet sherry, left over from the festivities. Currants rolled between the cushions, and, rather drunk, they drifted off to sleep wrapped in each other's arms.

* * *

After three weeks in Hidcote Cottage (or Hideous Cottage, as Julia had privately renamed it), she came to the conclusion that housework was much worse than

120

having a job. Managing Temperley's had been an exhausting and often anxious business, but there had been compensation in the form of camaraderie and a sense of common purpose. The isolation that she now endured she had never previously experienced. She had thought herself alone when Jack had sailed for Egypt; she had thought herself alone after her father had died. But she had never before endured such physical separation as she did now, enclosed in the dark little cottage in the dark little copse on top of the hill. Her cycle rides to the village shop became the high point of her day. She found herself looking forward rather desperately to her weekly bus ride to Hernscombe.

It was in Hernscombe that she met Jack. She had just come out of the post office and he was going in, so there was really no avoiding him. Momentarily, she thought that it might be all right, that he might have got used to it, that they might have gone back to being the friends they had always been as children.

One glance into his wintry blue eyes told her otherwise. The dislike she saw in them shocked her and she felt a flicker of anger. How unfair — and how typical — of Jack to blame her for what had happened!

But she said lightly, 'Jack. Fancy seeing you here.'

'I'm picking up a few things for Carrie.'

'Of course. Life on the farm . . . does it suit you?'

'It's all right.'

It's all right. Yet he had chosen Carrie Chancellor and Sixfields rather than her. '"All right'?' she repeated. 'No better than that?'

'It's not an easy time of year. And — ' he glanced up at the leaden sky ' — going to get worse by the look of it. Snow's blowing in.'

She couldn't believe that he was talking to her about the *weather*. She was seized by the fatal impulse to provoke, to break through his reserve. 'You seem a little browned off, Jack,' she taunted. 'What's wrong? Hasn't

Sixfields lived up to your expectations? Wasn't it worth it?'

She saw that she had fully engaged his attention. His cold blue gaze focused on her and he said softly, 'Oh, I don't know. At least you know where you are with a farm. At least houses — places — don't change. They're *constant*.'

'*I* was constant!' she hissed furiously. 'I waited *years* for you!' Passers-by were staring at them, so she picked up her shopping bags, intending, having had the last word, to walk to the bus stop.

'Did you?' he said, and she paused. 'The evidence is rather against you, isn't it, Julia?'

She fought to keep at least a superficial composure. 'Are you talking about Will?'

He nodded. Then he said, 'Or were there others?'

She was momentarily speechless. She was aware of the bitter cold, and of the tiny flakes of snow that had begun to fall from the iron-grey sky, and of the interested spectators gazing at them, hoping for fodder for gossip. 'You didn't want to marry me,' she said coldly. 'I suggested it, you refused. Don't try to blame me, Jack, for what *you* chose.' She began to walk back up the hill.

He caught up with her. 'I asked you to *wait*,' he said. 'That was all. To wait.'

Her shoulders ached, weighed down by the heavy bags. She longed to be away from him; she longed for the privacy of Hidcote Cottage and for the comfort of Will's undemanding affection.

'Leave me alone, Jack,' she said. 'Please leave me alone.'

'That wasn't unreasonable, was it, Julia, to ask you to wait?'

She swung round to face him. 'You wanted Sixfields more than you wanted me,' she said harshly. 'You wanted to be rich more than you wanted me.'

She saw by the alteration in his expression that she had struck home. He said softly, 'For a while, God forgive me. For a few hours. No more.' He looked down. The anger had gone from his voice, and he sounded bleak and drained. 'After you'd gone — after we quarrelled — I left the house, walked for a while. And I realized what a fool I'd been. So I went to find you. I went to Missencourt.'

She stared at him. In his eyes she saw grief and bitterness. 'I went to Misssencourt to find you', he said, 'because I wanted to tell you that, if I had to choose between you and Sixfields, then I'd choose you.'

There was a cold, frightened feeling inside her. She whispered, 'I don't believe you, Jack.'

'As you wish. But it's true. I went to Missencourt to tell you that Sixfields could go hang if it meant losing you. But you'd already found something to take your mind off things, hadn't you? You'd already agreed to marry Will.' Snowflakes were settling on Jack's shoulders and hair. 'If you'd waited a couple of hours, Julia,' he said, as he turned away. 'Just a couple of hours.'

★ ★ ★

On the bus home, she stared out of the window, watching the snow. It pirouetted in the golden gleam of the headlamps and streetlamps; it clung to the trees and the hedgerows, draining them of colour. It swirled and it danced, twisting and turning in little vortices, gathering in the runnels between the plough lines in the fields. As the journey lengthened, the flakes grew larger and more numerous until the horizon was lost, and sky, field and hill blurred into a mass of whirling, darting yellowish-grey dots and the familiar landscape was no longer familiar, but had become alien, adopting the harsh monotones of more northerly latitudes.

Julia thought, *If I'd waited an hour or two.* She pressed her fingers against her mouth. She was afraid she might scream.

If I'd waited . . .

★ ★ ★

Driving out of Hernscombe, Jack pulled into the side of the road and lit a cigarette. In the five minutes during which he was parked, the snow covered the windscreen of Carrie's old Bentley, trapping him in a greyish cave.

Because he knew that he could not bear to be alone, he decided to go and see Marcia. He had met Marcia Vaughan in a cafe in Bridport a couple of months ago. Marcia had asked him for a light; they had got talking. He had known after the first few moments of their acquaintance that she was interested, that she knew the ropes, that she understood the rules. They had become lovers a week later.

Marcia had three children, all at boarding school, and a husband who, during the week, worked in the City. She was sophisticated, elegant, bored. She lived in a large house on the outskirts of Bridport, at a convenient distance from prying neighbours. Even so, Jack always parked in a side road and walked the short distance to her house.

She must have glimpsed him from an upstairs window because he heard her footsteps on the stairs. The door opened before he could press the doorbell.

'I wasn't expecting you, darling,' she said. 'This dreadful weather . . . '

He didn't say anything, just took her in his arms and kissed her, his fingers searching for buttons, zips, hooks and eyes. After a few moments, she pulled away.

'My,' she said. She was slightly flushed. 'Impatient today, aren't you?'

He made to take her in his arms again, but she shook

124

her head. 'Not here, Jack. Too undignified, on the hall carpet.'

* * *

It took him more than two hours to drive the fifteen miles back to the farm. The blizzard had gathered strength, the screaming wind hurling the snow horizontally across the road. Though the Bentley was large and solidly built, the wheels frequently lost their grip. Several times Jack had to climb out of the car and shovel aside the drifts that blocked his path.

Driving into the yard at Sixfields, he saw Carrie, struggling to bolt the heavy barn door.

'Where have you *been*, Jack?' She had to shout to be heard over the scream of the wind.

'Hernscombe.' Reaching up, he slid the bolt home easily.

He followed Carrie into the house. Indoors, snowflakes scattered from her as she limped through dark corridors. Beneath her waterproofs her hair and clothes were soaking.

'You should have been here,' Carrie snapped. 'Mark Crabtree and I had to bring the cattle in from the pasture. And the tarpaulin has blown off the haystack.'

'I'll go and sort it out.'

As he walked back out of the house, he heard her screech after him, 'Fornication, Jack! It's a sin against our Lord!' and he had to grit his teeth, to dig his nails into his palms to stop himself telling the old dragon what he thought of her.

Battling against the blizzard to tie down the tarpaulin released some of his pent-up anger. After he had walked around the farm, checking that everything was secure, he went to the cottage. It was past ten o'clock. All his muscles ached. He hadn't eaten since midday. In the kitchen he cracked eggs, fried bacon and poured himself a glass of cider.

Carrie's parting shot rang in his ears. *Fornication, Jack. It's a sin against our Lord.* Carrie was only religious when it suited her. She never went to church and was thoroughly rude to the vicar whenever he was rash enough to visit Sixfields. Jack himself had mislaid the reassuring Anglicanism of his home and schooldays somewhere on his long journey through the battlefields of Italy. He would have preferred to believe, but he simply couldn't. He had seen things he knew he would never talk about and tried hard not to think about. In the landscape of his worst memories the hand of God did not linger for so much as a fraction of a second.

As for Carrie's strictures on his sexual impropriety . . . How dare she think she had the right to comment on his private life? She didn't *own* him. She merely employed him.

Yet Julia's voice echoed. *You wanted Sixfields more than you wanted me. You wanted to be rich more than you wanted me.* Cradling his glass in his hands, Jack groaned out loud.

Five months ago, the day after Julia had announced her engagement to Will, he had moved to Sixfields. He lived in the cottage that the land girl had vacated, working on the farm from dawn to dusk seven days a week. The work was both exhausting and demanding, and much of the time he loved it. What reservations he had had been provoked by Carrie herself. Her demands, her intransigence, grated increasingly. She showed little appreciation for his efforts and seemed to delight in finding fault. To his suggestions for improvement — that they buy new equipment, take on more labour, or use fertilizers to improve yields — she was scathing. She could not seem to see that investment now would reap rewards in the future. 'Too risky, Jack,' she'd say. 'D'you think I'm made of money?'

The passion that he had once felt for Julia he now gave to Sixfields. Julia's engagement to Will had proved all his worst suspicions. *Flighty*, Carrie had said, and you couldn't get much more flighty than proposing to one brother and agreeing to marry the other in the course of an afternoon, could you?

Every now and then, though, much less comfortable thoughts seeped through the cracks in the hard shell of his anger. That he had had his chance, and had thrown it away. That it had been his rejection which had driven Julia into Will's arms. That when Carrie had dangled Sixfields in front of him, she had in doing so appealed to a dark and covetous part of him.

He found ways of distracting himself, of course. He drank more than he used to. And there was a barmaid in Great Missen at first, and then a pretty shop assistant in Dorchester. And then Marcia. Once or twice Marcia had come to the cottage: that he had sneaked her in over the fields had been to protect her reputation, not his. It hadn't occurred to him that Carrie would take an interest. An ageing virgin, he had assumed her innocent of, ignorant of, adult love.

Jack looked out of the window. He hadn't seen so much snow in years. He found himself recalling Egypt and longing for its warmth and sun and blue skies. He loathed this shivering, pennypinching little island. He loathed the people, who complained about rationing while forgetting the far worse deprivations endured by those who had, for them, suffered prison camps, maiming and death. He loathed the spivs and black marketeers who played on the greed and weariness of the populace.

The trouble was, he thought, as he finished the last drop of cider, he didn't seem to believe in anything any more. He didn't believe in God, and he didn't believe in his country, and he no longer believed in the woman he thought he had loved. That he could hardly bear the sight of Will had cut him off from his family. He had lost touch with his friends in the Services, and seemed to have little in common with acquaintances from prewar days. He had reduced love to sex, and in doing so, he thought wryly, even he could see that he had lost something.

★ ★ ★

The blizzard blew from the snowfields of Archangel in northern Russia, through Scandinavia, across Britain. After three days the entire country, from the Scilly Isles to the Orkneys, emerged out of the scream of the east wind and the mad dance of snowflakes to stare at a landscape bleached white. Five days later there was another snowstorm. The Thames froze. Off the Norfolk coast ice floes loomed against grey, churning seas. The sun slipped behind the clouds and remained there through weeks of darkness.

Britain shivered to a halt. Snowfalls exacerbated the fuel crisis already brought on by a transport strike and a shortage of coal. Roads and railways were blocked, and coal barges icebound in northern ports. Factories and offices closed. Traffic lights went out, and lifts and escalators stopped. The government reintroduced blackout regulations: the use of an electric cooker or heater between nine and twelve in the morning or two and four in the afternoon was punishable by a fine.

Supplied by a private line from a country estate half a mile away, Hidcote Cottage's electricity failed on the night of the first blizzard. Julia found oil lamps and candles. The kitchen stove, fortunately, burned solid fuel. Will made a toboggan out of a metal tray and wooden runners, and Julia battled her way to the local shop, hauling tins and dried food back to the cottage. At first it was almost fun, like having an unexpected holiday from school. They lived in the kitchen, the only bearably warm room in the house. They didn't bother to get undressed at night, but curled up beneath blankets and eiderdowns, with their coats over their sweaters and trousers. They drank cocoa and ate baked potatoes and tinned peas, and played a great many games of gin rummy. They were marooned, thought Julia. Just now there were rather a lot of things she didn't mind being marooned from.

When they ran out of coal (there wasn't any coal in Hernscombe or Bridport; there didn't seem to be any coal in the southwest of England) they burned logs. Within two days all the logs in the outhouse were gone. Will sawed up packing cases and stuffed them into the stove's hungry mouth. When there were no packing cases left Will's optimism faltered. Tentatively, he suggested to Julia that she decamp to Missencourt or to the School House. She refused.

The following morning Julia woke with a headache and sore throat. Will wrapped himself up in duffle coat, scarf, hat, gloves and boots, and set off for the garage. There were a few bits of wood there, he explained, and perhaps he could scrape up enough paraffin for the lamps. When he had gone, the house seemed very cold, very silent. The heavy clouds and the canopy of snow covering the trees permitted little light through the windows of the house, so that, although it was mid-morning, the rooms were gloomy. Absently, Julia flicked the dial of the radio, but it remained, of course, silent. Reading made her headache worse and, anyway, there wasn't enough light. And playing cards were no fun when there was only one of you. She supposed she could tidy up a bit — the room was scattered with blankets and pillows and dirty plates and cups — but she felt too tired. When she glanced into the stove, she saw that the embers had burned down to a purplish pink. There wasn't a fragment of coal left in the scuttle.

She went into the outhouse. There was only Cousin Carrie's wardrobe and a few scraps of bark and the frozen corpses of spiders. She could die up here, she thought, and no one would know. Will wouldn't be back for hours, and this beastly little house would get colder and colder, and she would get sleepier and sleepier, and then she'd just freeze to death, like the spiders.

She wondered whether Will had been right and whether she should go to Missencourt. She hadn't wanted to because of Suzanne, of course, but Suzanne was her sister-in-law, she thought miserably, nothing could alter that. She missed Marius; she even — and the tears that stung the corners of her eyes took her by surprise — missed her mother.

In the stove the last scraps of wood were reddish-grey ash. *Don't you dare go out, you mustn't go out*, she whispered. When she threw the pieces of bark on to the embers the fire flared briefly and then died down again.

Back in the outhouse, Julia looked from the wardrobe to the axe, hanging on a nail on the back of the door. Then, gripping the axe with both hands, she plunged it into the wardrobe door.

There was a satisfying *chink* as the metal head bit into the wood. A couple more blows and the door split in two. Splinters of wood flew into the air, then scattered over the floor. Julia struck again and again. The sound of iron on wood echoed in the silent copse.

After a while, she fell back, exhausted, coughing, dizzy with tiredness. Every muscle in her body ached and her hands were sore and blistered. Moments passed before she was able to gather up the fragments of wood and go back into the kitchen. Her entire body seemed to reverberate with the remembered impact of the axe. She knelt in front of the stove, feeding it pieces of splintered oak, as though placating some angry god. When the fire had caught, she curled up in a chair, hot and shaking.

Will came back, dragging the toboggan behind him. After he had chopped up the remainder of the wardrobe and dumped it on the kitchen floor, a great bonfire of dark, shattered slivers, they curled up together on the sofa. Drifting off to sleep, Julia dreamed of dense woods and, in the dark heart of them, a silvery, glistening house. The windows of the house were white and opaque, and she could not see into them. She woke, shivering with cold and fear, and the whine of the wind was like a wolf's call.

In the morning her head still ached and her limbs still trembled, and she realized, with a dull lack of surprise, that she was ill. Beside her, Will slept. Careful not to wake him, she stood up, wrapping a blanket around herself. Sometime in the night the fire had gone out.

Opening the front door, Julia went outside. The sky remained grey and overcast and she could hardly see the path through the woods. Standing at the edge of the field, she looked down and saw the distant figure making his slow, determined way up the path to the cottage. She began to run. 'Marius!' she shouted, 'Marius!' Stumbling on the icy ground, falling to her knees, Julia struggled down the hill to reach him.

★　★　★

She had flu, quite badly. At Missencourt she lay in bed for a week in her old room, coughing. There was a fire in the grate, and her mother brought her bowls of soup and cups of tea at regular intervals.

To begin with her throat was too sore to speak and she drifted between dozing and waking, searching for a comfortable position for her aching limbs. Then she began to feel a little better, but was still too tired to do anything much, which meant that a lot of the time she

131

just thought. Her thoughts were neither comfortable nor flattering.

One afternoon there was a tap on the door and she looked up, expecting to see her mother.

Suzanne put her head around the door. Julia sat up. 'Where's Mother?'

'She's fallen asleep on the living-room couch. She was very tired. I wondered whether you wanted anything . . . a cup of tea . . . anything.'

There was still that mean, jealous part of Julia that wanted to say *sofa*, not *couch*, and *drawing room*, not *living room*. But she quelled it and shook her head, and said, 'I've drunk gallons of tea this week. I must have drunk everyone's ration.'

'Cocoa, then?'

'No thanks. Nothing.'

'OK.' The door was about to close again when Julia said, 'Well, only — '

'Yes?'

'It's rather boring, by myself.'

'I could stay and talk, if you like.' Suzanne sounded hesitant.

Julia made herself say, 'That would be nice.'

Suzanne sat in the Lloyd Loom chair by the window. She was wearing dark slacks and a great many jerseys, piled one on top of the other. The small, mean voice whispered, *she's not pretty at all, she's quite ordinary*. The pleasanter part of her, the part that was making an effort, conceded that, just at the moment, she probably didn't look too wonderful herself.

There was a silence. Then Julia croaked, 'Will . . . I haven't seen Will for ages.'

'He was here for a couple of days and then he went back to the garage. They've been trying to clear the roads, you see, so Will was helping out with the breakdown truck and snowchains.'

Julia remembered Tara. 'Where's your daughter?'

'Tara's with Marius. They're making a snowman.'

'Why isn't Marius at work? Or is it Sunday?' She had lost track of the days.

'It's Tuesday.' Suzanne drew back the curtains, letting in the clear, cold light. There were frost flowers on the panes. 'Temperley's has been closed for a fortnight because of the electricity cuts.'

'*Oh*,' said Julia again. Temperley's *closed*, she thought. The workshop had closed only for a day when her father died. Only half a day when a Heinkel had plunged into the adjacent field, guns blazing, scattering the site with shrapnel.

'How awful. Marius must be worried.'

Suzanne threaded her hands inside the folds of her jersey. 'He spends most of the time chopping up wood for the fire. I think that makes him feel better.'

'Everyone but me seems to have been terribly *useful*.' Julia felt depressed.

'Men like to do heroic things, don't they?' said Suzanne, rather cynically. 'Felling trees and digging through snowdrifts. It's the little things they can't be bothered with, like doing the washing up, or going to the shops.'

Julia smiled. Then she remembered the night she and Will had eaten Christmas cake because there had been no food and she said, 'I was pretty hopeless at all that, too. I thought I was going to be the perfect housewife, but I was hopeless.'

Suzanne's brows raised. 'Why on earth did you want to be a perfect housewife?'

'There's no point in doing things *badly*, is there? No point settling for second best.'

Looking out of the window, she saw that it had begun to snow again. She heard Suzanne say softly, 'Sometimes you have to settle for what you can get.'

'Anyway, I was hopeless. Utterly hopeless. And I hated it.' Julia blinked and blew her nose.

Suzanne looked at Julia. 'Marius told me what a terrific job you did at Temperley's during the war. That can't have been easy.'

'I miss it,' said Julia. 'I really miss Temperley's. I didn't expect to, but I do. Do you miss the army?'

'Sometimes.'

'Did you enjoy it?'

'Very much.'

'I'd have hated to join up.'

'I suppose it depends on what you'd had before,' said Suzanne, matter-of-factly. 'I was living at home, sharing a room with my sisters, working in a greengrocer's. I'd left school at fourteen — I wanted to stay on, but my parents wouldn't let me. I couldn't wait to get away from home. I loved the ATS. Driving trucks was better than weighing out pounds of potatoes, I can tell you. And I was good at it — I got my corporal's stripes pretty quick.'

'I'd have been hopeless in the Forces,' said Julia. 'I can't bear people telling me what to do. I just end up doing the opposite.'

'First day in camp', said Suzanne, 'I cheeked my corporal because she'd told me how to fold my stockings. I couldn't see what business the bossy cow had to tell me how to fold my own stockings. So I ended up peeling potatoes for four hours, which was even worse than selling the bloody things.'

When Suzanne smiled, her features seemed to alter, as if lit up from within. Perhaps not completely ordinary, acknowledged Julia, grudgingly.

Suzanne stood up. 'I'd better go and rescue Marius.' At the door she paused and said tentatively, 'It will get better, you know. When the babies come. They'll make it all worthwhile. You'd do anything for them.'

When Suzanne had gone Julia climbed out of bed and, wrapping the quilt around herself, went to the window. Looking down, she saw that Marius was crossing the lawn. Tara was sitting on his shoulders. She was laughing.

Though the thought of returning to Hideous Cottage appalled her, Julia knew that she must. Grimly she vowed to coerce the horrible little place into some semblance of home. As for her marriage, she was uncomfortably aware that she hadn't tried hard enough with that either, and that she and Will were marooned in some uneasy hinterland between friendship and love.

She watched as Suzanne joined Marius and Tara. Tara slid down from Marius's arms and ran to her mother, and then they all went back to the house. It seemed to Julia that a distance remained between Marius and Suzanne, that Suzanne's kisses and caresses were all for her daughter and not Marius. Momentarily distracted from her own troubles, Julia felt for her brother a shiver of apprehension.

★　★　★

In the yard at Sixfields the water in the well turned to iron, and in the fields they used pickaxes to release parsnips and turnips from the grasp of the earth. During a lull between blizzards Jack helped to clear snow from the roads so that lorries could get through to deliver food and fuel.

Carrie was his goad, his torment. Any illusions he might have entertained that somewhere in her a fragment of the Dunkirk spirit must reside, bringing out the best in her when times were at their worst, she quickly destroyed. However hard he worked, she still found fault; after a twelve-hour day he'd return to the house, every item of clothing soaked and frozen, and she'd look at him, malice dancing in her eyes. 'Finished already, Jack?' she'd say. 'Never could abide idle hands, Jack.'

She took pleasure in provoking him. Most of the time

135

he managed to ignore her jibes, knowing that any retaliation on his part would only fuel her vindictiveness. Then, one evening, his temper snapped.

He had spent the day digging the frozen corpses of newborn lambs from the drifts. He had burned them, knowing that as soon as the thaw came they'd attract rats and flies. The stench rose into the frozen air, black and foul. Then the axle on the tractor failed and Jack had to lie on his back in the barn, ice-cold metal scorching his hands as he loosened bolts. It was a two-man job, and there was only one of him, and he'd found himself thinking of Will, wishing Will was there to lend a hand.

A split second later, of course, and he remembered that he hadn't seen Will for almost six months, and *why* he hadn't seen Will for almost six months. Cold and exhausted, ugly images insinuated themselves into his mind. He wondered how long Will and Julia had waited. Had they fallen into each other's arms the moment he'd left the School House? Or as his ship sailed for North Africa? Or had Will turned Julia's grief for her father to his advantage, letting the comfort of friends turn to something more rewarding?

Jack heard a sound behind him. Carrie had come into the barn. She glared at him. 'Is it done yet?'

He held up the broken shaft of metal. 'I'll take it to the blacksmith's tomorrow.'

'Tonight, Jack.' She turned to leave.

He'd been up since four in the morning. 'No,' he said.

Her stick, tapping the stone floor, paused. 'We can't do without a tractor.'

'I'm tired,' he said shortly. 'It can wait.'

'*Tired!* You poor thing!' Her mockery scoured him. 'Shall I tuck you up in bed and bring you a cup of cocoa?'

'*Bitch,*' he muttered.

He had meant to speak softly, but in the great space of the barn, the word echoed. Carrie's face hardened. She crossed the floor to him.

She said, 'You don't own the farm yet, you know, Jack.'

You can keep your bloody farm . . . The angry words, on the tip of his tongue, died stillborn. The look in her eye — her obvious enjoyment of her power over him — chilled him. He heard himself murmur, 'Sorry,' and, as she walked away, he put out a hand to the tractor to steady himself.

After a while he gathered up the damaged length of metal, wrapped it in a cloth and set off for the smithy. The car slid on the impacted snow. All his muscles ached. He could almost taste his self-loathing. At the back of his mind, Julia's voice echoed. *I hope you hate Sixfields,* she had said. *I hope it makes you miserable. I hope it makes you lonely and miserable and mad like your Cousin Carrie.*

★   ★   ★

A few days later he drove through treacherous roads to Bridport and to Marcia. In her bedroom he stripped her of her clothes and made love to her without much in the way of preliminaries. When it was over, and he lay back on the pillows, his eyes closed, she said, 'Well, having got *that* out of your system, perhaps you'd care to remember that there are two of us here.'

He brought her to climax expertly and efficiently. Afterwards, when he had lit cigarettes for both of them, she glanced at him, and said, 'Bad day, Jack?'

He shrugged. The previous night he had dreamed of Julia. The dream lingered, a mixture of anger and longing. He remembered that she had twisted her light brown hair around her face, pushing it back with her long, thin, pale fingers.

After a while, he realized that Marcia was dressing. He watched her, trying to distract himself, noting the heavy swell of her breasts, the curve of her rounded stomach, and the small crinkled stretchmarks. He said, 'When shall I see you again?' and she glanced at him.

'I don't think you will, darling.'

He crushed his cigarette in the ashtray. 'Is Ronald coming home?' Ronald was Marcia's husband. She shook her head.

He sat up in bed. 'Then why not?'

She paused, attaching suspender to stocking. 'Because you haven't a heart, Jack. Because — ' and her blue eyes focused on him appraisingly ' — because there's a piece of ice where your heart's supposed to be.'

'I thought we were having fun.'

'Did you?' Her brows rose. 'Then what an odd idea of fun you must have.'

He tried to retrieve the situation, climbing out of bed, going to her. But she moved away from him.

'The thing is', she said, 'that wasn't *me* in bed with you, was it? I don't know who the hell it was, Jack, and I don't want to, but it wasn't *me*.'

As Jack returned to Sixfields it began to rain. As the rain fell to the frozen earth it coated everything it touched with a thick layer of ice. Ice encircled the telegraph wires so that their weight pulled them from the posts. Ice spread its great sculptured folds over hedgerows and houses, wrapping them in a glistening, beautiful, treacherous embrace. Ice encased the branches of trees, tearing them from the trunks, sending them crashing to the ground with a sound like breaking glass.

Sixfields itself seemed to have become a part of the snowbound landscape. The stone walls were carved from blocks of impacted snow, the traceries of the doors and frames had been moulded from ice, the glass in the windows was thin sheets of translucent ice, stolen from

138

the surfaces of ponds and lakes. There was not a flicker of movement. No birds flew in that leaden sky, and behind those chill windows the interior was fixed and immobile. The air had stilled; time, too, had paused, chaining them to the frozen present. The shroud of ice that bound the house held its inhabitants in thrall. It imprisoned them.

An ice palace, thought Jack, that was where he had come to live. In an ice palace.

6

After Christmas Topaz worked as a filing clerk for a firm of van drivers in Kilburn; when the road-haulage drivers went on strike and the snow came the firm closed. It remained closed even when, in April, winter finally relaxed its grip.

She found a job as a typist for a firm of solicitors in Marylebone. Twenty girls typed in a room with windows so high that only a patch of sky and a few chimney pots could be glimpsed through them. The typists were supervised by Miss Brakespear. To keep up with the other girls, Topaz devised a method of pounding the typewriter keyboard quickly and at random, and discarding the ensuing gibberish in the waste-paper bin when Miss Brakespear looked away. But Miss Brakespear's eagle eyes soon spotted that Topaz could not actually touch-type, and the inevitable happened, and Topaz found herself once more in the cafe with Francesca, eating iced buns.

She was telling Francesca about her ignominious exit from the solicitors' firm, when the cafe door opened and a group of people came in. Francesca whispered, 'Look — they're here.'

Regulars in the little Leicester Square cafe, they were young, noisy, and exuberant, and they trailed a kind of careless glamour that Topaz and Francesca had come, over the past couple of months, to envy deeply. They always sat at the table in the far corner and they had the knack of seeming to transform the dowdy little cafe. It was as though, at their entrance, the peeling paint brightened and the tired-looking customers sat up and smiled.

There were six of them, four men and two women.

One of the women always wore her fat, blonde plait coiled on top of her head; the younger woman's black hair was cut in a Louise Brooks' bob. They wore dark, short-sleeved, knitted tops and narrow-waisted, long, flared skirts. Their faces were pale apart from crimson lipstick.

Topaz and Francesca practised holding their cigarettes as the blonde girl did, taking small, jerky puffs, their eyes half-closed and heads flung back. They unravelled navy blue school jerseys, knitting them up into short-sleeved tops. Topaz borrowed lipstick and powder from her mother's dressing table, and Francesca cut her dead-straight, light-brown hair into a bob.

In the cafe's tiny, clanking ladies' room, they stared in the small square of mirror at their pale, scarlet-mouthed reflections. 'Too, too decadent,' murmured Topaz, and they leaned against the basin, hardly able to stand for laughing.

The summer of 1947 was hot and sultry, as if to make up for the harsh winter. Heat shimmered on the grass and the air was still and languorous. Topaz drifted through life, nothing quite touching her. A wall, invisible and shimmering like the heat haze, seemed to divide her from all the little enclaves and cliques that made up London. They whispered secrets, secrets she did not share. She wondered whether it would always be like this, or whether one day she'd be in the middle of things, in the centre of the circle. Something simmered inside her, something impatient and greedy for life searched for escape.

She started work for a domestic service agency in the West End. At the end of her first week she met Francesca in the cafe. *They* were already there, sitting at the corner table that they had made their own, the four men, and the girl with the bob and the girl with the plait.

Topaz filled up her tray at the counter. She had to

walk past them to carry it to her table. She felt large and clumsy, and she knew she was blushing. She sucked her stomach in, trying to walk as they'd taught her in deportment at school. *Head up, seat in, Topaz Brooke!*

Topaz stumbled, the tray wobbled, and a splash of tea seemed to leap out of the cup and on to the dark-haired girl's skirt.

'For heaven's *sake* — '

'Sorry. I'm so sorry.' Topaz wanted to die.

'My *skirt* — '

'There's a hanky in my pocket — '

'It's *ruined* — '

The bearded man sitting at the far end of the table said, 'Don't make such a fuss, Claudette.'

'I shall have to go home and change.'

'Darling Claudie.' Claudette's neighbour dabbed with a handkerchief at the hem of her skirt. 'See? It's fine now.'

Claudette pouted. 'Just there, Charlie. There's another drop just there.'

Another flick of the handkerchief. Charlie had wild, curling black hair and eyes that sparked with barely contained laughter. Topaz wondered whether he was laughing at her. But then he looked up and said, 'It's all right. Don't worry. No harm done.'

Somehow, she managed to walk the rest of the distance to the table she and Francesca were sharing. Her hands shook as she put down the tray. Sitting down, she put her head in her hands, and muttered, 'Such a clumsy idiot — ' Francesca squeezed her arm.

Claudette, Charlie and the others rose to leave the cafe shortly afterwards. Passing Topaz and Francesca's table, Charlie paused.

'Why do you always do that?'

'What?' Topaz looked up at him blankly.

'Roll your icing into a little ball.'

'*Oh*. It means you have the nice bit all at once, not in dribs and drabs.'

'Is that what you like, the nice bit all at once?'

'You notice it more then, don't you?'

'I suppose you do.'

He left the cafe. When the door had closed behind him, Francesca hissed, 'He was watching us! He noticed us!'

'*He* noticed *us*.' Topaz gazed at Francesca, eyes wide. 'Oh *Fran*.'

★   ★   ★

On Monday Charlie came to the cafe on his own. Once more he paused at Topaz and Francesca's table.

'Got a light?'

Francesca pulled out a chair. 'Your friends aren't here yet. You could sit with us till they come.'

Topaz held her breath. 'Thanks,' said Charlie and sat down.

'Would you like a bun?' Topaz pushed her plate towards him.

'Don't you want it?'

She shook her head. 'I'm not hungry.' Not true: she was starving. So she was relieved when he said, 'Tell you what, we'll share it.' He cut the bun in half. Then he held out his hand. 'My name's Charlie Finch.'

'Topaz Brooke.'

'Francesca Lovatt.'

Topaz began to peel the icing off her half bun. She smiled. 'You were watching us.'

'I like watching people,' said Charlie. 'I wonder who they are . . . where they live . . . what they do. And I borrow bits of them.'

'*Borrow* . . . ?'

He laughed. 'Don't worry, I'm not a Bluebeard. I mean . . . gestures, voices. I'm an actor, you see.

143

Though I'm working in an office just now. As a very, very junior clerk.'

'Do you like it?'

'It's loathsome. Absolutely loathsome. What do you do?'

'I'm a receptionist', explained Topaz, 'at a very smart domestic service agency. I have to write down appointments in a book and show clients in, and answer the telephone.'

'Of course. You've got the right sort of voice for something like that.'

'What do you mean?'

'Rather posh. Plummy.' He turned to Francesca. 'What about you?'

'I work for a theatrical agency.'

'*Ah*,' he said. Topaz noticed how his eyes lit up. 'Which one?'

Francesca told him. Charlie said, 'I've an audition tomorrow morning. Keep your fingers crossed for me.'

'What's the play?'

'A rather dire comedy. But it would be a start. Someone might see it, it might lead somewhere.' He grinned, and turned to Topaz. His eyes were a very dark brown, almost black. The colour of Marmite. 'I might borrow your voice, Topaz,' he said, 'for the audition. Would you mind?'

She thought how Francesca had cut her hair in Claudette's bob, and how they had practised smoking like the girl with the plait.

'Not at all,' she said. 'I'd take it as a compliment.'

★ ★ ★

Charlie introduced her to the others. The girl with the plait was called Helena. The bearded man was Donald, the small dark man was Mischa, and the man with the long, fleshy face and brown curls was Jerry. Donald and

144

Jerry knew each other from the army; now Donald was studying at Imperial College and Jerry was training to be a teacher. Mischa was Polish. He and his family had come to England in the 1930s; his elder brother had flown Spitfires during the Battle of Britain. Mischa's girlfriend, Claudette, was the same age as Topaz. She was a dancer.

Helena worked as a theatrical costumier. She had sewn the tight-waisted, flared skirts that she and Claudette wore. 'I copied them from a photograph in *Vogue*,' she explained to Topaz. 'There was a piece about Christian Dior. The most beautiful, beautiful clothes.'

'Would you make one for me?'

'If you like. You'll have to give me the material, though. I can get taffeta for the petticoats — you need to wear petticoats with skirts like these — but you must find some nice material.'

In one of the carved Indian chests at the Bayswater flat, Topaz searched through her mother's shawls and mantillas. There were dozens of them, silks and cashmeres, patterned and plain, turquoise and cerise and chartreuse. She remembered Peter de Courcy saying, *You should wear silks and velvets.* Remembering also the fiasco of the magenta satin dress she had worn to Jack's homecoming party, she chose a black silk mantilla. Black, as her mother always said, was so slimming.

To go beneath the skirt, Helena made Topaz three layers of taffeta petticoats. The taffeta was a patchwork of different colours because Helena had made the petticoats out of scraps left over from theatrical costumes. When Topaz put the skirt on, the petticoats whispered as she walked. Her mother looked suspiciously at her once or twice, but said only, 'What an extraordinary style. And so difficult to wear for anyone with hips.' Topaz breathed in and, suddenly doubtful, stared in the looking glass at the generous curves of her body.

In the cafe, Topaz said to Helena, 'I've brought you a present to say thank you.'

'What is it?'

'Close your eyes and hold out your hand.'

Helena's hand was a mass of small calluses and pin-pricks. Topaz placed a peach in her palm.

Helena opened her eyes. '*Topaz*. A *peach*. How glorious.'

'I haven't eaten a peach since Italy,' said Donald. 'Nineteen forty-four.'

'We went to Le Touquet the summer before the war,' said Helena. 'That was the last time I ate a peach. My last holiday.'

'Where on earth did you find a peach?' asked Jerry.

'My mother has an admirer at the American Embassy. He's called Major Radetsky.'

Donald looked around the table. 'What do you miss most? From before the war, I mean.'

'The lovely clothes,' said Helena.

'Malt whisky,' said Jerry. 'I'd sell my soul for a decent bottle of Scotch.'

'My dog,' said Mischa. 'I had a dog in Poland. Now my landlady won't let me keep a dog.'

Helena was cutting the peach into segments. 'Claudette? Topaz? Francesca? What do you miss?'

'They're too young,' said Donald. 'They were still in their prams.'

'Charlie, then. You're not quite such an infant.'

Charlie shook his head. 'I don't miss anything.'

'*Charlie* — '

'It's true. Not a thing.'

Helena gave everyone a segment of peach. They ate in silence.

'A Proustian moment,' said Donald eventually.

'He means', Charlie explained to Topaz, 'that in

decades to come we'll eat a single mouthful of peach and then we'll remember everything about this afternoon.'

Jerry snorted. 'We'll have forgotten it by next week.'

Topaz knew she'd never forget it. Helena to one side of her, Charlie to the other, and the peach, tasting of summer.

★ ★ ★

Helena invited them all to a party to celebrate her twenty-seventh birthday. Helena shared an apartment with Claudette near the Phoenix Theatre in Charing Cross Road. Topaz and Francesca wore their dark, knitted tops and the skirts that Helena had made for them. Francesca's skirt was greenish-grey, the colour of her eyes.

It wasn't the sort of party where you were expected to drink lemonade and play charades, nor were there any sharp-eyed mothers to keep an eye on things. The two tiny rooms were crammed with people; more guests flooded out into the dusty square of garden. A gramophone was playing and people were yelling to be heard over it.

Helena was in the communal kitchen along the landing. Topaz and Francesca gave her her birthday present.

She unwrapped the package. 'Handkerchieves, how marvellous, I never have enough.' She kissed them. 'What would you like to drink? There's beer, cider, and Tizer. Everyone's here.' Helena made a vague gesture. 'Somewhere.'

They found Jerry in the garden. 'I wasn't sure', he said, 'whether Donald would turn up, what with the Helena thing.'

Francesca said, 'What Helena thing?'

'Didn't you know?' He was stuffing tobacco into the

bowl of his pipe. 'Helena and Donald were in love for years and years.'

'But they're not any more?'

'*Well.* You do know Donald's married, don't you?'

They shook their heads. 'Had to,' said Jerry. He struck a match. 'Kid on the way. Little boy. Must be four or five now.'

Topaz looked round the garden. 'Are they here?'

'Just Donald. Jean doesn't often come to things. Babysitting, you know.'

'What about Mischa and Charlie? Have they wives we don't know about?'

'Mischa's a one-woman man.'

'Claudette?'

Jerry nodded. He struck a match. 'And Charlie's married to the theatre, of course.'

'Have you seen him act? Was he good?'

'Very good. Oh, Charlie'll see his name in lights, there's no doubt about it. If talent doesn't get him there, then ambition will.' His voice was dry. He turned to Francesca. 'Dance?'

They went indoors to the room with the gramophone. Topaz wandered around, drinking her cider, pretending to be absorbed in the posters on the walls and the flowers in the window boxes. Then a voice from behind her said, 'What's this? Alone and palely loitering?'

Turning, she saw Charlie. 'I don't think I'm capable of palely loitering, actually,' she said. 'If I loiter, I do it rather robustly.'

He laughed. 'Where's Francesca?'

'Dancing with Jerry.'

'Do you want another drink? I was just going to get one.'

'Please.' She sat on the grass at the end of the garden, waiting for him. When he returned, she said curiously, 'Did you mean what you said the other day about not missing anything from before the war?'

He sat down beside her. 'Absolutely. I had a very boring childhood. Not horrible — just boring. A semi in the suburbs and a scholarship to the grammar school. And a very boring war, too — three years in a freezing cold camp in Scotland, filling in forms and making out lists. So it's got to get better than that, hasn't it?'

'I should think so.'

'What about you, Topaz? Are you nostalgic for the past?'

She shook her head. 'Though I had some nice times. But just lately, I've sometimes felt — ' she paused: the cider was making her feel rather blurry ' — as though I'm not going anywhere. Everything seems to stay just the same. Nothing ever *changes*.'

He was lying full length on the grass, propped up on his elbow. 'What do you want to change?'

'I want to go to lots of different places. I want to wear lovely clothes, I want to do all sorts of different things. I want to — oh, I don't know — touch a glacier and see a volcano and go for a walk in a desert.'

He didn't laugh, as she was half-afraid he might do, but said, 'I want to be able to do what I know I'm good at doing.'

She knew that he meant acting. 'How lovely to have a talent,' she said.

'Although — ' and he smiled ' — I wouldn't mind some of the other things as well. Peaches and whisky and going abroad.'

'Have you?'

'Gone abroad? Never. Holidays were Margate or Hastings. How about you?'

She shook her head. 'Before the war we used to go to Dorset every year, to stay with my cousins. It was lovely. I miss that.'

'Don't you go any more?'

'I went last year, but it wasn't the same.'

'Why not?'

'It was just . . . different. I'd been away too long, I suppose. I thought it would be like coming home and it wasn't.'

'Coming home . . . ' he said slowly, 'I always rather dread it.'

'Why?'

He shrugged. 'I suppose it's because there's just me. So it can be oppressive sometimes.'

'You've no brothers and sisters?'

'Not one.' He smiled again. 'I'm unique.'

She thought that he probably was. He explained, 'All those expectations. My mother keeps a scrapbook, you know. She has photos and reviews from every play I've ever been in. School nativities onwards. My parents came to see my last play three times. *Three times*, Topaz, and it was an awful, awful play. Taking some hideously contorted route from Chingford to Richmond that involved endless trains and buses because my father won't go on the Underground and they can't afford taxis.' He sighed. 'Their lives are deadly dull, I suppose, and I fill the gap. But I hate that, don't you? Being *needed*. It's so suffocating.'

She, too, was an only child. She tried, and failed, to imagine her mother pasting photos into a scrapbook. 'They're just proud of you,' she said.

Charlie rose to his feet. 'We should go and rescue Francesca. Jerry is the most awful dancer.' They went inside the house.

★　★　★

Sometimes — when they were in the cafe, or when they were walking through the park — Topaz would catch sight of other girls glancing at them, envy in their eyes. Now, she and Francesca sat at the corner table; now, when they went to the counter to buy tea and biscuits, they addressed the cafe's proprietor by name. They were in the middle of things, thought Topaz. They had reached the centre of the circle.

With Donald and Jerry they went to jazz clubs in dark, smoky basements, where raucous, beautiful music poured from saxophone and trumpet. With Charlie and Mischa they watched French films in draughty little halls. Sometimes they gatecrashed parties. 'It's just a question', Charlie said breezily, 'of looking confident. Easy for you, Topaz. You look right. Sound right.' So she drifted around other people's houses, eating other people's food, talking to other people's friends. It seemed to her that she was discovering a new and inexhaustibly fascinating world just beneath the surface of the familiar humdrum one.

She was caught up in her new friends' complicated, tangled lives. Charlie gave up his office job when he was offered a role in *Henry V* at a repertory theatre in north London. Topaz went to a matinee performance: perched high up in the circle, her gaze focused and fixed on Charlie whenever he was on stage. When the play ended, she did not leave her seat immediately, but sat as people clambered over her, paralysed by a mixture of anguish and elation.

★　★　★

Donald and his wife, Jean, shared a flat in a house near the Goldhawk Road with Jean's widowed mother. Jean's mother was staying for a week with her sister in Clacton, so Donald took advantage of her absence and threw a party.

The rooms were high-ceilinged and shabby, sparsely furnished with threadbare sofas and battered tables and chairs. In the hallway Mischa was playing French cricket with Donald's small son, Paul. Claudette was sitting on the stairs beside them.

151

'I need someone to field,' said Mischa. 'Claudette won't.'

'I hate sport,' said Claudette.

'It's not exactly *sport*, my sweet. Just playing with the child.' There was an edge to Mischa's voice.

Claudette shrugged. Topaz said, 'I'll field,' and ran around the hall, retrieving the rubber ball from under furniture and out of coats and hats until Jean came to put Paul to bed.

In the kitchen Donald was putting plates of sandwiches and sausage rolls on the table. Helena was helping him. More guests arrived. In the front room the gramophone played. Topaz and Francesca danced with Jerry. He moved between them, gripping their hands, taking turns to swing them from one side of the room to the other. After a while, it seemed to Topaz that Jerry was dancing only with Francesca, so she slipped out of the room, weaving through the crowds.

Helena was in the hallway, searching through the heap of jackets on the floor. Tears glittered like diamonds on her face.

'I should never have come. So stupid of me.' Helena blew her nose. 'I can't find my cardigan — ' Again, she began to search frantically through the heap of clothes.

'What colour is it?'

'Lemon.'

Topaz unearthed a pale yellow cardigan. She followed Helena down the stairs, outside into the street. 'Would you like some gum?' She offered Helena a packet.

'Your mother's American major?' Helena's smile faded quickly. 'Perhaps I should find someone like that,' she said bitterly, 'someone who'll buy me nice things and look after me — ' She broke off. 'I'm sorry, Topaz. I didn't mean to imply that your mother isn't fond of her — her — '

'Her lover?' Topaz sat down on the low wall outside the house; Helena sat beside her. 'I don't think Major

152

Radetsky is her lover. I don't think any of them are. They just buy her presents and take her out, that sort of thing.' She looked at Helena. Her kind, gentle face was blotched red with tears. 'You probably think', she said, 'that I'm being very naive, but I really do believe that's how it is.'

Helena said, 'I keep telling myself that I don't mind any more about Donald and Jean — but I do, I always do. I am so *sick* of being in love with him.'

'How long have you known Donald?'

'Oh, for ever. I was still at school when we met. And then there was the war, and then he had that stupid fling, and then — ' and she flung out her bony, callused hands in a gesture of despair ' — then Jean got pregnant, and they had to get married, and that was that.' She hunched her shoulders. 'And, of course, I know I should leave London and get away from him, but the work's here, and I'm so fond of Jerry and Charlie and Mischa — though Claudette does drive me rather insane sometimes . . . ' Her voice trailed away.

Topaz looked up at the sky. It had begun to darken and the first stars were showing. 'It seems to me that you don't choose these things. They just happen. Like chicken pox.'

Helena said sadly, 'But you recover from chicken pox, don't you? And I can't seem to recover from Donald.'

Half a dozen children ran past them, calling to each other as they hauled a go-kart down the middle of the road. As their cries faded into the night, Helena said, 'I was trying to be grown up about it. I'm twenty-seven. Time to be grown up. And I usually avoid Jean, but I thought: Time to be adult, Helena, time to show everyone we're just friends now.'

'Is that what you want?'

Helena looked anguished. 'It would be better for everyone, wouldn't it?'

'I just wondered — ' it was a puzzle to her, she had

not yet worked it out ' — whether it's better to be in love with someone you can't have, or whether it's better not to particularly care about anyone. Obviously, it's best to be in love with someone who's in love with you, I can see that, but it doesn't often seem to happen like that.'

Helena rubbed her fingertips across her rumpled forehead. 'Sometimes I wish we'd never met. But other times, when I'm with him, I feel so *alive*. And nothing else seems to come up to that. Nothing at all.' She stood up. 'I think I'll go home now.' She smiled. 'You're very sweet, Topaz. Very nice to talk to.' She kissed Topaz's cheek and then headed down the street.

Topaz sat for a while, watching the sky go inky black, then she went back into the house. Jerry was alone in the kitchen.

'Where's Fran?'

Jerry's large, smooth face was patched with pink. 'With Charlie.'

She made to go and find them, but he said, 'I shouldn't, if I were you.'

'Why not?'

'Because they're . . . you know.'

She looked at him blankly. He took a few moments to focus on her. 'Rather *involved*.'

'Dancing?'

He snorted. 'You could call it that.' He was heaping sandwiches on to a plate. He stared at her. 'Didn't you know? Charlie's always fancied Francesca.'

Topaz concentrated on keeping her face just the same, so that he wouldn't guess. But something must have betrayed her because he said, 'Don't look like that. Leave 'em to each other, that's what I say. No need to be short of company.'

He was stroking her cheek with the back of his hand. When he began to kiss her, she remained quite still, aware of the movement of his fingers and mouth. His

154

breath smelt of beer and his beard scratched. His hands trailed across her neck, her back, then her breast. His caresses seemed to her rather half-hearted and haphazard. She knew that she should do something — either push him away or join in — but she could not somehow find the will.

Then he mumbled, 'Sorry . . . must find the lav,' and staggered out of the kitchen. Topaz went to the sink and leaned against it, looking out to the backs of the houses opposite. In the darkness their windows were curtained. Shadows moved behind the cloth. She supposed that those shadow people, too, fell in love and quarrelled and kissed and hated.

Didn't you know? Charlie's always fancied Francesca. Now she saw clearly how it must have happened. Charlie had noticed Francesca in the cafe and had used the accident of Topaz spilling the tea to get to know her. She had been foolish not to realize.

She ran down the stairs and let herself out into the street. Travelling home by Tube, she felt peculiarly bruised, as though someone had hit her, and she could not quite recover her breath.

At Cleveland Close, the front door to the Brookes' flat was slightly ajar. Voices filtered through the gap.

'Veronica honey — '

'Marty, you mustn't be a naughty boy.'

'A man can get tired of being good, y'know, Veronica.'

'My daughter will be home soon.'

'Have to pay your dues, honey.'

So no more peaches *there*, thought Topaz, and went back along the corridor to the stairs.

The walls of the stairway were panelled, and in the darkly polished rosewood she could see her reflection. It moved, wide and pale and ungainly, as she sat down on the top stair. *So stupid*, thought Topaz savagely, staring at her image, *to have thought he could ever have preferred you.*

155

As the snow thawed and the subsequent floods receded and summer came at last, Marius spent Sunday afternoons with Tara in the garden, keeping an eye on her as she made mud pies and poked beetles and snails, making sure she did not pull up the carrots or fall into the pond. Before he left for work each morning, Tara insisted on a kiss; when he came home in the evening, she would be waiting for him at the gate. He'd take her in his arms and whirl her round, and she'd scream with delight. Then he'd lift her on to his shoulders and carry her into the house.

Over the past six months he had learned Tara's ways and limitations and boundaries. He knew that she'd always refuse cabbage and sprouts, that she had a tendency to eat her wax crayons, that she wouldn't settle for the night without her old pram quilt. Milestones passed: the first time she let him put her to bed (adhering unswervingly to her routine: bath, teeth, story, goodnight kiss), the first time she let him take her out for a walk in her pushchair without constantly asking for Suzanne.

At last some of the tension slipped from his shoulders. He supposed it was the same for everyone, that the war years had put them in a constant state of readiness, and that they must relearn pleasures they had, in peacetime, taken for granted. He found himself, like Tara, delighting in the turn of a butterfly's wing and in the twist of sunlight on the sea.

He'd gone from school to Temperley's to the army, then to marriage and fatherhood, without so much as a pause for breath between. He had not chosen the route he had taken, it had been imposed on him. Yet the sense of futility that had haunted him since demobilization had gone. Tara had given him a purpose in life. She would have everything she needed, Marius promised himself, everything she desired. Her life would not be scarred by war, as his had been, or by want, as Suzanne's had been.

His remaining unease centred around Suzanne. Physically, she bloomed. Fresh air had brought colour to her cheeks. Yet her unhappiness persisted — deepened, he thought. Sometimes she was silent and withdrawn, at other times she snapped at him. Catching her unawares, Marius would glimpse desperation in her eyes.

She was always restless, busy, in need of occupation. She could neither lounge on the sofa, reading a magazine, or just relax in a deckchair in the garden. Missencourt itself, entombed (as Suzanne saw it) in the countryside, offered little distraction. Sometimes, when there was a little petrol to spare and Adele offered to babysit, Suzanne would borrow the Temperleys' pre-war Rolls for an afternoon. She had always liked to drive and Marius sensed that she found some release, snaking down hill and valley and through the narrow, curving, steep-sided lanes. She was a fast but skilful driver and, though Dorchester and Bournemouth were no substitute for London, she seemed to enjoy the somewhat larger sphere they offered.

He suspected that she was lonely, so he invited old friends to Missencourt. Sometimes, especially in the company of Julia and Will, she'd relax a little and chatter and laugh, and he'd remember the old Suzanne. The mood never lasted, though, and it seemed to him that she deliberately nipped every possibility of friendship in the bud, failing to return calls, rarely following up invitations. She avoided intimacy. He knew that soon he would stop trying, that he'd accept what they were: two strangers who shared a bed. The thought depressed him.

One Saturday afternoon they went to the beach at Lyme Regis. He had noticed that she liked the sea; if there was anywhere that seemed to release her from the unhappiness she carried with her, it was the seaside. Suzanne walked with Tara along the rocks, stopping every now and then to peer at a tiny celadon-green crab, or a plum-coloured sea anemone. She was wearing shorts and a shirt, which showed off her small, shapely body.

He made a sandcastle for Tara, and elaborate affair of turrets and bridges. The tide came in as he gouged out the moat. As sea water sloshed against the boundaries, Tara shrieked, clapping her hands together. Marius dug furiously, trying to contain the incoming water. A wave brushed against a turret, which slid slowly into the sea.

Suzanne smiled. 'You'll end up in Australia if you dig any more, Marius.'

'The moat just needs to be a bit deeper.'

'Obsessive,' she teased. She knelt beside him, clawing at the wet sand with her hands. A wave crashed over the sandcastle and the towers and bridges crumbled.

'Give up, Canute.' She was laughing.

Standing up, he squeezed her shoulder. 'Poor darling, you're soaked.'

She flinched, as though the endearment had stung her. Her smile disappeared and she muttered, 'I'd better get Tara dried,' and she walked up the beach.

'There's no rush,' he said. 'It's only — ' he glanced at his watch ' — half-past three.'

'It's a long walk home and Tara'll be needing her tea.' Suzanne was rubbing Tara with a towel. Her voice had altered, becoming clipped and quiet again. She would not meet his eyes.

★   ★   ★

When Marius and Jack had been boys, they had bought penny bangers on Guy Fawkes' Night. Their favourite game had been to light the bangers and hold them for

158

as long as they dared, hurling them out of danger at the last second, just before they went off. Once, Marius's father had caught them. It had been one of the very few times Francis Temperley had struck his son, so furious had he been that he should risk his limbs for such trivial pleasure. But Marius still remembered that fascinating, terrifying moment, just before the firework exploded.

He remembered it now, watching Suzanne. Her mood seemed to darken as the week wore on. She veered between silence and edginess, brightening only when she was with Tara. He sensed that if he misjudged things — if he said the wrong word, did the wrong thing — then she'd explode, like the firework.

On Saturday evening they went to dinner with the Barringtons. Derek and Lois Barrington lived near Great Missen, in a huge and echoing house which always smelt of spaniel. Derek was big and kind: his wife, Lois, was famously tactless and loud-voiced from a lifetime of shouting to dogs.

In the drawing room, they met the other dinner guests. Marius knew the local doctor and his wife to be both pleasant and interesting; his heart sank when he saw the third couple. Though Valerie Luscombe was inoffensive enough, her husband, George, was a pompous bore.

Dinner was a cacophony of barking dogs, china and cutlery clanking in the over-large room, and Lois yelling to be heard over the din.

' — the peas are our own, of course. Well, Derek's. Derek's awfully good with peas.'

'Damned cabbage whites have played havoc this year.'

'Used to pay the evacuees to catch 'em. Penny a butterfly. Never thought I'd miss the little blighters.'

'If the dog's bothering you, Mrs Temperley,' roared Derek, 'just give her a swat.'

'He wouldn't hurt a fly,' said Lois Barrington

159

tenderly. 'More roast potatoes, anyone?' Mrs Barrington's small, bright eyes focused on Suzanne. 'You should eat up, dear. You look peaky. Poor little Mrs Temperley looks peaky, doesn't she, Derek? You didn't walk here tonight, did you, Marius?'

'It's only a couple of miles.'

'No wonder your poor wife's exhausted.'

' — and there's about a teaspoon of petrol left in the car.'

George Luscombe said, 'Not still playing by the rules, are you, Temperley?'

'You don't, then?'

'Couldn't possibly manage on the ration. Two hundred and seventy miles a month? Impossible!' George tapped a knowing finger against the side of his nose. 'I need my little extra.'

'Everyone does it,' said Lois comfortably.

Yet it wasn't morality that prevented him from buying black market petrol, thought Marius, it was practicality. Absent from home for six years, he didn't have the right connections, he hadn't spent the war learning to exchange favour for favour.

George Luscombe helped himself to more potatoes. 'And until this ridiculous government sorts things out — '

'Should bring back Churchill,' interrupted Derek. 'Country's in a mess.'

'Giving handouts left, right, and centre,' said George Luscombe, through a mouthful of Yorkshire pudding, 'while we sell our souls to the damned Yankees, begging your pardon, ladies.'

Suzanne said, 'Handouts?'

'Family allowances and what-nots.'

'You don't approve of making women and children's lives better?'

'It's a question of whether the country can afford it, my dear Mrs Temperley.'

160

'You don't think people have *earned* the right to freedom from poverty?'

'Books have to balance. Just the same as when you tot up your housekeeping, my dear.'

Suzanne put down her knife and fork. 'People deserve something. All those ordinary people who joined the Forces and endured the Blitz, they deserve something. They deserve decent houses and proper medical care and not having to worry about being thrown out of work when the next Depression comes along. That's why they voted for Mr Attlee. Because they trusted him to give them what they deserved.'

George Luscombe smacked his hands together. 'You can't make something out of nothing, that's all I'm saying.'

'But they have to.' Suzanne's eyes blazed. 'Don't you see? They have to. Otherwise all those sacrifices would have been for nothing.'

'Just pointing out a few pertinent economic *facts* — '

'All those people who gave their lives — it would all have been pointless — '

'Mustn't let sentiment blind you to reality — '

'*Sentiment!*' Suzanne's voice, furious now, echoed in the cavernous room. 'People always say that, don't they, when they know that they are in the wrong! As if sentiment — emotion — *feeling* — was something to be ashamed of!'

Lois Barrington broke the ensuing silence. 'More veg anyone? No? I'll fetch the pudding.'

Walking home later, Suzanne said, 'Sorry. Yelling like that at that awful man. I hope I didn't spoil your evening.'

The sun was setting and the chalk downs were at first gold, then copper. 'Oh — ' Marius smiled ' — under-done beef and dog hairs in the soup . . . I shouldn't worry.'

'I meant what I said, though.'

'I know you did.'

She gave him a quick glance. 'Do you disagree with me?'

He shook his head. 'Not at all. Only — '

'What?'

'He had a point, I'm afraid. George Luscombe had a point.'

'Oh, *please*. He was unbearable. Pompous, patronizing, obnoxious — '

'He's all of those. But still . . . ' Marius squinted as the rays of the setting sun stabbed his eyes. 'Britain *is* having to go cap in hand to the Americans. And if they don't help us — '

'What?'

'Oh . . . it doesn't matter.' He tried to smile.

'*Marius*. Don't you dare treat me like that! I am *not* an empty-headed little woman!'

'I know you're not. I've never thought you were.' He sighed. 'People moan about rationing, how it's worse now than it was during the war. They think — oh, they think that we can't possibly go on rationing bread and meat and sugar and petrol — all the things people need — for much longer. But I can't see things getting easier for some time. The war used up all our reserves, and we can't count on the empire to fill up the coffers any more. And if the Americans won't help us, then it's all going to get a great deal worse.'

They left the road, taking the short cut that led over the fields to Missencourt. The remains of the glorious June day lingered in the warm air.

'How much worse?'

'Without American help we could be bankrupt,' Marius said bluntly. 'All the social improvements that you rightly point out are so necessary — and deserved — would have to be postponed indefinitely. But that could be the least of it. It's quite possible that labour would have to be directed — even more so than in wartime. It's even possible that we'd all be on famine rations . . . less than a thousand calories a day.'

They were walking alongside a dense, dark conifer wood. 'As for us,' he said, 'well, Temperley's would go under. It's been a rough year already, with the fuel crisis and the bad weather. Oh, you mustn't worry,' he said quickly, catching sight of her expression, 'we'll survive — '

'*Marius*,' she said again. He could hear the exasperation in her voice.

He handed her on to the stile. 'It's just that I want you to be happy.'

'I *am* happy.'

Somehow, at last, he found the courage to say, 'No, you're not, Suzanne.'

She paused, perched on top of the stile. 'I think', he said carefully, 'that you're extremely *unhappy*.'

She bit her lip. Her eyes were wary. Then she smiled. 'You're wrong, Marius.' She slid off the stile. Her voice was soft and seductive, and her body pressed against his.

Anger overcame desire and he pushed her away. 'If *that* was all I wanted,' he said softly, 'I could *pay* for it.'

She paled. Then she said bitterly, 'It's all most men want.'

He had to turn away, his fists clenched. The tangy scent of the pines recalled to him suddenly, sharply, the first time they had made love. 'I'm your husband,' he said angrily. 'I'm not your boyfriend, nor a passing stranger, nor some army officer you've picked up in a pub — but your husband, the father of your child.'

She put her hands to her face. 'I'm sorry.'

'It may be all some men want, but it's not all *I* want. I know we didn't marry for love. And I know it must have been very hard for you, all those months of managing on your own. I shall always feel guilty about that. But I have come to love Tara. And I thought — I

163

hoped — that we might come to love each other as well. All I'm asking for is a little affection. That you don't flinch when I kiss you — don't pull away when I hug you — '

'It's just that I'm not used to all that,' she said hopelessly. 'Showing affection. My family didn't do that. Touching . . . that was for sex, or out of anger. Not for *love*. When I first came to Missencourt, I couldn't get used to it, the way you and Adele were with each other. Kisses . . . hugs . . . I thought it was a bit funny, to be honest. Then I realized that you just did it to cheer each other up. You didn't even have to think about it.'

He wanted to believe her. But he said, 'It's more than that, though, isn't it?'

As if at the flick of a switch, the wariness returned to her eyes.

'It's me, isn't it, Suzanne?'

'Marius — '

'At first, I thought it was Missencourt. That you didn't like the house. Then I thought it was the countryside, or the people we mix with. But you dislike *me*, don't you, Suzanne? *I'm* making you unhappy.'

The feathery branches of the conifers cast shadows on her face. 'You're a good man, Marius,' she said.

'Damned with faint praise,' he said softly.

She shook her head. 'I don't dislike *you*.'

'Who do you dislike, then?'

The corners of her mouth twisted. 'Oh Marius,' she said, as she climbed over the stile and started along the path through the woods, 'haven't you worked that one out? I dislike myself, of course.'

★ ★ ★

He slept badly that night. Dozing fitfully, he woke at six o'clock and was unsurprised to find that he was alone in bed. Peering into the nursery, he saw that Tara slept, untroubled.

He dressed and went downstairs. Fragments from the previous night's scene echoed in his mind. *I don't dislike you. I dislike myself.* He wandered from room to room, looking for her, but could not find her. He made tea, but did not drink it.

After a while, he put on a jacket and went outside. Leaving the garden, he walked through the copse and saw her standing on the ridge of the hill. She was silhouetted by the pale dawn light. Her hand shaded her face as she looked south, to the sea.

'Too misty,' he said, approaching her. She spun round. 'You have to wait till it clears.'

Her gaze flickered away from him. Her eyelids were swollen and red-rimmed. 'Couldn't you sleep?' she asked.

He shook his head. She glanced once more at the opalescent horizon. Then she said, 'I've been trying to decide what to do.'

'About what?' he asked, though he dreaded her reply.

'About us.' She looked away, gave a short laugh. 'If you hadn't been so bloody honourable — ' She broke off.

His sense of foreboding increased, gouging a hole in his heart. But he said, 'If I hadn't been so bloody honourable . . . and insisted you marry me? Was that what you were going to say?'

Her silence was his answer. He said roughly, 'Would you have preferred me to react differently?'

'I *expected* you to react differently.'

He felt weary: the sleepness night, the fear of what was to come. 'I don't understand.'

She turned to face him, looking him in the eye at last. 'When I told you about Tara, I expected you to offer me cash.' Her voice was harsh. 'I thought that was what your lot did.' A fleeting, crooked smile. 'I underestimated you.'

He said again, 'And you would have preferred that?'

She paused. Then she said, 'In some ways it would have been easier, yes.'

'Easier . . . ?'

She closed her eyes. When she whispered, 'Than to live with a lie,' he only just caught the muttered words.

He made himself say, 'What lie?'

★   ★   ★

The doorbell rang at midday; Veronica Brooke, who was sitting on the sofa, reading letters, said crossly, 'On a Sunday — '

Topaz peered down from the window and saw Marius. 'It's all right, I'll go.' She ran out of the flat.

She knew the moment she saw him that something dreadful had happened. He was dazed and fragile; if she touched him, she thought, he might shatter like a pane of glass.

Sitting on a bench near the Round Pond, she watched him fold up his body, his fists supporting his head. Because she had to know, she said, 'Is someone ill?'

He shook his head. Then he said, 'Tara isn't mine.'

'Oh.' The word was a sigh. 'Poor Marius.'

'Suzanne told me this morning.' He shrugged. 'I couldn't bear to stay at Missencourt. I just — got on a train, came here. I'm sorry, interrupting your Sunday.'

'Our Sundays are very dull, Marius, and I tend to be glad of interruption.' She took his hand. 'Are you sure?'

'About Tara? Yes. Pretty well.' He screwed up his eyes. Then he said in a rush, 'Suzanne told me she'd had an affair with one of the top brass at the place where I was stationed in nineteen forty-four. She was his driver. Oh, and he was married, by the way.' His voice was savage. 'So they kept it quiet. She didn't even tell her girlfriends. And, of course, she didn't tell me.'

'Suzanne was in love with him?'

'Yes.'

'What happened?'

'He was sent south in early March to help with the D-Day preparations. I met her a couple of days after he'd gone.'

She prompted him, 'And . . . ?'

'And he was killed on the first day. June the sixth, nineteen-forty-four.' Marius lit a cigarette and drew deeply on it. 'So there you have it,' he said bitterly. 'That was why she married me. I was a convenient husband. A convenient father for Tara.'

They sat in silence, looking out over the pond. Eventually she said, 'What will you do?'

'Get a divorce, I suppose.'

'Why?'

'For God's sake, Topaz, isn't it obvious? Because it was all a lie — the marriage — my supposed fatherhood — '

'*Could* you be Tara's father?'

A pause. 'Yes. I suppose so.'

Such anger, she thought. A calm, strong man, she had rarely seen him angry. But she persevered. 'Do you love her, Marius? Do you love Tara?'

'That's the worst of it.' He threw his cigarette on to the grass and began to walk in no particular direction. 'If Suzanne had told me six, eight months ago that Tara wasn't mine, then it might have been bearable. I'd have felt a fool, but it wouldn't have been so . . . so . . . ' He fell silent. Then he said furiously, 'But to find out now, now I've got to know Tara, now she's used to me . . . It really is unutterably bloody.'

'You love her.'

'Yes.' He paused, desolation in his eyes. 'Yes, I do.'

'Well then.'

He stared at her. 'What do you mean, 'well then'?'

'Then that makes it all right, doesn't it?'

He said, exasperated, 'No, Topaz. No, it doesn't make

167

it all right. It doesn't make it all right at all.'

She thought back over the events of the past week and then she said quietly, 'It's just that it seems to me that when you find love, you should try to hold on to it. However awful the circumstances are. You love Tara, Marius, so why throw that away?'

He shook his head. 'If only it were that simple. If only it were that easy.'

'I'm not saying it's easy. You'd have to forgive Suzanne for deceiving you, and I can see that would be very difficult. But perhaps if you understood why she did it . . . She's a good person, after all. I don't think she'd do something wrong like that without a good reason.'

'What reason could possibly be good enough?'

She did not reply and after a while he answered his own question. 'To give the child a home, I suppose.'

She put her arms around him, resting her face against his chest. When she shut her eyes, she could hear the beating of his heart.

'You're making my shirt wet,' he said.

'Sorry.' She looked up.

He wiped away her tears with the balls of his thumbs. 'I seem to have assumed I'm the only one with problems.'

She told him the easier thing first. 'I've lost my job again. That's the fourth.'

'What happened?'

'Oh.' She sighed. 'I was feeling rather miserable and rather hungry — I always feel hungry when I'm miserable — and I got muddled up, and announced the Honourable Mrs Gish-Lake as the Honourable Mrs Fishcake.'

For the first time, he smiled. She said mournfully, 'My employers didn't think it was funny.'

He straightened his face. 'No.'

'And — '

'And . . . ?'

'And I seem to have fallen in love with someone.' She added quickly, 'Don't worry, he isn't a bit like Peter de Courcy. That was just — well, I was so pleased that someone might want to kiss me.'

He offered her his handkerchief and she blew her nose. Then he said, 'I think we should find a pub and have some lunch. If I can't stop you being miserable, at least I can stop you being hungry. And then — '

'Marius . . . ?'

He sighed. 'Oh, I haven't a clue, Topaz. I really haven't a clue.'

7

In the end Marius went back to Missencourt.

It was late evening when he arrived at the house. Suzanne was in the bedroom. He saw the open suitcase, the neatly folded piles of clothes. He said, 'You're planning to leave?'

She flushed, seeing him. 'I think it's best, don't you?'

He sat down on the edge of the bed. He thought how empty the house would be without them. 'Best for whom?'

'For all of us.'

'What I don't understand', he said angrily, 'is how you could do such a thing.'

She closed her eyes. Then she said wearily, 'It was for Tara. I did it for Tara.'

'Because — ' he struggled to damp down his anger, to understand ' — because you wanted her to have a decent start in life?'

'Yes. Because of that.' She paused, folding sweaters, and pushed back a lock of dark hair from her face. 'But also because I was afraid that I might lose her.'

'Lose her?' He stared at her. 'Why on earth should you lose her?'

'Last year, when you found me, my landlord was about to chuck me out of my flat. And I couldn't find anywhere else.'

'I still don't see — '

Her eyes met his. 'That's because you've never lived like that, Marius. Hand to mouth. Scraping along the bottom.'

'However poor you were,' he said angrily, 'however difficult things were, that doesn't excuse what you did!'

Her gaze dropped. 'I know,' she said softly. 'I know.'

She put the sweater in the case and straightened. 'Marius, I've regretted what I did a thousand times. And I could apologize for what I did a thousand times. But it wouldn't make it any better, would it?'

As she opened another drawer, he said, 'I want you to tell me what happened.'

'Marius — '

'Everything. I deserve *that* at least, don't I?'

She bowed her head. 'Of course.' She took a deep breath. 'My landlord — '

'Starting at the beginning. At the camp. With *him*.' He could not bring himself to say *Tara's father.* 'Were you in love with him?'

'Yes.' Her hands paused, pairing stockings. 'Very much. He wasn't the first man I'd slept with, but he was the first man I loved.' For a moment, he glimpsed a trace of the old defiance, but almost immediately it slipped away.

'What was his name?'

'Neil. Neil Finlay.'

'He was a colonel, you said?'

'Yes.'

'So he was older than you?'

'He was in his mid-thirties.'

'Married?'

'I told you.'

'Children?'

She shook her head. 'No.'

'And you were his driver?'

'I was assigned to him shortly after I arrived at the camp.'

'So . . . one night when you were driving him home . . . he put his hand on your knee — '

'It wasn't like that.' Anger flashed in her eyes. 'I'd been working for him for several months before we realized — before we realized — '

'What?'

171

Her voice faltered. 'How much we liked each other.'

There was a silence. He pictured them: Suzanne, bright and lively in her ATS uniform; the confident, cultured older man sitting in the car beside her.

He made himself go on. 'What was he like?'

'Marius,' she cried, 'do you really want to know all this? Won't it just make it worse?'

'*Tell* me.'

'Neil . . . well . . . ' Her voice shook. 'He was wonderful. He was kind and funny and clever and generous. And he was marvellous in bed.'

He got up and went to the window, fumbling in his pocket for his cigarettes. As he flicked the lighter, he heard her say, 'I'm sorry. That was . . . cheap.' She sighed. 'We were in love and that's all there is to it. I'd never felt like that before. I'd always rather despised all that soppy stuff in films and books. Thought it was nonsense, thought they'd made it up. Then it happened to *me*.' She gave a short laugh. 'Served me right for thinking I was immune, didn't it?' She sat down on the bed. Her face was white, her hands knotted together.

'Did you plan to get married?'

'When the war was over — when he came back — he was going to tell his wife. Jane lived in Cornwall, you see, and Neil hadn't seen her for ages. He said it wasn't something you should tell someone in a letter or on the phone. He had to do it face to face. And he knew something big was brewing up — ' She broke off and he saw her face crumple. 'I've often thought — maybe he knew he wasn't going to come back. Maybe he had a premonition.'

Marius remembered the night before he had sailed to France. Crammed with hundreds of his fellow soldiers on a ship in Poole harbour. Dreading it so much that you wanted it to begin, just so that it could be over sooner.

'I expect', he said slowly, 'he just didn't know.

Thought it was tempting fate to plan.'

She looked up at him. 'Yes.' Her next words were tumbled and rushed, as if to get them over with quickly. 'Anyway, Neil tried to get me posted south with him, but there was nothing doing. I knew, of course, there was a chance I'd never see him again. And I felt . . . I felt *desperate*. And so lonely. And *angry* that he should leave me. I know that must seem illogical — unreasonable. But that was how I felt. I missed him so much. I missed what we'd shared together.' She frowned. 'The company. And the sex. Not just the pleasure. The comfort of it, as well. The being with someone.'

'Which is where I fitted in, I assume,' he said bitterly. 'If it hadn't been me, it would have been someone else, wouldn't it, Suzanne?' He watched her carefully as he asked his next question. 'When we met, did you know you were pregnant?'

'No. I didn't have any idea. I've never been particularly regular, and Neil and I were careful, so I thought I couldn't possibly . . . ' She forced herself to meet his eyes. 'That's the truth, Marius. If I'd just wanted a father for my baby, I'd have told you about the pregnancy back in 1944, wouldn't I? And I didn't, did I? It was *you* who came looking for *me*, remember.'

And he had to admit that she hadn't exactly made it easy for him to find her. Yet if she hadn't intended to trick him into marriage, why had she slept with him?

'So you're saying he — your lover — had only been gone a few days when we met. But surely he *might* have come back, mightn't he? You weren't exactly *constant*, were you?'

Her great dark eyes stared into a distance he could not see. 'I needed to take my mind off things,' she said at last. 'I needed to blot it out . . . the anxiety and the anger. I suppose — it seems so stupid now — I wanted to punish him for leaving me. And sex — ' she shrugged ' — well, I've always enjoyed it. It's always made me feel better. And I knew, looking at you, that I'd enjoy it with *you*.' For the first time, she gave a small smile. 'I know women aren't supposed to say things like that, but that's how it was.'

'So I was . . . ' he struggled to find an analogy ' . . . a makeshift. A . . . a proxy.'

She bit her lip. 'I liked you, Marius, and I was attracted to you. I'm sorry if that seems . . . insubstantial.' Her forehead furrowed. 'A lot of men are attractive, but not many are *nice*. Neil was. You are.'

Nice, he thought. *Dear God*.

'What happened to him? You said he was killed on the first day.'

'A friend of his', she said slowly, 'told me he didn't even make it to the beach. He died in the sea, between the landing craft and the shore.' She paused. 'I couldn't go to the funeral. Family only. His wife insisted.'

He found that he could not bear the expression in her eyes. He lit a cigarette and crossed the room to her. 'Here.' When she did not take it, he placed it between her shaking fingers.

'Thanks,' she whispered. She closed her eyes, inhaling the cigarette. Eventually she said, 'By then I was pretty sure that I was pregnant. I tried to ignore it at first, just pretended it wasn't happening. I couldn't think straight. Neil was dead and that was the only thing that mattered. I couldn't think about the future because there didn't seem to *be* any future.' She drew deeply on the cigarette. 'Then it began to show and my commanding officer cottoned on and I was out on my ear. I'd lost everything, Marius — the man I loved, my job, my home. My parents wouldn't take me in — my mother slapped my face when I told her about the baby. I thought of getting rid of it — I went to see someone, but I was too far gone by then.' Her eyes widened. 'Sorry if I shock you, Marius, but you wanted the truth — ' Her voice broke.

He left the room and went downstairs. From the sideboard in the drawing room he took a bottle of Scotch and two glasses. When he came back to the bedroom, she was still sitting on the bed. Her head jerked up as he opened the door.

'I thought you'd gone,' she said.

He poured two large Scotches, handing one to her. The fiery liquid scorched his throat, steadying him.

'What did you do?'

After a long pause, she said, 'A friend let me sleep on her sofa for a couple of weeks. It was impossible, though — she had three children, and the back of the house had been damaged by a flying bomb. Then I found a room in Putney and managed to get a job in a shop. That kept me going for a couple of months. I was getting bigger, of course, but I wore loose shirts and sweaters and managed to hide it. Eventually they noticed and I got the sack. And then — well, I took a room in a lodging house. Bought a ring from Woollies and said I was a war widow.' She frowned. 'I can't remember too much about that time. There were V2s landing on London just about every day and everyone was scared stiff, I do remember that. *I* wasn't scared though. I thought a V2 would be a nice easy way out.' She drank some more Scotch. 'Then Tara was born.'

'Boxing Day,' he said.

'Yes.' A ghost of a smile. 'And then — well, I know it sounds corny, but I had a reason for living.' She cradled the glass in her hands. 'I didn't expect to love her, you know, Marius. All the time I was pregnant, I thought it was such a rotten trick, to lose Neil and to be landed with a baby I didn't want. I'd never been particularly keen on babies. Not like some women are. I'd seen what too many children had done to my mother, and I'd always promised myself I wouldn't end up like *her*.' Tears were trailing down her face. 'But I loved Tara. I loved her the first moment I saw her. They — the hospital authorities — wanted me to give her up for adoption, but I wouldn't.' She scrabbled in her sleeve for her handkerchief and blew her nose.

'Managing with an infant — it must have been difficult — '

'It was bloody awful.' She wiped her eyes with the back of her hand and swallowed another mouthful of Scotch. 'My landlady told me to get out of the house the day I came home from hospital. She'd guessed, you see, that I wasn't married. She looked at Tara as though she was *dirty*.' Suzanne took a deep, shivering breath. 'We lived in some awful places. Tara was always getting colds and sore throats, and it was because of the damp, I'm sure. And it was so difficult to find work that fitted in with her.'

She fell silent. While he had been heading north, Marius thought, through occupied France, Belgium and Germany, Suzanne had been fighting battles of her own.

'So when I came to see you — '

'As I said, my landlord was about to chuck me out. There were a lot of people desperate to find somewhere to live, people who could pay more than me. I'd been looking all week, trying to find somewhere. I was at my wits' end. Everything seemed to be getting more difficult, not less. Tara caught the measles at the beginning of the summer, so there were doctor's bills to pay. I'd had a job in a pub in the evenings — a neighbour looked after Tara — but I had to give that up when she fell ill. I was beginning to think she'd be better off if I did give her up for adoption. It would have broken my heart, but you've got to do what's best for your child, haven't you? Then you turned up. And when you assumed that Tara was yours — ' her upturned hands were a gesture of resignation ' — I saw a way of keeping her.'

He remembered the hot, damp little flat, and the child's cries. *She's mine isn't she, Suzanne?* he had said.

And she had inclined her head.

'You said you expected me to offer you money?'

'Yes.' The word was a whisper. 'And then when you didn't . . . when you insisted on marrying me instead . . . that wasn't only a way out of poverty, was it? It was a way out of Tara being *labelled*. As illegitimate. As a *bastard*. And when you told me about Missencourt and all the lovely things Tara could have . . . well, I justified it to myself. I told myself that you could afford it, that you'd always had it easy, you and your kind, so why shouldn't we have a share in that?' She sighed. 'I didn't know you then, Marius. Not properly. I knew what I was doing was very wrong, but I told myself that you'd do all right out of it. I could see you still wanted me — '

'Sex in exchange for a roof over your head.'

'Yes.' She gave a peculiar little laugh. 'Ugly, wasn't it?'

When he did not reply, she went on, 'Later on, when I got to know you better, I began to hate myself. When I saw how much you loved Tara. When you were kind to me. And not just you, Adele as well. She's been so good to me. And I just couldn't go on with it, I just couldn't.'

He turned away, staring sightlessly out of the window. After a while, from the small sounds behind him, he knew that she had resumed packing her case.

'Where will you go?' he asked.

'I don't know. I'll find somewhere.'

'And Tara?'

'*Marius.*' Her eyes were anguished.

He went on relentlessly, 'That's what you're planning to do, isn't it, Suzanne? Take Tara and go. And be damned to me — to my mother — to all the people who've come to love her.'

'She's all I have!' The words came out in a wail. 'I can't leave her — perhaps I should, but I can't — ' She was shivering now, her arms clasped around herself.

On the train coming home, one thing had become clear to him. *When you find love*, Topaz had said, *you should try to hold on to it.* He knew she was right.

'I don't want to lose her,' he said slowly. 'Even if she's not mine, I don't want to lose her.' Another thing he had thought about on the long journey home. Whether, knowing that he had not fathered Tara, he still cared about her. It hadn't taken long to find an answer. You couldn't turn love off and on, like a tap. Discovering that Tara was not of his blood, he felt regret and pain, but could not resent or hate *her*.

Suzanne sat down on the edge of the bed. Her face was pale and set. 'I won't give her up, Marius.'

He would persevere, he thought, wear away at her. She was a practical, sensible woman, and sooner or later she'd see that she'd be doing the right thing in leaving Tara with him at Missencourt.

Yet, almost immediately, he knew that he could not do it. Knew that it would be an act of barbarity to separate mother and child. To make their grief pay for his hurt and anger; to hurt Tara to punish Suzanne.

He sat down on the bed beside her. He felt mentally and physically exhausted. All his choices seemed to have narrowed to one impossible choice.

He said, 'If you won't go without her . . . and I can't bear to lose her . . . then that leaves only one thing to do, doesn't it?'

She, too, looked exhausted. 'I don't understand.'

'That you stay.'

She said, startled, 'Here? At Missencourt? I couldn't possibly do that.'

'Why not?'

'Because it wouldn't work.'

'Why wouldn't it work?'

'You would hate me, Marius.'

He said, 'It would be difficult . . . ' and her laughter cracked.

'Difficult! Bloody hell!'

'For Tara's sake, isn't it worth a try?'

'We have tried. Bloody hard.' She got up and began to walk around the room, flinging things into the case apparently randomly. A bottle of scent, a pair of shoes, a book. Then she said, 'And even if *you* could be that forgiving, *I* couldn't bear it. Such a half-life.'

He was taken off guard. 'Half-life?' he repeated, blankly.

'Us. You and me.'

'Missencourt, you mean?'

'No, Marius. *Us*. Never having a proper conversation. Never talking about anything that matters. I can't live the rest of my life like that, not even for Tara.'

'That's not true,' he said defensively. 'We've had plenty of conversations — '

'Rubbish. It's been obvious to me for a long time that you're only tolerating me out of a sense of duty.'

He ran his hands through his hair. His head ached. 'I didn't know you felt like that.'

'I haven't exactly felt I had the right to complain about niceties.' She yanked a drawer out of the dressing table and upended it into the suitcase. 'Back at the camp', she said, 'we used to argue dreadfully, but at least we talked. And about things that *mattered*. When did we last talk about anything that *mattered*?'

He had to think hard. 'Yesterday,' he said. 'Coming home from the Barringtons. Before that — I can't remember.'

'We used to talk about everything. Politics . . . people . . . the war . . . films . . . books . . . ' She scooped up the contents of a drawer and dumped it on top of the heap. 'You've changed, Marius,' she said. 'You hold a part of yourself back.'

'It's how I get through,' he said bitterly.

'How you put up with *me*, you mean. How you put up with a marriage you didn't want, that you were tricked into.'

'That wasn't what I meant,' he said sharply. He went

to the window and opened it, yet the night air did not seem to cool the room. 'I meant that when I came home last year I couldn't get back into the swing of things. It wasn't like I'd expected it to be. I didn't feel part of it any more. But since Tara came into my life — ' He broke off.

Crossing the room to him, she placed her hand on his clenched fist. Then she said, 'We seem to have made an awful mess of things, don't we?'

He screwed up his eyes. 'I have the most infernal headache,' he muttered. 'I can't seem to think any more.' He tugged at his tie.

'You're just tired, Marius. And upset.' She glanced at her watch. 'It's almost two.'

He said, 'Will you wait? A day or two — '

'Marius — '

'You mustn't just go, Suzanne,' he said fiercely. 'You mustn't just take her without telling me.'

She closed her eyes. 'I won't do that.'

'Promise?'

'I promise.'

He slid the suitcase off the bed. Its contents overflowed, spilling on to the floor. Then he kicked off his shoes and lay down and closed his eyes, and, to his surprise, fell asleep almost immediately.

★ ★ ★

That August the heat haze cast mirages on the English countryside, so that where the meadows tumbled down to the coast the colours of sea and grass mingled together, jade green, taupe and ultramarine. Day-trippers fled the airless cities, trains and buses spitting them out at seaside towns. At Bournemouth, Hern-scombe and Lyme Regis, they stretched out on scorching sand, broiled their pallid limbs crimson, and soaked knobbly, town-worn feet in salt water. Children dabbed shrimping nets into the shallows, skinned knees on barnacled rocks, and howled when their melting ice lollies slid from the stick, staining the pavement orange.

The vast tribe of Chancellors obeyed the dictates of the season. Chancellor children ran free, released from school to tease and taunt and tell secrets to each other as they built dens and dammed streams in the dark, flickering woods and valleys. Chancellor husbands, free for a fortnight from shop, school or office, decamped to lodgings and hotels with their complaining wives and squabbling children. John and Prudence escaped to the Lake District, where they walked among green velvet hills and mirror-glass water. Maurice Chancellor stayed with his mousy wife and sharp-eyed children in an hotel in Torquay, where Maurice eyed the waitresses and totted up the price of the drapery.

At Sixfields August was harvest, the busiest time of year. Jack worked from dawn to dusk, steering the combine harvester across the great sweep of Carrie Chancellor's land. Silver blades scythed golden stems. Towards the end of the day the setting sun spilled long shadows across the corn stubble. As Jack's memories of war became more distant, he recognized his own good fortune in escaping both physical impairment and the mental scars carried by former prisoners of war. When his mother berated him once more for his failure to attend family events, for her sake he prised himself out of his shell. Sunday lunch at the School House; a cousin's wedding. He even managed to exchange a civil word with Will and Julia.

In London they scattered, Charlie to work in Blackpool, Francesca to stay with a married sister, Jerry and Mischa and Claudette to bicker and flirt and make up in a damp little house in Devon lent by an admirer of Claudette's. Helena went to Brighton, where, crunching pebbles beneath her feet and shading her eyes from a luminous sea, she made the vow she had made last year and the year before and the year before that: that she would forget him.

Adele Temperley, aware and worried yet tactfully silent about the storms that raged around her, went to stay for the month with her sister in Cumberland. At Missencourt Marius's moods lurched wildly. He wanted Suzanne to leave, he wanted her to stay. He could not bear to touch her, yet he loathed the nights they spent apart, she sleeping in the guest room, or he collapsed on the drawing-room sofa in a stew of alcohol and exhaustion. He hated her for the way she had taken his ordered life apart, strewing it in jigsaw pieces. When Temperley's shut down for its customary fortnight's holiday, he found himself enclosed at Missencourt with her. Lacking the routine of work, he took to drinking too much and sleeping too little.

Late one evening he made a move to grab his car keys from where he had earlier flung them on the kitchen table, but Suzanne, who was washing up, reached them before him.

'You're not driving. You've had far too much to drink.'

'Suzanne — ' he said furiously.

'I mean it.' She was clutching the keys in one hand, a tea towel in the other. 'If you kill yourself, I'd have it on my conscience for the rest of my life.'

'Give them to me.' He held out his hand.

She moved away. 'You'll have to take them from me by force and you won't do that, will you, Marius?'

When he lunged at her, she stepped aside. Losing his balance, he grabbed at the draining board to steady himself. His hand smashed against a glass, breaking it. He leaned against the sink, shocked by the impact, staring at his palm, seeing the fragments of glass embedded in his skin.

He heard her say, 'Oh God, Marius — '

'Oh, *bugger*,' he said wearily. 'Oh bugger, bugger, *bugger*.'

'Sit down.' She pushed him into a seat. 'I'll phone the doctor.'

'No.' Blood was trickling down his hand to his shirtsleeve. He wondered why it didn't hurt. He looked up at her. 'Drunk as a lord and fallen over my own feet. No. For God's sake, Suzanne, he *delivered* me.'

She stared at him. Then she said, 'I'll patch it up then.'

She sat beside him, picking glass out of his hand. He felt lightheaded and cold. 'Stupid *fucking* thing to do . . . ' he said.

'*Marius*.' Her voice was slightly mocking. 'I've never heard you swear so much.'

For some unfathomable reason he found himself thinking of his father. He said, 'I can only remember Dad swearing once.'

'When?'

'The day war was declared.' He tried to focus his thoughts. He was drunk, shocked. 'He'd been in the first one. Had a bloody awful time, I think. Never talked about it.'

'I may have to get my tweezers for these tiny bits of glass.' She glanced at him. 'You're a rather funny colour, Marius. Would you like to lie down?'

'I'm all right.'

'Then talk to me. Tell me about your father. You've never really spoken about him. What was he like?'

'He was . . . ' He screwed up his eyes. 'Hard to live up to. Tall. Good-looking. Competent.'

'Like father, like son,' she said and he shook his head.

'Not really. Oh, I'm like him in some ways, I know, but . . . he was charming . . . funny . . . people adored him . . . women especially . . . I'm none of those things.'

She squinted. 'I think that's all the glass out.'

Marius said slowly, 'You once called me a stuffed

shirt. I suppose I am. *Duty*, that was what my father always drummed into me. You had to do your duty. To your country. To your family. To those who loved you. But — '

Suzanne opened a bottle of disinfectant. 'But . . . ?'

'I don't think he always found it easy.'

'No one does, Marius.'

'*Ow* — '

'Don't be a baby,' she said firmly. 'It's only Ibcol.'

'Bloody hurts.' He took a deep breath. 'Just occasionally he'd get into a rage about something. Not often. Bloody terrifying. Cold anger. I'd keep out of his way. Once or twice a year, maybe.'

'Once or twice a day, with my father,' said Suzanne. She took a clean tea towel from the drawer. 'Hold that in place while I get the bandages.'

Marius sat in the kitchen, holding the tea towel around his hand. It had begun to hurt now. Rather a lot. It occurred to him that he had never really mourned his father. That he had been out of the country when he had been told of Francis Temperley's death; and that, when he had come home more than a year later, his duty had been to his mother and to Julia, and had allowed him little time or opportunity to consider his own grief.

Now, for the first time, perhaps, when he thought of his father it was as an adult remembering — and beginning to understand — another adult. Francis Temperley had been a complex man. Julia had inherited his conflicting needs for passion and for privacy. Marius had admired and adored his father, but had not been close to him. The most unutterably bloody thing, he thought, was that now he never would be.

Suzanne came back into the room. 'Give me your hand — '

But, still seated, he put his other arm around her, drawing her to him, pressing the side of his head against her belly, his eyes closed. He felt her stroke his hair and heard her say his name softly, over and over again.

★ ★ ★

Topaz and Veronica spent August in Eastbourne, in a large hotel of faded pre-war splendour. Surrounded by potted palms and gilt ormolu mirrors, Veronica was at first subdued. Sometimes in the evenings, after several gins and tonic, she told Topaz about her childhood in India. Of summers spent at hill stations, of tea parties and gymkhanas and tennis parties. Tell me what it looked like, sounded like, smelt like, Topaz wanted to demand, but managed to hold her tongue, afraid of breaking the rare spell of her mother's confidences. Only once could she not contain herself, after Veronica described to her the long journey to England when she was nine years old, to boarding school. An army wife had escorted her, her own mother being considered too delicate to venture from the darkened bungalow, with its drifting muslin curtains and attentive servants. 'Of course, I never saw her again, she died when I was fourteen,' said Veronica, before summoning the waiter for another drink. Topaz blurted out, 'But how awful, how did you *feel*? You must have cried *buckets*,' and Veronica looked momentarily blank, bewildered. Then she said, 'I don't think so. Not especially. The day they told me, I was allowed to miss hockey. I was very glad because I hated the mud.'

Later, walking along the seafront, which she did each night, Topaz thought of that stoical, dry-eyed girl. And compared her to herself, and resolved that tonight she would not cry: she, who had wept rivers of tears for Charlie.

★ ★ ★

By August Will could no longer ignore his financial problems. The heavy losses caused by the severe winter and the fuel crisis had pushed him deeper into debt. Earlier in the year he had taken out a bank loan to tide the business over.

Towards the end of the month Will visited his cousin Maurice in Hernscombe. Maurice, fat and tanned, listened with apparent sympathy as Will explained how, because of the snow and because of the continuing rationing of petrol, he hadn't sufficient cash to pay the last three months' rent. He was still certain, Will added confidently, that he could make a success of the garage. He needed a breathing space; he'd pay his debts as soon as he was straight.

Maurice reminded Will that he was only a part-owner in the garage. 'Not my decision, I'm afraid, dear boy. Can't let the others down. If it was up to me . . . ' The unfinished sentence hung in the air as Will squeezed thanks and farewells from a gullet dry with desperation and escaped from Maurice's shop.

On the way home he stopped at the Holly Bush for a drink to calm his nerves. The Holly Bush lay off the beaten track, standing alone on an unlit, unpopulated section of the Hernscombe road. Its licensing hours were known to be lax. The cheerful mixture of fishermen and farm labourers who propped up the bar drew Will into their easy company, so that for a while he was able to forget his problems. But, waking the next morning with a headache and a parched mouth, all his worries flooded back. The overdraft. The interest payments. The lack of regular custom.

A few days later Maurice telephoned the garage. He'd been mulling over Will's difficulties, he said, trying to think of a way to help him out. He'd had a word with a friend who might be able to put some business Will's way. Maurice's friend was called Mr Hunter. Mr Hunter would drop by in a day or two.

Will imagined Maurice's friend to be a wealthy older businessman, Conservative and Rotarian, with two or three cars that needed servicing, perhaps. He was too ashamed to point out to Maurice that his affairs had reached such a crisis that the odd bit of extra work would make little difference.

A few days later a newish Lancia purred into the forecourt of the garage. Its driver introduced himself to Will.

'Rick Hunter.' They shook hands. Mr Hunter was, Will estimated, only a few years older than he was himself. He wore a well-cut grey suit and a pale blue silk shirt. A matching silk handkerchief peeked out of his breast pocket. Shorter than Will, he was more heavily built. He had a long, flat nose, dark, rather prominent eyes and a small red mouth. His features made Will think of a sleek, well-fed rodent.

Mr Hunter circled round. 'Nice secluded little place.'

'So secluded', said Will bitterly, 'hardly anyone stops.'

'It's just a question', said Mr Hunter, 'of knowing how to attract business.'

In the office Mr Hunter's busy, assessing gaze drifted from the window to the storeroom to the workshop. Will offered a chair. 'Are you a colleague of Maurice's . . . a friend . . . ?'

'A business adviser.' Mr Hunter flashed a smile. 'That's how I see myself, Will. As a business adviser. I'll get straight to the point. If you want to make a go of this place, you need to make it worth people's while to come here. You're a bit out of the way, aren't you? So you need to offer an incentive.'

'What sort of incentive?'

'The way I see it, people have a right to run their businesses, earn a living. A right to take their wives shopping, buy them nice things, give their kiddies a good start in life.'

Will's impatience must have shown in his eyes,

because Mr Hunter said, 'Hear me out.' There was an authority in his voice that made Will fall silent.

'I've connections with the motor trade. People who need an honest mechanic, someone who'll do a decent job. I could point customers your way, Will. Could make all the difference to you. And if they knew they could get a spot of petrol here, then they'd be all the keener to go out of their way, if you follow me.'

Will wasn't sure that he did, quite. The bright, dark eyes settled on him. 'If they knew there'd be no difficulty about coupons, for instance,' said Mr Hunter.

Will's stomach squeezed. 'Coupons?'

'I supply the coupons so you can sell the petrol. That's how it works, Will. Customer pays for the coupon — two and a tanner each — two bob for me, a tanner for you. Commission, that's the way to think of it.'

Forged petrol coupons? Stolen petrol coupons? The day had suddenly become unreal. Here he was, in his own garage, the sun shining, discussing with a jumped-up East End wide boy — the smart clothes couldn't quite hide the origins — the trading of black market petrol coupons.

He managed to find his voice. 'Where would the coupons come from?'

'I don't think you need to know that, do you, Will?' said Mr Hunter easily. He stood up. 'But I've had a couple of garages in Warren Street operating the same system for years and doing very nicely, thank you. No trouble and everyone benefits.'

He took a card from his pocket and handed it to Will. 'Think about it. There's my phone number. Give me a ring when you've made up your mind.' He left the office. A few moments later the Lancia drove away, its wheels throwing up clouds of dust.

Just for a moment or two Will imagined telling Julia about Mr Hunter, picturing her laughter as he described the silk handkerchief and the flashy car and preposterous proposition. The idea died almost immediately and Mr Hunter was added to the list of things Julia mustn't know about: the overdraft, the loan, his own carelessness with the accounts.

Julia knew things were tight, but she had no idea just how tight. She didn't need to know because he was going to sort it out, wasn't he?

Though he was tired, and though the afternoon's interview had, in some way he could not quite put his finger on, upset him, Will forced himself to go through the paperwork once more. When he had finished, he stared at the damning figures and considered his options. He could cut down his expenses — but he had done so already, had pared his costs to the bone. He could ask for another loan to tide him over — but he had already approached, and been refused by, both Maurice and the bank manager.

Or he could sell up. If he cut his losses, told Maurice he must look for someone else to take on the garage, what then? He would be penniless. Assuming he found work, he'd still have to pay off the overdraft and bank loan. He and Julia would probably have to give up Hidcote Cottage and move back to the School House. He imagined the shock in Julia's eyes when she learned of his failure, and the disappointment in his parents', and fear rose in his gullet, sharp and acid.

And if he kept going, struggled on . . . If he couldn't repay the loan, eventually he would be declared bankrupt. Will went to the window and flung it open, taking in gulps of cool night air in an attempt to still the pounding of his heart. The persistent nagging voice that whispered always in the back of his mind reminded him of Jack's success and his own imminent failure. Jack would inherit Sixfields, while he faced bankrupty. *She doesn't love you, you know. She really doesn't love you.* And why should Julia love him if he dragged her down

189

with him into poverty?

The following morning Will telephoned the School House and invited himself to lunch. Over stewed mutton and runner beans, his parents told him about their holiday in the Lake District. *Our first holiday in sixteen years*, his mother reminded him, as she dished out afters.

While his mother was washing up, Will screwed up his courage. 'Can I talk to you about something, Dad?'

John Chancellor glanced at him. 'Sounds serious.'

Will shook his head, smiled.

'Still, I might need my pipe.'

In John Chancellor's study, Will said, 'I wondered whether you could lend me some cash, Dad.' His throat felt tight.

Pipe cleaner in hand, his father glanced at him. 'How much?'

Will named a sum that was half what he needed, but enough, he reckoned, to get the worst of his creditors off his back.

The pipe cleaner paused. 'That's a lot of money, Will.'

'If it's too much — '

'Are you in trouble?'

'No.' Will shook his head vehemently. 'No, Dad.'

'Because if you are then you know I'll help, son. It wouldn't be easy, but we could cut back a bit. Sell the old Aston Martin, perhaps — I haven't driven her in years, after all.'

There were leather patches on the sleeves of the tweed jacket his father had worn for years. Will knew that his mother always turned the collars on shirts and sides-to-middled sheets.

'I'm not in trouble, Dad. Honestly.'

'Then may I ask what you need the money for?'

He gabbled, 'There's things to do at the garage and the cottage . . . Julia would like a proper bathroom . . . '

John Chancellor unclipped a leather pouch and began

to layer tobacco into the bowl of the pipe. Eventually he said, 'I know you're a married man now, Will, but would you listen to a bit of advice from an old man?'

'Course, Dad.'

'Don't borrow. Use the money you've got and no more. I borrowed and it got me into an unholy mess. That's why we came here. Lost my business, our home, the lot. It wasn't just bad luck — hard times and all that — it was my misjudgement, my folly, as well. Thought I could borrow myself out of trouble, and we just ended up deeper in debt. We're still paying for my mistakes, you know. Still paying off the last of the loans, still trying to put away a pension so I don't have to teach small boys Latin on my deathbed. And as for you and Julia — well, you're young, aren't you? It's easier roughing it when you're young.' John Chancellor smiled. 'I remember, when Prudence and I were first married, we couldn't afford a proper stove, so we cooked our supper on one of those little kerosene burners. We used to imagine we were camping out in our own sitting room.' His eyes were dreamy. 'I don't think we've ever been so happy.'

★ ★ ★

Driving back to the garage, Will pulled into the side of the road and lit a cigarette. His shame at having asked his father for money was intense. He drew deeply on the cigarette. Mr Hunter's voice whispered, insinuating and tempting, *You need to offer an incentive. Could make all the difference.*

At home that evening Julia told him the news. Earlier in the day the government had announced the abolition of the basic petrol ration. For an unspecified future, pleasure motoring was banned. He would be permitted to sell petrol only for necessary business purposes. 'Will it matter to us?' Julia asked, and Will shook his head, hiding his panic.

The next day, before he had time to change his mind, he scrabbled feverishly through the heap of papers on his desk and found Mr Hunter's card. As he dialled the operator, he recalled the flick of Mr Hunter's dark eyes around the office and he shivered.

It was just for a while, he told himself. Just until he got straight.

★   ★   ★

Helena found Topaz a job working for a retired actress called Miss Damerall. Miss Damerall was old and frail and her hands curled with arthritis, but the remains of a high-cheekboned, hollow-eyed beauty could still be glimpsed beneath the papery skin and thinning white hair. Topaz arrived at Miss Damerall's flat each midday and cooked her lunch. In the afternoon she walked her employer's overfed pug, helped her with her correspondence and ran errands. The walls of the flat and the mantelpieces and side tables were covered with framed theatre programmes and photographs of actors and actresses from a previous era.

Mischa invited Francesca and Topaz to supper. Mischa's flat was at the top of a tall, thin house in Finsbury Park. There were letting and secretarial agencies in the lower part of the building and a pawnshop next door. On the doorstep a tabby cat was meticulously washing her tigerish limbs.

Charlie opened the door to them. After he had kissed them, he muttered, 'Stormy weather,' and cocked an eyebrow to the upper storey. 'Mischa's tearing his hair out because he found a letter from Jerry to Claudette,' he explained as he led the way upstairs. 'So he's been drinking all day and Claudette's in a sulk. Expect burnt stew and lumpy mashed potatoes.'

Claudette sat in a corner, flicking through a magazine, barely acknowledging their presence. Mischa's kisses smelt of cheap brandy. He showed them round the flat. There were two tiny rooms, linked by a short, twisting flight of stairs. Mischa's brother, Lescek, the Spitfire pilot, slept in the attic room. In the kitchen, Mischa's camp bed was folded up in a corner, next to the gas ring and the sink.

Mischa was cooking lamb and barley stew and red cabbage. He had two half-moon-shaped saucepans that fitted on to the single ring. 'Leszek found me the red cabbage,' Mischa told them. 'So difficult to find red cabbage in London.'

'I hate cabbage,' said Claudette.

'Makes your hair curl,' said Charlie.

'The most beautiful colour,' said Topaz, peering into the saucepan. She had only ever encountered the green sort of cabbage. 'Shall I lay the table, Mischa?'

'Thank you, darling. And if you would light the candles.'

At dinner Claudette picked at her food while Mischa glowered and drank a great deal of brandy. Charlie attempted to steer the conversation to safe topics.

'Only another couple of weeks' run and I'm resting again.' Charlie was in a play at a theatre in Hammersmith.

'I thought you were hoping for a tour?'

'I was, Frannie, but the money seems to have run out. Desmond thought he could touch a friend for another thousand, but it's no go, I'm afraid.'

'It sounds so glamorous,' said Topaz. 'Going on tour.'

'Out-of-season seaside towns . . . interminable Sunday train journeys . . . '

'Horrible landladies', said Claudette, 'who tell you off for washing your stockings in the bathroom.'

'A dozen people in the audience and some of them are only there to get out of the rain.'

'I'd be quite happy never to go on tour again.'
Claudette put aside her knife and fork. 'I should marry
a rich man, shouldn't I? Then I could pick and choose.'

Mischa went white. Charlie said quickly, 'Claudette's
been touring for donkey's years, haven't you, darling?
Much longer than me.'

'Since I was twelve,' said Claudette smugly.
'Pantomimes . . . revues . . . plays. I was in a run of *The
Blue Bird* that lasted almost a year. I looked right, you
see. You have to look right. One of the reviews said I had
the face of an angel.'

Mischa muttered something in Polish. 'Anyway,' said
Charlie, 'this thing I'm in at the moment is pretty
frightful. I am so sick of murder mysteries.'

'Charlie specializes', said Francesca with a smirk, 'in
enthusiastic young men in cricket whites.'

'I do a lot of bounding in and out of French
windows,' said Charlie gloomily. 'It would be nice to
have something to get my teeth into for a change.'

Claudette lit a cigarette. 'At least you *do* something,
Charlie. Something creative.'

Mischa said furiously, 'She despises me because I
work in a restaurant. She looks down on me.'

'Nonsense, Mischa — '

'Shall I clear away?' Topaz stood up.

Mischa was not to be deflected. 'She only cares about
money. That's why she makes eyes at Jerry. Because he
is a teacher, not a waiter!'

'I don't *make* eyes at Jerry. It's hardly my fault if he's
in love with me!'

'Jerry falls in love with anything in a skirt,' said
Charlie calmly. 'You know that, Mischa.'

Mischa looked slightly comforted. Clearing away the
plates, Topaz remembered Jerry's beard scratching her
chin, Jerry's hands stroking her breasts.

There was poppy-seed roll for pudding. Mischa cut it
into slices. 'A Polish speciality. My mother's recipe.'

'You know I don't eat cake,' said Claudette. 'So fattening.'

Even Charlie's good humour began to falter. 'Afraid you won't fit into your tutu?'

'Of course not.' Claudette looked irritated. 'A dancer has to watch her figure.'

'She is afraid she get fat', said Mischa, his English disintegrating as his fury reignited, 'because then the men don't look at her. Isn't that so, Claudette?'

Claudette's eyes narrowed. Her curved red mouth hardened.

'See, she doesn't answer. She sit there saying nothing! She don't care how much she hurt me. Me — me, who would die for her!' Mischa jumped to his feet and seized the knife with which he had been cutting the poppy roll, pressing the tip against his chest.

Claudette gave a little gasp. Topaz's hands flew to her mouth. 'Mischa,' said Charlie.

'Shall I die for you, Claudette? Would you like that?' The blade of the knife flexed and a ruby red bead gathered on Mischa's white shirt. Claudette screamed.

'Mischa, old chap,' said Charlie gently, 'put the knife down. Claudette didn't mean it. She adores you, don't you, Claudie?'

Claudette was crying. 'Mischa darling — '

'Put the knife down, please. You're frightening the girls.'

There was a long, awful moment when it seemed to Topaz that Mischa might press the knife into his chest, and then he suddenly relaxed, the tension draining from him. The knife fell to the floor, and Claudette leaped to her feet and flung her arms around him.

They left shortly afterwards, while Claudette was sticking a plaster to Mischa's chest. Heading down the pavement, Charlie muttered, 'Such bloody histrionics. Supper with Mischa and Claudette always gives me indigestion.'

195

Francesca stared at him. 'That's happened before?'

'Well, not the *knife*. That's a new one. There's always something, though. Last time she threw a bowl of soup at him. Unbelievable overarm, she should have taken up cricket, not ballet. Spent half the evening putting butter on his burns.'

Topaz said, 'Why do they stay together if they make each other so unhappy?'

'Topaz, my darling, they adore it. They simply love scenes. Fighting's meat and drink to Mischa and Claudette. They think it proves how madly and passionately they're in love with each other.'

Charlie put his arm around Francesca as they walked down the street. Topaz, walking beside them, wondered whether she would ever not mind. She found herself remembering the knife point against Mischa's breast and understanding how you might believe that one pain might relieve the other.

★ ★ ★

Julia had spent the last few months trying to make Hideous Cottage habitable. She had painted walls, hung curtains, and reclaimed a little flower garden from the brambles and nettles that surrounded the house. She had put up shelves and filled cracks in the plasterwork. She made sure there was fuel for the stove and food in the larder. If the cottage would never be beautiful, it was at least wind and weatherproof.

Now there was always an ironed shirt for Will and supper in the oven when he came home. Or, if he was late — something that happened with increasing frequency — supper solidified in the bottom of a dish. As Julia hacked out burnt stew or desiccated cottage pie, he'd put his arms around her waist and nuzzle her neck. Sometimes he'd bring her a peace offering — a bunch of flowers, a dozen pears, sweets — presents, she

196

assumed, from a grateful customer. *I was working*, he'd explain. *There was a rush on.* Yet she could smell the alcohol on his breath.

In the autumn Julia went back to work at the stables. She took the job partly to help out with money, which Will seemed to worry about constantly, and partly because to remain incarcerated alone in Hideous Cottage would drive her insane. She enjoyed her job, cycling the three miles there each afternoon on a rusty old bike that had once belonged to Marius.

About her marriage she remained, however, uneasy. It wasn't that she and Will argued, like some couples. Their disagreements were short bursts of irritability, quickly retracted when he apologized or she managed to control her temper. After a year of marriage she still didn't enjoy sex much — which was why, she supposed, she didn't always make a fuss about the burnt casseroles and frazzled sausages; because, when Will was tired and a bit sloshed, he bothered less with all that. Yet her relief was mixed with a sense of failure and loss. Though she knew from the casual comments of friends that plenty of women regarded sex as a duty rather than a pleasure, she couldn't help but feel that something was missing, something important. And when Will's mother visited and Julia showed her the spare bedroom, which she had painted blue and pink with leftovers of paint from Missencourt, Prudence said in her most ringing housemaster's wife's tones, 'Pink for a girl and blue for a boy! Hedging your bets, Julia? Jolly sensible.' Julia made it clear to Prudence that she wasn't pregnant yet; she kept to herself her suspicion that, the way things were going, she wasn't likely to be pregnant for years, if ever. A conclusion that made her feel sad.

Often it seemed to her that since their marriage Will had changed. The things that she had liked about him — his easy-going, amiable nature, his optimism — were no longer much in evidence. Frequently he was tired and anxious. When she tried to talk to him, he brushed off her concern. Everything was fine, he insisted, rather irritably. She mustn't *fuss*.

In September they attended the wedding of one of Will's cousins. When, at the reception with Will, Julia saw Jack crossing the room to them, she anticipated bitterness and sarcasm. But the conversation, though brief and stilted, was inoffensive enough. Pleasantries were exchanged, vague enquiries into health and fortune, a few barbed comments about the happy couple. Then he disappeared into the crowd.

Julia told herself that she should feel happy now that Jack was on speaking terms with her and Will again. Yet the sadness returned, a sadness she could not quite shake off with all her usual distractions of riding and walking and frantically cleaning the cobwebs from the cottage's permanently dusty corners.

8

To begin with they stayed together, Marius supposed, because neither of them was able to think of a better solution. The forces that had brought them together in the first place — Tara and Suzanne's inability to care for her on her own — remained.

And yet, during the months that had passed since Suzanne had told him about Neil Finley, some things had altered. Suzanne had made an effort to involve herself in village life, attending local Labour party meetings and joining a branch of the Red Cross, where she organized jumble sales and bullied the neighbours into donating tins and produce to be parcelled up and sent to areas of Europe still stricken by famine. As for Marius, recognizing an uncomfortable truth in Suzanne's accusations of lack of involvement ('Such a half-life, Marius'), he too made an effort, taking her to London for shopping and the theatre, forcing himself to face up to, rather than skirt around difficult subjects.

Talking to her, he got to know her better. Got to know the contradictions that made her endlessly interesting to him (whatever his feelings for her — and desire, irritation and fury all figured among the more pressing — she never, he recognized after a while, *bored* him). Her equal shame and pride in her largely self-taught education, her passion and practicality, her determination and apparent physical frailty, all fascinated him. It occurred to him (another uncomfortable truth) that during their whirlwind affair in 1944 he had been too intoxicated with the physical proximity of her to notice what she was really *like*. It had taken the shock of her deception to make him stand back and begin to see her clearly.

Returning to England, he had sought her out not so much because of what she was, but because of what she had represented to him: a vitality and energy that he had somehow let slip from his own life. He was learning to know her, he supposed, all over again. The process was painful and exhausting because it told him as much about himself as about her, things that sometimes he might have preferred not to know. He felt as though he was stripping away a part of himself, all those layers of skin and muscle torn aside until he was flayed to the bone, robbed of both self-deception and self-delusion.

At the turn of the year Suzanne's mother died. Though Marius offered to accompany her to the funeral in London, Suzanne refused. Adele hadn't been well recently, she reminded him, so he should stay at Missencourt with Tara.

Once, he had believed that this was what he wanted: the child all to himself. Yet, as the days passed, he was aware of a feeling of flatness. Marius got Tara up in the mornings and put her to bed in the evenings. Tara pointed out, mournfully, that she missed her Mummy; Marius agreed that he did, too. In Suzanne's absence the days seemed long and dull, and nothing ran as smoothly, and the house was oddly cold and empty and lacking in comfort.

It was while he was rifling through the airing cupboard in search of a clean pair of pyjamas for Tara, that he came across a blouse belonging to Suzanne. Her perfume lingered in the silk, and he found himself closing his eyes and pressing it to his face and breathing it in, as if by doing so he could call up her presence.

Then, from the nursery, Tara called out his name, breaking the spell, and he opened his eyes. He seemed to see himself clearly, standing beside the airing cupboard, a scrap of scarlet and white silk clutched in his fist. What a fool he had been, he thought, dazed. With what a mixture of arrogance and pride had he tried to limit their relationship from its earliest days, telling himself at first that it was only a physical attraction, then that it was to give some sort of vague metaphysical validity to his life, and then, when they married, that it was a matter of convenience, because a child needed a father.

All of that was true, yet not true enough. In the stripping away of pretence, she had taught him to feel again. He missed her because she had woven herself into his life, like the perfume in the silk. He missed her because, in forcing him to reassemble his jigsaw of emotions, he had learned to love her.

★ ★ ★

At the beginning of February Charlie caught flu. Topaz visited him at his bedsit in Whitechapel. Fog smudged the silhouettes of the buildings and erased the distant, slender spiderlegs of the cranes at the docks. To one side of the tenement was a bombsite in which the foundations of the vanished houses and factories criss-crossed the waste ground like a chequerboard. To the other there was a row of shops and a bookmaker's.

Inside the hallway smelled of damp and of stale food. A very old woman was making her halting way up the stairs and a man was singing in a nearby room; Topaz did not recognize the language.

She knocked softly on Charlie's door, not wanting to disturb him if he was asleep. But a voice croaked, 'Come in,' and she opened the door.

'*Topaz.*' Charlie was wearing his old army coat over his jersey. He was pale and thin and hollow-eyed, locks of black hair sticking to his forehead.

'Helena told me you were ill.' She held up a basket. 'I brought you some things. Can I come in?' Inside the room there was a one-bar electric fire, a sofa upholstered with cracked brown shiny stuff, and a table and chair and bookcase.

He followed the direction of her gaze. 'Not what you're used to, is it? Did Helena tell you where I lived?'

'She was worried about you.'

'She fusses too much.' Charlie shot her a glance. 'She didn't tell Francesca . . . ?' Topaz shook her head. 'Thank God for that. I'd hate her to see this place.'

'She wouldn't mind.'

'Of course she would,' he said sharply. 'And, anyway, I'd mind.' He blinked. 'I'm sorry. Sit down, won't you, Topaz?' He shifted a pile of books from the sofa.

She delved in her basket. 'I've brought petits fours — Mrs Damerall gave them to me — and aspirins . . . and magazines . . . and a teeny bit of brandy . . . ' She took them out one by one. 'And snakes and ladders.'

He said, 'You're very sweet.'

She beamed. 'Which would you like first? The petits fours or the brandy?' She divided the brandy between them and emptied aspirins into the palm of his hand. 'Are you up to a game of snakes and ladders?'

He rolled the dice; she ate the biscuits. 'This is very kind of you,' he said. 'Ill people are so dull, aren't they?'

'You're never dull, Charlie,' she said honestly.

'Generous of you to say so. I'll make it up to you one day, I promise. When I'm rich and famous I'll own one of those wonderful little mews houses in Chelsea, and I'll invite you to dinner and we'll eat smoked ham and olives and exotic things like that, and we'll remember this horrid little hole and laugh about it.'

'I adore olives,' she said.

'I hadn't tasted one till six months ago.' He threw the dice. 'At the last-night party for *Henry V*, the old queen who played Exeter brought a tin of olives.'

She counted out squares. 'A queen?'

'A man who prefers men,' explained Charlie. When

she still looked confused, he added, 'To go to bed with, that is.'

'*Oh.*' She frowned. 'Blast. A snake. Did he want to go to bed with you?'

'Topaz. You do sometimes ask questions other girls don't. But yes. Probably.'

She sighed. 'You are so lucky. You have such an interesting life. Travelling all over the country — '

'Living in exotic places . . . ' His wry gaze took in the gloomy bedsit.

'You don't *mind*, though, do you?'

'About this? I mind when other people judge me by it. And because it shows I haven't got anywhere.'

'There's plenty of time,' she said comfortingly.

He shook his head. 'No, there isn't. I started late, remember, because of the war. I need to get a move on.' A grin. 'Before I lose my looks. Anyway, *I* should be envious of *you*. *I* didn't eat an olive before I was twenty-three. I bet you can beat that.'

'When I was seven I sneaked one out of Mummy's glass at a party. I thought it looked lovely but I couldn't believe how foul it tasted.'

'You had parties?'

'My mother did. Grown-up parties.' She remembered brightly lit rooms, and shimmering, jewel-coloured dresses.

'All my childhood', said Charlie, 'my father was ill. He was gassed in the war — the first war — and his nerves were shot to pieces. He tried to work, but then he had a breakdown, and after that he was at home. Which meant always being quiet. No games. Certainly no parties. No loud noises at all.' He rolled the dice again.

'You seem to have won,' she said. She glanced at her watch. 'I should go.'

'Don't. Please.' He caught her hand. 'Not yet. I've been so bored. I hate being by myself.' He gave a croak of laughter. 'Always have done. Imagine, an only child who hated being by himself. Hopeless.'

'Your poor throat,' she said.

'I've an audition next week.' He sounded worried.

'You'll have to gargle,' she said firmly. 'And wear a muffler. Oh, and Vick's Vapour Rub — ' She delved in her bag, and brought out a jar.

'God, Topaz, always so well prepared . . . You weren't a Girl Guide, were you?'

'When I was at boarding school.'

His eyes glittered. 'Boarding school?'

'I was only there for a year,' she explained. 'It closed down. There was a scandal.'

'The art master helping himself to the sixth form?'

'Something like that,' she admitted.

'Parties . . . scandalous boarding schools . . . hotels in the Lake District . . . you've definitely led a far more glamorous life than me.'

'Rubbish,' she said, and handed him the jar of Vick's Vapour Rub.

'Must I?'

'I'll give you another game of snakes and ladders,' she promised.

'Oh *well*.' He pulled off his jersey. She shook the dice.

★ ★ ★

A few weeks later they went to a party in a tall, elegant house in Belgravia. Magnolias in zinc pots, their buds tightly furled, stood beside pale stone steps. Fog curled around the basement windows. Topaz wore an emerald green velvet dress that Helena had borrowed from the theatre for her. 'There's a bit of a funny mark at the back,' Helena told her, 'but you could wear a cardigan.' Then she stood back. 'You look wonderful, Topaz. *Regal.*'

In the hallway of the house a crystal chandelier

caught the light. A maid took their coats, and in a white and gold bathroom Topaz and Francesca joined the crowd of girls standing in front of the mirror, drawing scarlet mouths on pale, wintry faces.

Later, they danced. A tall man with a moustache introduced himself to Topaz. He was thirtyish, with a lean, intelligent face and a glint of humour in his blue-grey eyes. At the end of their first foxtrot, he said, 'How do you know the Dobsons?' and she looked at him blankly.

'Our hosts.'

'*Oh.*' She remembered what Charlie always said. 'I'm a friend of a friend.'

The corners of his eyes crinkled. 'That sounds suspiciously like gatecrashing.'

'You won't tell, will you?'

'Of course not. Nothing wrong with gatecrashing, all the best people do it. Did you gatecrash by yourself or in company?'

She pointed out Charlie and Francesca. He took two glasses from a passing waiter's tray, and handed one to her. 'Shall I introduce you to some people?'

They moved about the house. In a room lined with books and pictures, she drifted away from the talk of income tax and capital levies, glancing at the engravings on the walls. They were of Venice — St Mark's Square, the Rialto, the Grand Canal. One day, she promised herself, she would sit in a gondola, and glide along the Grand Canal.

After a while, he came to stand beside her. 'Sorry about that,' he whispered. 'Frightfully dull, to talk about money at a party. Shall we eat?'

There was cold chicken, and ham studded with cloves, and vegetables in aspic — like jewels encased in ice, thought Topaz — and a dozen different salads.

'Such wonderful food.'

'You should gatecrash here more often. The Dobsons

205

always put on a marvellous buffet. Just a question of knowing the right people.' There was an ironic glint in his eye. 'I suppose I should disapprove.'

'Why?'

'I work for the Ministry of Food. We're supposed to see that everyone gets their fair share.'

'And do you? Do you disapprove?'

'Utterly,' he said, helping himself to more cold chicken. 'It's deplorable. But I can't *resist*.'

'I always feel', she said, 'that one should enjoy what one can when one can.'

'Absolutely. And if there's another war — '

She stared at him. 'There won't be, will there?'

He shrugged. 'Stalin's rattling his sabre. What's happening in Czechoslovakia's pretty chilling.'

The headlines on the newsvendors' billboards had screamed of a Communist purge in Prague. 'But that won't matter to *us*,' she said.

'That's what we said in nineteen-thirty-eight. Munich, remember.' He glanced at her. 'I'm sorry. I don't mean to frighten you.'

'It's only', she said, 'that my life's just getting interesting.'

'The Russians won't push their luck.' But his smile seemed forced.

'And I suppose, if there was another war,' she said, 'it wouldn't be like the last one. I mean, it would be *quick*.' She thought of mushroom clouds filling the sky.

'I say, cheer up. It won't come to that, I'm sure it won't. Have some trifle. Georgie Dobson always puts masses of sherry in the trifle.'

After supper there were speeches. Halfway through she wormed through the crowds to the powder room. It was empty apart from Francesca, who was sitting in a corner, crying.

'Fran . . . ?'

Francesca's face was blotched pink and white. Tears

made rivulets through her powder. 'Charlie's got a part in a play.'

Topaz remembered Charlie telling her he had an audition. 'But that's good, isn't it?'

'It's in *Durham*. For two months.' Francesca wiped her eyes. Then she said dully, 'He didn't even seem to think I'd *mind*. He thought I'd be *pleased*. And I am, in a way, I suppose — pleased for him, I mean — it's a good part . . . '

'No French windows or cricket whites?'

Francesca managed a smile. 'Gritty and northern. Charlie likes gritty and northern.' She closed her eyes very tightly and rested her head on her forearms. Then she said in a muffled gasp, 'It's just that *I* mind and *he* doesn't. He says he does, but he doesn't, Topaz, not like *I* do. And it's probably all over now anyway.'

'Just a couple of months, Fran — '

Francesca blew her nose. 'Your horrible friend Joyce is here. She saw Charlie and me together.'

'Joyce Blanchard?'

'Yes. So she'll tell her mother, and her mother'll tell my mother, and that'll be that.'

'Perhaps she won't. Perhaps she'll keep quiet.' But Topaz recalled Joyce Blanchard, with her flat, marmalade hair, and her pale, inquisitive eyes.

Francesca stood up and went to the mirror. She began to powder her face. 'It wouldn't have lasted anyway. I always knew it wouldn't. They'd never let me marry someone like Charlie. And Charlie — ' She broke off and swung round to face Topaz.

'Do you think it would have been different if I'd gone to bed with him?'

'I don't know, Fran.' She tried, and failed, to think of something comforting to say. 'I'm not much good at these things, am I? I really don't know.'

★ ★ ★

207

In a garden room where sheets of plywood still replaced glass shattered in the Blitz, she found Charlie. He was leaning against the frame of the French windows, looking out at the garden, smoking.

He said, 'I seem to have put my foot in it, don't I?' Then he rubbed the back of his hand across his forehead and turned to Topaz. He looked bewildered. 'I didn't know she felt like that. I thought it was just *fun*.' He groaned, running his hands through his hair. 'Does she hate me? I can't bear it when people hate me.'

She shook her head. 'We're going home, though. I said I'd tell you. We'll get a taxi.'

'This was supposed to be a *treat*.'

'It has been.' She smiled. 'I had the most lovely supper. And I danced. Lots of men asked me to dance. It must be my dress.'

A sudden grin. 'It does make the most of your assets.'

She looked down at herself, suddenly doubtful. 'Is it too low-cut? Do you think I should wear my cardigan?'

'Certainly not.' He stubbed out his cigarette in a plant pot. Music drifted in from the adjacent room.

She said, 'I haven't danced with *you*, though, Charlie.'

He held out his arms to her and she laid her head against his shoulder as they circled the empty room. You had to enjoy what you could when you could. Closing her eyes, she thought that, even if she was only borrowing him, then it was a glorious, intoxicating sort of loan.

★   ★   ★

At the garage Will kept the counterfeit petrol coupons in a drawer behind a heap of old newspapers and salesmen's flyers. Customers arrived in dribs and drabs. 'I'm a friend of Rick Hunter's,' they told him. Or, 'Ricky sent me.' In a back room, Will exchanged coupons for half crowns, his fingers nerveless and fumbling. Then he filled private cars with petrol allocated for business use. He supposed they were businessmen of a kind, these well-fed, well-dressed, confident men who drove smoothly into the forecourt of the garage as his nerves jangled a frightening rhythm.

Often he called at the Holly Bush on the way home. A drink or two and he'd stop imagining the police calling at the garage, producing a search warrant. Or Julia finding out about the forged petrol coupons, or Julia meeting Rick Hunter. Stop picturing her disillusion, her anger, her rejection of him. A few pints and he'd be able to sleep at night. He'd remind himself that it was just for a while, till he sorted himself out. All he had to do was to be careful: always shut the office door when he was dealing with a customer sent by Rick, and keep from Brian, the boy who helped out, the purpose of Rick's henchmen.

They were called Lenny and Gene. Their job was to deliver the counterfeit coupons when Will was running low and collect Rick's cut of the proceeds. *Two bob for me, a tanner for you.* Lenny was much the same height as Will and his thick, stubby head melded neckless into broad, bovine shoulders. Lenny's sharkskin suit always seemed to be missing a button and the jazzily coloured silk of his tie had frayed. Gene was small and dark and quiet and neat. Will supposed he should have been afraid of Lenny, who could have knocked him to the floor with a flick of the finger. But there was an emptiness in Gene's eyes that made his heart stand still.

One morning before he went to work, Julia said, 'I've been thinking, Will. Why don't I help you out at the garage?'

He took the kettle off the hob. 'What? Man the petrol pump?'

'Of course not.'

'Tea . . . where's the tea . . . ?'

'In the caddy, where it always is.' Julia stirred the porridge. 'I could do the books — help you with the accounts.'

Will seemed to go cold inside. 'Oh, it's all right,' he managed to say. 'No need for that.'

'I know about bookkeeping, remember. Daddy taught me when I started at Temperley's.'

He said breezily, 'Honestly, Julia, you don't have to,' but his nerveless hands slipped, opening the tea caddy, and tea leaves showered the table.

Julia sighed at his clumsiness and began to scoop up the spilt tea leaves. 'I thought you'd *want* me to help.'

She sounded hurt. He didn't want her to help, of course. God, no. He didn't want her to help because she'd only have to glance at the books to see that he was in debt. Had been deeply in debt for getting on eighteen months.

'If I gave you a hand,' she said, 'it would mean we could spend more time together.'

He wished she would just let the subject drop, instead of gnawing it like a dog with a bone. He tried to sound calm and reassuring. 'Things'll be better soon, darling. Business is picking up. I should be able to come home a bit earlier. Maybe even take on extra help.'

'But you'd have to *pay* someone else, wouldn't you, Will? You wouldn't have to pay me.'

He tried to make a joke of it. 'Can't use my lovely wife as cheap labour.'

She spooned out the porridge. 'I wouldn't *mind*, Will.'

'And you've got your job at the stables — '

'I could make time.'

'All those boring figures.'

'I'd enjoy it. I'm good at figures.'

'And the garage's mucky and oily. Not the place for a woman.'

'Honestly, Will!' The bowl of porridge slammed down

in front of him. 'I spend half the afternoon shovelling horseshit! A few whiffs of oil aren't going to hurt me! Surely you can see that it's a good idea?'

In the silence, his porridge stared at him, mottled and grey. 'No, Julia.'

She said accusingly, 'Is it because you don't want me there when you're working?'

'Of course not.'

'Why, then?'

'All the reasons I've given you. Now just leave it, won't you?'

He dug a spoon into his porridge, though he didn't feel in the least bit hungry. He had rarely been on the receiving end of Julia's anger. That he knew himself to be in the wrong only made things worse.

She said coldly, 'I just thought that if we shared things more, we might be happier.'

He couldn't cope with it, not a dissection of their marriage, not first thing in the morning, not with a hundred forged petrol coupons in his office at the garage and Lenny due at nine to collect Rick's cut. He said sullenly, 'We are happy.'

'Are we?' Her tone of voice challenged him.

'I can't see what you're making such a fuss about.' He glanced at his watch. Half-past eight. He thought of Lenny, who, let's face it, had *spiv* written all over him, hanging round the forecourt, advertising his own complicity to anyone interested.

'Can't you, Will?' Julia's voice stabbed at him: cold, hard little words. 'We've only been married a year, haven't we?'

'So?' He could feel his own temper slipping; he was, he thought self-righteously, only trying to do his best for her, after all.

'You went to the pub every night last week.'

Cornered, he said softly, venomously, 'You were counting?'

'I could hardly fail to notice!' Her eyes blazed. 'Sometimes you can't even walk straight!'

'Spying on me — '

'I can't think why you're behaving like this!' she cried. 'I thought you'd be *pleased*!'

'Pleased you think I can't manage on my own?'

'That's not what I meant.'

'Isn't it? That's what it sounds like. 'Poor old Will's obviously making a hash of things so I'd better help him out.'' He rose from the table, flinging back his chair.

'Where are you going?'

'Work, of course.' He grabbed his coat from the peg. 'Where I'm always bloody going.'

As he slammed the door behind him, he heard her yell, 'I spend hours slaving away in this horrid little house and then you can't even be bothered to eat the breakfast I cook!' Her voice, a shriek of shrewish fury, echoed in the copse.

★ ★ ★

After he had gone, she picked up his breakfast bowl and hurled it against the wall. Clumps of porridge slid slowly to the floor, leaving snail trails on the distemper.

Julia leaned against the door jamb, catching her breath. Her gaze drifted around the room and she thought that, in spite of all her efforts, it was still wrong. The ceiling was too low, the aspect too gloomy, the fireplace and table and chairs ugly, taking up too much space. She lived in a dolls' house where nothing seemed to fit and daily she shuffled the furniture about, trying to find the right place for it, never quite succeeding.

That afternoon, when she was walking Salem back to the stables through a rainstorm, Julia heard a car draw up on the other side of the road. Through the folds of her sou'wester and the curtain of rain she saw Jack.

He climbed out of the Bentley. 'I'd offer you a lift,' he

212

said, crossing the road to her, 'but I don't think he'd fit in the passenger seat.' He ran a hand down Salem's black satin neck.

Julia's heart was beating very fast. 'He's thrown a shoe,' she explained.

'Should stick to cars and tractors, like me.' Jack's gaze slid to her. 'You look like a drowned rat. Let me take him for you.'

'There's no need. And the car — '

'It won't run away.'

'You'll get soaked.'

'An act of contrition,' he said.

'Are you contrite, Jack?'

He shot her a glance. 'I wasn't exactly polite the last time we were alone together.'

Julia remembered the street in Hernscombe: snow in the air and winter in Jack's eyes. 'I was pretty foul too, I expect.'

He grinned. 'You always had a way with words.' He touched her hand. 'You're frozen.'

'I forgot my gloves.' Quickly, she dug her hands into her pockets.

He took the reins. 'You're working at the stables?'

'Every afternoon.' She smiled. 'Teaching little girls to ride.'

'You always said you'd never do that. You always said you hated teaching.'

'It gets me out of the house.' She could not keep the bitterness from her voice.

She felt him looking at her, so she turned away, heading along the road. Rain plastered her hair to her head and dripped down the collar of her mackintosh. The morning's quarrel lingered, so that she felt bruised and upset.

'Anyway,' she added, trying to sound cheerful, 'I get to ride and I do love riding.'

The road snaked between tall beech trees. Rain

pounded the naked silver branches. A car hurried past and Salem threatened to rear. Jack quietened him.

Looking out at the smooth columns of the tree trunks that surrounded them, she didn't realize she was shivering visibly until he said, 'You're getting cold.'

'I almost fell', she said suddenly, 'when he threw the shoe. It was my fault, I was pushing him too hard and the ground was wet.' She had needed to exorcize the morning's argument, to erase both her anger and her memory of herself, yelling at Will like a fishwife. They had been on stony ground when Salem had stumbled; the nearness of disaster had sobered her.

'I told you before, you should wear a hat.'

'Life's dull enough', she said crossly, 'without riding like an old woman.'

'I'd hate you to have an accident, that's all.'

'Would you?' She glanced at him sharply.

He sighed. 'Whatever's happened . . . whatever our differences . . . I wouldn't want anything bad to happen to you, Julia. Surely you know that?'

She bit her lip. 'I thought you hated me.'

'Never that.' He sounded sad.

She pressed him. 'But you were angry with me?'

'Furious. I'd have quite cheerfully throttled you. But that doesn't mean I want you to end up in a ditch with a broken neck. So buy a bloody hat.'

'So bossy, Jack,' she murmured.

'So obstinate, Julia.'

It was her turn to sigh. 'It's just that I like to feel free.'

He was silent for a moment and then he said, 'And you don't feel free now?'

She produced a bright, glassy smile. 'Oh, I'm fine, Jack, fine. Just this dreary weather.'

They walked in silence. Then Jack said, 'You and Will are living in that little place on Maiden Hill, aren't you?'

'Hideous Cottage.' Julia made a face.

'That good?' There was laughter in his eyes.

'It's an awful little house, but it was the best we could find. As soon as Will's garage picks up, we'll move somewhere bigger.'

'Must be lonely, stuck out there in the middle of nowhere.'

'Lots of people come to visit,' she said breezily. 'Mother . . . Marius and Suzanne . . . ' She caught his look, and added rather shamefacedly, 'She's quite nice, really, once you get to know her.' She changed the subject. 'How about you, Jack? How's Sixfields?'

'Farming suits me well enough, though Cousin Carrie's a difficult old biddy, to tell the truth.' His eyes were troubled. 'I can't quite make her out. Sometimes I think she hates me.'

'Hates you?'

'She humiliates me. Enjoys showing me who's boss.'

'She can't hate you,' said Julia logically. 'She wouldn't have chosen to leave Sixfields to you if she hated you.'

'She could change her mind, couldn't she? She likes to remind me of that.'

'Are you sure you're not being — well, a bit *touchy*, Jack?'

'Maybe.' He smiled. 'One of my faults, d'you think?'

Mine, too, she thought, but said, 'Perhaps Miss Chancellor's just cranky. She's lived on her own for ages, hasn't she? That makes people cranky, doesn't it?'

'I live on my own. Do you think that's how I'll end up, tormenting my relatives and having cobwebs for curtains?'

Julia laughed. 'I've only seen Sixfields from the road. What's it like?'

'It's just a house.'

'*Jack*.'

'Well.' He frowned. 'It's big, I suppose. When I was a little boy I used to love exploring it. Every now and then I'd come across a room I'd never seen before. Or a staircase that didn't lead anywhere, or a door that was always locked, that sort of thing. All those nooks and crannies — exciting to a little kid. All that clutter. I don't know how Carrie finds a thing, though she claims she can put her hand on anything.'

She imagined him, a dark, solitary child, roaming his enchanted castle.

'When I was abroad', he said, 'I used to think about Sixfields. Dream about it, even. Funny that, now I come to think about it. I'd never dream about the School House — about home. I suppose it's because Sixfields is different — unusual — '

'It's because you love it, Jack.' Julia paused, gathering her breath. The wind caught her wet hair, flicking it across her face.

'I suppose I do.' Again he sounded sad. 'But you pay a price for love, don't you?'

They had reached the stables. She took the reins from him and, murmuring a quick goodbye, walked away.

★   ★   ★

Returning to Sixfields, Jack met the doctor coming out of the house. Dr O'Connor was new to the area, young, ex-army. He looked tired and harassed — he had the appearance, Jack thought as he suppressed a smile, of someone who had been on the receiving end of the lash of Carrie Chancellor's tongue.

'How is she?' Jack opened the door of the doctor's car.

'Thanks. Miss Chancellor's quite poorly, I'm afraid.' Dr O'Connor put his bag in the back of his Wolseley. 'You work for her, don't you?'

'I help with the farm. I'm her cousin, Jack Chancellor.' They shook hands.

'She needs to ease up a bit. Isn't there someone — a sister, or a friend, perhaps — who'll keep an eye on her for a while?'

Jack shook his head. 'Carrie's very independent. Likes her privacy.'

Dr O'Connor said bluntly, 'Her lungs are in a poor condition. The spinal deformity doesn't help — compresses them, you see. I'm telling you this in confidence because she won't listen to me. If she doesn't start looking after herself, she won't last out the decade.'

He started up the car and drove away. Jack went into the house. At Carrie's bedroom door he paused and then knocked.

'Who is it?'

'It's me. Jack. I came to see whether you wanted anything.'

Out of a tangle of coughing, he picked out the complaint, 'To be permitted some peace!'

He persisted. 'Is there a fire in the grate?'

'In the bedroom? Certainly not!' Her protests and coughs followed him downstairs. From the scullery he collected a coal scuttle and kindling.

He knocked on her door again. 'I'm coming in.'

More squawks. He gave her a couple of minutes to make herself decent and then he went in.

The room was freezing. He would not have been surprised to see icicles hanging from the vast, dark pieces of furniture, or a glitter of frost on the books, papers and bric-a-brac.

Carrie was sitting up in bed, clutching a shawl around her small, skinny frame, outrage in her eyes. 'What do you think you're doing, Jack?'

'Laying a fire,' he said calmly and knelt in front of the grate.

'I don't believe in fires in bedrooms, you know that, they're bad for the health. How dare you come in here? Go away — get out of my room — '

Carrie croaked and hissed, the paper crackled, and the match rasped against sandpaper. When the fire had caught, Jack stood up.

She screeched, 'I can change my will, you know — tear it up — I'll write to my solicitor — ' and then she fell back against the pillows, racked by coughing.

He went to the bed and poured her a glass of water from the flask on the table. Then he said, 'If you want to change your mind, that's your business. But if I'm to inherit this place, I'll do it fair and square. I'll not stand by and watch you kill yourself.'

He left the room. In the kitchen, he boiled an egg and buttered bread and put it on a tray and carried it up to her. She was asleep, though, so he placed the tray on the bedside table and put more coal on the fire, and went out, closing the door quietly behind him. Then he put on wellingtons and oilskins and attended to all the necessary work on the farm.

It was past ten o'clock before he went to the cottage. Only there did he allow himself to think of Julia. Rain trailing from her hair and her unhappiness written in her great, grey eyes. He wondered why she was unhappy. Because of the house, of course — what had she called it? Hideous Cottage. Months ago he had driven past, pausing at the side of the road to look up at the cramped, mean little place. An unsuitable home, he had thought, for someone as beautiful and free-spirited as Julia. Yes, perhaps she was unhappy because of the house. Or perhaps she was lonely. Or bored.

Or perhaps the marriage wasn't working.

Restless, Jack went to the window and looked out. The night was clear and cold. His hands gripped the sill. What else had Julia said? That she worked at the stables each afternoon. Easy enough, then, to meet up with her, to talk to her. Just friends, of course, nothing more. There could be nothing wrong in renewing an old friendship, could there?

Because he knew he wouldn't sleep, Jack put his coat back on and opened the kitchen door. His dog, Con, stirred and shook herself, and padded outside beside him. They walked along meadows and beside brooks, through all the favourite, familiar places, the moon lighting their way, and the great bulk of Sixfields, with its mad, fairy-tale sloping roofs and frost-lit windows always in sight.

Other voices echoed. *If she doesn't look after herself, she won't last out the decade.* To the rhythm of his footsteps, pounding the frozen ground, a dangerous, alluring thought moved unbidden to the forefront of Jack's mind.

That, if he was patient, he could yet have them both, Sixfields and Julia.

★　★　★

At six o'clock one evening Marius waited, his coat twitched by the blustery wind, outside Selfridge's for Suzanne. He had been in London since the previous day; Suzanne had come up that morning for shopping and theatre.

He caught sight of her weaving through the crowds towards him. 'A good day?' he asked, and kissed her cheek. She was carrying half a dozen parcels and bags.

'The most lovely silk . . . ' As he took her bags from her, she delved through them and pulled out a square of violet-blue material. 'It's only a remnant,' she said, 'but it'll be enough to make a dress for Tara. And look — ' she showed him another scrap of fabric. 'White cotton. *Egyptian* cotton. You'll be able to have some new shirts at last, Marius. I found it in Petticoat Lane.' She grinned. 'It's just a question of knowing where to look.'

'No nylons from dubious street hawkers?'

She looked regretful. 'I didn't have time. The wretched train was late. What about you? How has your day been?'

He saw an unoccupied taxi and flagged it down. 'Our suppliers are making a mess of things,' he explained, as

219

he helped Suzanne into the cab. 'The last batch of resistors they sent was faulty. I'll have to come back next week. I really should look into reopening the London premises again.'

She tucked her coat and parcels around her as she sat down. 'You had somewhere before the war, didn't you?'

'My father did. Just a couple of rooms — he used it as a base for sales in London. It was bombed in nineteen-forty, so everything was moved to Great Missen.'

She glanced at her watch. 'Are we going to the hotel?'

He shook his head. 'We haven't time. We're supposed to be meeting the Glanvilles at half-past six.'

'Only there's something I'd like to talk to you about.'

'Sounds serious.'

'Just an idea of mine. I've been doing a lot of thinking. You may hate it, though.'

He began to feel slightly uneasy. 'Tell me.'

She was squinting into the mirror of her powder compact. 'Later. When we can talk properly. I hate starting important conversations and not being able to finish them.' She opened her lipstick. 'Are they terribly smart, the Glanvilles?'

His sense of unease continued throughout the evening. Since Suzanne had told him about Neil Finlay, the question of whether she would remain at Missencourt had remained unresolved. Recently he had begun almost to feel safe, almost to believe that, in the absence of any neat solution, they could evade decision and the passing of time should make up their minds for them. Suzanne and Tara would continue to live at Missencourt because there was, simply, no sensible alternative. Now Suzanne's words lingered, uncomfortable and unsettling. *I've been doing a lot of thinking . . . you may hate it though.* Suzanne, perhaps, had made up her mind at last. The trouble was, he acknowledged grimly, that as each day, week, and month passed, the thought of Missencourt without Suzanne and Tara became ever more intolerable.

He was uncommunicative with the Glanvilles — Roger Glanville had been an old friend from his army days — and paid little attention to the play, a piece of nonsense punctuated by unmemorable songs and drearily choreographed dances. When the play was finished, Roger Glanville suggested supper at Quaglino's, but Suzanne, giving the excuse of tiredness, declined.

In the taxi she said, 'You looked like you'd had enough. The hotel will make us some sandwiches, I expect.'

'As long as you don't mind', he said, 'missing out on a treat.'

She hugged her coat around her. 'A hot bath and supper in bed. What could be more of a treat?'

In the hotel he smoked and drank brandy while Suzanne bathed. Standing at the window, looking out over the jagged skyline, with its roofs and chimneys and plumes of smoke, he found himself recalling the years he had known her. Four years now. Such a strange, patched relationship. First, the powerful physical magnetism of those initial six weeks and then the long separation while he had been in Europe. And then, coming home, he had searched for her. Their marriage had been loveless to begin with, but then love had caught him up, had ensnared him. He didn't quite see how he would be able to do without it.

She came into the room, wrapped in a dressing-gown, flushed and tousled. 'I'm *starving.*'

He offered her the sandwiches. 'They're ham. Curling at the edges, I'm afraid.'

She sat on the edge of the bed, towelling her hair. He said, 'What was it you wanted to talk about?'

'If you're too tired, I can wait.' She leaned forward, running her fingers through her thick, dark curls. 'It seems mean to ask you to make decisions when you look like you'd rather go to sleep.'

'Better', he said, 'to get it over and done with.'

She looked slightly startled. 'All right.' She clutched her hands around her glass of brandy. 'I've been thinking of starting up a nursery school, Marius. I wanted to ask you what you thought.'

He stared at her blankly. 'A nursery school?'

'At Missencourt.' She seemed to interpret his silence as lack of enthusiasm because she said, 'I'd quite understand if you weren't happy with the idea. After all, it is your home.'

He blurted out, 'You're staying, then?'

It was her turn to look confused. 'Marius?'

He made an effort to hide his misunderstanding. 'A nursery school . . . At Missencourt . . . Why not?'

'Tara could do with some company. And there really isn't anywhere else — just that awful place in Hernscombe where they sit in rows and have to wear uniforms — ' She broke off. Then she said slowly, 'You thought I was going to tell you that I was leaving Missencourt? Leaving you?'

He felt foolish. 'I wasn't sure . . . when you said . . . ' He stubbed out his cigarette. 'Stupid of me.'

Her damp hair was curling tightly. She frowned. 'Was that what you *wanted* me to say?'

'No. God, *no*. Suzanne — if you feel able to put up with me — please stay.' He broke off, embarrassed by his own incoherence. Why was it so easy, he thought furiously, to make his wishes known to difficult business associates and demanding government officials, and so hard to express himself to his wife?

Her eyes narrowed. 'Is that what you think? That I'm *putting up* with you?'

'I don't know. Sorry.'

'Honestly, Marius,' she said, exasperatedly, 'you can be such an idiot sometimes. I mean — I'm not the most patient, tolerant person, am I?'

He had to suppress a smile. 'They're not the adjectives that first spring to mind.'

'But you seem to think I'm just *putting up* with you?'

'I thought — because of Tara — '

'*Men*,' she said disgustedly.

'Sorry.'

'Oh, for God's sake stop apologizing.' She yanked a comb through her hair. 'Marius, if I felt like that, I'd have gone months ago. *Years*. I'm not good at putting up with things. Surely you noticed *that*.'

He made himself say, 'But you don't feel about me as you felt about Neil, do you?' and she put the comb down and looked away.

'No. No, I don't. I don't think I'll feel like that about anyone ever again.'

He felt his heart contract. She said, 'I don't think I'm *capable* of feeling like that any more. I really don't.' She turned towards him. 'We should be honest with each other, don't you think? *I* should be honest with *you*.'

There was a silence. He remained at the window, his gaze fixed on the blackened sky.

'Marius,' she said firmly, 'listen. Try to understand. Neil and I — I'm not saying it didn't mean a great deal to me because that would be a lie. But, then, I don't know what might have happened, do I, if we'd had longer? Whether it would have lasted. We didn't have time to find out. We were never *tested*. We'd loved each other in a sort of *bubble* — we'd kept it a secret, no one knew. I don't know what would have happened when the bubble burst. How we'd have coped with the divorce and the child. Those things don't make it easy, do they? Whereas you and I . . . we've had all sorts of difficulties right from the start, haven't we?'

'You could put it like that.'

She paused and then she said, 'You mustn't think that because it's different with us, it doesn't mean anything.

223

You mustn't think I don't care about you.'

He noticed that she did not use the word *love*. Yet he did not press his point, or insist on definitions, quantity.

'But you'll stay?'

'If you'll have me.'

That his relief was edged with sadness, an awareness of the unequal nature of their feelings for each other, he tried to disregard. Best, he told himself, to settle for what you could get.

She said, 'Anyway, I've met a woman through the Red Cross — Vivien Lewis, she lives in Longridge — she was a teacher before she married, and she's got a little boy much the same age as Tara. And we thought as there isn't a nursery school, why don't we start one up? I need something to do, Marius. There's Tara, of course, but she's easier now, not quite so much a full-time job as she once was. And I need to be busy.'

He said, 'I had noticed,' and she looked guilty.

'Is it so obvious?'

'You're like a cat on a hot tin roof if you're left to sit and twiddle your thumbs.' Yet it was something he had always loved about her: her enthusiasm and energy.

'The nursery school would have to be at Missencourt because Vivien's house is too small, so I spoke to Adele, and she said speak to you.'

'Anything you want,' he said. 'Anything that'll make you happy. All I want is for you to be happy, Suzanne.'

And if their marriage was a collection of bargains, deals and compromises, then it was possible, he told himself, that a great many marriages were much like that. And he, in turn, had been given pearls of immeasurable price.

He threaded his hands beneath the folds of her dressing-gown and found that she was naked. Her hair, still damp, smelt of shampoo. She buried her face in his shoulder. Then he stroked her in the places she most liked to be stroked, until she lay back on the bed, her

224

limbs sprawled, abandoned, her eyes, beneath half-shut lids, beckoning him, drawing him to her.

* * *

Francesca had been banished to Norfolk to stay with her sister; from there she wrote long, anguished letters to Topaz. Topaz wrote equally lengthy letters back, and sent short, funny postcards to Charlie in Durham.

One afternoon, she left Miss Damerall's flat early to meet her mother before going to the dressmaker for a fitting. In Cleveland Close she found Veronica in the drawing room, standing by the window, a cigarette in one hand. Broken glass was strewn over the parquet floor.

'*Mummy* — '

'Trying to clear up this damned place.' Veronica swayed.

'What happened? Are you all right, Mummy? Did you break a glass?'

Ash from Veronica's cigarette fluttered over the shards. 'Threw it at the bastard,' said Veronica.

'At Mr Dexter?' Mr Dexter was a friend of her mother's. He owned a shop in Knightsbridge.

'At Terence bloody Dexter.' Veronica blinked. Then she sat down heavily on the sofa.

'I'll get the dustpan and brush.'

When she came back, her mother had refilled her glass and was drinking. 'Of course, he was a shopkeeper.' Veronica smiled. 'My father always detested shopkeepers. Penny a pound mentality, he said. Should have known better, shouldn't I?' The sapphire-blue eyes narrowed. 'You think they buy you presents because they admire you, but it's never enough, is it?'

Her mother seemed to expect an answer. 'I don't know, Mummy. I don't understand.'

'About time you did, then,' said Veronica harshly.

225

'How old are you? Eighteen?'

'Nineteen.'

'Old enough to know about *men*.' Veronica's pretty, delicate face hardened, became momentarily ugly. 'Never give them what they want till you've got a ring on your finger. That's my advice. Because they're only after one thing. Give in to them and you'll have nothing to show for it.' Veronica's bright blue gaze slid from the Martini bottle and raked disdainfully over her daughter. 'Not that you'll have too much trouble, I imagine.' The corners of her mouth twisted. 'I mean, I don't suppose you have to *fight* them off.'

Something inside Topaz seemed to go cold. 'Kitty,' she said quickly. 'We were supposed to be going to see Kitty — '

'She cancelled.' Veronica poured more Martini into the glass. 'The buttons she'd ordered hadn't come in or something.' She half-closed her eyes, settling back on the seat, her small, graceful hands curled around the glass. Then she seemed to notice Topaz again, because her eyes widened and she said irritably, 'Oh, do find something *useful* to do. You make the place look so *untidy*.'

Because she could not, suddenly, bear to be in the Cleveland Close flat, Topaz put her coat and beret back on and went outside. The cold feeling persisted, a small nub of ice somewhere in the region of her heart. It would thaw, she thought, when she was in company, so she headed for the cafe. Talking to Helena, Jerry and Mischa, she would begin to feel normal again; she would forget, perhaps, that her mother had said, *I don't suppose you have to fight them off.*

But there was only one person sitting at the corner table. 'Charlie,' she said. And he smiled his lovely, lazy smile and she had to sit down, pressing her hands against her legs to stop them shaking.

'I thought you were in Durham.'

'The run ended a couple of weeks early.'

'*Oh.*'

'So here I am. Resting again.'

'Where are the others?'

'Haven't a clue. Well, I phoned Jerry — his mother's ill. And Helena and Donald are otherwise engaged, no doubt.' He glanced at her. 'So you'll just have to make do with me.'

'I think I could bear that.'

He looked at her more closely. 'Are you all right?'

'Bit of a headache.' Behind her eyes tears still stung, and she rubbed her fist against her ribcage, as though to wipe away the chill.

'Let me buy you a cup of tea, then.' He stood up.

'Let's go somewhere else,' she said suddenly. She had him all to herself, she thought. If one of the others came, she would have to share him.

'Anywhere in mind?' She shook her head.

'When do you have to get back?'

'No one's expecting me.' She knew she sounded bitter.

'Then let's think.' He shrugged on his jacket. 'A pub or a club . . . or there's a little place in Pimlico where they put on some interesting stuff — little plays — ' He frowned. 'Some of them are in French, though, so you may not . . . '

She said, 'I'm as good at French as I am at most other things. In other words, pretty hopeless.'

He glanced at her again. 'You look like you need to dance. Dancing always cheers people up.'

They went to a pub first, where she drank port and lemon and he made her laugh, telling her about the theatre company in Durham. She began to feel strangely exhilarated. A sort of private excitement, an awareness of opportunity that she knew she must not squander.

She said, as they left the pub, 'You must miss Francesca.'

He nodded. Then he said, 'At first. But then you get caught up in things, don't you?' She looped her arm through his, huddling against him as they walked.

In a club in Battersea, in a crowded basement foggy with cigarette smoke, a girl sang Edith Piaf songs. 'Nearest I get to going abroad,' said Charlie.

'Soon,' she said. 'When you're famous. Charlie Finch's European tour.'

All the chairs were taken, so they leaned against stone archways that seemed to Topaz to be chilled by their proximity to the river. 'Do you think', he said, 'that when we finally travel somewhere it'll be a disappointment?'

'White sand and palm trees and pavement cafes — how could that possibly be disappointing?'

'It's just that when you've wanted something for ages, sometimes when you get it it's not as good as you thought it might be.'

The singer got down from the podium; there was a ripple of applause and then a jazz band took her place. Everyone seemed to move on to the tiny dance floor. Charlie took Topaz's hand, pulling her into the crowd. She could only *shuffle*, she thought, hemmed in on every side by people. Yet the music seeped into her, its heat and energy warming her. Odd how her ungainly body, that normally never did quite what she wanted it to, should become now graceful and cooperative. Odd how constraints seemed to fall away, pushed aside by the compulsion of the rhythm, emptying her of thought, so that there was only the music, and the heat, and Charlie.

After a while, he drew her towards him and whispered in her ear, 'Trouble. We'll slip out, I think.'

She glanced over her shoulder. Several uniformed policemen were threading down the narrow steps. 'What do they want?'

The music faltered, then died. He shrugged. 'This

place hasn't a licence to sell liquor, perhaps. Or someone's selling black market cigarettes or dodgy ration books.' He took her hand, heading for the door. Torchlight shone into their faces as they climbed the stairs and then it slid away.

Outside it was night and patchy clouds drifted over the face of the moon. A foghorn sounded on the river and a fox pattered among the ruins of a bomb site, threading between the skeletons of churches and tenement blocks. They bought fish and chips, eating them as they walked. When they had finished, Charlie made paper boats out of the newspaper wrappings and dropped them from Chelsea Bridge. Darting through the traffic to the far side of the bridge, they waited, and shrieked as they saw the little white dots on the black water, swirling in the eddies.

He said, 'I'll show you where I'm going to live when I'm rich,' and led the way to Cheyne Walk.

The tall houses faced on to the river. From an open window, Topaz could hear a gramophone playing.

'Which house?'

'That one,' he said.

'Why?'

'The dolphin door knocker. I've always wanted a dolphin door knocker.'

She giggled. 'And primroses,' she said. 'In the window box. My favourite flowers.'

'Are they?' He stepped over the chain fence and began to pick flowers from the window box.

'*Charlie!*' she hissed.

'Sweets for my sweet,' he said and fitted the posy into her buttonhole.

Her breath caught in her throat. She bent her head to the flowers and breathed in spring and hope.

'What are you thinking about?' he said.

'Holidays with my cousins when I was little. So many primroses. The woods turned yellow.'

229

The tune on the gramophone had changed. She cocked her head to one side.

'A tango,' he said, and held out his arms.

'I can't, Charlie. I've never learned.'

'I'll teach you.'

They danced along the Embankment, the music fading as they travelled, replaced by Charlie, singing under his breath. Primroses drifted from her button-hole, scattering the pavement like confetti. When they stopped beneath a gas lamp, out of breath, she saw for the first time uncertainty in his eyes, so she stood on her toes and touched her lips against his. His hands threaded through her hair. They kissed for a long time and then he stood back, and said, 'I wasn't sure — '

'What?'

'What you felt about me.'

'What *I* felt about *you* — '

'You're a little bit . . . out of my league.'

'*Me?*'

'You know. Hotels and boarding schools and olives.'

She saw herself reflected in his dark eyes. '*Charlie*,' she said.

'I wasn't sure whether you'd slap my face, or whether there was a titled fiancé stashed away somewhere.'

'Of course not. *Silly*.' There was a bubble of laughter and happiness in her throat.

'I've never quite been able to pin you down,' he said seriously. 'You do and say things I don't quite expect. When we first met, at the cafe, you seemed . . . offhand, almost.'

She wondered whether he was telling her the truth. The doubting, unsure part of her reminded her that he was an actor, that he was good at making people believe in him.

She said bluntly, 'I knew that you *liked* me. But I thought — that was it, just *liking*. You know, good old Topaz, a good chum, that sort of thing.'

The corners of his mouth flexed. He said, 'Topaz, you are an idiot sometimes,' and then he kissed her again. The palms of his hands ran slowly down the silhouette of her body, pausing at the swell of breast and hip. And she thought, *Well, if he is acting, then I don't particularly care*, and then she closed her eyes again and didn't think much at all any more.

9

Sometimes Jack waited for Julia outside the stables, sometimes — getting to know her routine — he ran into her when she was shopping in Hernscombe or calling on friends in Bridport. He'd offer to buy her a cup of tea in a cafe; she'd be reluctant at first, glancing at her watch, heading towards the bus stop, but then he'd coax her. *Just half an hour*, he'd say. *I was supposed to be meeting someone and he hasn't turned up, and I'm rather at a loose end.* And she'd smile and say, *Well* . . . and he'd know that he'd hooked her.

Sitting across a table from her, or walking with her from the stables, he'd have to force himself not to fix his gaze on her, not to let his eyes feast. Force himself not to show his pleasure just in being with her. He knew that if he let her witness his hunger, then she'd run to ground, frightened, fearful of the consequences. So he kept their conversation to uncontroversial subjects, was content to make her smile, took only a small peck on the cheek as they parted. But he knew that he was reeling her in, that she had come to look forward to their meetings, almost to depend on them.

Parting from her, he was able to think of nothing but her. Her image imprinted itself on his inner eyelid. It was there when he woke in the morning and when he fell asleep at night. He knew that they teetered on the edge of something dangerous, and that if they took just a step or two out of line, they'd slip, slide, fall. He saw she was edgy, nervous; as for him, he had to exhaust himself with physical labour to erase the tensions of their meetings. Once or twice he found himself imagining Julia at Sixfields. The old house woken from its sleep by her energy and beauty. A fantasy that unsettled him because there was something repellent about it, something that momentarily cooled his fever and made him dislike himself.

★　★　★

As Julia groomed the pony after saying goodbye to her last pupil, she'd look up and see Jack waiting for her. Watching him, her nerves jangled: she, who was never afraid.

She was afraid because, though she rarely bothered much about conventions, she had always adhered to her own rules. Her morality, bequeathed to her by school, by church, and by, most of all, her father, she had never before compromised. She was afraid because she had always loathed furtiveness and concealment, and because she knew that even if her meetings with Jack were not wrong now, then they might become so all too easily. She could put a halt to all this with a few words, she told herself. It alarmed her that she did not do so.

She slept badly, couldn't eat. With Will, she veered between irritation and guilty affection. She was euphoric with the elation that overtook her during and immediately after her conversations with Jack, and then listless with the depression that always followed closely. She dreamed about her father. Remembered his guiding principles. *What you do when people can't see you is just as important as what you do when they can.* A frightening, uncompromising rule that allowed for no mitigating circumstances.

At the stables one afternoon she was sharp-tongued with her less apt pupils. Afterwards, she rested her forehead for a moment against Salem's black neck, closing her eyes. When, taking her leave of Penny, she saw that Jack was not there, she did not know whether to feel relieved or disappointed. Cycling up the hill, the thick, low clouds seemed to press down on her, and

233

there was a stillness, and a sticky warmth in the air.

A scream of brakes and, in the dark tunnel of the beech trees, the Bentley drew up beside her. She slid off the bike, leaning her weight on it. As the door slammed and Jack got out of the car, her body tensed.

'Sorry,' he said. 'Couldn't get away.'

'It's not', she said edgily, as she started to wheel the bicycle along the road, 'as though I was *expecting* you.'

He clenched his fists. 'That bloody woman.'

'Which bloody woman?' She gave a small smile. 'You're not talking about your benefactor, are you, Jack? Not talking about Carrie Chancellor?'

He said furiously, 'She suddenly decides our tenants have been swindling us. Had me up most of the night going through the figures. Searching through the *attics*, for God's sake, looking out tenancy agreements from donkey's years ago — *Napoleonic* times. She said if I couldn't be bothered helping her then she'd find someone who would. The usual implication — that she'll leave the place to Cousin So-and-So if I won't toe the line — '

'It's what happens', said Julia smoothly, 'when you sell your soul.'

He blenched. She walked on. She heard him say, 'Yes, of course, you're right.' The words were quiet and bitter. 'She speaks and I jump.'

A car passed; Julia recognized Lois Barrington at the wheel. 'You made a bargain, Jack,' she said slowly. 'You and Carrie. Was it worth it?'

'I don't know. I really don't know.' He closed his eyes, rubbing the tips of his fingers against his forehead. He said suddenly, 'Every now and then I think I'll chuck it in. Leave Sixfields. Be damned to her. And do you know what she does? She falls ill, that's what she does. She falls ill, and the doctor comes and tuts and says she may not have long to go. And so I stay, don't I? Because I can see the light at the end of the tunnel. Because I think that in a few weeks or months that house, that land, will be mine. Because you're right, of course, I made a bargain. Because I gave you up so that I could have Sixfields. And if it goes to someone else, then how shall I live with what I've done?'

She whispered, frightened, 'You mustn't say things like that.'

'It's true, though, isn't it? I wanted Sixfields — I wanted it so much I gave up the woman I — '

She let the bicycle fall with a whirr of wheels to the verge, and pressed her fingers against his mouth, silencing him. He covered her hand with his and slid his lips against the hollow of her palm.

'You mustn't.'

'Why not?'

'You know why.' She pulled away from him and tried to pick up the bicycle. But the belt of her mackintosh had entangled with the chain and she struggled to free herself.

'We only talk to each other,' he said. 'It doesn't do anyone any harm.'

She yanked at the buckle. 'Then you won't mind if Mrs Barrington gossips about seeing us together, will you? And I'll tell Will about our conversations, shall I? Tell him that you meet me in Hernscombe — tell him that you wait for me after work and walk home with me? Only you don't walk *all* the way home, do you, Jack? Only as far as the crossroads. Why's that, do you think?'

'No point in stirring things up.'

' 'What the eye doesn't see, the heart doesn't grieve after',' she quoted mockingly. 'Is that your motto, Jack? Oh, this *bloody* thing — '

'Let me. You'll break it.' He knelt at her feet, carefully disentangling the belt from the chain. She reached out a hand and almost touched the small patch of bare skin between the dark hairs that clustered in the nape of his neck and the collar of his shirt.

'There you are.' He handed her the belt. 'It's rather oily, I'm afraid, but — ' He broke off. 'Oh God, Julia, don't cry.'

She pressed her face against his shoulder and he put his arms around her. 'It's Dad's birthday,' she whispered. 'And I keep thinking — what would he have thought of *this* — what would be have thought of *me* — ' She pulled away. 'I have to go now.'

She cycled away. Tears blurred the road. When she reached the crossroads, she paused, looking across the valley to Maiden Hill. Hidcote Cottage was a grey, depressing little dot among all the spring greenery.

She could not see quite how it had happened. Her impulsiveness, she supposed wearily, her temper, had led to her making such an error.

Such a monumental, irredeemable error, to have married the wrong brother.

* * *

Julia telephoned Penny Craven and told her she was unwell. Then she spring cleaned the house and hacked another length of garden from the wilderness that surrounded it. She must make an effort, she told herself. You could make a success of anything, her father had always said, so long as you worked hard enough. She noticed that Will was looking thin and strained, and wondered how long he had been like that. Was he ill, perhaps, and, involved with Jack (she could not think of the word for what had been going on between them: flirtation? Intrigue? Not *affair*. Not *yet*), it had escaped her attention.

She couldn't bear being on her own. She hurtled around the countryside on her bicycle, calling on acquaintances she hadn't seen for years, or going from shop to shop in search of something she suddenly, desperately needed: a reel of grey thread, a dozen drawing pins, a tin of Brasso.

Then, one lunchtime, she called at the garage. The workshop was empty, so she went into the office, opening the door before she realized that Will was not alone.

'Julia — '

'Sorry, darling.' She smiled apologetically at Will's visitor, who said, 'Won't you introduce us, Will?'

'Rick, this is my wife,' Will muttered. The colour had drained from his face. 'Julia, this is Mr Hunter, a — '

'A customer,' said Mr Hunter, smoothly. 'Will and I do business together, Mrs Chancellor.' He held out his hand.

Mr Hunter's hungry, watchful face reminded Julia of a pine marten she had once encountered in an outhouse at Missencourt, guarding its territory with a vigilant glare. Just now those dark, calculating eyes focused on her in a way that made her feel uncomfortable.

'I'll go and wait outside, shall I?' she said quickly.

She sat on the grass, stretching out her legs in the spring sunshine. A few minutes later Mr Hunter came out of the office and climbed into a car. As he drove away, she seemed to feel the direction of his gaze, so she pushed her dark glasses to the bridge of her nose and tucked her bare legs beneath her.

She went back to the office. Will was locking something away in a drawer. He looked up as she came into the room.

'You should have told me you were coming, Julia. You shouldn't just barge in.'

His words, and his tone of voice, shocked her. 'Sorry, Will,' she stammered. 'Sorry.' She made an effort to retrieve the situation. 'I didn't mean to interrupt you. Had Mr Hunter called about something important?'

He was leafing through the order book. 'Nothing much.'

'I haven't seen him before. Does he come from round here?'

He shut the book with a thump. 'What's this? An interrogation?'

'Of course not.' She was aware of a dull ache inside her, born of a conviction that, no matter how hard she tried, she and Will weren't going to come right.

He put the order book in a desk drawer. Then he flicked a glance at her. 'What was it you wanted?'

As if, she thought, anger replacing depression, she was some sort of minor inconvenience, to be hurried out of the way as quickly as possible. She said, 'I need a reason to come and see my husband?'

He seemed to make an effort. 'Of course not,' he said soothingly. 'Only you don't usually come to the garage.'

'I thought we might — ' But she broke off. Go for a picnic, she had intended to say. Have a drink at the pub. But now, seeing the stacks of paperwork on the desk and the cars and vans lined up outside, presumably waiting for repair, such suggestions seemed trivial and inappropriate.

'I just thought I'd call in and say hello,' she finished lamely.

'Sweet of you,' Will said, but it seemed to Julia that his mind was already elsewhere.

'Can I help with anything?'

'There's no need — '

'Tidy up a bit?'

'Honestly, Julia. It may look a mess, but it's all under control, believe me.' He forced a smile. 'Would you like anything? A drink?'

She shook her head. 'I'd better go.'

'I could get Brian to make you a cup of tea — '

'It's all right, Will. I can see you're busy.'

She went outside. Because she could not think of anywhere else to go, she cycled back to Hidcote Cottage. Even in the spring sunshine the house seemed chilly and damp. She sat on the front doorstep, looking out through the trees. For the first time, she acknowledged her sense of futility. Seeing Will's crowded little office had recalled to her her days at Temperley's Radios: the busyness, the sense of excitement and achievement. All her present occupations were tedious, unrewarding and trivial. Who would notice or care if she hadn't cleaned the kitchen floor or dusted the bookshelves? It wasn't even, she thought miserably, as though she was particularly good at ironing shirts or cleaning bathrooms.

Even worse was her sense of isolation. Enclosed in the copse, the cottage had become a cage; she found herself longing to rattle the bars. There had been a time when she had been important to people. To her father, to the men and women who worked at Temperley's. A time when she had had a role to play. That time had passed and she found herself wondering whether in future she must always stand on the sidelines, must always take the inferior, inconsequential part. She had hated the war for the way it had separated her from both Marius and Jack; how ironic, if, when she was an old woman, she should one day look back and think, *That was the happiest time of my life*. How frightening to think that the remainder of her days might waste away in pointlessness and loneliness.

She glanced at her watch. Two o'clock. Not giving herself time to think, she picked up her bicycle and cycled to the stables.

⋆　⋆　⋆

If Penny Craven was surprised at her sudden return to work, then, being a tactful person, she said nothing, only offered to take the riding lessons while Julia groomed the horses. In the privacy of the stables, Julia breathed in the familiar, comforting smells of horse and straw, and tried to calm herself.

When she finished work at five o'clock, she peered out of the stable window to the entrance, and saw Jack leaning against the five-barred gate. It was as though she was standing on a rock, trying to decide whether to dive into deep water. Once she let herself fall, there would be no going back. Hidden behind the window, she waited. But when he turned on his heel and began to walk away, she ran out of the building and up the drive.

Hearing her footsteps, he glanced back and then paused. She ran to him, threading her fingers through his, reaching up and kissing his cheek.

She said, 'Did you miss me, Jack?'

'For years.' His eyes were dark with desire. 'For years and years.'

His lips pressed against her throat. Julia closed her eyes. When he kissed her, it was as though she had come home.

★ ★ ★

In the cafe Charlie ran his fingertip down the columns of advertisements in *The Stage*. *Wanted*, they read, *Bognor Regis twice nightly, one leading M, two juv. char. No salary, but expenses and accom.*

Mrs Damerall had a fall and was sent to a nursing home on the Isle of Wight to recuperate. Topaz was out of a job again. When she told Charlie, he said, 'Don't fancy a bit of ASM-ing, do you?'

She looked blank, so he explained. 'Desmond's managed to scrape together the funds for a tour. Claudette's coming along.' He grimaced. 'Bit of a mixed blessing — she's pretty, of course, which'll bring in the punters, but her dancing's better than her acting. We're still looking for an assistant stage manager, though. How about it?'

'Me?'

'Why not?'

'I don't know anything about the theatre, Charlie.'

'There's nothing to it,' he said breezily. 'Props, a bit of prompting, that's all.'

'I wouldn't have to act?'

He shook his head. 'Shouldn't do.'

'Because I can't, you know.' Topaz had a brief, terrible vision of herself on stage, bursting out of her costume and forgetting her lines.

'It's just setting up and striking the set, calling the half-hour, quarter, five and beginners, and making sure all the odds and bobs are on the props table.' He put his arm around her, and hugged her. 'Piece of cake. You'd be terrific.' He glanced at her speculatively. 'Of course, you'd have to be away from home for a couple of months. Would that be a problem?'

'I'd have to talk to Mummy.'

'It's a tour of the south coast. Seaside towns. You'll come, won't you, love? So much more fun if you came.' His tone altered, became practical, matter of fact. 'There won't be much cash in it, I'm afraid. To be honest, once all the expenses are paid, there probably won't be much more than a few bob a week.'

They left London a fortnight later. Early in the morning they met outside a pub in St Martin's Lane. Desmond had offered them a lift in his car. The others would join them in Broadstairs, the first stop of the tour.

Charlie introduced Topaz to Desmond. Desmond McKenna was fortyish, red-faced, with thick, greying, curly hair. He wore a houndstooth jacket and a crimson spotted cravat. He shook Topaz's hand.

'So pleased you're joining our merry band, Miss Brooke.' Desmond waved to a man and a woman on the far side of the road. 'Freddie! Sylvia! Over here!'

'Oh *God*,' muttered Charlie. 'The *Ryders*. Desmond,

you didn't tell me — '

'Salt of the earth, old chap.'

'Desmond, Freddie can't act and Sylvia drinks like a fish.'

'She's given up the booze. She told me.'

Charlie snorted. Then he smiled and held out his arms and said, 'Sylvia *darling*, how marvellous to see you, and looking so *gorgeous*. And Freddie — so pleased you're joining us — '

'Wouldn't miss it for the world.'

Hands were shaken, Topaz was introduced. Charlie glanced at his watch. 'Claudette's late.'

'Likes to make an entrance, dear boy,' said Desmond equably.

'Give her ten minutes.' Charlie paced up and down the road. 'There'll be more room in the car without her.'

'Plenty of space in the old jalopy. Squeeze us all in. Can I cadge one of your fags?' Desmond's hands were yellow with nicotine, his nails bitten to the quick.

A taxi drew up. Claudette and half a dozen bags spilled out of the door, followed by Mischa.

'Darlings! I'm not late, am I? It took such an age to find a taxi.'

Charlie drawled, 'Overslept, did you, Claudette?'

Claudette pouted. 'Don't be mean, Charlie.' She kissed Desmond's cheek. 'You're not cross with me, are you, Desmond, darling? And you don't mind if Mischa comes too? Just to wish me luck?'

'*Seven* in the bloody car . . . ' muttered Charlie. They gathered their luggage and headed up the road, a straggling, querulous band.

★   ★   ★

She wasn't sure what she had expected. Bright lights, of course; crimson velvet curtains and costumes dripping with sequins, perhaps. Topaz's first sight of the Gaiety Theatre, with its peeling paint and draughty gloom, swept away her expectations of glamour. The theatre was perched on the seafront at the unfashionable end of Broadstairs; in the warren of streets behind it she found lodgings in a terraced house run by a Mrs Gibson, who had herself, many years ago, been on the stage. Mrs Gibson explained to Topaz that, because of her legs, she had played principal boys. 'Lovely pins, I had,' she said wistfully, 'lovely pins.' For the last twenty years she had run a boarding house for theatrical folk. 'Nice grub and cheery rooms, just what you need after a late night.' In Topaz's room the bedspread, curtains and wallpaper were in different pink florals. It was a room, Topaz agreed, in which you couldn't possibly be miserable — dizzy, perhaps, but not miserable.

The first week was spent in rehearsal. Before they left London Charlie had explained her duties. Prompting was just a question of standing in the wings and giving the actor his lines when he forgot. She must speak loudly enough for the actor to hear, Charlie said, but not so loudly that the audience could. Props were all the odds and ends used on stage — teacups, daggers, bottles of champagne. The half-hour, the quarter, and the five were, simply, the length of time before the curtain was raised.

Topaz bought herself a notebook, pencil and torch, and made a list of props for each play. She learned which actors knew their lines and who never would. Charlie was word-perfect from the first day, Claudette substituted for the correct words malapropisms and spoonerisms. Freddie, most alarmingly, leaped from scene to scene at random.

She got to know the other members of the company. Sylvia showed Topaz how to do her hair. 'It's easy, darling. Look.' A twist of the hands and Sylvia's shoulder-length locks were fixed in an elegant pleat. A flick of dark red lipstick and a spit into her mascara and her tired face was elegant, haughty, beautiful.

Sylvia swept Topaz's hair back from her forehead. 'Natural Titian! Lucky girl! I'd give my eye teeth for hair like yours.'

'Yours is a lovely colour, Sylvia,' said Topaz politely.

'Out of a bottle these days, darling,' she said sadly. 'Out of a bottle.'

Pauline, Nora, Martin and Cyril joined them in Broadstairs. Pauline and Nora were just out of drama school, both thin and quiet and intense. Martin was darkly good-looking, Cyril short and plain and cheerful. It was Cyril who taught Topaz how to arrange her props table and explained the etiquette of calling the half and the quarter. Cyril also pointed out to her the cheapest fish and chip shops and cafes, and the flea markets and secondhand shops that she might scour for props. In the longueurs between rehearsal and performance Martin read American detective novels with lurid covers and titles like *Deadly Blonde* and *Born to Kill*, while Cyril knitted Fair Isle jumpers. He had learned to knit, he explained to Topaz, in the Merchant Navy. It took Topaz a few days to realize that Martin and Cyril were, in Charlie's words, men who preferred men, much less time to notice, and sometimes envy, Cyril's tenderness for Martin.

The two plays, *Ghost Train* and *Hay Fever*, were to be performed each night, the first starting at five o'clock, the second at eight. From a shop on the seafront Topaz bought Charlie a bird made of shells, for good luck. It had black bead eyes and stood on a plinth that said 'A Present from Broadstairs'. On the first night, watching Charlie, Topaz understood that in rehearsal he had always held a part of himself back. When she looked away from him to turn a page, it seemed to her that she was dragging herself away from an enchantment.

After the performance they celebrated in a pub with yellowing theatrical billboards framed on the walls, mementos of long-ago performances and forgotten actors. Relief spilled over into elation and when, at closing time, they went out into the street, the fine drizzle had sheened the pavements like satin. Topaz made to walk on with the others, but Charlie drew her back, separating her from the rest of them. As they turned the corner, she saw the sea, like black tar, and above it the ghost of the moon, flickering between the clouds. They ran down curving steps to the beach. Reaching the sands, Charlie leaned against the sea wall, closing his eyes.

'Thank God that's over. First nights . . . '

'Were you nervous?'

'Terrified.' He opened his eyes wide. 'I am always terrified.'

'You were wonderful.'

'I was — ' he considered ' — adequate.'

She shook her head. 'No. Much better than that.'

'Just before every first night I tell myself I'm going to give it up. Find something else to do. Something sensible. Not put myself through it.' He screwed up his eyes. 'And then I change my mind. Every single bloody time. And I don't really know why. It's not the *applause*. That's what people think, but they're wrong. I mean it's *nice*, but it's not that. I think it's because, when it goes well, I can lose myself. I forget who I am. And that makes me feel so good. There's not many things make you feel like that.' His dark gaze slid to her. 'Well, a few.' He shrugged off his jacket. 'Come here. Sit down.'

She sat down beside him. There was an urgency, an intensity about his kisses. And there was a moment at which she could have pulled away, dusted off the sand, headed back to her lodgings. All the admonitory, warning words of older, wiser women through the ages echoed in her head. *They're only after one thing. Don't give into them till you've a ring on your finger. Men don't respect girls who go all the way. Nice girls don't.* Such calculating, dispiriting bargains.

She had always worried about the mechanics of sex, the potentially humiliating complexities of stocking and garter belt, the wobble of white flesh and sag of bosoms released from their encasing of brassiere. But Charlie didn't seem to mind any of that; in fact, he seemed to delight in it, to bury his face between her breasts, to sigh with happiness as his palm trailed along the rounded curve of her thigh. The night curtained the worst of her embarrassment, the distant rush and rustle of the sea quietening the flick of elastic, the unpopping of press-studs. And afterwards, curled in his arms, she thought that it wasn't such a bad place to lose your virginity, Broadstairs beach. More original than the marital bed and at least it was sand, not pebble.

★ ★ ★

When he was feeling particularly depressed and nervous, Will reminded himself that almost everyone had some involvement with the black market. You couldn't manage without. Maurice had a stock of goods he sold only to favoured customers; Cousin Carrie, who despised ration books and government controls, sold eggs and milk off the ration to the family. Even his mother used her vast network of friends and relations to put food on the table. Surely, he reassured himself, selling a few petrol coupons under the counter was different only in scale.

One morning he was in the workshop when a police car drew into the forecourt. The sight of the car made the spanner slide out of Will's hand, clanging to the floor. A pulse pounded in his ears, and he wanted to run to the office and chuck the counterfeit coupons into the dustbin. But he could not move.

Brian was speaking to the driver. Slow, painful seconds and minutes passed before the police car drove away. Will closed his eyes, faint with relief. He was trembling. He heard Brian call out, 'You all right, Will?'

'Fine.' He pressed his fist against his chest. 'What did they want?'

'Directions to Longridge.' Brian still looked concerned. 'Shall I make us a cup of tea?'

'Please.' He swallowed. 'They weren't from round here?'

' 'Spose not. London types,' said Brian dismissively.

He hadn't called at the Holly Bush for weeks, not since he and Julia had quarrelled, yet he did so that night. He drank steadily and determinedly, needing to erase the events of the day. He could no longer hide from what he knew to be true: that huge, terrible secrets now divided him from Julia and that selling black market petrol coupons was in a different league from the petty rule-breaking his friends and relations practised. He resolved that as soon as he had put by just a little more money, he would tell Rick he had decided to sever their association.

Around midnight one of the fishermen, a wild lad called Johnnie Gamble, suggested they take his boat out. The Gambles' fishing boat, the *Katie Rose*, was moored in Hernscombe, so Will drove the four of them — Johnnie, Johnnie's younger brother, Mick, and his cousin, Eddie — to the harbour. The car slewed unsteadily from one side of the road to the other as Will, his reactions slowed by alcohol, negotiated the quiet country lanes.

At Hernscombe the narrow jaws of the harbour spat the *Katie Rose* on to a smooth black sea. The night air was cold and sharp, and Will lay in the bows, looking up at the stars. His gaze slid through the constellations — Orion, the Plough, Pegasus — and he remembered the trick his mother had taught him, of looking to the side of a dim star to see it properly. Yet as he gazed up to the heavens, squinting, the stars shifted and blurred, and after a while he closed his eyes and fell asleep, rocked by the motion of the boat.

★   ★   ★

Sometimes they gave him presents. Champagne, tins of salmon, a bottle of perfume — 'For', said Rick, 'your pretty wife.' Will gave the perfume to Julia and watched her spray it on her throat and wrists. In the shabby little cottage the scent seemed luxuriant and overpowering and decadent.

Lenny called at the garage one morning. In the office, Will gave him his money and watched him count out the florins and half crowns, muttering numbers under his breath before sliding the coins into a leather wallet. Then, from the folds of a vast Persian lamb overcoat, he drew out a parcel.

He placed it on Will's desk. 'Rick'll collect it in a few days,' he said. 'Keep it safe.' The parcel was squarish, bulky, wrapped in brown paper and secured with sealing wax and string.

'What is it?'

Lenny tapped the side of his nose. 'Those that ask no questions . . . '

Will said nervously, 'I'm not sure, Lenny. I'm not sure I want — '

'Rick's orders.' Lenny dabbed at his perspiring, moon-shaped face with a dirty silk handkerchief, and then glanced at his watch. 'Must be going. Toodle-oo.'

Outside Will watched Lenny's Jowett Javelin drive away and then he went back to the office, closing the door behind him. There was no address on the parcel and no indication of its contents. Squeezing it, bending it to try to read its contents through his fingertips, he felt both nauseous and disorientated. Lenny's bland assumption of his own acquiescence had shaken him. *Rick's orders,* Lenny had said, as though that guaranteed compliance. What else might Rick order him to do? How else might Rick choose to use him?

He hid the parcel in the drawer with the coupons. He was always aware of it, though, as he went about his daily business. His imagination enclosed within the brown paper forged banknotes, opiates, jewels, a handgun. When, a few days later, a seedy-looking fellow in a whip-striped suit collected the parcel, Will felt weak with relief.

In June the government restored the petrol ration and passed a bill requiring that all petrol for business purposes be dyed red. Any private motorist found with red petrol in his tank would be prosecuted. The black market in petrol would effectively be brought to an end.

A load seemed to fall from Will's shoulders. There would be no more counterfeit coupons hidden in the office. No more visits from Lenny and Gene. No more presents. *For your pretty wife, Will.* Business had picked up; though some of the loan had still to be paid off, he was sure he could manage.

He tried to patch things up with Julia. He took her to the cinema and for Sunday lunch at the School House. He found himself for the first time that summer noticing the landscape around him, the glorious sweep of the moors that surrounded the garage, the birds that sang in the copse beside Hidcote Cottage. He felt as though he was emerging from a long nightmare. He began to be able to sleep and eat again.

Arriving at work one morning, he didn't notice the Jowett Javelin parked to the side of the garage. Pulling off his jacket, rolling up his sleeves, he called out a quick hello to Brian and went into the office. As soon as he opened the door, he felt a rush of shock and fear. Lenny was there, his great bulk squeezed into Will's chair, his expensively clad feet on Will's desk.

He stammered, 'But the coupons — they're no use any more — '

'I 'aven't brought coupons, Will.' Lenny delved inside his jacket. 'Coupla packages.' He placed them on Will's desk.

Will stared at them disbelievingly. He stammered, 'But I thought it was *over*.'

'Just doing my job, Will. You and me', said Lenny cheerfully, 'we're colleagues now. Business associates.'

He was aware not only of fear, but of anger. From somewhere, he found courage. 'No,' he said. 'No, Lenny. I don't want to do anything more for you.' If only his voice would steady.

'Bring you a nice bottle of Scotch next time, Will,' said Lenny, as he shuffled to his feet. 'Or something for the wife.'

'But I don't want there to be a next time.' And, desperately, 'I want to talk to Rick.'

Lenny paused at the door. 'Rick's out of the country just now. Business.'

Will could hear the pitch of his voice rising. 'I want you to take them away.'

'Can't do that, Will. More than my job's worth. Rick done you a favour, see. So you owe him.' In Lenny's pale eyes there was only concern. 'You want to be careful what you say, Will.' He left the room.

Will's legs were shaking so much that he had to grip the table for balance as he sank into his seat. Resting his elbows on the table, he knotted his hands together, pressing them against his mouth. His gaze fixed on the parcels, would not let them go.

When he was able to move, he took out his penknife and slit the string that bound the larger parcel. He broke sealing wax, unpeeled paper. Then he folded the last of the wrappings aside and sat for a long time, staring at the contents of the parcel. Banknotes — not

English, but a mixture of French and Italian and Dutch currency. Hundreds, thousands, of them. Then, very carefully, he replaced the wrapping and put the parcel in the drawer.

After Lenny's visit he never seemed to feel right again. He saw it going on for ever, an unending spider's web of obligation and deceit. Everything he did for Rick — every gift accepted, every parcel handed on to a nameless caller — drew him further into the darkness. And at the back of his mind there darted something small and frightened and defenceless, searching for escape.

★   ★   ★

The tour began to unravel. Claudette's agent telephoned her, offering her a part in a West End production; she headed back to London, Mischa and suitcases in tow.

Charlie and Topaz took the train to Bournemouth. They had a compartment to themselves and Charlie had pulled down the blinds so that they could not be seen from the corridor.

Charlie's pencil jabbed at a script. 'Pauline can take over Claudette's roles. Nora can do Pauline's walk-ons.' He frowned. 'I'm more worried about Sylvia, to tell you the truth. She only got through the last performance because Freddie steered her round the stage. Desmond had a word with her and she's promised never to drink before a performance again, but . . . ' He glanced at Topaz. 'You're looking worried.'

'I don't want it to end, you see.'

'Don't want what to end?'

'The tour.'

'You mustn't worry,' he said lazily. 'The show must go on and all that.' He held out his arms to her. 'Come and sit on my knee.'

'You'll *suffocate.*'

'Rubbish.' She sat on his knee. He kissed her, then he began to undo the buttons of her blouse.

'*Charlie.*'

'Mmm . . . ?' He was nuzzling her breasts.

'The ticket inspector might come in.'

'Such lovely, lovely breasts.'

'I've always thought they were a nuisance.'

'Then how silly of you. They are the most beautiful breasts in the world.' His hand reached beneath her blouse, undoing the clasp of her brassiere. Pleasure and desire uncoiled inside her and she ran her fingers through his black, silky hair. He murmured, 'Beautiful, beautiful Topaz,' and there was something about his bent head and the happiness in his voice that made her breath catch in her throat and tears sting at the back of her eyes. Then the train drew up at a station, and the slamming of doors and tapping of heels along the corridor warned her to slide off his knee and quickly do up her buttons.

★ ★ ★

In Bournemouth it wasn't even a proper theatre. Just a church hall in a seedy part of town, with table tennis and carpet bowls in the green room, and a Brownie pack's papier mâché toadstool and bean bags in the dressing rooms.

'All I could get so late in the season, my dears,' said Desmond apologetically. 'But you'll see — we'll rake them in.'

They didn't. Thirty on the first night, a miserable fifteen on the second. *Just as well*, thought Topaz, as she watched Sylvia totter across the stage, slurring her words. When the curtain came down at the end of the play, she gave a sigh of relief.

Leaving the stage, Charlie threw off his jacket and

pulled off his moustache, and muttered, 'I'll strangle the bloody woman.'

'Let me have a word with her. I'll make her some coffee.'

Topaz found Sylvia sprawled among the bean bags, her head resting on the toadstool. 'Black coffee,' said Topaz. 'And aspirins.'

Sylvia emptied half a dozen aspirins into the palm of her hand and washed them down with a glass of gin. 'Sweet girl,' she said, patting Topaz's cheek. She looked dispiritedly at the coffee.

'I suppose it's chicory?'

''Fraid so.'

'In the twenties I toured France with *Cyrano de Bergerac*. I can speak French, you know.' Sylvia smiled. 'And the *coffee*! I can still smell it.' Her face crumpled. 'It doesn't matter about the performance, you know. None of it matters. No one's bloody watching us, anyway. And the bloody Russians are starting World War Three, so what does a silly little play matter?' Blearily, she looked at Topaz. 'Didn't you know? Don't you listen to the wireless? I suppose not. You're in love, aren't you?' Sylvia's voice was bitter. '*Come live with me and be my love, and we will all the pleasures prove . . .*' Not for much longer, though. Soon it'll be — ka-boom . . . ' Sylvia made the shape of a mushroom cloud with her hands. 'And we'll all be burnt to a crisp, won't we? Lovely little girls like you and washed-up old hags like me.'

★ ★ ★

The headlines on the hoardings screamed of Stalin and Berlin. Arriving in Hernscombe on Sunday, Topaz bought a newspaper. The Russians had closed off all passenger and freight routes to the city, effectively isolating the British, American and French zones, and drawing the Iron Curtain tightly across Europe. The fragile peace of the postwar years seemed suddenly precarious, liable to snap. There couldn't be another war, she thought. She imagined everyone going away again. Charlie called up, sent away to fight. Just when she had found happiness. She remembered pictures of Hiroshima and Nagasaki, those black deserts of devastation, and she shuddered.

The following day, she made posters and darted around town, pinning them to trees and lamp posts, paying tuppence to have them displayed in shops. It was when she was coming out of the grocer's that she looked across the road and saw Will. Calling his name, waving madly, she dashed across the road to him.

'Will!' She threw herself into his arms.

'Topaz.' He looked dazed. 'What on earth are you doing here?'

'I'm an assistant stage manager in a theatre,' she said proudly. 'And I was going to telephone you, but now I've seen you instead, which is much better.'

He glanced at her. 'Are you doing anything just now?'

She was supposed to be helping Pauline repair the curtains belonging to the tiny seafront theatre, which were moth-eaten and falling away from the hooks. But Will said suddenly, 'It's just that I could do with someone to talk to,' and something about his expression and the tone of his voice made her say, 'It's my lunch hour. Why don't we go to a pub?'

'Not a pub,' he said. 'Too crowded.' He frowned. 'A picnic? It's almost stopped raining. We could go to one of the old places, where we used to go when we were kids. A picnic on the beach . . . it'll be just like old times, won't it?' The cynicism in his voice jarred her.

They drove to the cove. The rain had stopped and the sun was washing across the sea by the time they climbed down the cliff. As they kicked off their shoes and walked across the sand, Topaz told Will about the theatre and their motley band of actors and absentee audiences.

After a while, she realized that he wasn't listening to her. 'Will, what's wrong?'

'Nothing.'

'*Will*. Are you worried about Berlin?'

He looked momentarily blank, and then he said, 'Actually, I'm in a bit of a mess, you see, Topaz.' His voice trembled.

She waited for him to go on. When he did not, she took his hand in hers and said, 'What sort of a mess?'

'I can't say.'

'Is it to do with Julia?'

He gave a peculiar sort of laugh. 'Well, things aren't all that *peachy*, but no, it isn't.'

'Jack, then?'

'I hardly see Jack. A few pleasantries at the grimmer family events, but that's all these days. No open warfare.'

'Then . . . ' She had noticed how pale he was, how thin, and felt a sudden stab of anxiety. 'Are you unwell, Will? Is it your heart?'

'Wish it was. So much easier, a nice, quick heart attack. That'd sort everything out, wouldn't it?'

'*Will*.' She stared at him, shocked. 'You mustn't talk like that.'

'Mustn't I?' When he turned to look at her, she saw the panic in his eyes. 'I suppose I mustn't. Keep pretending — that's what we're supposed to do, aren't we? Keep pretending.' He pulled away from her, walking down to the water's edge.

There was an unpleasant feeling in the pit of her stomach, as though someone had knocked away the accustomed props of her life. Dorset was supposed to be *fun*. Dorset was supposed to be holidays and sun and her favourite people, the people who enhanced her life. Dorset — and she realized that she'd never before seen it quite so clearly — was people who loved her and accepted her and didn't want to change her. Who gave her all the things her mother could not, or would not give. Dorset was her little piece of happy family life, her little piece of heaven.

She went to stand beside him. He managed a watery smile. 'Sorry to be such a misery. It's not fair, is it, to bring you here and then bore you sick with moaning.'

She said carefully, 'Whatever it is, Will, I won't *judge* you.'

'Won't you? How can you say that till you know what I've done?'

'Because I know you. Because I know the things you might do, and the things you'd never, ever do.'

The silence lingered. She watched the tide as it slowly ebbed, leaving a lacework of foam over the shells and sea-polished pebbles.

He said, 'I've been trying to work things out. Do you think, Topaz, that if you'd done something wrong, do you think it would be better to come clean, go through all the flak — which would probably be a pretty awful sort of flak — but eventually you could clear it up and be able to start again. Or do you think it'd be better to go on as you are and hope that everything works out in the end?'

He was staring at her, his cornflower blue eyes anxious, haunted, as he waited for her to reply. She had an awful sense of far too much hanging on her response. She didn't even, she thought, with a flicker of panic, properly understand the question.

'I don't know, Will,' she said, and when she heard his exasperated, despairing sigh, went on quickly, 'All I do know is that I've had rather a lot of different jobs, and when I've made a mess of things I've always been found out. And I think, if I look back, then it might have turned out better if I'd owned up to not being very good at things earlier.'

He nodded, his eyes serious. As though, she thought, her anxiety doubling, pearls of wisdom were falling from her lips. So she said feebly, 'But that's just me. I don't know if it's the same for you.'

He looked exhausted. 'You're only saying', he said slowly, 'what I've been thinking for ages and haven't yet had the guts to face up to.'

Which made her feel even more worried. 'If you could tell me, Will.'

'I can't. Really, Topaz, I just can't.' He seized her hands. 'And you mustn't tell anyone what I've said to you today. Do you promise? Especially not Julia. *Promise.*'

She promised, yet she was aware of deep unease. But some of his tension seemed to fall away, and he said: 'When I was a kid, I sometimes used to think about running away. Like in a story book. Running off to be a cabin boy on a treasure ship, that sort of nonsense. It was when I was ill, when I was sick of being Will Chancellor, who was always stuck in bed, left behind. I wanted to be someone different, I suppose.' He threw a pebble, watched it skim across the water. 'That's what I'd like to do now. Run away. Start again. Be someone different.'

★   ★   ★

After she had parted from Will in Hernscombe, Topaz sat for a while on a bench on the esplanade. She remembered the expression in Will's eyes — that disturbing mixture of fear and panic — and the wobble in his voice. *I'm in a bit of a mess, Topaz.*

She wondered what she should do. Talk to Julia, she thought. Yet Will had made her promise not to. She wondered whether one should keep that sort of promise.

Glancing at her watch, she saw that it was almost four

o'clock. Weaving through the crowds of day trippers, she reminded herself that the company was staying in Hernscombe all week. It would be easy for her to visit Will and make sure he was all right. She would take a bus to the garage tomorrow.

At the theatre, she found Desmond in the green room. 'Sorry I'm late, Desmond,' she called out.

He made a vague gesture. 'Not to worry, dear girl.'

'Where's Charlie?'

Desmond looked up briefly from his paperwork. 'I believe he's making a phone call. He had a telegram.'

Charlie was in the box office. He put down the receiver as Topaz came into the room. There was a shocked, dazed expression in his eyes.

'Charlie?' She went to him. 'What is it?'

'Something awful's happened.' He drew his hand across his face.

'Your father?'

He shook his head. 'Helena.' He stared at her, eyes wide. 'She tried to kill herself, Topaz. Stuck her head in the bloody gas oven.'

'Oh God, Charlie — '

'She's alive. Someone found her in time.' He looked angry. 'The police will be involved, of course. Attempted suicide's a crime.' He held her so tightly her breath caught in her lungs. 'I knew she was miserable,' he muttered. 'She's always miserable in the summer.'

'But why did she do it?'

'Because of bloody Donald, of course,' he said savagely. 'Because *that* had all started up again.' He looked down at her. 'Didn't you realize?'

'No. No, I didn't.' Her voice sounded hollow. She thought of Helena and of Will. It seemed to be a day for discovering she didn't know much at all about the people she had believed closest to her. Silly old Topaz, still on the outside, looking in.

'I'd like to throttle Donald,' said Charlie angrily. 'He

won't leave Jean because of the kid, and he won't do the decent thing and get out of Helena's hair so she has a chance to start again.'

They went to the green room. Charlie said, 'I've got to go to London, Desmond. Now. Something's come up.'

'As you wish, dear boy,' said Desmond vaguely.

'You can understudy me at the performance tonight, can't you?'

Desmond looked evasive. 'There may be a teeny problem with tonight's performance. We may have to cancel.'

'Cancel?'

'And I shouldn't *rush* back . . . '

'Desmond . . . ? What's going on?'

Desmond rustled papers. 'I may have overlooked the copyright payments . . . '

'Stupid bastard,' said Charlie succinctly. 'Every bloody time . . . ' He grabbed his jacket. 'I'll phone you from London.' He turned to Topaz. 'You'll come, won't you?'

It was only when she was sitting on the train, leaving the station, that Topaz remembered Will. Somehow, put beside the real horror of Helena's suicide attempt, Will's problems, whatever their nature, seemed to have diminished. Yet she thought how precarious happiness seemed to be, how fragile. The carriage was crowded and they had been unable to sit next to each other, but she nudged her foot against Charlie's, and saw him look up and smile. Reassured, she settled in her seat and let the train draw her back to London.

★   ★   ★

Will phoned Rick early that evening. Took the card from the drawer and asked the operator for the number before he had time to chicken out. The phone rang out for ages and he didn't know whether he'd be relieved or disappointed if no one picked it up. Then a voice at the end of the line said, 'Yes?', and Will said, 'Rick?'

'I'll get him. Who's calling?'

'Will Chancellor.'

He wished he'd had a drink. He sat on the edge of the desk, twisting the phone cable around his fingers.

'Will?' Rick's voice. 'How can I help you?'

'I need to talk to you, Rick.'

'Fire away, then.'

'It's the parcels.' Will's throat was dry. 'I don't want you to leave them here.' The cable was in a knot. 'Not any more. I've had enough.'

A silence. Then, 'You're telling me you want out?'

'Yes.' A flicker of relief: Rick understood.

'But we had an arrangement, Will.'

Will noticed the slight hardening of Rick's voice. 'I don't want to be involved any more. I opened one of the parcels, you see. I don't know what you're doing with all that money, Rick, and I don't want to know, but I'm not having anything more to do with it.'

'It might not be that easy, Will.'

He felt an unexpected sense of calm. He was taking control of his life at last, doing what he should have done months ago. 'If you leave another parcel here,' he said, 'then I'll take it to the police.'

'Ah.' A long silence. Then, 'I'll think about what you say, Will.' The line went dead.

★   ★   ★

Will was working late at the garage the following evening when he heard the car draw up in the forecourt. He was alone; Brian had gone home and Will had stayed behind to clear up the last of the paperwork. During the twenty-four hours since he had made the telephone call to Rick, his calmness had persisted. For the first time in months he didn't dislike himself. He knew that at last he had done something right. He was beginning to claw back his life, to shake it into its proper shape.

He opened the office door and looked out. A man was climbing out of the parked car. Will was about to go out to the petrol pump when he recognized Gene. His heart began to pound and sweat lay slick in the palms of his hands. Rick was laughing at him, he thought. But he saw that Gene was empty-handed, that his small, lean frame concealed no packets or parcels.

He just managed to get the words out. 'What do you want?'

'Message from Rick,' said Gene.

'A message?' repeated Will, blankly.

A smile. Then Gene hit him. There was the splinter of broken glass as his spectacles hit the floor and a sprinkling of white, bright lights, like stars.

10

Each time they met they went a little further, creeping closer to a precipice. She sat in the back seat of the Bentley, cradled in Jack's arms. His lips nuzzled the curve of her neck as he stroked her breasts. She closed her eyes, drowsy in the confined warmth of the car, lethargic with pleasure and with longing. Her limbs seemed heavy, her muscles loose and pliant. His fingertips ran along her inner thigh. When he touched the place between her legs, darts of electricity ran through her and it took an effort of will to reach down and push him away.

'Jack, you mustn't,' she said, as she had said countless times before. 'It's wrong.'

And he said, as he always did, 'Don't you want me to?' His hands moved back to her thigh, inching along her skin. Her resolve faltered, died.

Then she felt him tense. 'Bloody Nat Crabtree,' he whispered. 'Walking his bloody dog. Keep your head down.'

His fingers pressed against the back of her neck. Julia lay against the cracked leather of the seat. She seemed to see herself clearly, to see the situation in which she had let herself become complicit. And she hated herself. Hated the indignities she invited and the unending sense of wrongness.

Nat Crabtree turned aside without seeing them. When he had gone, Julia buttoned up her dress and got out of the car. Cycling home, she ached with frustration and longing. Sometimes it seemed to her that the remembering was almost as good as being with Jack. Better, in some ways, because there wasn't that small but undismissable fear of discovery; nor was there that conviction — always to be brushed away sharply — that everything they did was tainted by deceit.

Back at the cottage she had just time enough to pull a comb through her hair when she heard footsteps. As the door opened, she called out a greeting to Will. A greeting that froze on her lips as soon as she saw his bruised, swollen face.

He said, 'Sorry. Didn't mean to give you a fright.' He sat down at the table. His split lip twitched; she realized that he was trying to smile. 'Bit of an accident,' he explained. 'The jack slipped.'

She imagined the weight of a car, rushing down. While she had been with Jack. She managed to say, 'Have you seen a doctor?'

'No need. It's just bruises.'

'You might have broken something.'

'I don't think so.'

'Just to make sure — I'll run and phone — '

'Please, Julia,' he said softly. 'Please don't go. Please don't leave me alone.'

The words cut through the elation she always carried with her after being with Jack. 'I'll make some tea,' she said, rushing to the stove. Guilt made her solicitous, bustling. 'Let's get you patched up.' She knelt in front of the cupboard under the sink, searching for plasters and arnica.

Will said suddenly, 'I haven't been much of a husband to you, have I?' and her heart seemed to still.

'Nonsense, Will. What a thing to say.' The briskness was getting out of hand. She sounded like a games mistress.

'I've always been afraid', he said slowly, 'that you only married me because you couldn't have Jack.'

She peered into the cupboard, seeing nothing. She could not get out of her head the image of herself and Jack, coiled in the back of the car.

Will said in the same low, toneless voice, 'I thought

I'd make it up to you. Make you prefer me. But I haven't done too well, have I?'

Had he heard something? Had someone seen her with Jack, and spoken to Will? What would she say to him if he were to confront her? *I don't love you, Will I love Jack.* Yet was that even true? If she didn't love Will, then why did the sight of him, bruised and battered, tear at her heart?

When she put the cup in front of him, he grabbed at her hand. 'I meant to make everything perfect for you,' he muttered. 'Meant to give you everything you wanted, meant to buy you nice things.'

She managed to smile. 'You gave me those stockings. That lovely perfume . . .'

'The *perfume*,' he repeated. He clenched his fists. 'Good *God.*'

Bruises had almost closed his right eye. Despair and self-loathing mingled with the blue of the left. 'It might have worked, mightn't it,' he muttered, 'if it hadn't been for the money. If we hadn't been so wretchedly hard up.' His words were slurred by his swollen lip. He sounded preoccupied, as if he was trying to work something out.

She smiled weakly. 'You know I never mind about money.'

His gaze flicked towards her. 'You don't understand, Julia.'

'No.' She stared at him. 'No, I don't.'

He pressed her hand against his damaged face. 'I'm so sorry. So sorry I've let you down.'

'You mustn't talk like that, Will. You really mustn't.' Her voice quivered. Because she was starting to realize that she had made a mistake. A rather dreadful mistake. She thought of the gifts he had given her and the long hours he had worked. It was possible, wasn't it, that Will's moodiness and distance had had a different cause from the one she had assumed. And if that was so, then it changed everything.

There was a heaviness around her heart and a sense of foreboding. 'You didn't think I cared, did you, Will,' she whispered, 'about being hard up?'

'*I* cared,' he said fiercely. 'When we were married, when I started up the garage, I thought, this is it, now I can show everyone. Show them that I'm as good as anyone.' He gave a short, unamused laugh. 'As good as Jack.'

'It wasn't a competition, Will.'

'Wasn't it? That's what it felt like,' he said bitterly. 'A competition I was always losing. Anything I did, Jack did it earlier, better, faster.'

'I didn't know you felt like that.'

'Didn't you? Then how — how *unobservant* of you, Julia.'

She drew her hand back as if he had stung her and he groaned. 'Sorry. Such a nerve, for *me* to criticize *you*.'

'Will!' She couldn't bear it any longer. 'You musn't say things like that! As if I was — as if I was *perfect*!'

'But you are,' he said seriously. 'You've always been perfect to me, Julia.'

She gave an involuntary cry of dismay, and turned away. She had got it all wrong, she thought. So hopelessly, disastrously wrong.

Standing up, he put his arms around her. 'You musn't be upset,' he said gently. 'It's all *my* fault. Not yours.'

She swung round, burying her face in his shoulder, hugging and stroking him, murmuring soothing noises. After a while, his hands began to follow the paths Jack's had taken only a few hours earlier. The two brothers blurred together, dark and fair, sun and moon. If she closed her eyes, she could imagine that Jack was touching her. Desire, suppressed and frustrated so many times these last few months, reignited easily.

'I wouldn't blame you', he whispered, 'if you wanted to call it a day.'

Her eyes jerked open. She had to know. Had to ask.

'Is that what you want, Will?'

'No.' He threaded his fingers through her hair and paused, bound to her by hanks of light brown locks. 'Dear God, *no.*'

Tears brimmed at the corners of her eyes. *Not yet, she told herself. Just a little while longer. Then I'll make my heart break.*

So she unbuttoned her dress and let it fall in a flood of blue to the floor. Unhooked her brassiere, stepped out of her knickers. Soon, in his bruised blue eyes, she saw delight when she cried out as she climaxed.

★   ★   ★

Rick came to the garage the following afternoon. Catching sight of the Lancia from the workshop, Will straightened, wiping his oily hands on his overalls. There was the impulse to run, but he fought it, knowing its futility.

When the office door was shut behind them, Rick said, 'I came here to apologize. Gene can get a little carried away sometimes.'

Involuntarily, Will put up a hand to his face.

'Brought you a few things.' Rick opened a briefcase. 'No hard feelings, eh?'

Will's gaze slid over the bottle of Scotch, the packets of cigarettes and nylons. Rick offered cigarettes. When he took one from the case, Will's hand trembled.

Rick flicked a lighter. 'Thing is, Will, we had an arrangement. I did you a few favours, so now you do favours for me. That's how my business works.'

Will whispered, 'I thought it was *over,*' and Rick shook his head.

'No. Not by a long chalk.'

'But I'm *frightened.*' The words escaped before he could stop them: self-abasing, childlike.

'I know you are, Will.' Rick perched on the edge of

the desk. 'Let me explain about myself — I'd like to tell you how I built up the business. I'm a Londoner, from the East End. Dad scarpered when I was a little kid — I can't even remember what he looked like. I didn't go to school much. I was a cocky little beggar, didn't think books could teach me anything. Proper little street Arab, I was, lived from hand to mouth, if you know what I mean.' Rick's sharp, dark eyes focused on Will. 'Don't suppose you do. I expect it was all a bit different for you.'

There was a tinge of contempt in Rick's voice that made Will say, in spite of his headache, in spite of the fear, 'I wasn't born with a silver spoon in my mouth, if that's what you mean. It wasn't always easy.'

'If you say so, Will. Anyway, the war came and I was called up. I knew after the first couple of weeks the army wasn't for me. So I got out.'

'You deserted?'

Rick shook his head. 'Dishonourably discharged. Conduct unbecoming.' He laughed. 'Don't look so shocked. Means to an end.' He stubbed out his cigarette. 'So I started up on my own. Good times, wartime. Could see there were plenty of opportunities. People'd pay good money to get the things they wanted. I did small-time stuff at first — sold fruit and veg off the ration at Romford market and down Petticoat Lane. Then I managed to get my hands on some petrol coupons. Fallen off the back of a lorry, hadn't they? They earned me a bob or two, so I set up the garages in Warren Street. And then, when the Yanks came over, I got a nice little arrangement going on. A case of whisky from the PX. Cigarettes. Nylons. That sort of thing. And after D-Day — well, there was a whole new market, wasn't there? All those poor sods on the Continent desperate to sell whatever they'd got for a loaf of bread or a few bits of coal to keep their kiddies warm. And everyone back home just as anxious to buy a bottle of champagne or perfume and not bothered about asking where they'd come from.'

Will thought of the parcel. 'And the money?'

'Can't go abroad without foreign currency, can you? And it's not legal nowadays, is it, to have more than a bob or two in francs and what-nots. Ridiculous, I call it — people still need holidays, but there you are, it makes a nice little profit for me.' Rick smiled. 'Way I see it, I help out, provide a service. You wouldn't believe the people who rely on me to get them their currency, Will. Lady this and Lord that ... doctors ... lawyers ... professional men.' Now Rick's voice was openly contemptuous. 'All needing me so they can have their week in the sun.'

He went to the window and said, his back to Will, 'Before the war that sort would have despised me. Wouldn't have let me darken their precious doorsteps. Now they need me. *They* come to *me*. How times change, eh, Will? Now I dress better than them, drive a better car than them. Not long now, and I'll own a bigger house than them. I'll take my holidays abroad, stay in the best hotels. When I marry, my kids'll go to fancy schools. A few years' time and there won't be a distance to spit between us.' He swung round and Will saw that his eyes gleamed, hungry, intelligent and amoral.

'*Their* sort's finished,' he said. He made a small gesture of dismissal. '*Your* sort, Will. Oh, you mustn't take it personal. You're a nice enough fellow. But you haven't got what it takes, not nowadays.' He took out another cigarette, tapping it against the case. 'Got into another line of business recently,' he confided. 'Better than bottles of Scotch and petrol coupons. That's why I made your acquaintance. More *lucrative*.'

Will whispered, 'What sort of business?'

'Lots of bits and bobs knocking around the Continent these days. Paintings ... jewellery ... little old books and statues. That's where the money is. The Nazis took whatever they wanted from art galleries and private collections. Sold them on when things started turning bad for them. Amazing what you can lay your hands on, if you know where to look. And that's where you come in, Will.'

'I don't see — '

'Can't fly my purchases in any more — the Services got wise to that. They search the planes now. But boats are easy enough, plenty of boats around and plenty of people happy enough to earn a few quid taking them across the Channel. But you have to have a nice quiet little spot to land. Lots of quiet bits of coastline round here, Will. Little coves and estuaries. I got your cousin Maurice to show me round a few places. Said I was thinking of buying a holiday home.' Rick's lips parted, showing long, slightly curved teeth. 'Might do, as well. I fancy being a country gentleman. Anyway, you see what I'm saying. My friends in the armies of occupation get hold of paintings and whatnots while they're abroad. They ship 'em over here on a fishing boat. Then they call on you.'

'So you're using my garage', Will said slowly, 'to park your stolen goods? A sort of . . . post office?'

Rick looked pained. 'Not *stolen*, Will. I pay a fair price.'

'Do you?' He glanced at Rick: sleek, well-fed, assured. He thought of the photographs he had seen in the newspapers. The gaunt, ragged women and children scrabbling among the ruins of Berlin.

'It's nice and quiet here,' said Rick, looking around. 'Out of the reach of snoopers. Some of my places in London have been getting a bit hot, if you know what I mean. I've had to shift some things.'

Will's head throbbed. The previous night, after he had made love to Julia, he had believed for a little while that miracles were still possible. That he could still alter the course of events, that there was still a way out.

269

He had to know whether he had been mistaken. He made himself ask, 'How long for? Weeks? Months?'

'Let's not pin ourselves down,' said Rick cheerfully. 'An open-ended contract, shall we say?'

'But I need to know.' He felt as though he was walking along a tightrope. One glance down and he'd tumble into the abyss. 'I need to know whether it'll go on for ever.'

'It'll go on for as long as I need you, Will.' Suddenly, Rick's voice was cold. He took a package from his briefcase. 'I want you to look after this for me. It's something rather special. Look upon it as a little test. Prove yourself to me. I don't want to have to ask Gene to call again. Nasty temper, Gene. Goes over the score too easily.' Rick placed the package on the table. 'Keep good care of it. Gentleman should come for it in a few days.'

Halfway to the door, Rick paused. 'Oh, and no more nonsense about going to the police, eh, Will? You're in it up to your neck, you know. Selling forged petrol coupons . . . handling stolen goods. Shop me and I'll make sure the police know your part in it. The magistrates are often harder on the men from good families. It'd mean a prison sentence, for sure. Think what that would do to your family. The shame. Think what it'd do to your lovely wife, all on her own while you were banged up inside. I was sent down for six months a few years ago. Prison's no joke, I can tell you. You wouldn't survive it. Not someone like you.'

He left the room. Will's scalp crawled with sweat and his breath was ragged. He sat down, his head in his hands, shaking.

★ ★ ★

Jack's cottage lay a little apart from Carrie Chancellor's house, standing on its own in a hollow at the foot of a hill. Julia left her bicycle behind a hedgerow and walked across the fields. Halfway to the cottage she paused in the shade of a copse and looked up. Sixfields House stood against the skyline, dark and monolithic. It seemed to Julia that there was something discomforting, menacing even, about the house.

Jack always left the back door open, so she slipped inside. He was not yet home, and only the dog padded across the kitchen floor to greet her. She stooped, burying her fingers in Con's silky coat, glad of the silence and the opportunity to compose herself. She felt restless and tired at the same time. She had slept little the previous night, drifting in and out of gaudy, exhausting dreams. In the early hours of the morning, she had lain awake, still trapped in Will's embrace, watching the darkness slowly fade to grey. Now clouds bubbled on the horizon, sometimes masking the face of the sun.

She heard Jack's footsteps on the path and she tensed, threading her fingers together, grinding knuckle against knuckle.

'Darling,' he said, embracing her. 'I came as soon as I could.'

'I can't stay long, Jack.' She pulled away from him. 'We have to talk.'

There was a sudden wariness in his eyes, but he said lightly, 'About anything in particular?'

'I can't see you again.' Like spitting out hot stones, she thought. The words seemed to hurt her mouth.

'I don't understand.'

'It's quite simple, Jack. I don't want to see you any more.'

His fingers clenched. Just that small movement. He had always, she thought, had a talent for stillness.

'Why not?'

'Because it's wrong.'

'We've been through this before.' His tone became

271

conciliatory, soothing. 'You're just feeling nervy, darling.'

'I am — not — *nervy*.' Though she had felt nauseous all day, sick with dread.

'Julia, sweetheart — '

'Is this what you want, Jack?' she cried. 'Furtive little meetings — an hour or two snatched when no one's looking? Have you any idea how I feel when I'm hiding my bike behind the hedge, or cowering in the back of your car?'

He looked away. Then he said, 'You say you hate the deceit. Well, we can put an end to that, can't we? We can come clean. Tell the truth.'

'*Tell the truth*,' she repeated. 'Tell Will . . . tell my mother and your parents — '

'Why not?'

'*Think*, Jack. Just think what people would *say*. I mean — coveting your brother's wife — it's pretty much beyond the pale, isn't it? What do you think it would do to our families? To your mother and my mother?'

'They'd get used to it eventually.' But he did not sound convinced.

'No.' She shook her head. 'No, they wouldn't get used to it. It would tear them apart. And I don't think *I* could bear that. All the people I love most thinking badly of me. And as for Will . . . It would destroy Will if I left him for you. Do you really want to hurt him that much?'

After a while he gave a small shake of the head. Dry-eyed, beyond tears, Julia stared out of the window at the golden fields. Far away, at the foot of the valley, the jewelled line of the sea flashed and sparkled, catching the sinking sun. She said dully, 'Last night, I realized that I'd made a mistake. I thought Will didn't love me, you see. But I was wrong.'

He swung round. 'And you? Do you love him?'

Her gaze dropped. 'I think I do. In my way.'

'Not in the *right* way.'

'And you know the right way, do you, Jack?'

He made a small gesture. 'After you married Will I wasn't exactly *celibate*.'

She looked away. 'I don't want to know.'

'Don't you? Too bad. The thing is that none of them meant anything to me. Oh, there was pleasure, of course, I'm not denying that. But every one of those women made me realize how much I loved you. After a while, I began to hate them for not *being* you.' He paused, and then he said matter of factly, 'I've never loved any woman other than you, Julia. I don't know if I ever will.'

'Nonsense,' she whispered. 'You'll meet someone, you're bound to. You're still young.'

He shook his head. 'I don't love easily, do I? Don't *trust* easily. And you have to trust someone to be able to love them. I doubt if I've loved half a dozen people in my whole life. Not really *loved* them. But I do love you, Julia. And if you go away from me, I won't just shrug my shoulders and find someone else. It'll be even worse than the first time, when you married Will. Because I'll know what I'm missing. Because I'll know how it *should* have been.'

She cried out, 'Jack — you are making this impossible — unbearable — '

Fleetingly, she caught a glimpse of uncertainty, a rare moment of similarity with his younger brother. 'This is the way I see it,' he said slowly. 'I know that I made a mistake. I've known that for a long time. I chose Sixfields when I should have chosen you. And I think you made a mistake, too, Julia. I think you agreed to marry Will because you were upset because Marius had married Suzanne, and upset because I'd turned you down. And then Will turned up offering a convenient solution. Isn't that about it?'

There were tears in her eyes. 'If it is . . . it doesn't alter anything, does it?'

'Why should we have to pay for our mistakes for the rest of our lives? It seems too high a price.'

'What alternative is there?'

'There are always alternatives.' He shrugged. 'For instance, we could go on as we are.'

'Could we? How long, d'you think, till we go that little bit further? How long till we sleep together? And then how long till someone finds out? Because sooner or later someone would. It's such a small world, isn't it? Everyone knows everyone else's business. Everyone knows us. Someone would see us.'

'If we're careful — '

'We would make mistakes, Jack. We'd be bound to. Or we'd be unlucky.' Her voice was flat, empty of emotion.

'Or we could go away,' he said. 'Start again.'

For a moment she imagined it: her and Jack, alone at last, openly, freely, able to love each other. Then the dream crumbled and she said slowly, 'You'd never see Sixfields again, Jack.'

'Damn Sixfields — '

'You're a man of few passions. You said so yourself. But Sixfields is one of them, isn't it? And even if you wouldn't mind never coming home again, I'm not sure I could bear to be exiled. How long do you think it would be till we begin to hate each other?'

'I could never hate you.'

The words echoed. In the silence, she pulled at her wedding ring, twisting it round and round her finger. When Jack said, 'What *we* need — doesn't that matter too?' she could hear the desperation in his voice.

She tried to smile. 'There doesn't seem to be an answer, does there? If I keep on seeing you, I'll be unhappy because I know what I'm doing is terribly wrong. And if I don't see you any more, well, I don't know how I shall bear it.'

He crossed the room to her and took her face between his hands. 'I never wanted you to be unhappy.'

'Then let me go. Let me go, and don't be angry with me, and don't be bitter. And promise me you'll try to be happy. Because then I might manage. Let me go, dear Jack.'

'Don't ask me that.' His eyes were anguished. 'Please don't ask me that.'

She stood on tiptoes and touched her lips against his. Then her head drooped forward, resting against his shoulder.

★   ★   ★

Will sent Brian home early and closed up the garage.

He had reached a point when just to think sent him into an exhausted, spiralling panic. He was caught in a maze, every exit barred to him. He could not go to the police because to do so would mean admitting his own guilt. He imagined his family's shame, their rejection of him. He imagined standing in court, surrounded by policemen, listening to the judge pass sentence. He imagined being in prison. Confined in a cold, comfortless little cell, with some muscle-bound thug, perhaps, who'd take pleasure in beating the living daylights out of him. He suspected that Rick was right, that he would not survive prison.

Yet the thought of continuing to work indefinitely for Rick was equally appalling. A combination of blackmail and physical violence meant that he had lost control over his own life. Rick might demand his services for months, years, even. There was no guarantee that he would stop at selling black market petrol coupons and handling stolen goods. Rick might demand worse crimes of him. Gun-running, the selling of narcotics, extortion . . . Murder, even. He was being sucked into a whirlpool, deeper and deeper. He was drowning.

Will's head, and the bones of his face, hurt, reminding him of the sadistic, efficient aim of Gene's fists and boots. He left the garage, driving aimlessly along the high-banked, narrow lanes, squinting short-sightedly through the windscreen because Gene had broken his glasses. Then he thought of Topaz.

He turned on to the Hernscombe road. He would tell her everything, he decided — no more evasions, no more half-truths. He should have told her the truth the other day. He should have told *someone* the truth a very long time ago.

He parked the car near the harbour and walked along the seafront. Emerging from between the clouds, sunlight burned the flat span of sea copper. When he reached the theatre, Will saw that it was closed, the posters scrawled through with the word, *Cancelled*. He stood on the pavement, trying to decide what to do. Holidaymakers still scattered the beach, soaking up the remains of the sun. Day trippers, hurrying for trains and buses, jostled him.

Enclosed in the stuffy, metallic airlessness of a phone box, he called the Brookes' London flat, but Veronica had no knowledge of Topaz's whereabouts. Will put down the receiver and gazed out to sea. He imagined taking one of the fishing boats and sailing away. Sailing until there was only the water and the sky, until the keel of the boat grated against an unfamiliar shore.

Someone rapped on the glass and he stumbled outside, mumbling apologies. Walking along the narrow mole that enclosed the harbour, he shaded his eyes from the bright light of the sun. Where the sea surged against the stone wall, he sat down on an upturned lobster pot and took out his cigarettes and matches. He could not simply run away, of course, because of Julia. For a few hours last night, buoyed with unexpected optimism after he and Julia had made love, he had believed that he would find a solution to his problems. After Rick's visit his conviction had crumbled.

He saw how a succession of seemingly harmless steps had led him into this nightmare. His first mistake had been to rent the garage from Maurice. The garage had never been the bargain Maurice had boasted it to be. Isolated and run down, it had lost money from the first day. His own lack of experience and carelessness with the paperwork had made things worse. The severe winter and petrol rationing had been death blows.

Yet he had continued to entangle himself with such blind and easy foolishness. The bank loan . . . Maurice's refusal to wait for the rent . . . and that fatal moment when he had picked up the telephone and called Rick. With a mixture of blithe optimism, ignorance and naivety, he had stumbled into a lion's den. Will groaned out loud, clutching his head in his hands.

He found himself remembering an incident from years ago, at prep school. He had been ink monitor, which had meant that he had been responsible for filling the inkwells at the desks from a big bottle. One afternoon he had dropped the bottle in the storeroom, ruining half a dozen textbooks. Horrified, he had smuggled the textbooks out of the school beneath his blazer. He had, for some reason he could not now remember, hidden them in the gardener's shed. His guilt and anxiety had increased as the days went on. His form teacher would notice the books were missing . . . the gardener would be falsely accused and made to leave the school . . . He had felt then as he felt now, sick with shame and worry. The difference was that then his imagination had magnified a small misdemeanour into a great crime. Now the crime was real and undeniable.

In the end, he recalled, Jack had found him weeping in the boys' lavatories. *Oh, is that all*, Jack had said, when Will, between snuffles, had confessed everything. Jack had retrieved the books, had claimed responsibility for their damage, had been fined a week's pocket money and required to write a hundred lines. And that had been that.

He had almost forgotten that there had been a time when Jack had protected him, had used his greater strength to guard him from the world. A time when he and Jack had been better friends. He could not pinpoint when all that had changed. When they had moved to the School House, perhaps. Or maybe they had grown apart during the long years of Jack's absence abroad. Or their mutual envy had gradually worn away at them, poisoning whatever had been good. The thought saddened him.

Jack, he thought. Will's fingers, clutching the cigarette end, trembled. He imagined telling everything to Jack, laying open all the deceits and stupidities of the past year to his brother's critical gaze. This time, Jack would not just say, *Oh, is that all*.

If he went to Jack, told Jack the truth, he would justify all the contempt Jack had ever shown towards him. Jack reserved a special scorn for those who dabbled in the black market. Jack despised weakness, had little sympathy with incompetence. He couldn't possibly tell Jack.

Yet what was his alternative? To go on as now, each day caught more deeply in Rick's web. To continue to endure every moment of every day sick with anxiety and fear. He needed Jack's strength, Jack's decisiveness, Jack's cold, clear judgement. If anyone was capable of finding a way out of this mess, then that person was Jack. And he did not see, Will realized suddenly, how he could bear to go on alone.

He walked back to the car. As he turned the ignition, he glanced at his watch. It was almost seven o'clock. He drove fast, afraid he'd lose his courage en route, the ferns and Queen Anne's lace on the verges blurred to a smear of cream and green by his myopia. Braking to a halt outside Sixfields, he recalled childhood visits: the dust had always made him sneeze, and he had been convinced that ghosts lurked behind the creaking doors and in the ill-lit passageways. When his mother had read him fairy stories at night, the witches had always borne Cousin Carrie's sour, critical features.

But there was no sign of her, thank God, and the dogs in the courtyard seemed to remember him because they quietened when he spoke to them. It seemed to Will that the cobwebbed bottles and jars on the scullery windowsill were the same bottles and jars that had been there years ago, when he'd visited Sixfields with his mother; that the same ragged curtains were drawn across the mullioned windows, shutting out the sunlight just as they had a decade before.

He took the path that led from the farmyard to the cottage. The warm evening air was heavy with the sourish scent of newly turned earth. The fields, hedgerows and copses were still and silent. Coiled in the hollow of the valley, the leaves on the trees and the dusty blades of grass were motionless. In the distance a tractor ploughed the slope of the hill, white dots of gulls following in its wake. Will walked quietly, as if reluctant to break the spell.

He reached the cottage. He was about to knock on the door, when, glancing through the window, he glimpsed movement.

He looked and then he stepped back into the shadows. Then he looked again. Because he had to be sure of what he had seen.

His wife and his brother, embracing.

★　★　★

From a high window at Sixfields, Carrie Chancellor watched Will turn and run back along the path. His gait was peculiar; he lurched as though he was drunk, or ill. She scrubbed at the sooty film that covered the glass, trying to see more clearly. Will was stumbling through the courtyard, tripping over the dogs and the clumps of rusty, tangled machinery.

He went out of view. After a few moments, she heard an engine start up. A car wove along the narrow road, slewing unsteadily to left and right. Carrie watched until the car, and the cloud of dust that followed it, dropped beyond the horizon.

★   ★   ★

Back at the garage, Will searched through the shelves, flinging box files and account books aside, looking for the cash box. Papers scattered to the floor as he shovelled coins and notes into his pocket. He had the wild idea of setting fire to the office, but he couldn't find a match. He remembered that he had left his cigarettes and matches beside a lobster pot on Hernscombe harbour.

Rick's package lay on the desk beside the bottle of Scotch and the packets of cigarettes and nylons. Will picked up the package, clawed open the wrappings. He had expected to find money, ration books, forged passports. Instead, unfolding a piece of sacking, he glimpsed a flicker of colour, a glint of gold. He found himself looking at a wooden panel about eight by ten inches square. A blue-clad Madonna was sitting in a garden. The garden was dotted with flowers, pink and gold and white. Above the Madonna were three angels. They seemed to Will to be dancing, dancing in the sky. Their feet were pointed and their wings were unfurled, and their loose robes curled and twisted, echoing their movements. Absorbed in the dance, their features were still and serene. The Madonna's hand was upraised, as if calling for silence. There was a stillness, an entrancement about the picture that reminded Will of Sixfields. The Madonna and angels, even the garden itself, seemed to be waiting, poised for some extraordinary event that was just about to happen.

Rick, Sixfields, Julia . . . Will shoved the painting, cigarettes and nylons into a knapsack and left the garage. At the Holly Bush, he stood at the bar, drinking. He didn't want to remember, he didn't want to be able to think. If he drank enough, then he might be able to erase the memory of Rick saying *I wouldn't want to have to ask Gene to call again*. When he pressed his knuckles against the bones of his face, the marks left by Gene's fists hurt. He doubted if he were capable of drinking enough to block out the image of Julia enclosed in Jack's arms. The image persisted, as though burnt into the lens of his eye. When he thought of Jack, it was with a mixture of shock and disbelief. Whatever differences had divided them these past few years, he had never thought that Jack was capable of such a profound betrayal. Jack must hate him. He wondered how long the affair had been going on. Weeks . . . months . . . throughout his marriage, perhaps. He gave a little moan of despair and the landlord looked up at him and frowned.

As the evening wore on, the pub began to fill up. Johnnie Gamble bought Will a pint and, in a dark corner of the public bar, Will offered Johnnie and his brother a whisky chaser from the bottle Rick had given him. Events blurred together, disjointed and fragmented. There was a drinking game which Mick Gamble won. Will gave Mick a packet of nylons as a prize. Mick kicked off his hobnail boots and pretended to put on the stockings, and the pub echoed with cheers and wolf whistles. Then there was a fight. Will kept out of it, unsteady on his feet, not wishing to add to his bruises. Stools and tankards flew through the air. The landlord intervened, throwing out a couple of burly labourers.

Mick Gamble suggested they take the boat out. Will

281

thought of the *Katie Rose*, and the sea and sky and stars. The dark velvety peace of it. The Gamble brothers dragged him out of the pub and through the warm night air, and pushed him into the driver's seat of the car.

★ ★ ★

Waking early the next morning, Julia saw that, beside her, the bed was empty. Pulling on slacks and a jersey, she went downstairs, twisting her long, tangled hair into a knot at the nape of her neck. Her head ached and, in spite of her sleep, she still felt tired. She moved slowly around the cottage, tidying away books and crockery, plumping up cushions. Her thoughts jerked exhaustingly from Jack to Will. She sat down on the sofa, a cup of tea cradled in her hands. Looking out of the window, she saw that grey clouds hung low in the air; she thought the tops of the trees might touch them. A movement flickered between the beech trunks and Julia glanced up, expecting to see Will, coming up the path. But it was only an old fox, red-brown coat almost lost against the carpet of dried leaves.

Anxiety seeped into her numbness and desolation. Will had never before stayed out the entire night. She remembered his swollen eye and lip, and the chain of bruises across his jaw. The thought that had been hovering at the back of her mind for the past thirty-six hours — that those were not the sorts of injury you'd expect to receive when a jack collapsed — could not, this time, be put away for later. She could imagine fists making those sharp, carefully placed marks, but not the crushing weight of a car. She pressed her hands together, disturbed by her memories of the expression in Will's eyes, and the despair in his voice. *I've let you down, Julia . . .*

She couldn't sit still. The house was too silent, too

lonely. She went outside, drifting around the little garden she had claimed from the wilderness. Her nervous fingers touched a flower here, a raspberry cane there. There was mildew on the brambles and the leaves of her little almond tree were black and curling. Needing to see the sky, she took the path that led to the green lane. When she looked down the hill, she saw the car parked by the road. A tiny figure was walking up the slope to the cottage. *Will*, she thought, and felt a rush of relief. The figure grew. Julia made out a policeman's uniform. She began to run.

When she was within earshot, the policeman called out, 'Mrs Chancellor?'

'Yes.' She couldn't seem to catch her breath. 'What's happened?'

'I'd prefer to come up to the house, if I may.'

She shook her head. It was hard to speak. 'No. Tell me here. Please.'

He said, 'There's been an accident, I'm afraid, Mrs Chancellor.'

★   ★   ★

There were iron bars on the windows, and two rows of identical white-covered beds. Enclosed in the beds, the patients, and the whispering relatives gathered around them, had a sameness that made it hard, at first, for Topaz to pick out Helena.

Then they saw the policeman sitting beside the bed. Charlie said, '*There*,' and walked to the end of the ward.

Helena was lying back on the pillows. Only her face, curtained by her loose fair hair, was visible; her body and arms were imprisoned beneath the smooth folds of sheet. As they approached the bed, the policeman moved a few yards away, a concession to privacy.

Charlie said, 'We came as soon as we heard.'

Very slowly, Helena's gaze drifted towards him. 'They

283

said . . . only relatives.'

'I told them I was your brother.' He kissed her cheek. 'We thought you'd like some company.'

Helena's eyelids flicked towards the policeman. A ghost of a smile touched her pale lips. 'I have company.'

'We brought you flowers,' said Topaz, 'but they took them away.'

There was another long pause, then Helena said, 'Sweet of you.' Her brow creased. 'Do you think they'll put me in prison, Charlie?'

'We'll get you a lawyer. A good lawyer.'

'I don't *care*. I really don't. It's just . . . My parents would mind. Bad enough for them to see me here. I didn't think — I didn't think I'd have to *know* — '

Charlie said, 'We won't let you go to prison, Helena, I promise.'

With an effort, she focused on him. 'The tour . . . ' she whispered.

'It's finished,' said Charlie. 'We're back in London, now. So we can come and see you every day, darling.'

Helena's head fell to one side. Her eyes focused on the window. Swayed by the breeze, a horse chestnut branch rapped against the panes.

'I keep thinking', she murmured, 'that someone's trying to get in.'

Charlie touched her shoulder. 'You'll be all right now.'

Helena gave a small, disbelieving smile. A passing nurse barked at Charlie for sitting on the bed, so he went to fetch chairs from the stack in the corner. Topaz thought of all the things she mustn't say. *Why did you do it? How could you do it?* Helena's eyes were half-closed. Topaz heard herself begin to talk, quickly and inanely, about the tour. When Charlie returned with the chairs she fell silent.

Charlie asked, 'Has Claudette visited?'

'With Mischa. Yesterday.' Helena's thin, pale fingers

crawled out of their covering of sheet. 'And Jerry. Not Donald.'

'Oh. Perhaps he thought — ' Charlie's voice trailed away. Then he said, 'If there's anything you want — ', and Helena gave a small shake of the head.

It seemed to Topaz as though a part of Helena had been erased — abandoned, perhaps, in the little flat she had once shared with Claudette. All the qualities that had made Helena unique — her calmness, her generosity and concern — had been squeezed out of her. Nothing had come to take their place. Not regret. Not even grief.

Then Helena said, 'I thought I was pregnant.'

Charlie's eyes widened. 'Donald's . . . ?'

'Yes.' Again, Helena frowned.

'Is that why you — '

'Oh no.' For the first time, Topaz saw emotion cross the blank canvas of Helena's pale face. A bitter curling of the mouth. A flare of anger in the empty blue of her eyes.

'I tried to kill myself when I found out I *wasn't* pregnant. Because that made everything so pointless. So utterly bloody futile.'

Exhausted, Helena closed her eyes. Somewhere in the distance a bell rang. From around the other beds relatives began to shuffle to their feet and head towards the double doors at the end of the ward.

Charlie was white, speechless. Topaz kissed Helena's cold cheek. The horse chestnut branch tapped its knuckles against the glass as they walked out of the ward.

★ ★ ★

She went home the following morning. To collect some clean clothes. To see her mother. To find out how the land lay.

Her mother was sitting on the drawing-room sofa, smoking. In much the same place as she had left her, Topaz thought, a month ago.

When Veronica looked up at her daughter, her eyes sparked.

'*There* you are.'

'Hello, Mummy.' She kissed her mother's cheek.

'Where *were* you?'

'The tour, Mummy. You remember.'

'I meant', said Veronica irritably, 'where were you *yesterday*. The phone ringing all day, and me left to deal with everything on my own. *Too* tiresome.' Her sapphire-blue gaze sharpened. 'You look as though you spent the night in a haystack. Or someone else's bed.'

Topaz said quickly, 'The theatre — '

'The theatre closed the day before yesterday. I telephoned and spoke to someone. An Irishman.'

'Desmond?'

'I can't remember his name.' Veronica stubbed her cigarette out in an ashtray. 'If you choose to sleep around like a tart, Topaz, then that's your affair. But bring any bundles of joy home and you'll be out on your ear, my girl. Don't doubt that for a moment.' Veronica took out another cigarette. Gold bracelets jangled on her arms as she gave the lighter an impatient flick. She shot Topaz a glance.

'You look a fright. You should have a bath, tidy yourself up. God knows what the neighbours will think.'

'Yes.' At the door she paused. 'Telephone calls, Mummy?'

Veronica inhaled her cigarette. 'Prudence, mostly. And that friend of theirs ... nice-looking boy ... married beneath him.'

'Marius?'

'Yes.' Veronica glanced at her watch. 'You'd better iron your blacks. I suppose we shall have to go to Dorset.' She frowned. 'If there is to be a funeral. I don't know what one does, in such cases.'

'Mummy . . . ?' Suddenly, she was frightened.

Veronica said, 'Will Chancellor is dead. Apparently he went sailing on Thursday night with a couple of friends. The boat hit an unexploded mine. The police believe they were all killed instantly.'

★　★　★

Will had spent Thursday evening in the Holly Bush, leaving at around midnight in the company of Johnnie and Mick Gamble. The three men had driven to Hernscombe harbour, where they had taken out the Gambles' fishing boat, the *Katie Rose*. Sometime before that — a day, a week, a month — a mine, a remnant of the war, had broken loose from the chains that had for years tethered it to the sea bed, and had floated free, driven by the current towards Hernscombe Bay. When the *Katie Rose* had reached open sea, it had collided with the mine. The explosion had woken most of the town of Hernscombe and had been heard several miles inland. The lifeboat had been launched, but no survivors had been found. Will's car had been discovered parked near the harbour.

Through the days immediately following Will's death Julia recalled those stark facts over and over again, as if by doing so she could make them seem real. The pub. The boat. The mine. Her mind seized on details, picking at them, rubbing them raw. Why hadn't she heard the explosion? And why had Will decided to go sailing so late at night? Why hadn't he come home after a few drinks, as he usually did?

Though her family tried to explain things to her, she saw the pity in their eyes and after a while she stopped asking questions. Yet they continued to rattle around in her head. They'd tell her to sit down and rest, and she'd try, curled and tense on the sofa, to read a magazine. Or

287

she'd lie on her bed, staring at the ceiling of her bedroom at Missencourt, trying to calm her haunted, fitful thoughts by following the cracks in the plaster.

She had gone back to Missencourt because they wouldn't let her stay at Hidcote Cottage on her own. The policeman who had broken the news to her had tried to persuade her to let him drive her to Missencourt, but she had refused. But sometime later Marius had arrived, and she had known by the look in his eyes that he would brook no argument, so she had thrown a few belongings into a case and let him take her home. There she moved from house to garden, trying to make sense of what had happened, obsessively re-examining the events of the past forty-eight hours. Yet she couldn't seem to think straight. If only she wasn't so tired. If only she didn't always feel slightly sick. If only there was someone she could talk to. Someone who wouldn't judge her. If only she could rid herself of the conviction that it was somehow her fault, that Will was dead because she hadn't loved him enough.

Everyone was very kind to her, but she was unfit for company, unable to concentrate long enough to listen to their expressions of condolence. Each of them, her mother, Suzanne, Marius, took turns to sit with her — as though, she thought, it would be *dangerous* to leave her on her own. If, fleetingly, playing with Tara, she managed to forget, a moment or two later it would all come tumbling back. That Will was dead. That she would never see him again. That somehow (she could not quite follow the paths) she was to blame.

At night, when the house was quiet, she went downstairs and out on to the terrace. The night sky was cloudless and alive with stars. She looked up, searching for the Pleiades. *Look just to the side, and then you'll see more clearly.* But tears made her vision blur.

Hearing a footstep behind her, she turned and saw Marius.

He came to stand beside her. 'Couldn't you sleep?'

She shook her head. 'I didn't mean to wake you up.'

'It doesn't matter. Can I get you anything? A Scotch? Some cocoa?'

She said, 'Cocoa please,' because she sensed that he'd feel better if he had something to do.

In the kitchen Marius heated milk. 'Suzanne's got some sleeping pills,' he said. 'Shall I get you a couple?'

'I'd rather not.' She frowned. 'It's just that I'm trying to work things out. There are things bothering me. Everyone tells me not to worry, but I can't help it.'

He poured the milk into the mugs and handed one to her. 'Tell me.'

'The garage,' she said. 'What will happen to it? Will worked so hard to get it going and I'm afraid it's just been . . . abandoned.'

'Brian's keeping an eye on things. And I went over earlier in the day and collected the account books and invoices. They'll have to be gone through at some point.'

'I'll do it.'

'Julia, there's no need.'

'*Marius.*' Her voice trembled. 'I want to do it. For Will.' She blew her nose. 'And then there's the cottage — '

'Have you left anything valuable there?'

'We didn't have anything *valuable*. There's just . . . things. You know.'

'Suzanne or I can drive you there tomorrow, if you like.'

'Why didn't I hear the explosion?' she said suddenly. 'Why did I just keep on sleeping?'

He explained, 'Because Hidcote Cottage is much too far from the coast. And the hills, of course, mask sound. We didn't hear anything at Missencourt either.'

She put her hands to her mouth. 'I can't believe that

289

he's dead, you see. It seems so — so *silly*. So *pointless*.'
She bit her nails, tearing at a piece of loose skin. 'If I
could see him, I might be able to believe that he's dead.'

He lit two cigarettes and gave one to her. The skin
around her nails was raw and bleeding. He said, 'That
wouldn't be a good idea, Julia.'

She rubbed her forehead, as if by doing so she could
rid herself of the headache that had followed her around
for days.

'You go back to bed, Marius,' she said. She wanted to
be alone. 'You must be exhausted.'

'I'll wait for you.'

'No. Please.' She tried to smile. 'I'll go up in a few
minutes, I promise.'

After he had gone, she wandered from room to room.
Though she had always associated Missencourt with
safety and happiness, tonight the house failed to work
its spell. In Marius's study, she paused. Books and
papers were heaped on the desk. Idly, she leafed
through them. Will's untidy schoolboy handwriting was
scrawled across every page. Sitting down, she
remembered Will's refusal to allow her to help with the
accounts. *Will, you idiot*, she whispered out loud as she
ran her finger down the scratched-out, blotted columns
and figures. From the first glance it was painfully
obvious that Will had had little idea of bookkeeping.
She wondered what odd notion of pride or masculinity
had prompted him to reject her offer of help. She
imagined him sitting in his untidy little office at the
garage, ink on his fingers and his brow furrowed as he
struggled to balance the books.

Which didn't balance. Wouldn't balance. Julia found
herself gazing at the account books with a mixture of
bewilderment and shock. If these figures were correct,
then by the spring of 1947 the garage had been several
hundred pounds in debt. A number scrawled at the foot
of the page gave the total shortfall. Will had underlined

it half a dozen times, as though unable to accept its reality. The nib of his pen had scored the paper, piercing it, a visible sign of his anxiety and desperation. Julia tried to remember. There had been the snow and the garage had been closed for several weeks. Perhaps that had been when things had begun to go wrong. With the garage, and between her and Will. After that time, Will had worked long hours. She thought of the presents he had bought her. The stockings, the perfume and flowers. To placate her? Or because he dared not admit the truth to her?

The following morning Suzanne drove Julia to Hidcote Cottage. At Julia's request, Suzanne waited in the car on the main road while she walked up the green lane alone. It had rained that morning and she skirted round the puddles that pitted the track.

She took out her key to unlock the front door, but found, giving it a little push, that it was open. She had thought Marius had locked it, but she must have been mistaken. Standing in the narrow passageway between the kitchen and the outhouse, it seemed to her that the cottage had already taken on a forlorn, abandoned air. In the kitchen a dripping tap had almost filled the sink, so she plunged her arm into the cold water and pulled out the plug. She noticed that all the cupboards were open, their contents higgledy-piggledy, and wondered at herself for leaving them like that.

In the sitting room, the books had been pulled from the shelves and scattered anyhow. The contents of the sideboard — papers, pencils, packs of cards — were strewn across the floor. As if, she thought, a giant had picked up the little cottage and given it a shake, so that everything tumbled out of place. Upstairs, clothes — hers and Will's — trailed from open drawers and wardrobes. A jersey she had knitted for him, a blouse he had always liked to see her in. She picked up the jersey, folding it, clutching it to herself as she sat down at the top of the stairs. Odd how the scent of him, subtly, indefinably encapsulated in the twists of wool she gripped in her hands, could bring him back so vividly.

After a while she noticed the stack of cardboard boxes. Their wedding presents. She never had got round to unpacking them all, yet now that same unknown careless hand had upended them, tipping their contents anyhow over the floor. Which seemed to her to say everything there was to say about a marriage that had, in the end, been half-hearted.

11

In the two months that had passed since the memorial service Jack had not seen Julia. Whenever he called at Missencourt she was busy, or resting, or out. At the service she stayed close to Adele and Marius, as though their presence gave her shelter. Jack thought she looked ill, she was white and thin and her features pared back to the bone.

After a while he got the message: she didn't want to see him. He stopped visiting Missencourt, stopped writing letters and making phone calls. At the farm he worked fourteen-hour days, throwing himself recklessly into all the most physically exhausting tasks, trying to wear himself out so that he could sleep at night. Yet he had begun to hate Sixfields, to see how it had corrupted him, to see how it was both emblem and author of his guilt.

He was walking the path along the chalk ridge that lay between Carrie's land and her neighbour's when, on the far side of the valley, he saw the horse. A streak of black against the fawn of the corn stubble, it was bolting, neck outstretched, tail and mane flaring like banners. Hooves pounded a mad tattoo against the earth; Jack knew that the rider clinging desperately to the saddle was Julia.

He began to run. There was a moment when, as the horse approached the copse, he thought it might realize the impossibility of going full pelt between the trees and slow down. But then a pheasant, startled in the undergrowth, took flight in a sudden whirr of wings. Salem reared and threw his rider. When she hit the ground, Julia didn't move, but lay nestled in a tangle of fern and nettle as the horse cantered on. Jack thought she was dead. It had been that sort of year. When he found her pulse, he gripped her wrist, disbelieving. Then, very carefully, he scooped her out of the ferns.

She opened her eyes. 'I knew it was you,' she whispered. Then she frowned. 'Where's Salem?'

'Thrown himself over the bloody cliff, I hope.'

He carried her to the house. Carrie was in Dorchester, at the cattle market. He laid Julia on a settee, where, white and bruised, she stared around the room.

'What an extraordinary place.' A half-smile. 'I always wanted to see Sixfields.'

He dabbed at the graze on her forehead with a damp handkerchief. She said, 'Aren't you going to tell me off?'

'Why should I tell you off?'

'For not wearing a hat.'

He said in a rush, 'Oh God, Julia, I thought you were dead,' and buried his head in her breast.

She stroked his hair and then, after a minute or so, pushed him gently away from her. Then she shuffled upright, flexing her limbs.

'Nothing broken, I think.'

'You should see a doctor.'

She shook her head, and winced. Golden afternoon light filtered through the dusty parlour windows, marking the floor with diamonds.

He said, 'Why wouldn't you see me?'

'Oh, you know why, Jack,' she said sadly. 'What would be the point?'

'To talk about things.'

'What is there to talk about?'

'Us. You and me.'

'I don't think so.' Her fingers picked at a tear in the elbow of her shirt. Then she said, 'There is one thing . . .' and his gaze darted towards her, and he felt a sudden and irrational hope.

'One thing you ought to know.' She frowned. 'About

Will. And about me. I've no money, Jack, none at all. Less than none, actually. Will was in debt. He owed money to the bank and to Maurice Chancellor. Rather a lot of money, at one point.'

He glanced sharply at her. 'Are you sure?'

'I went through the books. The bad weather at the beginning of last year hit the garage hard. So he took out a loan. Which got him into a worse mess because of the interest payments.'

'And you didn't know?' She shook her head.

Will had been in debt. Will had been in trouble. Jack didn't want to believe it.

His mouth was dry. 'How will you manage?'

'Marius has lent me money to repay the bank loan. And I went to see Maurice Chancellor and he agreed to forget about the overdue rent. After — ' Julia's lip curled ' — after I pointed out to him what the rest of Will's family would think of him when I told them he was insisting I pay.' She paused. Then she said softly, 'I keep thinking how frightened Will must have been. How anxious. I could have *helped* him. I might have known what to do. But I didn't realize. He didn't tell me he was in trouble.' Her gaze jerked towards Jack. 'Why do you think that was?'

He had to look away from her. Carrie Chancellor's possessions surrounded him: a Toby jug, a dusty crystal vase containing a bunch of dead stems, a glutinous painting of a child at prayer.

She said, 'All that time he must have been worried sick. And he didn't say a thing.' She gave an unamused laugh. 'Not that I blame him. I mean, he couldn't be sure of a sympathetic ear, could he? When he worked late, I nagged him. When he went to the pub, I complained. Now I can see that he was trying to take his mind off things. But I didn't ask him *why*. I was just angry with him.' The corners of her mouth twisted. 'But I suppose I had an excuse. After all, I was distracted, wasn't I, Jack? Because of you.'

She was very pale, he noticed. A rather greenish-white. Delayed shock, he supposed. He touched her hand, and said gently, 'You look rotten. I'll make you a cup of tea.'

In the kitchen, boiling the kettle and finding cups and saucers, the thoughts rushing through his head were unpalatable. An hour ago he wouldn't have thought it possible to dislike himself more than he already did.

A little colour came back into her cheeks as she drank the tea. He asked, 'Have you told anyone?'

'A little to Marius because of having to pay off the loan. But I haven't said anything to anyone else. I won't', she said fiercely, 'have people think badly of Will.'

Jack sat down in Carrie's armchair. The leather had split, and gouts of horsehair burst through the cracks. 'I still can't believe it,' he said slowly. 'Will, keeping all that a secret. He wasn't up to it.'

'It would have made him nervous, do you mean, Jack? Edgy? Anxious? Much like he was in the six months before he died?'

'Julia —'

'And there's something else. The night before the accident, I think he'd been in a fight.'

'A fight?' He stared at her blankly. 'Not *Will*.'

'He told me that a jack had collapsed when he was underneath a car. But I think that he was lying to me. Not that I questioned his version at the time. After all,' she went on harshly, 'as I said, my mind was on other things.' She was silent for a moment and then she said more quietly, 'Whatever you and I did or didn't do, Jack, however we failed Will, well, we're just going to have to live with that, aren't we?'

In the silence, there was only the ticking of the grandfather clock. Julia stood up. 'I should go.'

He couldn't stop himself. He said, 'Will I see you

again?' and she shook her head.

'Never?'

Her eyes were dry and empty. 'I've been thinking about it a lot, Jack. The thing is that we didn't love each other enough.'

'That's not true — '

'Oh, it is.' Her gaze rested on him, clear and cold and unforgiving. 'You and I, we made our decision long ago, Jack. The week you came back from Italy.'

He groaned. 'It wasn't like that. You have to believe me.'

'Wasn't it? I know that I should never have married Will. I didn't make him happy.' Her voice was harsh. 'I married him because I couldn't have you. And as for you — well, I wasn't what you wanted most at the time.'

'No,' he said desperately. 'No, Julia. It was just that Carrie said — '

'Carrie?' Wearily, she pushed back her hair from her eyes. 'What has Carrie to do with it?'

Everything, he thought. Everything. He remembered that evening so vividly. Carrie had offered him Sixfields, a gift with the power to change his life. She had capitalized on his greed, and she had nurtured the seeds of his jealousy and distrust. *Julia Temperley?* Carrie had said. *I've heard she is . . . flighty.* And all too easily he had believed her. Tempted by riches, doubting the woman he loved, he had allowed himself to be bought and bound.

Reluctantly, he forced the words out. 'Carrie implied to me that you'd been seeing other men.'

Julia looked tired and confused. 'What on earth are you talking about, Jack? You must have made a mistake. Miss Chancellor doesn't even know me.'

'She said she'd heard gossip. And I thought . . . ' His voice trailed away. He muttered, 'I thought of Will.'

She looked at him, he thought, as though she despised him. Turning on her heel, she walked out of the house. He followed her into the courtyard. The warmth of the late summer afternoon jolted him after Sixfields' chilly rooms.

He called out, 'At least let me drive you home!'

'I'll walk, I think.'

'You may be hurt. Or in shock — '

'I'm fine, Jack.'

'Promise me you'll see a doctor. Just in case.'

She swung round to face him. 'I don't think so. Because he'd tell me off, you see.'

'Tell you off?'

'Pregnant women aren't supposed to ride, are they?'

His mind went numb; the sun hurt his eyes.

'I'm expecting a baby,' she said defiantly. 'Will's baby. So that's another reason I won't be seeing you any more. Because I'm pregnant, Jack.'

★ ★ ★

After Julia had gone, he went to the cottage and poured himself a large whisky. The alcohol, however, failed to blur his thoughts. They persisted, with dark, accusing clarity.

Julia was pregnant with Will's child. His dead brother's child. The brother whom, in trouble, he had failed to help. The brother he had willed to fail.

Quick to condemn, he had been unable to forgive Will for marrying the woman he loved. From that, everything else had stemmed. Now, looking back over the events of the past two years, Jack found that it was himself that he was unable to forgive. Blessed with strength and energy and good health, he should have protected his weaker younger brother. Instead, with an impressive flair for destructiveness, he had kept his distance, allowing Will to sink deeper and deeper into the mire. Part of him, he acknowledged, had always looked down on Will. With quick, harsh judgement he had long ago noted and been contemptuous of Will's overactive imagination, his need for reassurance. Will's vulnerability had endeared him to many; years ago, it had angered Jack that the brother who seemed to him both feeble and flawed was effortlessly able to draw to himself the greater love.

He poured another whisky. Though he closed his eyes, he could not shut out the images that raced through his mind. Will, his trusting nature exploited by Maurice Chancellor, out of his depth, running a business that had been doomed to failure from the start. Will desperately trying to keep himself afloat. Will, too frightened and ashamed to confide his troubles to anyone.

And if he had confided, then what would he, Jack, have done? Would he have sympathized and offered money or practical help? Or would he have rejoiced in Will's downfall? Jack shivered. He had wanted Will's marriage to fail. Would he have cared two pins about the collapse of Will's business?

He had not merely failed to help Will, he had magnified his difficulties. When Will had needed support, he had offered only hostility. While Will's business had been sinking deeper and deeper into debt, he, Jack, had been trying to seduce Julia. He had pursued her tirelessly and deliberately. He had disregarded her scruples, had used every trick in the book to try to take her from his brother. He had capitalized on Will's abstractedness and inattention, and had taken advantage of her loneliness. He had been vengeful and self-centred. He had tried to hurt Will in the worst possible way.

Everything that had happened had sprung from that week in 1946 when he had been demobbed. He had looked across Missencourt's lawn and he had seen Will and Julia. And the jealousy that childhood had sown — his old conviction that Will was more loved than he

— had flowered. Those sour, poisonous blooms had blighted all their lives. He had distrusted the two people to whom he should have extended his confidence and protection, and he had let that distrust harden to hatred. He could offer no justification for his treatment of Will. His own lack of faith had led to his rejection of Julia. Carrie's remark would not have had the power to hurt if he had not already doubted Julia. And though, looking back, he could see how the years of war had marked him, that, too, offered him no real mitigation. If now he could see that much of the anger and resentment that had accompanied his return to England had been the product of fear — fear that he might have been forgotten, fear that there would no longer be a role for him — that did not excuse his behaviour. He had been jealous and he had been obsessed, both with Julia and with Sixfields. He had believed that Will had stolen what had belonged to him. Will had been the casualty of his obsession and of his covetousness.

The bitter taste of self-disgust mingled with the whisky. He recalled Julia's curse. *I hope you hate Sixfields*, she had said. *I hope it makes you miserable. I hope it makes you lonely and miserable and mad like your Cousin Carrie*. Well, he was certainly miserable. And lonely. He had lost Will and he had lost Julia. And, somewhere in the course of the past two years, he had also lost his self-respect. Carrie, and his own venality, had taken that from him. His greed had made him a prisoner of her capriciousness and manipulativeness. His longing for this house, this land, had distorted his vision. As Julia herself had once said to him, he had sold his soul. If he was not yet as mad as Cousin Carrie, then he glimpsed attributes in himself that might, in time, make him so. A desire for privacy that could lead to reclusiveness. A distance from his fellow man that might end in misanthropy. And an insecurity that could easily, in time, become miserliness.

Sixfields had brought him to this, so the solution was simple. He must leave Sixfields. He had known that for weeks, for months. Since Will's death, he had known that he must offer penance, must somehow seek redemption. Cradling the glass, Jack stared out of the window at the land he loved. Odd, he thought, how he could still feel so much for the swell of the earth, the rise of a hill. Autumn was on the turn, a sharp wind blowing flurries of dead leaves from the trees. A couple more weeks and the bare black branches would lie like pen strokes against a darkening sky. And he would not be here to scent in the air the sharp, exhilarating first frosts, or to see the translucent silver ice lying between the furrows.

★ ★ ★

The following day he went to see his mother. After he had finished telling her why he had come, Prudence said, 'I am to lose *both* my sons?' The expression in her eyes, a mixture of horror and anger, which had been there since Will's death, persisted.

Jack said, 'I need to go away for a while. But I'll come home, I promise. And I'll phone and I'll write.'

The look in her eyes was unaltered. 'Is it because of Julia?'

He said simply, 'I need to get out of her life.'

There was a silence. She was making an apple pie; with a knife she trimmed excess pastry from the lid. Hack, hack, hack: the shreds of pastry fell to the table.

'Have you told Carrie?'

'Yesterday.'

'How did she take it?'

Jack's recollection of the unpleasant little scene was vivid. Carrie had screamed at him. *If you think I'll wait for you — if you think your name will still be on my will when you come home, then you're mistaken!*

301

'I wasn't sure she'd care,' he said. 'I thought I'd been a disappointment to her these past years. But she was — upset.'

Prudence put down the knife. Then she said, 'The thing that I can't bear, Jack — the thing that makes me so angry — is when I remember all the years I waited for you. All the years I prayed for you. All the years I lay awake in the dark, thinking of you, afraid for you. And then, after you'd come home safely, for *Will* to die like that . . . to be killed by a mine . . . taken by the war, after it was all over . . . ' She covered her face with her floury hands, and wept.

★ ★ ★

Until, watching from an upstairs window, she saw his figure, distorted by knapsack and suitcase, diminish against the grey of the road, Carrie did not believe that Jack would go. The money would hold him back, she had told herself. Sixfields would hold him back. When Jack was out of sight, she turned aside and limped downstairs. Though she did not allow his leaving to alter her routine, a dull heaviness hung over the day. It mystified her why the land and the house, with all her familiar possessions, should fail to give her comfort.

As the days passed, though, unredeemed and empty, she began to understand. She had allowed herself to become attached to him. To Jack Chancellor. *Such a fool*, she thought. Her stick tapped against the cobbles as Carrie moved around the house and the farmyard.

Such a fool to make the same mistake twice.

★ ★ ★

Julia didn't weep when Jack went away. She knew that she had lost both of them now, Jack and Will, her oldest

302

friends, but her eyes remained dry and tearless as they had since the memorial service.

Instead she began to pack. Marius found her trawling through Missencourt, gathering her belongings.

'I'm going back to Hidcote Cottage,' Julia told him, as she picked out handkerchiefs and stockings from the linen cupboard.

'Are you sure?'

She threw him a smile. 'It'll be more peaceful. The nursery school. The *noise*!'

'I am always glad', he admitted, 'to escape to work in the mornings.'

She was pairing stockings. He asked, 'How will you manage?'

'I thought I'd get a part-time job. In a shop, perhaps.' She dropped the stockings in neat balls into a wicker basket. 'I have to do something, Marius,' she said bluntly. 'I need the money. I won't be *dependent*. I should hate that.'

He said, 'Why don't you come back to Temperley's?', and she stared at him.

'Are you serious?'

'Perfectly. We could do with someone and you know the ropes.'

She was clutching a crumpled linen blouse in her hands. 'You're not just being kind?'

He shook his head. 'I've been thinking of reopening the London office for some time. If you were at Great Missen, it would free me to spend a couple of days each week in London.'

She leaned against the radiator. The late afternoon sunlight streamed through the open window, touching the back of her neck, warming her. 'I'd love to, Marius. I'd really love to. But — ', she looked down at her smock, 'the baby — '

'You know that Mother's longing to have a grandchild to fuss over. I'm sure she'll be only too delighted to help out. See how it works out. See whether you enjoy it.'

But she knew that she would. For the first time since Will's death, she felt a stirring of optimism. She glanced out of the window. Suzanne was strolling around the lawn, collecting toys. She said, 'When you and Suzanne were first married, you didn't always get on, did you?'

He gave a wry smile. 'You could put it like that.'

'Did you quarrel?'

'Not often. It was more that we were married, but we were still living separate lives.'

'But you're fine now, aren't you?'

When he did not reply immediately, she looked at him, surprised. He had come to stand beside her; he was looking out of the window. She saw how his gaze clung to Suzanne as she moved around the garden.

'You see', she explained, 'I thought it was going to get better. Me and Will. Like you and Suzanne. I meant to try to make it better. Now I can't, can I?'

He said brusquely, 'Marriage isn't always easy. It's supposed to be bliss, isn't it, particularly at first. But I don't suppose it always is. You didn't have time to make it work. You did your best, Julia.'

'No, I didn't. That's the thing.' She was twisting her hands together. 'I was seeing Jack, Marius.' She repeated, so that there was no room for misunderstanding, 'When I was married to Will I was seeing Jack. We weren't having an affair. It hadn't gone that far. But it would have, in time.' She had to tell someone, and of all people, Marius knew her best. She waited, wondering whether he would condemn her, judge her.

But he said, 'People don't always love each other in the same quantity. You can't *force* love. Sometimes it just doesn't come.'

There was a bitterness in his voice that shocked her. He moved away from the window; she saw that Suzanne had gone out of sight. She wondered whether to ask him more, but knew almost immediately that Marius's pride, and his need for privacy, equalled hers. The Temperleys didn't believe in baring their souls, she thought. They licked their wounds alone, while showing to the world a composure that some mistook for coldness. So she said, 'Anyway, that's why I'm glad about the baby. I didn't want it at first — I thought it was a dirty trick, to lose Will and be landed with a baby — but then I realized that it might let me make things up a little to Will.' She added fiercely, 'I'm going to be a good mother, Marius. I'm going to get *that* right.'

He smiled. 'What do you want, a boy or a girl?'

She thought of the boisterous little boys in Suzanne's nursery school and gave a small shudder. 'A girl,' she said firmly. She imagined her daughter, fragile and blonde and blue-eyed, like Will. 'A sweet, quiet, little girl.'

★   ★   ★

In the weeks immediately following Will's death Topaz sometimes thought she saw him. She'd glimpse a flash of yellow hair on the platform as the Tube train drew to a halt and she'd leap from her seat, escaping the carriage at some unfamiliar, unwanted station. Or, waiting at a bus stop in Tottenham Court Road, she'd catch sight of a passer-by whose tentative, loping gait seemed suddenly familiar, and she'd dash through the traffic to the far side of the road while horns blared and taxi drivers waved their fists. Only to lose him in the crowds, or to find that it was not Will, but a stranger, who did not even bear much of a resemblance to him.

One evening she was at the cinema when she thought she saw him. How reasonable it seemed just then that Will Chancellor, who had died six weeks earlier, should be watching a film in Leicester Square. Will, after all, had always liked thrillers. She squeezed down the long column of seats, tripping over bags and umbrellas, murmuring apologies. But, running down the aisle, calling his name, the fair head turned towards her, and she saw the young, scarred, disfigured face. Ex-RAF, she guessed, later. Burned in his plane in a tangle of distorted metal and parachute silk.

Charlie found her sitting on the steps outside the cinema. *I thought it was him*, she said, pressing her hands against her wet face. Then, because she had to tell someone, and because Charlie was not, after all, *family*, she told him about the conversation she had had with Will that afternoon at Hernscombe Cove. Will had told her that he was in trouble. That he wanted to run away, to start again. To become someone new.

The accident happened two days later, she explained. Just two days. And they never found a body. Half a dozen witnesses had seen the three men leave the Holly Bush together; Will's car had later been discovered abandoned by the harbour. But no *body*, Charlie. Nothing to lay to rest, nothing to bury. Just a memorial service that had seemed little more than an empty gesture, lacking in focus or catharsis. But so *strange*, she said, anticipating Charlie's agreement. So strange for Will to disappear just after he'd said those things to her.

Her words tailed off, seeing the expression on his face. He put his arm around her. He told her about an incident that had taken place during the war, when he had been stationed in Scotland. A munitions dump had caught fire during an exercise and there had been a massive explosion. Half a dozen men had died. A detachment of soldiers, including Charlie, had been sent to clear up. There had been little left of the men who had been standing nearest the munitions, he explained. Just — fragments. There were no bodies to bury because there weren't any bodies left. The mine the *Katie Rose* had struck would have been large, designed to penetrate the armour of a destroyer. No one could possibly have survived such an impact.

Topaz knew Charlie was telling her this because he believed that it was kinder to snuff out false hope, and because he believed that her doubts were born of a reluctance to acknowledge her loss. So she tried to think of Will as dust on the surface of the sea, floating down through the waves to mingle with shells, coral, sand. As the months passed, her apparitions retreated and she no longer turned to look at every fair-haired young man. Though a small kernel of doubt remained, niggling like grit in an oyster shell, she no longer voiced her doubts. They had begun to embarrass her; she saw them as others did — as, at best, a naive optimism, and at worst a morbid inability to accept the truth.

Sometimes, though, waking in the night, her heart would turn over, thinking of Will. As a schoolboy, ink on his fingers, scribbling car numberplates into a notebook. At the wheel of the car, after her seven years' absence, waving to her as he kept pace with the train. Or standing in that hinterland between shore and sea: *Actually, I'm in a bit of a mess.* What had he done? What had he believed he had done? Had she said the wrong thing? Had she said too little, or too much? The memory haunted her.

She made herself concentrate on day-to-day matters. On her new job, working in a restaurant in Ladbroke Grove, and on Charlie, whose life had begun to change. In the summer, at the theatre in Bournemouth (the papier mâché toadstool and Sylvia, drunk among the bean bags), someone had seen him, someone influential. On the strength of his performance, Charlie had been offered a role in a production of *Journey's End* in a theatre in Hampstead. It wasn't, he explained to Topaz, his eyes bright with excitement, the sort of rep he was accustomed to. No twice-nightly performances, no non-existent profits divided between a disorganized troupe of drama students and has-beens. No collapsing scenery or drunken actors. Everyone was professional, ambitious, perfectionist.

The play was a success and Charlie was offered a permanent place in the company. Vistas opened out to him, new possibilities and paths. Good fortune changed Charlie, giving him confidence, lessening the self-doubt Topaz had often glimpsed in him. She took pleasure in his happiness, delighted that he had, at last, what he wanted. She let herself be carried along on the wave of his success, accompanying him to parties and dinners, or making love with him in the privacy of his new flat in Finsbury Park. He had waited long enough for his lucky break and she wouldn't tarnish his sudden optimism with her lingering grief.

They saw little of their old acquaintances from the cafe in Leicester Square. Jerry had taken up a teaching post in Basingstoke. The one time Charlie and Donald had crossed paths since Helena's suicide attempt they had almost come to blows. After leaving the hospital it had been a condition of Helena's probation that she stay with her parents in Maidstone. Topaz visited her once a month. It was, she thought, like watching someone trying to climb out of a very deep well. Every so often Helena would reach out a hand to the light, and then she'd slip back, and begin again the long, tortuous haul out of the darkness.

Along with success, Charlie had acquired new friends. Glamorous friends, sophisticated friends. These friends did not run up copies of dresses from scraps of taffeta; instead, labels bearing the name of the House of Dior snuggled inside the collars of their frocks. She and Charlie no longer went to smoky jazz clubs or watched French films in chilly church halls. They met their new acquaintances in smart little restaurants and fashionable Chelsea pubs. They no longer had to gatecrash parties, they were invited to them.

Charlie's new friends were actors, journalists,

dancers, models, socialites. They formed a little clique of their own, excluding the too old, the too obvious, the too poor, the too plain. They were good-looking, witty and amusing. They adored Charlie and Charlie adored them. The women reminded Topaz of a particular type of girl she remembered from school. Pretty, clever, confident, rebellious. The sort of girl who never doubted for a moment that the world was at her feet. With slender, fluttering fingers they issued vague invitations to suppers and cocktail parties. *Bring someone*, they'd say. *Bring a friend, a girlfriend, a fiancée. Bring that girl who makes us laugh. Bring Topaz.* That they struggled to classify her was, she thought, hardly surprising. It wasn't as though she herself was completely sure what she was to Charlie.

Often she did not see him for days at a time. Late nights, rehearsals, evening and matinee performances filled up his week. It was better that way, she told herself briskly, better than living in each other's pockets. Better not to be dependent on each other, not to be the sort of girl who moped at home, doing her nails and washing her hair on the nights her boyfriend was busy. Once, though, she found herself staring into the mirror, wondering whether things would have been different if *she'd* been different. Imagining her face hollow, high-boned, beautiful. Flattening her unruly hair, picturing it smooth and sleek against her shoulders. Blurring her gaze, making her eyes bigger, her mouth fuller, her nose straighter.

She loved her work at the restaurant, though; she wondered why she hadn't thought of it before. All those dreadful offices, where her clumsy fingers had stabbed at typewriter keys instead of cutting, peeling, whisking, as they were meant to do. Her duties included waitressing as well as helping in the kitchen. The restaurant was owned by and named after a Frenchwoman called Angelique. Angelique had married an English soldier in 1940, fleeing with him from Dunkirk after France had fallen. Angelique despised English cooking, and was contemptuous of the pathetic offerings of London butchers and wholesalers, sneaking food to England by circuitous means from her family's farm in France: gleaming dark aubergines, spiky bluish-grey artichokes, peppers as red as rubies, and pale haricot beans. Some of the fruit and vegetables Topaz had never seen before, others were a distant childhood memory. Angelique taught her to make a silky-smooth béchamel sauce and a puff pastry that melted in the mouth, a sweet and caramelized onion soup and *îles flottantes* whose meringue boats quivered on a pale yellow custard sea.

She got to know the regulars at the restaurant. The lunchtime customers were teachers, office workers, medical students from the nearby hospitals. Serious people, who read textbooks or scientific journals while drinking their vichyssoise or eating their *croque monsieur*. The evening diners brought their wives, pleasant women in shabby clothes that had once been good. They sympathized with Topaz about all the standing and running and fetching. Their husbands reminisced about holidays in France before the war. *Do you remember*, they'd say, *that little* pension *in the Loire? The vineyards and the fields of sunflowers. And the golden-pink light in the evenings.*

Her mother, who was between admirers, complained about the length of time Topaz spent at the restaurant. *My daughter*, she'd say, with a downward twist to the mouth, *a waitress.* Topaz placated her by spending the occasional afternoon playing bridge with her mother's bored, disappointed friends. Will's death, and her mother's reaction to it, had brought home to her with particular clarity her mother's emotional emptiness, the absence of feeling that extended to her own life as well as to everyone else's. Which didn't quite make it all right, didn't stop Topaz craving the occasional endearment, or one of those rare indications of shared feeling. Nor could she completely abandon her need for love and approval, or rid herself of the suspicion that the lack of those things pointed to some failing in her. But she had learned to stand back a little, not to expect too much, not to put too much weight on either sympathy or disapproval. She was growing up, she supposed.

Part Three

Breaking the Spell

1950–1951

12

In the spring of 1950 Topaz, turning twenty-one, inherited a sum of money left to her by her father. She thought of spending it on a cookery course at one of the London schools, and confided the idea to Angelique, who was dismissive. Cookery schools taught girls to make moulds of vegetables in aspic or fussy desserts topped with glacé cherries and whipped cream. If Topaz wanted to improve her cooking, then she must stay with Angelique's mother, in France.

She spent six weeks at Angelique's mother's farm near Chinon, in the Loire valley. Those weeks were a revelation. She visited markets where bundles of herbs — oregano, sage and thyme — perfumed the warm air, and where shiny purple aubergines and glistening green and red peppers and plaits of plump white garlic were heaped on stalls like smears of paint on an artist's palette. Where ducks and chickens squawked in wire cages, and green, black and brown olives and tiny salty anchovies curled like jewels in terracotta pots. After ten years of rationing and austerity, the sights, the tastes and smells, almost overwhelmed her, making her lightheaded and dizzy. She felt as though she was sampling something magical, something forbidden.

Madame Caillot taught her to make soups and quiches. Topaz learned to simmer veal bones for stock, to make *brandades* of salt cod and omelettes with field mushrooms. To cook langoustines in garlic and butter, and to stew mussels in cream. In the afternoons she explored the lovely, sun-touched countryside where, centuries before, the French kings had lived. She visited châteaux whose slender, silvery pinnacles seemed to touch the sky and whose impossibly narrow bridges darted over cool, moated water. In the heat of the afternoon, the pools and rivers seemed to still, dark and fathomless, and the pennants on the flagpoles drooped sleepily in the windless air. She'd sit in the shade, writing letters, or increasingly, as the weeks passed, doing nothing, just revelling in the heat of the sun on her skin and the scent of grass and warm earth.

London seemed grey, dusty and busy when she returned. Her mother commented on her freckles; in bed with him in the afternoon, Charlie kissed them one by one. Lazy sunshine trickled through the slats of the Venetian blinds and, if she closed her eyes, she could almost imagine herself in France again. They should go abroad together, she said to Charlie, and he smiled and found another freckle to kiss. She pictured herself travelling through France with Charlie. Dining in cool, dark little restaurants, stopping for picnics beside green, reedy rivers. They had never, she reminded him, taken a holiday together. *Of course*, he murmured. As soon as he could fit it in.

They spent weekends that summer staying with Charlie's friends. They had lovely homes, these newest friends of Charlie's: Edwardian villas in East Dean and Hendon, ancient cottages in the Cotswolds and on the Sussex Downs. The houses were owned by David, who made films, by Celia, who knew the Oliviers, by Jennifer Audley, who, fair-haired and stick-thin, was the leading lady of the moment. Topaz saw how Charlie altered in the company of these people, adopting their brittle wit, their insouciance, their carelessness of other peoples' feelings. How he censored his past, bending and reshaping it to meet their approval. How he reinvented himself for them, so that sometimes, in their company, she found it hard to recognize him.

And yet, when they were alone together, he was still her Charlie. In the grey twilight she'd wake and watch him as he slept, tracing his familiar features: his high

316

cheekbones, his straight, narrow nose, and deep-lidded eyes. He'd turn in his sleep and wrap his arms around her, their bodies folding perfectly together, the rise and fall of their breath matching. *This* was the real Charlie, she reassured herself, the Charlie who, waking in the morning, gathered her to him, his eyes filled with dreamy pleasure.

In September they stayed for a weekend at a house in Lewes. In the afternoon Charlie explained that he needed a couple of hours ('Theatrical business — so dull'), so Topaz wandered by herself around the town, exploring bookshops and antiques shops. Returning to the house she saw, through a side gate, Charlie and Jennifer Audley, walking through the garden. She stood for a moment, watching. Jennifer's silver-fair hair flicked in the breeze and her hand threaded through Charlie's arm. As Topaz watched, the sun slipped behind a cloud and a gust of wind blew the first leaves from a walnut tree. The image remained with her as summer drifted into autumn: the woman's fingers curled around Charlie's sleeve, and a flurry of dead leaves on the grass.

★ ★ ★

One day a friend asked her to cook for a supper party. Topaz agreed, with some trepidation. There were to be four couples, and the hostess would supply the wine and the coffee. Because there was still rationing, and because, in her least confident moments, she had awful visions of collapsed soufflés and burnt pastry, she kept the menu simple. She made the parsnip soup and the lemon tart beforehand — she had to have two attempts at the parsnip soup because one of her mother's friends phoned while it was simmering, and the milk scalded. For the main course she cooked Dover sole, sauté potatoes and green beans, all fairly foolproof. In the unfamiliar kitchen, juggling pots and pans on a cranky gas cooker, she felt a rush of nervousness. What if she forgot to salt the potatoes? What if the beans were stringy? She had written a detailed timetable and had checked her ingredients twice, but nevertheless there seemed to be a great deal of scope for disaster.

One of the fish fell apart in the frying pan and the beans were slightly overcooked, but none of the guests seemed to notice. The host complimented her and two of the guests asked her for her phone number, so that they could engage her to cook for them. Clearing up the kitchen, she felt exhausted but elated.

Afterwards, the business seemed to grow of its own volition. One of the guests at that first supper party engaged her to cook for a small pre-theatre buffet. Then, somehow, Charlie's friends, Charlie's wealthy, busy friends, heard that she cooked. *Just a little supper,* they'd say, coaxing her to find a date in her diary. Or, *A cold buffet lunch, darling, nothing too elaborate.*

She learned to put together a balanced menu; she learned which dishes could be successfully prepared beforehand and which had to be cooked in a flurry of activity on the night. There were disasters, of course. There was the time the custard for the *îles flottantes* curdled and she had to rush out to find a late-night corner shop that sold cream. There was the time her hostess's cat got at the baked salmon and she had to disguise the ruins with slices of cucumber and lemon. And there was the time that the host, who had had far too much to drink, seemed to assume that she came with the dinner, and chased her around the kitchen until she drove him away with a rolling pin.

Exploring previously unvisited parts of London, Topaz discovered a shop in Soho which stocked terracotta kitchenware and the copper pans that both Angelique and Mme Caillot used. Another shop sold food imported from the Continent: courgettes, lemons, olive oil, fresh pasta, and almonds. Often Charlie would drive her and her bags and her boxes in his old Riley to the houses where the dinner parties were to be held. Afterwards, he would go on to the theatre, sometimes returning several hours later to pick her up. He'd be fizzing with reaction if the performance had gone well, furiously gloomy if it hadn't. They'd share the leftovers; Topaz suddenly, ravenously hungry, Charlie too restless to do much more than pick at the fragments of beef Wellington and chocolate mousse.

Her mother began to complain about the smell of garlic and the clutter of pans in the kitchen. In her coffee break at Angelique's restaurant, Topaz ran her fingertip down the *Evening Standard*'s To Let column. On her free afternoons she tramped around tiny bedsits in Earls Court and smart flats in Highgate. She was shown round immaculate Formica kitchens that reminded her of school laboratories, and grim Victorian bathrooms with claw-footed tubs and menacing geysers. She peered into cupboards and under sinks, and into dank back yards and luxuriant roof gardens. In one of the flats cobwebs were slung from lightbulb to windowsill, and the floors almost blotted out by drifts of old newspapers. In another there wasn't a speck of dust and she could see her reflection in the polished floor. Nowhere was quite right. She sensed the letting agents were growing impatient with her. She was looking for something particular, she supposed. She was looking for a home.

★　★　★

Exhausted and always surrounded by chaos, Julia sometimes found herself remembering the conversation she had had with Marius. The conversation in which she had said (the recollection embarrassed her), she was going to have a sweet, quiet, little girl. Well, she hadn't had a sweet, quiet, little girl, she'd had William. Almost nine pounds at birth, he hadn't slept through the night till he was four months old, and even after that remarkable event, William's night always ended at half-past five in the morning, when he opened his mouth and bawled, something he had done rather a lot in the eighteen months since his birth.

The first few months of William's life had passed in a stew of exhaustion. She hadn't known it was possible to be so tired; hadn't known that she — bright, competent Julia Chancellor — could be reduced to a quivering weepy heap who didn't notice till midday that she'd put on her jersey inside out, or that for some mystifying reason she had left her house keys in the soap dish. Then, when at six months old William, screaming with frustration and fury, began to haul himself across the floor in pursuit of some gorgeous and invariably lethal object, a whole new layer of anxieties was added to the constant worry that seemed to Julia the most prominent feature of motherhood. She dreaded that William would put his fingers in the socket and electrocute himself, or that he would pull at the flex of the lamp and bring it down on his head, fracturing his skull. Or that he would worm determined little fingers around the door of the cupboard under the sink, and poison himself by drinking the contents of the bleach bottle. He was always bruised, scratched, bumped. Out shopping, she'd exchange pleasantries with the mothers of dear little girl babies; the dear little girl babies would have brushed blonde curls, perfect, unmarked, rosy-cheeked complexions, and clean pink and white frocks. Julia's William would have a row of purple and yellow bruises along his forehead, scabs on his knees, and a tear in his sleeve where he had taken a tumble that morning. He'd probably be trying to pull the dear little girl's curls.

Another of her pre-William resolutions had been to be a good mother. It was, she had believed, the only way she could make things up to Will. But did good mothers

320

sigh with relief on the mornings they woke up and remembered that it was one of their days to work at Temperley's? Did good mothers feel a weight fall off their shoulders when they handed their only son into the care of one of his grandmothers? Did they stop the car for a few minutes on the short drive from Missencourt to the workshop and sit back, closing their eyes, drinking in the silence, the peace?

And yet, and yet. She worshipped him, of course. He was the apple of her eye, the centre of her universe. She loved his speedwell blue eyes and his yellow hair, both inherited from his father. She delighted in the robust maleness of him, in his physical prowess, in his ability to roll over, to sit up, to crawl and walk long before any of the baby books said that he should. Secretly, she even admired his stubbornness and his refusal to compromise, recognizing something of herself in this whirlwind of a child. A part of her, even when she was so tired she could no longer think straight, knew that she might have been bored by a good, quiet baby. A part of her longed for half a dozen more sons; a part of her knew that nothing would ever equal her love for William.

Oh yes, *love*. A disastrous marriage and an unconsummated love affair behind her, Julia had thought she knew about love. Yet none of her passions — not for her father, nor for Will, not even for Jack — had been as raw, as painfully and gloriously intense as the love she felt for William. Love had been instant and instinctive: the midwife had put him in her arms and she had looked at him, and that was that, bound for life. His tears seared her heart, his laughter guaranteed her happiness. She would, if necessary, have lied for him, stolen for him, killed for him. At the worst times — when he knocked himself out, trying to climb on to the dresser, and had to be rushed to hospital, or when, at eighteen months old, he caught measles and ran a high temperature — she found herself gazing into a black pit and knowing with bleak certainty that she simply wouldn't survive anything bad happening to William. Knowing that if she lost him, she would lose also the best part of herself, that she was in thrall to her tempestuous son, that he had stolen her heart and would hold it to ransom for the rest of her days.

She had moved from Hidcote Cottage to Longridge when William was three months old. Hidcote Cottage simply wasn't a practical place in which to bring up a child: pram wheels jammed in the muddy track and the isolation frightened her, when, in those early days, she had little confidence in her own ability to care for a baby. She left the house with mixed feelings, relieved to escape the temperamental coal stove and outside lavatory, yet aware that, in abandoning her marital home, she was losing a little bit more of Will. Memories of him assailed her as she left the cottage for the last time: Will walking up the path to the cottage, his torch bobbing like a beacon in the night; Will and herself, curled on the sofa in the depths of that first, terrible winter, watching the snow fall. Her later memories, of dissent and betrayal and, finally, absence and death, she tried not to dwell on.

Now she rented a small, detached house at the edge of Longridge. There were two bedrooms, a sitting room, a kitchen and (bliss) an upstairs, plumbed-in bathroom. There was a garden for William to play in and a pathway on which Julia could park the old Aston Martin that her father-in-law had kindly lent her. The house wasn't the least bit grand and could have fitted into Missencourt several times. The decor was old-fashioned and well worn, and became, as the months passed, adorned with small, muddy handprints and wax crayon scribbles. The furniture was similarly shabby: Missencourt's leftovers, looking too big in the small rooms.

Yet she was happy, as much as she was capable these

days of happiness. Her emotions drifted between anxiety, contentment and exhaustion, exhaustion generally being uppermost. On fine days, in the hope of wearing him out, Julia took William for walks along the footpath that traced the brow of the hill. While William was pulling up fistfuls of grass and harebells, or jumping in chalky, cafe-au-lait puddles, Julia would shade her eyes and look across the valley. In the distance, she could see Sixfields, massive and brooding, almost hidden by the folds of the green and gold hills.

Though, for William's sake, she tried to fit into the village, she knew that she never did, quite. Most of the other young mothers were the wives of farmhands and labourers, and viewed Julia, with her smart accent and her family at the big house, with a mixture of unease and awe. That she went out to work, that she drove a car and wore a fur coat (even though it was forty years old and moth-eaten) distanced her further from these pleasant, cheerful wives and mothers. She sensed that she threatened their domesticity, that she challenged the relief with which they had slipped back into the routines of home and family after the war. Though they accepted her invitations to bring their little boys to play with William, she knew that she was excluded from the casual meetings, their coffee mornings and cups of tea. She heard them sometimes in the summer as she walked to the shops, heard the peals of laughter from the gardens, and the confidences and female intimacies.

She didn't quite fit in at work, either. Something had changed since the war; the easy acceptance that she had then experienced, stepping into her dead father's and absent brother's shoes, had vanished. Then she had been a heroine; now she was an oddity. During the war many of the technicians had been women, taking their absent husbands' places. Now the workshop was entirely staffed by men. Julia had learned to endure small humiliations: the telephone callers who assumed she was Marius's secretary, the salesmen who patted her bottom and asked to see the boss. Other incidents clawed at some deeper part of her. The crude sexual insults thrown at her when she had to sack a technician for persistent lateness. The women packers she overheard gossiping in the ladies' washroom: *That poor little boy — his father dead, and his mother leaves the poor mite so she can come here. It isn't right, is it?* Julia had remained where she was after the women had gone, struggling to stem the tears, wondering whether they had been right, wondering whether she was neglecting William. In the cramped little cubicle that smelt of Lifebuoy soap and Jeyes Fluid, she looked soberly at the choices she had made and wondered whether she was, indeed, hurting the person she loved most in the world.

Since he had left Dorset two years ago, Julia had followed Jack's progress through the letters he had written to Prudence. She knew that he was living in Canada, in Saskatchewan, where he was working on a farm. Julia's only direct contact with Jack had been a parcel that had arrived a few weeks after William's birth. The parcel had contained a splendid teddy bear for William, and a china horse — black, like Salem — for her. There had been no note, but it was a sort of truce, she supposed. The teddy bear had become a favourite of William's; it was no longer splendid, though, its golden fur was now grey and matted from being dragged through puddles and dunked in the bath. As for the horse, it sat on the mantelpiece, a reminder of a different, more careless Julia. She hadn't ridden since the day Salem had thrown her. Motherhood had changed her; now she was watchful of herself as well as of her child. For William's sake, she knew she must take care of herself. Lacking a father, she was his sole bulwark against the world.

Once Jack had loved her for her fearlessness. Sometimes she wondered what he would think of her now that she anticipated danger everywhere. Walking to the shops, she held William's reins tightly; driving, she kept her speed down, her eyes watchful and wary. A part of her was relieved that Jack stayed away. All her passion and energy was now concentrated on her son and she often thought that, even if Jack were one day to come home, she would have nothing much to spare for him.

★   ★   ★

Marius showed Suzanne the invitation at the breakfast table. 'Tom and Linda Page,' she read. 'Who are they?'

'Tom was my sergeant in the Signals,' Marius explained. 'I haven't seen him in years. Decent bloke.' The invitation was to a party to celebrate Tom and Linda's tenth wedding anniversary. He said, 'Hell of a slog, all the way to London for a party. We should turn it down, don't you think?'

She did not reply, but there was that look in her eye that always worried him. That expression of carefully concealed desperation.

He said, 'Unless you'd like to go?'

'It might be fun. It seems ages since we went anywhere.'

He made an effort. 'Yes, why not? We could make a weekend of it. Have dinner somewhere decent. You could do some shopping. And it would be good to see Tom again.'

On the weekend of the party they stayed at the small pied-à-terre in Holborn Marius had bought the previous year. They spent the afternoon wandering down Regent Street, looking at the shops before dining at the Savoy. Afterwards they went on to the party.

The Pages lived in Mortlake, in south London. The house was in a red-brick terrace, one of a long row of similar houses. Not far away was the river, slick and black in the night, strands of mist snaking across its surface.

All Tom and Linda's vast extended family seemed to be crammed into the small house. People danced to the music of a scratchy gramophone, their arms and legs flailing. Tom seemed to Marius almost unchanged, just a little stockier and balder. He and Suzanne hit it off instantly. Tom had been born and brought up in Stepney; he and Suzanne had played in the same streets, had attended the same school. His wife, Linda, had for a short time worked in the same greengrocer's shop as Suzanne. When Tom asked her to dance, Suzanne followed him into the melee of bodies in the centre of the room.

In the kitchen someone gave Marius a glass of beer. Eventually he wandered back into the front room. Suzanne was still dancing, but with a different partner. He realized that he had not seen her look so happy in months. How long was it, he asked himself, since they had gone dancing? Years, he thought, unless you counted the stiff little occasion at the Barringtons a few weeks back, where they had shuffled in a restrained way to a stilted tune from two decades ago. Now Suzanne jived and jitterbugged, her skirts swirling, her dark hair escaping from its tight curls. Marius saw how her partner's eyes followed her as she moved about the floor. Half the men in the room were watching her. In spite of the heat of the small, crowded house, he shivered.

He knew that in marrying Suzanne he had taken her away from the life that she knew, to one with which she would never, perhaps, be completely at ease. Thinking it over, he felt exasperated with himself. Earlier in the evening he had taken her to the Savoy, telling himself that he was giving her a treat. Yet it hadn't been a treat for Suzanne, had it? If he himself felt an outsider in this house, marked out by accent and dress and upbringing,

326

then how must Suzanne feel, enclosed with uniformed staff in rooms of hushed grandeur?

Worse, how did she feel at Missencourt, trapped in the countryside she neither responded to nor understood? She never complained, she had made the best of it, adapting to rural life as well as she could, starting up the nursery school to give her an occupation. But would she have thrived better in a different environment? Would she be happier, more fulfilled if she lived in the city she knew and loved?

Yet he could not see that he had had any choice but to remain at Missencourt. Half the population of Great Missen relied on Temperley's Radios for its employment. And it would be an act of cruelty to leave his mother, to separate her from the grandchild she loved. Besides, Adele's health had not been good these past few years. How would she manage that vast old house, that acre of garden?

In marrying him Suzanne had bound herself not only to him, but to a house and to a family. The old fear, the one that was always at the back of his mind, that he usually managed to keep in check, that she might secretly regret the bargain she had made, resurfaced now as he watched her dance. He would never be certain of her, he thought with a pang. There would always be something elusive about her, something that drifted just out of his reach.

Yet afterwards, walking back towards the main road in search of a taxi, she linked her arm through his, and smiled up at him, and said, 'Crumbs, I think I've worn through the soles of my shoes.'

'You enjoyed yourself, didn't you?'

'Brought back my youth. My dancing days.'

'I should take you dancing more often.'

She said, 'Not for a while, Marius.' She was looking away, towards the river, as though reluctant to meet his eyes.

He said hesitantly, 'I know you find Missencourt a bit isolated sometimes — '

'It's all right. And it's perfect for children.'

'Tara loves it, doesn't she?'

She patted her stomach. 'And this one will too, I hope.'

He stopped suddenly in the street. 'Suzanne . . . ?'

'I'm pregnant, Marius.' Her eyes were bright. 'So I'll be hanging up my dancing shoes.'

He said suddenly, anxiously, 'Shouldn't you be resting — taking it easy?'

'*Marius.* Not *yet.* What do you expect me to do? Sit on the sofa for the next seven and a half months? Don't be ridiculous.' She glanced at him. 'Are you pleased?'

'Yes,' he said. He kissed her. 'Oh yes.'

And had to push away the uncomfortable discovery that a small part of his very real pleasure was that this second child would tie her to him, would make him certain of her.

★ ★ ★

A fortnight later he met Topaz for a drink in a pub near the restaurant where she worked.

She was looking for a place of her own, she explained to Marius. She had inherited some money from her father, so she could now afford to. 'And besides', she added, 'my mother doesn't like all my things cluttering up the kitchen, and anyway, I'm twenty-one, so it's about time, isn't it? I went to look at some places this afternoon — I've made a shortlist of six. It's so hard to find anywhere that's just right — the kitchen of one place is nice but the bedroom's perfectly awful, or there's a lovely garden and one of those ridiculous kitchens that's supposed to be a bathroom as well — '

He thought she looked rather tired and fed up. 'I didn't think', he said mildly, 'that was possible.'

She let out a breath. 'I'm afraid it is. You have a wooden cover over the bathtub that's supposed to be a kitchen table too. It doesn't do for either very well, of course.'

He said, 'It might be best to settle for the best you can find. Looking for the perfect thing is often a bit soul-destroying.'

She dug into her pockets, pulling out dog-eared scraps of paper and a pen. 'I tried to make notes, but I got into a muddle because the letting agent was in a hurry. And then there's the electricity.' She made a face. 'Boilers and geysers and things. I don't want one of those awful geysers that nearly explodes every time you put a match to it.'

'Isn't there someone you can ask to help you?'

She said, 'Charlie was supposed to come with me, but he was busy.'

There was a shuttered expression in her eyes. Marius had met Charlie Finch only once. It was not that Charlie had been dislikeable — quite the contrary — but Marius had decided quite quickly that he wasn't good enough for Topaz. A bit of a lightweight. Not a *stayer*. A judgement which, though he had tried to keep it to himself, he suspected he had conveyed quite clearly.

He said, 'How is he, your chap?'

'Charlie's fine.'

He waited for her to say more. When she didn't, he said, 'He's busy just now? Acting?'

'He's in a play at the Drury Lane Theatre. It opens in a couple of weeks. That's why he's so busy. That's why he had to go to the party.' She looked, he thought, thoroughly miserable.

He frowned, looking at her. '*Party?*'

'It's to do with work.'

'But if he was supposed to be helping you — '

'There's no need to look like that,' she said crossly.

'Like what?'

'You know.' Her lower lip was sticking out mulishly.

He shrugged. 'I should have thought Charlie could have made time for you.'

She said proudly, 'I can manage perfectly well by myself.'

'Two heads are better than one — '

'After all, it's only a question of looking at places, finding the nicest one — '

'That's not quite', he said quietly, 'the point.'

There was a silence. She stared down at her glass. He heard her whisper, 'Charlie and me, we have a good time. I'm very happy, Marius.'

He said only, 'Are you?' and her head jerked up.

'I love him.' Her eyes glittered.

'I know you do,' he said gently.

He did not, of course, voice the obvious question. *And Charlie? Does he love you?* But it hung in the air between them. And then, because it seemed kinder to change the subject, he told her about the baby.

'Marius, that's wonderful.'

'Suzanne's been dreadfully ill. Sick every morning.'

'Julia was awfully sick when she was expecting William, remember. But it went away and then she ate absolutely masses.'

'Yes.' He gave a quick smile. 'She's insisting on keeping the nursery school going. I've tried to persuade her to ease off a bit, but you know what she's like.' He delved into the carrier bag beside him. 'I bought some things in Fortnum's and Harrods — grapes, Bath Olivers, ginger cake. I thought she might be able to keep some of them down.'

He saw her give herself a shake, manage a smile. Then she raised her glass. 'To the new baby,' she said.

★ ★ ★

Suzanne said, 'That's the last of them gone,' and Julia, who was scraping jelly off the kitchen floor, sat back on her heels and gave a huge sigh of relief. That afternoon, she had held a tea party for William's friends. Six little boys and girls had run riot while their mothers had attempted to make conversation over tea and sherry.

'I don't know who was worse,' said Julia, 'the children or the mothers. But never again.'

'William enjoyed it.'

'William — ' Julia rinsed the cloth in the sink ' — disgraced himself. I won't hold another tea party till he's sixteen, and civilized.'

Half an hour later Julia gave William his bath and put him to bed. It took a while to get the house back in order, to put away toys and books and mop up the fallout of crumbs beneath the kitchen table. By then it was almost nine o'clock, so she went upstairs for a bath. But the water ran cold after a few minutes, consumed by washing up and the cleaning of both William and the kitchen floor, so she abandoned the idea. Then, turning, glancing into the bathroom mirror, she caught sight of herself and she paused, transfixed. Never vain, the sight of this dishevelled woman, with her stained jersey and slacks, and those peculiar white streaks (Icing sugar? Custard?) in her hair horrified her. *Once I was pretty,* she thought, and horrified herself even more by wanting to cry.

Instead, she went downstairs to the kitchen, where she picked at the leftovers and poured herself a large glass of sherry from the bottle she had bought for the mothers. Then she curled up with a book and the radio on the sitting-room sofa. But, try as she might, the flat, miserable feeling lingered, and eventually had to be faced and dissected. She didn't usually think about how she looked, so why was she so upset now? *Because,* she thought grimly, *I am only twenty-six. Because it's Saturday night and I'm alone. And because, in spite of*

331

William, in spite of Marius and Suzanne and Topaz and all the Chancellors, I'm lonely.

It wasn't, she thought cynically, that she hadn't had opportunities. There had been a weary succession of men who seemed to assume that, husbandless and (presumably) desperate for sex, she must be eternally grateful for their clumsy advances. And more than once, through her work at Temperley's, she had glimpsed in a business acquaintance a look of unmistakable interest. Interest that had faded quickly when Julia, offered a drink at the pub or dinner at a restaurant, had pointed out her need for a babysitter. Julia Chancellor the businesswoman was an attractive proposition; Julia Chancellor the mother rather less so.

For a long time, enclosed in the blissful private circle of their love for each other, she hadn't wanted anything other than William. But recently she had become aware of something missing in her life. A need for adult company and adult diversion. She couldn't remember when she had last done her nails, visited a hairdresser, or worn an evening frock.

Her eye was caught by a small square of white card propped on the mantelpiece. It was from Maurice Chancellor, inviting her to celebrate his silver wedding. She had put off replying, aware of her obligation to Will's relatives, yet disliking Maurice himself. She took the card from the mantelpiece and tapped her fingernail against the edge of it. Dinner and dancing in Hernscombe's best hotel. She hadn't danced for years . . .

*   *   *

All her old evening dresses were hopeless, pre-war and adorned with schoolgirlish frills and bows. When her mother offered to lend her a dress, she accepted thankfully. Going through Adele's wardrobe at Missen-court, silks and satins slipping through her fingers, Julia was taken back to long-ago evenings when her father and mother had gone to Town for a dance or the theatre. Evenings that seemed now impossibly distant and impossibly glamorous: her father tall and handsome in a dinner jacket and silk scarf, her mother beautiful in velvet and pearls.

She chose a light grey satin dress, the colour of her eyes, cut on the bias. The clinging, narrow style was old-fashioned, but it suited Julia, whose figure remained boyish even after William. Adele dug out earrings and a bag and shoes to match, and promised to babysit.

On the night of the dinner-dance, Julia washed and arranged her hair, struggling against her besetting sin, impatience, as her long, fine locks slipped through her nervous fingers. She drove herself to Hernscombe. John and Prudence had offered to take her with them, but she had declined, explaining that she would be happier if she came under her own steam because of William. If there was an emergency, for instance. Privately, she thought that if it was awful and she could bear no more than an hour or so, then she must have a means of escape.

Her edginess increased as she neared the town. Parking in the grounds of the hotel, she almost wished she hadn't come. Almost wished she'd turned down the invitation and had another quiet Saturday night at home, listening to the radio or reading a book. She sat in the Aston Martin, watching guests spill from cars and taxis into the brightly lit foyer. *Pathetic, Julia*, she said to her herself crossly. *You never used to be afraid of anything.* So feeble, to be nervous about a *party*.

As she made her way into the reception room, she couldn't help noticing that she seemed to be the only lone woman there. Every other female was draped on the arm of a dinner-suited man, or had him at least within her sights. She should have dredged up some sort of partner, perhaps. Mentally she ran through the unattached males of her acquaintance: her foreman at Temperley's, the boy who delivered the groceries, the postman. She suppressed a grin. Noticing that people were staring at her, she held her head high and walked slowly and gracefully.

Maurice Chancellor kissed her cheek and let his covetous little eyes run the length of her body. His wife sniffed and said so *brave*, to come on her own, and that she couldn't have possibly. Julia caught sight of Prudence and John across the room, and hastily escaped both Maurice's clammy hand and his wife's censorious glare.

She shared a dinner table with Prudence and John and half a dozen Chancellor cousins and their spouses. She wasn't short of conversation or offers to fetch her drinks. She realized quite quickly that, though the men thought her rather daring, the women disapproved of her. She was supposed to sit at home in her widow's weeds, perhaps, or commit suttee, hurling herself on her husband's funeral pyre. Only poor Will hadn't had a funeral pyre, had he, or anything much else: quickly, Julia turned aside from that thought and drank another glass of wine.

After dinner, during Maurice's speech, which was peppered with off-colour jokes and references to his burgeoning wealth, Julia's attention wandered. Something about the brightness of the women's dresses and the glittering chandeliers in the ballroom made her feel, for the first time in ages, *young*. The music, too, worked its familiar spell. Tapping her foot to the rhythm, slipping into the arms of first one partner, then another, some of the constraints and sadnesses of the last few years fell away and she felt a heady excitement.

Then Maurice Chancellor asked her to dance. He hauled her around the dance floor in much the same way, it seemed, as he hauled the bales of cloth in his shop. He was half a head shorter than Julia, his straight dark hair was Brylcreemed back from his forehead and his red lips slightly parted. Adenoids, Will had always said, before making Julia snigger with his imitation of Maurice's nasal whine.

'Rather a good show,' said Maurice complacently, his mouth brushing against Julia's ear, 'if I say so myself. Of course, the owner of the Imperial is a friend of mine.'

'Is he?' She wanted to yawn, but managed not to.

'You're living in that little place in Longridge, aren't you, Julia? Could do you some curtaining for a good price. Or dress material. Had some lovely taffetas in this week. Bright colours. They'd suit you.'

She said firmly, 'I prefer pastels.'

'Do you? Shame. I'd like to see you in a nice scarlet.'

His hand curved round her buttock; she gave a little wriggle, trying to shake him off, but he clung like a limpet.

'Or an emerald. Emerald would flatter a girl like you.'

A voice said, 'Your wife's looking for you, Maurice.'

Maurice's hand flicked quickly away and his eyes darted across the room. He gave a nervous smile. 'You'll have to pardon me, Julia, but I'm going to have to take my leave, I'm afraid.'

When he was gone, Julia's rescuer said, 'If you don't mind a substitute . . . '

She smiled. 'I think I can just about bear it.'

As they danced, she stole a glance at him. She couldn't immediately make up her mind about him. He was of average height, thick-set, broad-shouldered and neat-featured, with strong, square hands that guided her with a confident, but not proprietorial touch. His eyes were dark and intense; when their gaze caught hers, she looked away. He wasn't handsome, but she sensed a power and strength in him that were not unattractive.

They circled the crowded dance floor. He said, 'Are you related to Maurice? Everyone here seems to be related to Maurice.'

She laughed. 'Only by marriage. And you?'

'I do business with him.'

'What sort of business?'

'Oh . . . a bit of buying and selling.'

She said drily, 'Maurice would sell his own soul if he was offered a good enough price for it. In fact, he was offering himself to me when you appeared.'

His eyes glittered. 'At a bargain price, I hope?'

'It couldn't possibly', she said lightly, 'be sufficiently tempting.'

She was flirting, she realized. Such a long time since she had danced with a man, flirted with a man. She had almost forgotten how.

He glanced round the room. 'It's a good turnout.'

'I suppose so,' she said. She wrinkled up her nose. 'But so *vulgar*.'

'*Vulgar* . . . ' he repeated, as though the idea was new to him. 'Do you think so?'

'The *cake*,' she said, rolling her eyes. 'All that silver leaf. I'm surprised the table didn't collapse.'

He smiled. 'I hadn't thought. A cake's a cake, in my book.'

'And the flowers, so hideous.' Huge vases of gaudy lilies, chrysanthemums and tightly budded hothouse roses were dotted around the room.

'I thought they were rather striking.'

She shook her head. 'Hideous,' she said firmly. 'The band's good, though. And the dinner was lovely.'

She left the party an hour later, having danced every dance and having been made once more aware of something she had almost forgotten: the power of her beauty. She had assumed that after Will, and after William, that part of her life was over.

It was exhilarating to discover it did not have to be so.

Her elation drained away when, starting up the car, the engine refused to ignite. 'Don't you dare,' she muttered out loud, 'don't you dare.' She tried again. The crank seemed unusually stiff; she struggled to turn it. The engine remained obstinately silent. Julia swore.

There were only a few cars left in the car park. Prudence and John had left half an hour earlier. She could phone for a taxi, Julia supposed, but Hernscombe's entire fleet of taxis had probably been commandeered by the other guests. There was the horrible possibility that she might have to throw herself on Maurice Chancellor's mercy.

She climbed out and opened the bonnet. Staring at the engine, she tried to remember all that Will had taught her about cars. She prodded a hose, which left a smear of oil on her hand. Wretched, *wretched* thing, she hissed.

Hearing footsteps behind her, she turned. And saw her dancing partner, the man who had saved her from Maurice.

'She won't start,' she explained.

'Shall I have a go?' He bent over the bonnet. 'Beautiful motor.'

'She belongs to my father-in-law, but he lets me borrow her. She's terribly temperamental, though.'

'These old darlings often are.' He closed the Aston's bonnet and stooped in front of the car to turn the crank. 'It might be the starting handle,' he said. 'The mechanism could be dirty.'

Stars speckled the night sky and the last revellers were stumbling out of the hotel, calling out slurred goodbyes. Julia hugged her coat around herself, cold in the chilly autumn air.

Then the crank swung and the engine spluttered

into life. Julia gave a sigh of relief. 'Thank you so much.' She smiled at him. 'That's twice you've rescued me tonight, Mr — '

'Hunter,' he said. He held out his hand to her. 'Rick Hunter.'

13

Topaz found a second-floor flat in South Kensington. It was Victorian, high-ceilinged, with tall sash windows. The kitchen, which seemed to Topaz the most important room in a house, was twice the size of her mother's kitchen. Long and narrow, it ran the width of the flat and had two large windows overlooking the back garden.

She found a scrubbed oak table in a junk shop, which Angelique's husband lugged up three flights of stairs one afternoon, pausing at every landing to catch his breath. She bought a New World gas stove; she adored it, wiping up specks of sauce the moment they flecked its pristine surface. She painted the walls bright yellow and the cupboard doors French blue, and fixed hooks on to the walls to hang up her copper pans. She put up shelves for the terracotta pots, and arranged her cookery books and her crockery — all of it blue and white, none of it matching — on an old dresser. From the bereted onion-sellers who cycled over from France, she bought wreaths of onions and slung them from a rack suspended from the ceiling.

Her mother, visiting, commented on the bathroom, which was a depressing, damp-encrusted pea-green, and on the draughts that seeped through the cracks around the bedroom windows. She'd get round to them, Topaz explained. She kept to herself her slightly embarrassed knowledge that she didn't particularly care about the bathroom or the bedroom, and that just to walk into her kitchen made her happy.

She loved having her own home. She no longer tensed, fitting her key in the front door, uncertain of her mother's mood. No one told her she made the place look untidy; no one complained about the smell of garlic. No one stubbed out their cigarette ends in her olive dishes or left puddles of gin on the kitchen table. She could go to bed when she liked and get up when she liked. She could spend an hour soaking in the bath and listening to *Family Favourites*, or she could curl up by the fire, reading a novel. She could entertain her friends and afterwards not have to endure criticism of their dress, manners, accent.

Charlie's play was nearing the end of its six-month run. In his tired eyes Topaz witnessed both his battle against the exhaustion that always accompanied the drawing to a close of a long piece of work, and the re-emergence of the ambition that fired his search for the next project. She thought he looked thin, so she made him suppers on her new stove, and fed him pot-roasted chicken at her big oak table. Sometimes she found herself suspecting that he would have eaten, with the same automatic enthusiasm a Spam fritter, a Marmite sandwich, a piece of mousetrap cheese.

They spent a weekend at Jennifer Audley's home in Marlow. Charlie drove them in the new Vauxhall that had replaced his old Riley. Driving through Marlow, he said, 'Might look for a place here myself.'

'Here?'

'Why not?' His eyes darted from one side of the road to the other. 'I'm thirty in a couple of years, Topaz. Can't stay in rented flats for ever. People don't take you seriously if you haven't got the trappings. You have to move on, keep up with the times. If you stop, you lose the race, don't you?'

The garden of the Audleys' house ran down to the banks of the Thames. Weeping willows drooped over the water. The brown, papery heads of Michaelmas daisies and asters rustled in the wind, and a light but incessant rain disrupted the smooth surface of the river.

Topaz found herself remembering the parties she had

attended when she had returned to London in 1946. Adults now replaced the acned youths, cocktails and canapés substituted for lemonade and fairy cakes. Jennifer Audley, ethereal in white wool, took the place of the tweed-suited mothers, directing the proceedings, corralling the guests into sun room and drawing room, demanding they play games, make conversation. The mixture of boredom and terror from the earlier parties was unaltered, only now Topaz's boredom was with the endless theatrical gossip, her terror that she might be required to join in the sing-songs round the piano. There were still charades, frighteningly literary and well acted, still that sense of rivalry, of being permanently on show.

At six o'clock all the guests assembled in the drawing room. Jennifer Audley had settled herself in a large, wing-backed chair, one long, nylon-clad leg drooping gracefully over the other. Her ash-blonde hair was looped into a smooth chignon, and her eyes were a cool blue-grey. Yet there was a tension in her coiled body and in the curve of her lips, like a cat waiting to pounce.

Now she complained, 'I'm *bored*. I want you to amuse me.' A flick of the eyelids. 'I *command* you all to amuse me.'

'God, Jennifer — '

'And you know that I'm easily bored, David, so you'll have to try very hard.'

A large, red-faced man said, 'I could amuse you, but Brian mightn't like it.' Brian was Jennifer's husband.

A ripple of laughter. 'So naughty, Edgar.'

Brian said, 'I've made you a cocktail, Jennifer darling. That'll amuse you, won't it?'

'Of course.' Jennifer's voice was silky smooth. 'I don't expect originality from *everyone*.' Her gaze moved slowly from guest to guest. 'Darlings, are you all bashful? I'd better offer a prize. An incentive. Let's see. For the person who amuses me most . . . a kiss.'

Topaz muttered, 'Oh *Lord*,' and the woman sitting next to her turned, and said softly, 'What? Not thrilled? You're supposed to be thrilled.'

'*Well* — '

Someone called out, 'What if it's one of the girls?'

'I'm not *fussy*, darling,' said Jennifer archly. 'I'm sure I could be the teeniest bit Sapphic if I tried.'

'And now', Topaz's neighbour whispered, 'you're supposed to be shocked.' She smiled at Topaz, and offered her hand. 'I'm Mary Hetherington.'

'Topaz Brooke.'

Mary was sensible looking, her slightly greying brown hair in a neat bun on the back of her head. She said, 'You came with that gorgeous chap, didn't you?'

'Charlie? Yes.'

Charlie was sitting on the carpet, his back resting against Jennifer's chair. Jennifer's hand was flung carelessly over the arm of the chair, an inch from his head. She could not move her eyes, Topaz found, from those pale, pointed, restless fingers.

Jennifer called out, 'Who's going to be first?'

'Just recite a poem, Topaz,' suggested Mary kindly. 'Something you learned at school. Travellers knocking at lonely doors, that sort of thing. Or do what I do and tell her to get knotted.'

Jennifer's guests went through their party tricks. Fortune-telling and mime and horribly expert recitations of verse. When it was Mary Hetherington's turn, she made a vague gesture and said lazily, 'Can't think of a thing, I'm afraid. *Awfully* sad not to qualify for the prize.'

Then Jennifer said, 'I'd forgotten Charlie's little friend. How will you amuse me?'

Topaz's mouth was dry. She couldn't remember a single line of poetry. She had never been able to remember poetry. Jennifer drawled, 'Do you sing? Dance? Tell fortunes?'

She said, without thinking, 'I cook.'

'*Cook?*'

'Yes.' She said firmly, 'It's what I do. It's my talent.'

'Goodness.' Jennifer's eyebrows were curls of disbelief. Her gaze shifted to Charlie, sitting beside her. Now, her fingers dipped down, stroking his hair.

'*You* haven't amused me yet, Charlie.'

'I can't think of anything worthy of you, darling Jennifer.'

'Can't you?' Her fingertips drifted towards his face, tracing its contours, pausing as they reached his lips. 'I'm sure if you *tried . . .*'

The room had become very still. Topaz's heart was pounding. She wanted to slap Jennifer Audley's smooth, pale face; she wanted to leap out of her chair and haul Charlie to his feet and take him away from this horrible house.

Then Jennifer drew her hand away, and said, 'I shall begin to think that you don't care, Charlie. You'll have to find a way to make it up to me.' She seemed to settle on one of the guests at random. 'Edgar. Come here.' Edgar bent his head as he approached Jennifer's armchair and her lips skimmed against his cheek. Then she yawned and said, 'Well, it's almost seven, time to dress, so I must love you and leave you,' and she left the room.

★   ★   ★

Topaz was dressing for dinner when Charlie came into her bedroom. She said, 'That awful *game.*'

He had flung himself full length on to her bed. He was wearing a dinner jacket; his black tie was slung unknotted around his neck. He said, 'I thought it was fun.'

'It was embarrassing. It made me feel stupid.'

'Nonsense.' His head on the pillow, he had closed his

eyes. He said, 'You shouldn't be so self-conscious.'

Afterwards, she thought that she should have let it go at that. Should have lain on the bed beside him in the crook of his arm and not said another word. Instead she said slowly, 'But that's what it was all about, wasn't it? Making us feel self-conscious. Showing us who's in charge.'

Charlie opened his eyes, propping himself up on his elbows. 'Meaning?'

She pulled a brush through her hair. 'Jennifer. She likes people to pay court, doesn't she?'

'That's one way of looking at it.' There was an edge to his voice that should have warned her.

'I can't see another way of looking at it.'

'Can't you?' He was sitting up, watching her. 'How about having fun? Giving people a good time?'

'Well, she certainly made it clear that she was offering you a good time.' The words came out before she could stop them, shrewish, jealous.

She sat down at the dressing table and opened her lipstick. She wanted him to come to her, to kiss her, to tell her that beautiful, blonde Jennifer wasn't important, that she was the only woman that mattered to him.

Instead, he said, 'Oh, grow up, Topaz,' in a tone of voice that made her feel cold inside.

Her hand shook and the lipstick smudged. 'She was flirting with you, Charlie.'

He shrugged. 'It was only a bit of fun.' He ran his fingers through his untidy hair. 'They're our friends, after all.'

'*Your* friends.'

His gaze settled on her, cold and dark. 'They could be yours if you made the effort.'

She scrubbed at her mouth with a tissue. 'I'm not sure I want them to be my friends. I'm not sure we have anything in common.'

'Oh, for heaven's sake — ' He sounded angry.

'They're interesting, talented people. I shouldn't have thought it was too difficult to find common ground.'

She found herself remembering, with sudden, painful nostalgia, the old days in the cafe in Leicester Square. 'I preferred our old friends,' she said slowly. 'I preferred Helena and Mischa and Donald. Even Claudette.'

He made an impatient gesture. 'I don't want to be sitting round in grubby little cafes for the rest of my life, thank you. I want a bit more than that.'

There was a silence. Then she whispered, 'And me? Where do I fit into your ambitions, Charlie?'

He rose, and went to the window, leaning his hands on the sill, looking down at the rain-soaked garden. After a while, he said, 'These are the sort of people I need to know if I'm to get on.' The anger had drained from his voice, leaving him flat and exhausted. 'They *know* people. What I do, it's not just how good you are, how talented you are. It's who you know, where you're seen. And these people — Jen and Brian, David Earnshaw, Edgar White — they are the sort of people I need to know. This sort of place is where I need to be seen. I thought you understood that, Topaz.'

Now she felt ashamed of herself. She rose from the dressing table and went to him, leaning her head against his shoulders, curling her hand into his. He turned to her and took her in his arms. She read his weariness in the pallor of his skin and in the shadows around his eyes.

Stroking his face with the back of her hand, she whispered, 'Your tie . . . ' Carefully, she knotted it.

'Thanks.' He kissed her. 'Never could get the hang of these things.'

His hand slid open the zip at the back of her dress, and his fingertips brushed against her skin. His lips caressed the curve of her throat.

Then, in the distance, a bell sounded. He pulled away from her. 'Hell,' he said. 'Dinner. Are you ready?'

At the table she was separated from him. The food was the sort she loathed, fussed about with, course after course designed for appearance rather than taste. Afterwards there were more drinks and party games, only now she was left to her own devices, excluded from the innermost circle, sidelined to a sofa with Brian and Mary: the dim and the disaffected, she thought, and wondered which category she fell into.

Then they rolled back the carpet and put on the gramophone. Topaz danced, though not with Charlie, because Jennifer danced with Charlie. After a while, when she looked round, she saw that they were no longer there. Her gaze flicked from couple to couple. There was a knot of panic and anger beneath her ribs. Her own voice echoed. *Well, she certainly made it clear she was offering you a good time.* Such an overheated, unattractive emotion, jealousy.

She went upstairs. Looking out of the bedroom window, she saw that someone had opened the French doors. Light spilled out on to the grass. One or two guests had drifted on to the terrace. The moon shifted fitfully between the rainclouds and danced, doubled in the river.

Then she saw them, Charlie and Jennifer, walking along the bank, Jennifer's dress bright in the moonlight. Topaz watched them for a while. Watched Jennifer throw back her head, displaying her slender white throat, and laugh. Watched the narrow black line of Charlie's arm curl around her shoulders.

Watched Charlie bend his head and kiss her. She jerked the curtains shut. She was shivering. Wrapping her arms around herself, trying to still the involuntary movement, she stripped off her clothes and climbed into bed, pulling the eiderdown over her head.

Though she longed for the oblivion of sleep, it would

not come. Images flickered through her head. Slender fingers stroking dark curls. A kiss, in the moonlight. She wondered what he would say, were she to challenge him. *It doesn't matter, Topaz, it wasn't important. Jennifer's just a friend.*

Or, *You have to move on. You can't stand still.*

Charlie was talented, ambitious, determined. He had collected odds and ends from here and there, putting them together to make himself the person he wanted to be. He had replaced his old car with a new one, soon he would buy a house to replace the rented flat. Years ago he had acquired the right accent. She remembered the first time they had met, in the cafe. *I might borrow your voice, Topaz, for the audition. Would you mind?* Mightn't he decide to replace some of his other possessions? The old girlfriend for a newer, rather more glamorous model, perhaps?

You have to take what you can, when you can. Yet the platitude seemed tired and worn thin by repetition. Topaz jammed the pillow over her head, trying to blot out the sound of laughter from the garden.

★   ★   ★

The Aston Marton broke down halfway between Longridge and Missencourt; Julia had to abandon it at the side of the road and walk the remaining two miles with William in tow. It was raining, of course, so by the time she reached Temperley's, three-quarters of an hour late, her best shoes were splashed with mud and her stockings holed. She was sitting at her desk, trying to clean her shoes with spit and a handkerchief, when the door opened and the foreman came in. Three years earlier Raymond Bell had replaced nice old Ted Butcher, who had been Temperley's foreman during the war. Without being openly insolent, he nevertheless managed to convey quite plainly his hostility to Julia.

347

And there was something about him that set her teeth on edge: the sneer that seemed always to hover around the corners of his mouth, and the slightly slanting eyes set in a pale face, like lumps of coal in snow.

Now his gaze drifted to Julia's bare feet, showing a mixture of lechery and distaste. Quickly, she shoved her shoes back on.

She said coldly, 'I would prefer you to knock before you come into my office, Mr Bell.'

'I didn't think you were coming in today, Mrs Chancellor.' Bell's voice was smoothly insinuating. 'I thought you must be taking the day off.'

'My car broke down.' As soon as she said it, she wanted to draw the words back, knowing that she demeaned herself by offering excuses.

He said, 'You should get yourself a little runabout. Something nice and easy for a woman.'

Controlling her temper, she rose from her desk. 'Shall we go to the workshop?'

He held the door open for her so that she had to brush past him to reach the corridor. In the workshop she breathed in the familiar smells of metal and solder, and some of the morning's irritations began to fall away. She loved the workshop, always had. She remembered her father taking her here when she was a little girl; she had perched on his shoulders, looking round the room, with its cavernous ceiling and high, arched windows. She had gazed, fascinated, at the glass valves, had touched the coloured wires that protruded from the ends of the resistors and had twirled the control knobs on the wooden cases.

Raymond Bell said softly, 'Did you remember to put that order in, Mrs Chancellor?'

Her hand flew to her mouth. The previous afternoon one of the technicians had told her that they were running short of capacitors. She had promised to phone the suppliers, but then Adele had telephoned to remind

Julia that she had an appointment at the doctor's, and Mullard's had called to query an invoice, and she had ended up dashing out to collect William without making the call.

'I'm terribly sorry.' She knew she was red-faced. 'I'll phone straight away.'

'It's all right. I called Dublier's myself. No harm in making sure.'

She could read the triumph in his eyes. She was about to point out that it was her job to order supplies, but managed just in time to stop herself, realizing that to do so would only make her look more foolish. Instead she said stiffly, 'Thank you, Mr Bell. That was very helpful.'

'You're welcome. You must be very busy, what with a house to run and your little boy to look after.'

Meaning, she thought furiously, *go back to the kitchen where you belong*. As she left the room, she saw Bell turn aside and whisper something to one of the younger technicians. The technician's eyes flicked to Julia and he sniggered.

Back in the office she sat at her desk, pressing her fingertips against her brow, trying to cool her hot, aching head. Paperwork formed mountains around her, and her in-tray overflowed. Perhaps the obnoxious Raymond Bell was right, she thought miserably; perhaps she should have been content with being a housewife. Perhaps, in attempting to combine motherhood and a job, she ended up doing neither very well. Yet, without her income from Temperley's, how would she live? That was what the Raymond Bells of this world conveniently forgot. Will had had no savings, no insurance. He had left her only debts. The widow's pension provided by the state covered only the bare essentials. Without Temperley's, she would have to rely on Marius's generosity. It was not that she doubted for a moment that it would be forthcoming, but something in her

349

rebelled against returning to dependency.

Leaving Temperley's at half-past four, she caught a bus to Hernscombe. As she hurried from shop to shop the rain persisted, whipped up by the wind, which tossed the boats in the harbour and threatened to turn her umbrella inside out. She was walking down the High Street when she heard a voice call her name. Turning, she saw Rick Hunter.

'Mrs Chancellor?' He crossed the street to her. 'How nice to see you again.' He smiled. 'I wonder whether I might call in a favour?'

'A favour?'

'Starting your car,' he reminded her. 'Rescuing you from Maurice Chancellor.'

'Oh dear,' she said ruefully. 'Two favours. What can I do for you, Mr Hunter?'

'You can let me buy you a cup of tea.'

She was wet and cold and tired, and her headache, the legacy of her frustrating morning, lingered. She really couldn't face a half-hour of stewed tea and stilted conversation with a man she hardly knew. She said politely, 'It's kind of you to offer, but I'm afraid I can't. But thank you once again for helping me at the party.'

As she turned to go, she heard him say, 'You see, I have a confession to make.'

She looked back at him. 'A confession?'

'We've met before, Mrs Chancellor. I don't mean Maurice's dinner-dance. Before that. Don't you remember?'

Something stirred at the back of Julia's mind, something she could not quite pinpoint. 'I'm sorry — '

'I knew your husband.'

'Will?' She stared at him. 'You knew Will?'

'We did some business together. I used to call at the garage. You dropped in one day. Will introduced us.'

You dropped in one day . . . Will introduced us. Suddenly she remembered. She had walked into Will's

350

office without knocking. He had been angry with her because he had been with a customer. Later that same day she had kissed Jack.

Will's customer had been Rick Hunter. The two images of the same man jarred slightly, the earlier one cruder, slightly disturbing. They did not seem to her quite to fit together, those two Rick Hunters.

'I'd forgotten.' She felt confused.

'It was a long time ago. Why should you remember?'

'*You* did.'

'I never forget a face.' He smiled. 'Won't you reconsider the tea, Mrs Chancellor?'

This time curiosity overcame unease and she followed him into the Copper Kettle. Waiting for the tea and cakes to arrive, she told him about Temperley's. 'We had a rocky few years after the war,' she explained, 'but we've doing well now.'

'And the future? Are you confident of the future? The competition — '

'Our radios are of the highest quality,' she said proudly. 'They're the best you can buy. People know that.'

'I was thinking', he said, 'of television.'

'I don't see television as competition. It'll always be a complement to radio, don't you think? Radios are so much more *handy* — you can get on with other things while you're listening to the radio, can't you?'

The waitress arrived with the tea. 'And you?' she asked. 'What do you do, Mr Hunter?'

'Rick,' he said. 'Please call me Rick. I'm in property. I buy and sell property.'

'You're an estate agent?'

'No. I buy land and develop it. Houses or offices, depending on the location. I work in London most of the time — I buy up bombsites and pieces of waste ground. The trick is to know the areas that are going to go up rather than down.'

351

'Is that what you're doing here? Buying property?'

'In a way. I'm hoping to buy a house in the area. I like it here. Lots of potential for development. Lots of nice things to look at.' His gaze rested on her; she found herself reddening, turning away.

She poured out the tea. 'How did you meet Will?'

'I did some business round here few years back.'

'Did you know him well?'

'As I said, we were business acquaintances. I used to be in the motor trade.'

'You were one of Will's suppliers?'

He nodded. Then he said, 'When I heard about Will's death, I found it so hard to believe. Such an — ' he seemed to be searching for the right word ' — such an *improbable* thing to happen.'

When she looked back at the weeks following Will's death they seemed unreal, as though she had been trapped in a nightmare. She whispered, 'It was all so unbearable.'

'I'm sorry.' His straight black brows lowered. 'I don't mean to rake up painful memories.'

'I don't mind. It's nice to talk to someone who knew Will. Someone who isn't a relative. My mother-in-law hardly mentions him. She can't bear to. And everyone else is so *tactful*.'

'It must have been a terrible shock for you all.'

She handed him a cup. 'At first, I couldn't believe it. Perhaps it's always like that with a sudden death.'

He said softly, 'And such an unfortunate combination of events.'

It struck her how exactly his thoughts echoed hers. She said, 'I kept on thinking that if Will hadn't gone to the pub . . . if he hadn't been on the boat . . . if the mine hadn't been washed into the bay that night . . . And some of it was so *unlike* him. So *unpredictable*. And Will wasn't an unpredictable person.'

'What do you mean?'

The sharpness of his voice jolted her, and she looked up. 'Will was so gentle. He wouldn't hurt a fly. He worried about things — too much, perhaps. He liked everything to run smoothly, he hated to be taken by surprise. He would have told you, if you'd asked him, that he wasn't a brave person. That he wasn't brave like Jack is brave. But that's nonsense, of course. In his own way, Will was very brave. He was very ill when he was a child, did you know that? It takes courage to get over something like that, courage to get on with your life and accept that you can't do all the things most people take for granted. And, of course, the times weren't kind to him, were they? In the war Will was classed as unfit for active service. I think that just reinforced his opinion of himself as a failure, as second-rate.'

She tucked her hair, which was escaping, as usual, from the barrage of pins and clips with which she attempted to confine it, behind her ears. She wondered, fleetingly, why she was confiding such private thoughts to a stranger. But she went on, 'What I'm trying to say is that he tended to keep to a routine. When things were going well between us then he'd stay late at work perhaps, then maybe have a drink or two, and then come home.' She pressed her hands together. 'Only that night he didn't. Didn't come home, I mean.'

She bit her lip, remembering with sudden and painful vividness Will's nightly tramp up the long path to Hidcote Cottage. Remembering how, in the early months of their marriage there had been a bounce in his step, a cheerful wave, a kiss for her. And how, as time passed, his shoulders had slumped, and his conversation had become terse and monosyllabic.

Rick's voice broke into her thoughts. 'Who's Jack?'

'Jack?'

'You mentioned him.'

'Jack is Will's elder brother. Jack was always cleverer, healthier, handsomer than Will. And without even

353

trying.' She knew that she sounded bitter. 'So hard, to have to bear that sort of competition from birth. So hard, don't you think, to feel you're always going to be second best.'

She glanced at her watch and pulled on her gloves and scarf. 'I must go. My bus — '

'You're not driving?'

She gave a little smile. 'My car's sick again, I'm afraid.'

'I'll drive you home.' He didn't give her time to argue, but threw a few coins on the table as they left the cafe. As they walked out of the door, he said suddenly, 'I wondered whether you might like to go for a drink. This evening, perhaps.'

'I can't, I'm afraid.' After all, she had the perfect excuse. 'I have a little boy, you see. I have a son.'

'Another day, then. Next week, perhaps. Or Saturday, if the weekend suits you better?'

But the feeling of unease had returned and she said quickly, 'To be honest, I'm so exhausted, what with William and my work, that I don't go out much. I hope you understand.'

'Of course,' he said, and opened the passenger door of his car for her.

★ ★ ★

Topaz knew that Charlie was drifting away from her. Their lives did not seem to fit together any more. He'd cancel arrangements at the last minute. Something had come up, he couldn't make it. *So sorry, darling. You do understand, don't you?* She could not seem to halt it, this slow falling apart.

They went to another party. She lost sight of him soon after they entered the St John's Wood house. She wandered around the perimeter of the room, making conversation with the other flotsam and jetsam who

354

lined the walls, those who, like her, remained by choice or by circumstance outside the inner circle. Charlie reappeared an hour or so later, elated and animated. They were going on to a restaurant, he explained. She invented a prior engagement, and he made quick, preoccupied murmurs of regret and kissed her cheek.

When she cooked for him, she was unsure whether he noticed what she had put in front of him. Once, she whipped his plate away halfway through a meal. 'What are you eating, Charlie?' she cried furiously. 'What are you eating?' He looked slightly alarmed. She grabbed her coat and gloves and ran outside, and walked for an hour through the darkened streets. It was raining, and by the time she returned home she was soaked. Running a bath, she thought how foolish, how histrionic, to be angry because Charlie couldn't tell a crêpe from a galette. He'd come back to her as soon as he was more certain of his future. He was always unsettled when he was out of work.

He made short, perfunctory phone calls. 'I haven't seen you for *ages*,' she said to him one evening.

'Auditions,' he explained. 'I've had auditions.'

'It seems so long. I miss you, Charlie.' Imploring, needy: she heard and hated herself.

It seemed to her that his quick arrangement to meet for a drink at the end of week was a sop, something to quieten her so that she did not fuss. Charlie never liked fuss. Waiting for him in a bar in Frith Street, she sat at a window table so that she could see the street. Time passed; every so often someone would turn the corner of the road, and her head would jerk up, and she would stare out into the darkness. There'd be that pang of disappointment that it wasn't him, and a second glance, just to make sure. Then she'd look down at her glass, dipping the olive in and out of the Martini, not bothering to drink.

Seven o'clock, he had said. She wondered whether

she had made a mistake. He'd said half-past, perhaps, and she had muddled it up. At a quarter to eight, she heard footsteps approaching her table and she looked up, her heart beating fast.

It wasn't Charlie, but a stranger. He was nice-looking, youngish, smiling. He said, 'Is anyone sitting here?' and she wondered for a moment whether she'd invite him to share her table. Perhaps Charlie, coming late into the bar, would see them together and taste a drop of the jealousy that these days always poisoned her.

But she said, 'I'm waiting for someone, actually,' and he went away. And she watched and waited some more, aware now of a sense of humiliation. She understood the role she was playing. She had been stood up, let down. After a while she picked up her bag and gloves and left the bar.

He phoned the following morning. His train had been delayed, he hadn't been able to find a phone. She forgave him, as she always did. Making love with him that afternoon, she found herself glancing at the collar of his discarded shirt, looking for lipstick stains. Wondering whether, if he dozed off, he might in his sleep cry out another name.

★ ★ ★

Mary Hetherington asked Topaz to cook for her. Charlie promised to drive her to Mary's house in St James's Square. The dinner was to begin at half-past seven. At six o'clock Topaz waited in the hallway of her flat, surrounded by tins and boxes. At ten past six she went back into the living room to stand by the window. Headlights loomed through the fine snow. None of the cars stopped. At a quarter past she dialled the number of Charlie's flat. The phone rang out, a mournful, repetitive bleating.

In the street she flagged down a taxi. Three-quarters of an hour late at the Hetheringtons' house, she worked with dogged, robotic speed. When, much later, the maid carried the last of the puddings through to the dining room, she sat down at the kitchen table. Her head throbbed; much worse was the dull ache somewhere in the region of her heart.

Mary Hetherington looked into the kitchen between the cheese and the coffee. 'Lovely dinner, Topaz dear. Everyone enjoyed it enormously.'

Topaz was washing up. 'I'm so sorry about being late,' she said. 'Charlie was supposed to pick me up. I hope he's all right. Would you mind if I used your phone to give him a ring?'

She heard Mary say, 'But he's at Jennifer's, isn't he?' and she swung round.

'Jennifer's?'

'Yes.' Mary frowned. 'Oh dear, I thought — ' She broke off.

It reminded Topaz of that surprised, sinking feeling you got when you thought you'd reached the foot of the stairs and there was still one more step to go. She had to squeeze the question out. 'You thought what?'

'Nothing. Nothing important.'

'*Please.*'

Mary said, 'I thought you two weren't together any more.'

Just then it seemed to Topaz that Mary was right, and that they had not really been together for a very long time. 'Why?' she whispered. 'Why did you think that?' Seeing Mary hesitate, she added softly, 'I need to know.'

Mary sighed. 'It's just that when he was at Jen's without you, I assumed — '

'Charlie's been to Jennifer Audley's?' Her voice rose. 'Since that weekend? The one where we played the awful games?'

'Once or twice,' said Mary reluctantly. 'I've seen him

357

at the Audleys once or twice.'

She gathered up the last remnants of her pride. She turned back to the sink. 'I'll just finish this and then I'll go.'

'Oh, just leave the washing-up, Topaz — '

'I'm almost finished.'

Tears blurred her vision so that it was hard to see what she was washing; they slid down her nose and plopped into the murky water. She heard Mary leave the room.

When she had washed and rinsed the last of the china, she packed her belongings back in the cardboard boxes. Then she wiped the table and the hob, and untied her apron. And then, leaning forward, wrote his name on the misted windowpane. And dragged the tips of her fingers across it, erasing the letters completely, so that she could see clearly through the glass the softly falling snow.

★   ★   ★

There was a message through her door when she got home. *Darling Topaz, terribly sorry, got stranded in this frightful weather and couldn't make it. I hope the evening went well. All my love, Charlie.* She crumpled up the note and threw it into the bin.

He was waiting for her when she left Angelique's the following evening. He was carrying a bunch of chrysanthemums: to say sorry, he explained. *I couldn't find any primroses,* he added — *too early, they said in the shops.* Tears stung at the back of her eyes, but she did not let them fall.

She knew as soon as she saw him that something had happened; he fizzed with energy and excitement. She thought that, if she looked down, she would see that his feet weren't touching the ground. He drew her beneath the shelter of his coat, kissing her. Headlamps swooped out of the night towards them, tail lights quickly retreated.

After a while he stood back from her. 'What is it? You've forgiven me, haven't you? I said I was sorry about last night. The car — '

She said, 'You were with Jennifer, weren't you, Charlie?' and she saw his expression alter, becoming defensive.

'What if I was? She's a friend.'

'A friend . . . ' A sudden rush of anger, disturbing her fragile calm. 'Charlie, I saw you kiss her. When we were at her house that weekend, I saw you kiss her.'

He said, as she had known he would, 'That didn't mean anything. You know what it's like in the theatre . . . all that kissing and hugging. It doesn't mean anything.'

'Then why didn't you tell me you were seeing her?'

He shrugged. 'I didn't think it was important.'

'It was', she said, 'to me.'

Now he looked sulky. 'It was to do with work. I told you, Jennifer knows some important people.' He took her hand and his face lightened. 'Don't let's quarrel. I have the most marvellous news. I've been offered a part in a film.'

She murmured, 'How wonderful.'

She couldn't have hit quite the right note because he said, 'A *film*, Topaz. At last. I'd almost given up.' His eyes were bright, shining in the darkness. 'It's not a major role, but not a bit part, either. A proper speaking role. It's going to be called *The Rose Garden*. It's a drawing-room comedy, set in an English country house. A bit sub-Noël Coward.'

'Enthusiastic young men in cricket whites?' She could not keep the sarcasm from her voice.

'It's a *film*, Topaz. Who cares what it's about? Think of the audience it'll reach. Thousands of people — tens of thousands, perhaps. Britain . . . America . . . half the world, if things work out.'

'Your name in lights,' she said.

He frowned. 'You sound as though you disapprove.'

She raised her shoulders. 'No. If it's what *you* want, Charlie, that's all that matters.'

They were walking through Knightsbridge. Fleetingly, the clouds cleared, showing a pale sliver of moon. Charlie's hands chopped at the air with excitement. 'It's a way in. Even if this one isn't up to much, it should mean I'm in the running for others. And the money should be good — three times what I'm earning now. And I'll get to see America. I've always wanted to go to America.'

'America?' she echoed.

'They're making the film in Hollywood.'

'You said an English country house — '

'Made of cardboard and paint, I suspect.' He grinned. 'I can't believe it. *Me.* Charlie Finch. Going to *Hollywood.*'

She thought, *It was an afterthought.* She wondered, had the conversation not drifted that way, how long it would have been before it occurred to him to tell her.

'How long for?'

'A few months,' he said vaguely.

Trailing branches of laurel drifted over a wall, their leaves wet and gritty. She remembered Francesca. *The thing is that I mind and he doesn't.*

Well, she thought, *you can't say that you weren't warned, Topaz Brooke.*

He put his arm round her waist. 'I'll miss you terribly.' Another afterthought.

'Will you, Charlie?'

'Of course I will.' He glanced at her. 'You do understand, don't you, darling? You do understand how important this is to me?'

'Of course.' Cold, she shivered, wrapped up in her coat. 'I understand perfectly.'

He glanced at her sharply. 'That's not fair.'

'Isn't it?'

'I can't pass up an opportunity like this.'

'I wouldn't want you to.'

'But you don't approve?'

'I told you, Charlie, it's your choice. You must do what seems right to you.'

They had almost reached her flat. As they turned the corner of the street, he seemed to have a sudden inspiration.

'Why don't you come with me?'

'Charlie — '

'No, really, why not? You could chuck in your job, couldn't you? Lying on Long Beach in California would be more fun than peeling potatoes, wouldn't it? Think of it — the palm trees — the Pacific Ocean — '

For a moment she allowed herself to imagine it. She, Topaz Brooke, reclining on golden sands in some wonderfully constructed American swimsuit that would instantly give her a figure like Jane Russell.

'Go on, Topaz. It'd be terrific fun. Say you'll come with me.'

She turned to him. 'As what?'

'What do you mean?'

'As your friend — or your girlfriend . . . ?'

'Well, I — '

'Or your fiancée, Charlie?'

Surprise and confusion. And, in the depths of those dark, beautiful eyes, a rather hunted expression. He rubbed his forehead, uncharacteristically speechless.

She almost felt sorry for him. She said lightly, 'It's all right. I don't really expect you to marry me.'

'It's just — ' a small laugh ' — *marriage*. I hadn't really thought about it. I don't feel — *settled*, yet. Everything's still too up in the air. And anyway, I hate all that obligation . . . red tape . . . it takes all the fun out of it, doesn't it?'

She pressed her face into the bunch of chrysanthemums he had given her. In the frozen air, they had a stale, acrid scent.

She heard him say, 'But — America . . . you'll come, won't you?'

'I don't think so.' They had reached her flat; she took her doorkey out of her bag.

'Topaz — '

'Goodbye, Charlie.'

'I wish you would.' His brow furrowed. 'I'll miss you, you know.'

'And I shall miss you too.'

'You'll wait for me, won't you?' He sounded suddenly anxious.

She turned away. 'I don't think so, Charlie.'

'*Topaz* — ' He was shocked, bewildered.

'I think that it's over, isn't it?' She was surprised how calm she sounded. 'I think we both know that.'

His eyes were wide and confused. 'Is it because of Jennifer? I told you, Topaz — she's not important.'

She shook her head. 'No, it's not because of Jennifer.'

'Then — if I'd said I'd marry you — '

'No.' She shook her head again, and smiled. 'No.'

'I don't understand. *Why*, Topaz?'

Because, she thought, *I don't intend to occupy the gaps in someone's life ever again. Never, ever. I've had enough of that.*

But she said only, 'Because I've changed, Charlie. And because you haven't.'

Then she went into the house. As soon as she closed the door behind her, she felt it, the loneliness rushing in on her, the terrible absence of him. She wanted to fling open the door, to call him back.

But she did not. Instead, she slowly climbed the stairs and let herself into her flat. And sat in her kitchen, looking around at all her things, and found, for the first time, that they did not give her any comfort at all.

Rick Hunter telephoned Julia.

'I've found a house,' he said. 'And I'd like a second opinion. Would you take a look at it?'

'I'm not sure — ' Once more, that instinct for caution.

He interrupted, 'I hope you don't think I'm imposing. You must be very busy.'

She took a deep breath. Ridiculous, she told herself, to be so stand-offish. Rick Hunter was only trying to be friendly.

'When were you thinking of?'

'An afternoon would be best. In the light. Sunday?'

'Sunday could be difficult. William — '

'Bring him with you. There's a big garden for him to play in.'

She thought, ten out of ten, Rick Hunter. 'Sunday, then,' she said, and put down the phone.

The house was ten miles from Longridge. She sensed, rather than was able to see, the approach of the coast. Smelt the salt on the air, saw that special brightness in the sky. An unmade track branched off from the main road. The car bounced and bumped on the ruts. There were trees to either side of the track: when they fell away, Julia saw Rick Hunter's house for the first time.

It took her by surprise. Literally took her breath away. She had expected something solid, brutal even, to be to Rick Hunter's taste. Not this fragile, graceful construction, its pale stone melding into the blue-greens of woodland and sea. Climbing out of the car, she stood still for a moment, her hands clenched. A veranda ran along the front facade of the house. Boughs twisted around the wrought iron: she pictured in the early summer the lavender blue wisteria flowers that would shiver in the sea breeze. In the gardens surrounding the house she saw the brownish-grey skeletons of sea holly and the first small, spiky bluish leaves of seakale. Beyond, the dark, shifting masses of rhododendron bushes. A month or two and they'd be aflame with pink, crimson, scarlet.

She followed Rick into the house. The rooms were spacious and well proportioned. Dove-grey, sea-stained light seeped through the tall windows. A staircase curved sinuously to the upper floor, pale as a spiralling seashell.

Upstairs William ran ahead, peering through doorways, shrieking at the echo of his footsteps in the empty rooms. Julia ran her fingertips along a peeling wooden banister, and touched a fragment of faded patterned paper that trailed from the wall.

In the centre of the main bedroom's ceiling, a cobwebbed chandelier swung from an ornate plaster roundel. When Rick spoke, Julia gave a little jump. As though, lost in the dream of this exquisite house, she had almost forgotten he was there.

'What do you think?'

'It's beautiful, Rick. So beautiful.'

He was carrying a sheaf of papers. 'I had an interior designer look round. Came down from London.' He glanced at the topsheet. 'Crimson for this room, he said. Red and black striped curtains. With gold lining and gold pass — ' his brows slammed together as he struggled with the word ' — pass — '

'Passementerie? That's just tassels and trims.' Julia turned, taking in the Georgian windows, the delicate carvings on ceiling boss and architrave. 'Crimson and gold . . . Really, that's not how I'd do this house.'

'Thought the fellow was a fool.' He ripped the papers in half, flung them to the floor. The sudden violence of the gesture broke through the stillness.

He said, 'What would you do, then?'

'Me?'

'You have to tell me. I don't know, you see.'

She felt embarrassed. 'Rick, I'm not an interior designer — '

'You know what looks right. At Maurice Chancellor's dinner-dance you said the way the hotel was done out was vulgar. I wouldn't have known that. And when I do up this place — ' his meaty hand slammed against the windowsill ' — I don't want it to look vulgar. I want it to be just like you tell me it should be.'

She said, 'But you're just *thinking* of buying it, aren't you, Rick?'

He shook his head. 'Signed the papers last week. I couldn't wait. Someone else was interested.' He threw her a glance. 'You look cold,' he said. 'We should go. Always damp, these old houses.'

They went outside. As they crossed the courtyard, he said, 'There's something more I want to show you.'

He led the way through the thicket of rhododendrons at the bottom of the garden. The dark leathery leaves arched over a sandy path, forming a tunnel, shutting out the sky. The hush of surf on shingle became louder as Julia, holding William's hand, followed Rick along the path. Then the shrubs fell away, and she found herself standing on a wooden jetty in the centre of a small, secluded beach. Only a dozen yards away, the sea rushed against the shingle. Dark brown bladder-wrack gleamed on wet, shiny sand, and a starfish, orange arms outstretched, moved in a shallow pool at the edge of the jetty. Limestone cliffs curved to either side of the beach, forming a bay. The cliffs, and the rocks scattered across the entrance to the bay, secured the beach's privacy.

She felt William's fingers slip through hers as he darted away to explore. 'It's magical,' she said aloud. Once more, she felt breathless. 'Quite magical.'

★ ★ ★

The baby was due at the end of April. Marius dug out Tara's cot and sanded and painted it, and wallpapered the old nursery at Missencourt. And then, so that Tara should not feel left out, he decorated her bedroom in the colour she had chosen, a deep, periwinkle blue.

Tara had celebrated her sixth birthday on Boxing Day. She remained in appearance a miniature Suzanne: small for her age, with pale skin, dark eyes and curling hair. In character, though, she was marking out her own path. Whereas Suzanne relished battles with authority, Tara cherished a rather touching veneration for her teacher, Miss Rokeby, quoting her at the tea table and presenting her with small gifts: a potato print, a home-made fairy cake with lurid icing, a cross-stitch comb case that Tara had battled over and Suzanne had later secretly unpicked and reassembled. Whereas Suzanne saw household tasks as a necessary but tedious evil, Tara loved to polish the small dressing table that Marius had made for her, and became upset if the contents of her drawers were not just so. Where Suzanne rushed, Tara was patient and organized. And whereas Suzanne was happiest in a shirt and slacks, Tara demanded frocks, the pinker and frillier the better. Suzanne, watching her daughter preen herself in front of the glass, said despairingly, 'She's a changeling, Marius. She's not mine at all. They must have swapped her at the hospital.' But Marius's pride in his tiny, pretty daughter was unbounded. Returning from London each week, he would always bring her a present: a hair slide, a ribbon, a new dress for her favourite doll.

Tara's school was in Hernscombe, a small but forward-looking institution which did not impose the uniforms and regimentation that were an anathema to Suzanne. Tara loved school, acquiring a series of best friends who came to tea at Missencourt, and who were introduced to the delights of Tara's doll's house, guinea pig and sandpit. Julia had promised that in a year or two she would teach Tara to ride; already she attended a weekly ballet class, where twenty little girls, all identically attired in pink tunics, pointed their toes to the music of an old wind-up gramophone.

Marius and Tara had fallen into the habit of a Sunday morning outing. Both were early risers and would tiptoe out of the house, wrapped up in coats and gumboots, while Suzanne and Adele still slept. Because Tara invariably demanded a picnic, Marius always took with him a flask of tea and a pocketful of biscuits. Then they'd head for the hills or the woods, tramping through mud and puddles, scrambling up chalky slopes, mud clinging to their boots as they searched beneath the tallest trees for conkers, acorns and, when spring came, pale slender orchids.

Most of all, Tara loved the sea. Marius would sit her in the back of the car and head off through the early-morning winter's gloom for the coast. They would eat their picnic, surrounded by slabs of limestone pitted with pools that were home to crabs and sea anemones. In winter their conversation was almost drowned by the crash of the breakers and the howl of the wind. Tara ate the biscuits and drank a cup of milky, sugary tea, screwing up her face at the taste of it, and then, whatever the weather, she would make a sandcastle. As they walked hand in hand along the shore, she'd tell Marius about the boat she intended to sail when she was a big girl. It would have blue sails and an anchor and she would catch fish. Marius made interested noises and pictured his small daughter, out there on the churning waves, alone in a cockleshell of a boat. He and Julia had, as children, sailed a dinghy: the memory of their recklessness now made him shiver. Because of Will, he supposed. Since Will's death the sea, which had consumed him so suddenly, so completely, had taken on a darker hue, casting a shadow across the bright glittering memory of their childhood.

Once Julia had said to him, 'Do you think you ever stop worrying about them, Marius? Do you think it ever goes?' and he, understanding straight away that she meant *children*, that she meant William and Tara and the unborn baby curled in Suzanne's womb, had shaken his head. 'Probably not,' he'd said. 'Mother still gets into a flap if I'm late back from London.' And Julia had said, 'Oh *dear*,' and had looked so despairing that he'd given her a hug, trying to comfort his sister, who had once never worried about anything.

It pleased him that Tara was a country child, that she delighted as he did in the turn of the seasons, the change of the wind. He did not, had no wish to, know whether they shared the same blood; it was enough that they shared the sun on their heads as they walked along the chalk ridge, that they loved the sea spray stinging their faces as they stood beside each other on the beach. That together they watched the rise and fall of the waves, forgetting the time until eventually he glanced at his watch and hurried her back up the cliff path because they were going to be late for breakfast.

Six months pregnant, Suzanne was still working at the nursery school, which was now housed in the village hall at Great Missen, having grown out of Marius and Julia's old playroom. Often, she looked pale and tired. *Anaemic*, the doctor said, and recommended she eat liver and take more rest. Once more Marius suggested she consider giving up the nursery school, for the remainder of her pregnancy at least. This time, Suzanne conceded; as soon as Vivien found a replacement for her she would step down. Marius gave a private sigh of relief. Yet he saw Suzanne glance quickly out of the window, with an echo of her old desperation. As though the house, and the countryside that bounded it, still caged her.

★ ★ ★

In the immediate postwar period, Temperley's Radios' difficulties had been to do with the changeover from a war economy to a peacetime one, and with shortages of raw materials and difficulties in obtaining supplies. Five years later, the company was profitable and the order books were full. Their problems were now of a different nature: because of limited capacity they sometimes had to turn orders away. Marius's decision to relocate the cabinet-making workshop to London, along with the newly established sales office, had helped, but had not completely resolved the problem.

At the end of February a fire at the London workshop brought production to a halt. Marius drove up from Dorset to inspect the damage. Suzanne went with him.

He returned to the flat at seven o'clock. Taking one look at him, Suzanne poured him a drink. 'Bad day?'

'Pretty awful. Apparently some idiot chucked a cigarette end into a binful of waste paper.' He swallowed the Scotch. 'It could have been worse, of course. The whole place could have gone up.'

'At least no one was hurt.' She was in the tiny alcove of a kitchen, cooking.

'Only the ass who'd set the bin alight. I should think his eardrums were perforated after I'd finished with him.' Marius pulled off his tie and slung it over the back of a chair. 'It couldn't have happened at a worse time,' he said angrily. 'The workshop will be out of production for a week at least. Great Missen will be twiddling their thumbs. I may have to lay people off.'

He went through to the kitchen. He made an effort to put his problems behind him, wrapping his arms around where her waist had once been, kissing the back of her neck.

But she moved away from him. 'The egg whites, Marius — '

He passed her a bowl. 'How was your day?'

'Fine,' she said. 'Just fine.' He thought, though, that

she looked tired and strained. There were shadows around her eyes and her skin had a translucent quality. Her small, pointed face seemed out of proportion to her swollen body.

'Can I do anything?'

'Just this — ' She handed him a lump of cheese and a grater. She said, 'I saw some lovely Moses baskets in a shop in the Brompton Road. I only had a carrycot and wheels for Tara.'

'Did you buy one?'

'Certainly not! They were ridiculously expensive. But I found a place that sold the wicker baskets and I've got some material to trim it with. It'll look just as pretty, and for a fraction of the price.'

'I'm sure it will,' he said mildly, 'but you don't have to economize, you know.'

'I don't like wasting money.' A quick smile. 'Habit, I suppose.'

He put the grated cheese in a bowl. 'We're all the same, aren't we? Mother still saves bits of string and slivers of soap. I use the backs of old letters for scrap paper.'

'And I can't eat a whole bag of sweets at once. I used to, before the war.' She sighed. 'Do you think we'll always be like this? Feeling guilty if we waste the smallest thing?'

'I expect so,' he said. 'Yes. Our grandchildren will probably laugh at us.'

She had put down the whisk and the bowl of egg whites, and leaned against the sink, rubbing her back. He said, concerned, 'Let me finish off in here. You go and have a rest. You look done in.'

She shook her head. 'I've almost finished.' Then, turning away, she said suddenly, 'I'm going to have to go home tomorrow, Marius. Vivien phoned — she needs me to help at the nursery school.'

He glanced up at her. 'I thought what's her name

— the ginger-haired girl — was taking over?'

'Sally O'Brien? She is, but her son's just gone down with mumps so she won't be able to come in for several weeks.'

'Can't Vivien manage on her own?'

'Not with ten children. Do you mind if I take the car?'

'Suzanne, of course I don't, but that's not the point.' He tried not to sound exasperated. 'It's a very long drive. And you look worn out already.'

'I'm fine,' she said. 'I just feel a bit whacked in the evenings. I'll be fine tomorrow.'

'If you really have to go home — and I can't see why they can't manage for another day without you — then surely it would be more sensible to take the train?'

'The last time I went by train it took *hours* and it was freezing cold and there was no buffet.' She sounded edgy and irritable. 'And there were no taxis at Longridge, so I ended up walking and there were cows all over the road.' She shuddered. 'I prefer to drive. You know that, Marius.'

'But you look so tired — '

'Marius, don't fuss!' Turning away from him, she began to plunge dishes into washing-up water. 'It's a perfectly normal thing to have a baby. Millions of women do it every year.'

After the long, difficult day, he felt his self-control slipping away. 'Millions of pregnant women', he said, 'don't look after a six-year-old, *and* help run a nursery school *and* rather a large house.'

'My mother', said Suzanne furiously, 'worked God-awful hours in a factory, and lived in a house the size of a shoebox with a man who'd hit her as soon as look at her. And she had *seven* children!' She glared at him. Then the fight seemed suddenly to go out of her because she sighed and said, 'I'm sorry. I didn't mean to snap.'

He took her in his arms. Yet, once again, she was stiff, resisting. He said, 'I can't drive you home tomorrow morning because the loss adjuster's coming and I need to be there. But he should be finished by midday. Would the afternoon do? We could stop overnight at Andover or Salisbury, make it a bit more civilized.'

'Dear Marius,' she said. Her voice shook slightly.

* * *

The loss adjuster, who had promised to arrive at ten o'clock, did not appear until eleven. Then he insisted on inspecting everything with a thoroughness that set Marius's teeth on edge, interviewing each of the staff in turn, and checking every fire extinguisher and sand bucket.

Then, just as Marius was about to leave, the phone rang. A department store in Leeds, one of their most important customers, had heard about the fire and was concerned that their regular order would not be fulfilled. Marius spent twenty minutes soothing the buyer. After he had put down the phone, he made a quick call to Julia, in Dorset, to remind her to give priority to the Leeds order.

By the time he left the office it was almost three o'clock. In the hope of making up lost time, he hailed a taxi rather than take the Tube, and was back at the flat before half-past.

But there was an empty, desolate air about the place that struck him as soon as he unlocked the front door. The carrier bags were gone, and Suzanne's coat and hat were no longer on the peg by the front door.

He read the note she had fixed to the dressing-table mirror. '*Dear Marius, I've decided to go back to Missencourt this morning. I've taken the car. I hope you don't mind. I can see that you're very busy, so don't rush home. If I feel tired, I'll stop at a hotel on*

372

the way, I promise. Love, Suzanne.'

He stared out of the window. The cold snap had set in a couple of days before, and the sky was the pale, icy blue of agates, smeared with smoke trails from chimneys.

★ ★ ★

She hadn't realized how hard it would be. How each stage of this second pregnancy would bring back reminders of the first. How the nausea and exhaustion of early pregnancy would recall to her the confusion and anger she had felt at Neil's departure. How, when she felt her child move for the first time — those strange, feathery flutterings — she would remember the blank, numb weeks that had followed his death in France. How, as month followed month, she would wake in the night, reliving her desolation, recalling with such vividness her grief, and her fear for and resentment of her unborn child.

It wasn't quite true that Vivien had insisted she return to Dorset. It was true that they were short of staff, but Vivien — calm, easy-going Vivien — had told her not to rush back. 'You have a break while you can, love,' she had said. 'You'll be up half the night soon enough.'

She had left London because she had needed some time to herself, and because she had had a sudden and irresistible urge to see the place where she and Neil had last been together. At the end of April 1944 they had managed to wangle a weekend in Salisbury. Neil had been stationed at nearby Tidworth; she remembered keeping her left hand in her pocket as he signed the register, so that the hotel would not notice her lack of a wedding ring. There must, Suzanne thought with a wry smile, have been dozens of Mr and Mrs Smiths booking into hotels at that time, with Salisbury Plain and its huge army camps so close by.

Now, driving into Salisbury, she parked and walked the short distance to the White Hart Hotel. Looking up at the old building, she remembered that the weekend had gone badly. She and Neil had not argued, but she had been unable to shake off the feelings of edginess and depression that had settled on her during the long drive from Northumberland. There had been a distance between them, as though their short separation had already set them on divergent paths. She had not told Neil about Marius, of course; and Neil himself must have had secrets concerning the preparations for D-Day. When they had made love there had been a desperation to their passion, as though they had been trying to recapture something that was already lost. When, on the Monday morning, she had set off on the long journey north, she had felt nauseous. She had put it down to the misery of parting, but it had been, of course, a symptom of her as yet unrealized pregnancy.

Suzanne walked away from the hotel and headed through the Cathedral Close. The day was cold and clear, the sky a gleam of palest blue. Ice glistened in the shadows and frost clung to the notched bottle-green leaves of an ivy that trailed along a garden wall. Walking down Bridge Street, she caught sight of the Poultry Cross and thought, *That was where I saw him for the last time. That was where we kissed goodbye.* He had offered to see her to the jeep, but she had refused. She had always hated partings.

She tried to visualize him, to see him clearly in her mind's eye. But his features blurred, unresolved, as if hidden under water. She could not now remember the exact shade of his eyes, nor could she clearly recall the shape of his mouth. She was aware of a feeling of panic. If she had loved him, why had she forgotten him? Was that how love always ended? Would she one day forget the blue of Marius's eyes? An old woman, would she forget her daughter's face, voice, name?

A voice interrupted her thoughts and she realized to her horror that she was crying. Standing in the street and crying. She muttered something to the older woman who stood beside her, concern in her eyes, and then she headed quickly back to the car. She had intended to dine in Salisbury and perhaps book into an hotel overnight, but now she wiped away the tears and headed out of the city to the Shaftesbury Road.

She drove fast; she had always loved to drive. They had taught her in the ATS; she remembered driving in Northumberland: those long, straight Roman roads through the hills, rushing down blind summits with Neil beside her, roaring at her to put her foot down. These roads were different, though. Turning off the Exeter Road and heading south, the route snaked and curved through countless little villages. Every now and then a lorry or a bus would swoop around a blind corner towards her and she'd have to squeeze the large, lumbering pre-war Rolls into the bank. Her feet began to cramp, pressing on the stiff pedals, and her arms, turning the heavy wheel, ached. *Stupid bloody car*, she muttered to herself. *Worse than driving an army jeep.*

She began to feel unbearably tired. Pulling into the opening of a field, she parked the car, and turned off the engine and sat, her eyelids heavy and her limbs aching. Yet some of the feelings of grief and regret had dropped away and she had begun to feel calmer. It was as though the visit to Salisbury had at last closed a book, putting the past into its proper context: over, finished with. Now she could look to the future instead. The future was Marius and Tara and her unborn child. Not a bad sort of future at all, she thought contentedly. Suzanne's eyes closed and she found herself drifting off to sleep.

But without the heat of the engine the car cooled quickly, and she woke after a few moments, shivering and chilled. Her mind still blurred by sleep, she set off again. She was within half an hour of Missencourt, she estimated. As soon as she got home, she'd have a hot bath and go to bed. Marius had been right: she was too far gone in her pregnancy to tackle a marathon like this again. She'd be sensible in future, put her feet up.

The road rose and fell as she drove south through hills and deep wooded valleys. She took a short cut along a little back lane that climbed downhill to the Hernscombe road. The road was unfamiliar, its twists and turns exhausted her and she fought to concentrate. *Almost home*, she murmured out loud to herself. Flanked by trees, the lane straightened, so she pressed the accelerator. As she descended through the woodland, the wintry sun, low in the sky, flared above the tree tops and momentarily she closed her eyes. Opening them, she saw too late that she had reached the junction and that the main road, with its high, coppiced verges, lay straight ahead of her. Suzanne stabbed her foot on the brake, but could not slow the impetus of the heavy car. The bank rushed at her, and as the front of the car struck it she was thrown first against the steering wheel, and then back against the seat.

She couldn't work out what was wrong. She couldn't work out why the sun still blinded her. Why she couldn't catch her breath. Why she felt so cold, a numb chill that seemed to flower quickly through her body. *Marius*, she whispered, but could not turn her head to see whether he was beside her.

14

Jack had been living in Canada for almost two years when Prudence's letter arrived. After he had sailed from England in the January of 1949, he had made contact with an ex-army friend who had emigrated to Canada at the end of the war. Wallace Maxwell owned a farm in Saskatchewan; there was work for Jack, he wrote, if he wanted it. Jack arrived in the prairies just as winter was loosening its grip, and found himself in a country of vast, rolling fields, patched with bright, flickering copses and jewel-like lakes.

In the years since he had been demobbed Maxwell had married and had fathered four children. After a week of sleeping in the spare bedroom of Maxwell's farmhouse, Jack escaped the four infants and Maxwell's talkative wife and took sanctuary in the nearby town of McKenna. McKenna consisted of a railroad station, a small hotel with paint peeling from its faded facade, a general stores, a garage and a couple of dozen houses. One of the houses was owned by a Mrs Turner, who let out rooms to lodgers.

Jack spent his first Canadian summer working on Maxwell's farm and living in Mrs Turner's lodging house. In the middle of the day the sun beat relentlessly down on his head; he found himself recalling the heat of North Africa. In the evenings the purple-grey shadows seemed to go on for ever. Most of the farmland was put to wheat, vast golden seas of waving corn. Sometimes the gold was interrupted by the yellow of mustard seed or the azure blue of flax. On the outermost reaches of Maxwell's farm, away from the comfortable farmsteads and red barns, there was nothing other than the expanse of honey-coloured fields and the great blue cupola of a sky that seemed to soar up to the heavens. The prairies were populated by sights unfamiliar to Jack: the brightly coloured grain elevators that peered down their noses like mechanical prehistoric beasts, and the surreal onion domes of Greek Orthodox and Ukrainian churches, reminders of the patchwork of nations which had settled this remote, landlocked country. Surrounded by such immensity, Jack seemed to feel something slipping from his shoulders at last, something heavy and burdensome.

In the parlour of the lodging house there was a photograph of Mrs Turner's husband, who had died during the Battle of the Falaise Pocket in Normandy in 1944. Mrs Turner was a good cook and a tactful, unobtrusive landlady. She was brisk and busy with Jack, avoiding, at first, any real conversation. Of medium height and build, brown-eyed and neat-figured, it took Jack a while to recognize that her briskness was due to shyness, a while longer to see in her self-contained demeanour a quiet beauty. The summer was almost gone before they dropped the formality of Mr Chancellor and Mrs Turner and began to call each other Jack and Esther. The winter's snows had begun to fall by the time they shared a bed. Because of the other lodgers in the house, their love-making was as quiet and gentle as the drifting snow.

The severity of the Canadian winter took Jack by surprise. The thermometer showed ten, twenty, thirty degrees below zero. On a nearby farm, on the coldest night of the year, half a dozen cattle and the stockman who had been leading them froze to death before they could reach the safety of the barn. In the winter the prairies became white oceans, only the lightest pencil line separating them from the pale sky. The cold could blind you, could rot the fingers from your hands and the toes from your feet. It concentrated the mind and reduced existence to essentials.

During the long, dark evenings, while Esther sewed

patchwork quilts, they talked. Jack watched her slender fingers flicker across the squares of striped and plain and figured cotton as she told him about her upbringing in Montreal, her marriage at the age of eighteen, the shock of transplanting herself to her husband's farm in Saskatchewan. In words devoid of any self-pity, she described the exhaustion and loneliness she had endured trying to run the farm after Frank had joined up, and her decision, after his death, to sell up. She had simply lost heart, she explained to Jack. It seemed to beat her down, the fierceness of the summers and winters and the isolation of the little farmstead. *I thought I could pick up the pieces*, she said quietly, *but I couldn't*. So she had sold the farm and moved to McKenna, where she had bought the lodging house. From the attic bedroom she could see the farmstead where she and Frank had lived. Sitting beside Jack on the settle in the front parlour, Esther explained, *I still feel guilty, Jack. Frank inherited the farm from his father and he meant to hand it down to his sons. There weren't any sons and I sold the farm to a stranger.*

It seemed to Jack, as time went on, that you couldn't always do what was expected of you. During the war he had served king and country, had gone home when the job was done and had tried, like Esther, to pick up the pieces. Returning to the web of family and obligation, he had struggled to fit into the drab, unfamiliar little country that Britain had become. Afraid of having nothing, he had tried to hold on to what he had believed to be his — Sixfields and Julia. It seemed to him, looking back, that that had been his mistake. There had been nothing to hold on to; the appearance of continuity had been an illusion. He had expected to return to the world he had left four years earlier. Yet everything had changed, almost beyond recognition. His family had grown and altered, so that their ways of life had become strange to him. His country had seemed at times to be a foreign land. As for Julia — Julia had been a girl when he had left Dorset, yet he had come home to find her a woman.

He had been unable to come to terms with change and had found continuity only in the land. His hunger for something lasting had led him to Sixfields: the solidity of hills and field and coast, and the illusion of permanence and security offered by wealth. In Canada, if he was not yet free of the past, at least he sometimes sensed liberation in the openness of the landscape and the magnificence and power of the elements. It helped to feel that he was small and insignificant, it gave a scale to his misadventures and mistakes.

Jack told Esther about Egypt and Italy and about Carrie Chancellor and Sixfields. He told her about Will, but not about his involvement with Julia. He knew that she sensed things unsaid. He still struggled to forgive himself for the way he had treated Will. And, though he tried to disregard it, he had a niggling sense of ends untied, stories unresolved.

Then the letter arrived. Sitting in the parlour in the evening, he read about Suzanne Temperley's death. The snow was thick on the ground and the wind blew flurries from the branches of the trees.

Esther was sitting by the fire, mending shirts. Scanning the flimsy blue paper, he must have made some sort of sound because she looked up at him.

'Bad news?'

He told her about Suzanne. 'Oh *Jack*,' she said, and rose and put her mending aside and came to sit beside him. 'Did you know her well?'

'Not really.' Indeed, he found it hard to visualize Suzanne. Just a snapshot of her dark vivacity and a memory of the way she had hurtled into their lives, shaking them all up, himself and Julia included. 'But I've known Marius, her husband,' he explained, 'since I was a child.'

Throughout the next few days, as he worked on Maxwell's farm, Jack tried to compose in his head a letter of condolence. But the sentences fragmented before he could complete them and the words seemed to fail to express the depths of his sympathy for Marius. Often his thoughts drifted to his own fragmented family. He thought of his nephew, whom he had never seen. He wondered what William looked like, whether he resembled Will or Julia. There was a responsibility there, to this child of his dead brother's, which he knew he had not faced up to. Prudence's letter had made the family he had left behind vivid and demanding. He was no longer able to slot them away neatly into the past.

He put his arms around Esther one evening, looking down at her nut-brown eyes and fair, translucent skin, flecked with tiny golden freckles. He wondered whether he would forget her quieter beauty, confronted with eyes the colour of storm-tossed waves and all Julia's brittle, fastidious passion.

'I should go home,' he said.

She nodded, as though that was what she had expected him to say. 'Will you come back?'

'I think so.' He cupped her face with his hands. Then he frowned. 'There are things — '

She interrupted him with a trace of her old briskness. 'I know. I guessed. But that's the old world, Jack, and this is the new. You have to choose.'

She slid out of his embrace and left the room. He found her in the kitchen, weeping as she rolled out the pastry. He kissed her and her floury hands left snowy prints on him as she pulled him to her.

★ ★ ★

At the funeral, sitting in church, Topaz found herself thinking angrily, why not a *wedding*, for once. Or a *christening*. But that thought was unbearable

381

(Suzanne's poor little baby, and all those tiny clothes and cot blankets at Missencourt, now bundled away, out of sight), so she stared up at the stained-glass window instead, and kept herself from howling out loud by reciting recipes in her head. Though why, she thought, blinking away the tears (. . . *omelette à la tomate* . . . *take one tomato, skinned and chopped small* . . .) one shouldn't bawl at such an awful, awful thing, she really couldn't think.

A couple of days later she telephoned Angelique and told her she would not be going back to the restaurant for the foreseeable future. She was needed at Missencourt, she explained. She was needed because Adele looked too tired and ill to care for such a large house and for such a small, bewildered granddaughter, and because Julia (white and thin, and possessed of a frightening, furious energy) was needed to manage Temperley's. And because Marius, who didn't do anything other than drink too much and wander around the house, looked as though someone had taken a hammer and splintered him into sharp unfixable little fragments. That she remained at Missencourt because there didn't seem much left for her in London these days was a thought that, even to herself, she tried to leave largely unvoiced.

Besides, someone was needed to shop and cook and make sure they were all offered supper, even if they didn't eat it. At least she could do that. Topaz caught the bus to Hernscombe twice a week, or cycled on Marius's old bike to Great Missen, and bought whatever looked best and cooked for them each evening, soups and stews and fresh fish, bought from the harbour at Hernscombe. And some of them ate it and some of them didn't, but at least, she thought, as she scraped the leftovers into a dish and put them in the refrigerator, it was one less thing for them to worry about.

She kept the house tidy as well, darting around with vacuum cleaner and duster so that there was always somewhere warm and pleasant to sit down. She dealt with the tradesmen, and with the succession of phone calls — that mixture of condolence and curiosity that she remembered from the aftermath of Will's death — making notes on a scrap of paper, and only bothering the Temperleys if absolutely necessary. In the afternoons, after school, she helped Adele with Tara; on washday she and Tara and Mrs Sykes folded the huge piles of linen. Once, very tentatively, she offered to help Marius sort out Suzanne's things, but he turned to her with a look of such blind fury in his eyes that she backed away, muttering quick apologies.

She woke early each morning, at five or six o'clock, and was unable to go back to sleep. She knew that Marius, too, rose early: she heard the soft click of the opening and closing of his bedroom door, and his quiet footsteps on the stairs. Standing at the window, she watched him go out to the garden, the labrador and Adele's King Charles spaniel at his heels. His wanderings were aimless and repetitive, back and forth along the terrace, then a circle or two of the perimeter of the garden before he headed for the copse or for the path that led out to the hills. As though, she thought with a shiver, he was looking for something.

Through her bedroom window, she watched him, kept an eye on him. Her heart ached for him, those grey, misty mornings. As she waited for him to return, she thought of Charlie, recalling every detail of their years together, trying to work out where they had gone wrong. Sometimes it seemed to her, looking back, that there had always been something detached, something incomplete about his love for her. He had neither loved her first nor loved her enough. Yet she had accepted that make-do affection, knowing its true colours; had not, until that last encounter (sleet in the air, and that hunted look in his eyes at the mention of the word *marriage*), asked for more than he could give. Often she felt ashamed of herself, sometimes she disliked herself. So craven, so abject, to settle for such a disproportionate love. It smacked, she thought, of desperation.

When she saw Marius returning to the garden she ran downstairs. As he came into the house she gave him toast and tea. He didn't often eat the toast, but he usually drank the tea. She sat with him in the little boot room at the back of the house, the room with the peeling wicker chairs and wellingtons and heaps of old mackintoshes, and the dogs, panting and ecstatic after their run. Thorns from the brambles that lined the path through the wood flecked his clothes. Often he hadn't shaved, and his hair, uncut now for several weeks, touched the collar of his coat. There was a dead look in his eyes which frightened her, which was why she watched him.

They didn't talk much. She knew that he hadn't really talked to anyone since Suzanne had died. Just dazed, exhausted responses to the questions the police had put to him and, later, murmured thanks for condolences after the funeral. Of course, people had *tried* to talk to him. John and Prudence Chancellor had tried, but had been met with such a stone wall of silent rebuttal that they eventually abandoned the attempt. Adele tried, several times, until Marius was so coldly, deliberately unpleasant that she was reduced to tears. Julia didn't try because, as she confided to Topaz, she didn't know what to do with Marius just now. She could hardly bear to look at him, she explained, let alone think of the right thing to say to him.

★　★　★

Julia had been the first person to learn of Suzanne's accident. The police had arrived as she was turning into

384

the drive at Missencourt to collect William. The memory of that conversation, and the knowledge of what had happened to Suzanne, remained with her all the time. Suzanne had been driving home from London when she had lost control of the car, turning on to the Hernscombe Road. The Rolls-Royce had struck the verge, throwing Suzanne first against the steering wheel, then back against the seat. The steering wheel had broken her breastbone, the seat had broken her neck. Lois Barrington arrived on the scene shortly after the accident had taken place. Suzanne had been alive — just — when Lois had found her, but by the time the ambulance had arrived twenty minutes later both she and her unborn child had been dead. At the inquest the coroner had suggested that Suzanne might have been blinded by the low winter sun. He had also pointed out that the car was big and heavy, not easy for a small, heavily pregnant woman to drive.

All the details, all the dreadful heaping of fact on fact, seemed to Julia an obscenity. Her chief emotion in those first few weeks was one of anger. Anger that they had another tragedy to endure, when they were only beginning to come to terms with the loss of Will.

She was privately relieved that her work at Temperley's now took up almost all of her time. She could cope with the demands of the business; she could not, as she had explained to Topaz, cope with Marius. Her own grief and guilt at Will's death was too recent, too raw. For William's sake, and for her own, she was thankful that she had the excuse of work for keeping her visits to Missencourt brief. She was immensely thankful that Topaz's decision to stay released her from any domestic obligations. Visiting Missencourt, Julia realized that Topaz had changed. That they had all fallen into the habit of thinking of her as Will and Jack's younger cousin, little Topaz, forever struggling to keep up with the rest of them. Those days were gone; Topaz was now a competent, resourceful and practical woman. Or perhaps, she thought uncomfortably, Topaz had been all those things for quite a long time and they hadn't noticed.

It would have been difficult to manage without Rick, too. She was even less comfortable with that. Before Suzanne's death Rick Hunter had existed only on the boundaries of her life. Afterwards he seemed always to be *there*. Coming home from work, she'd find him waiting outside her house. 'Just calling to see how you were,' he'd say. Or, 'Thought I'd find out whether there's anything I can do.' He'd give her a bunch of flowers or a box of chocolates, or he'd have bought a balloon or a toy car for William. So she could hardly snub him, leave him on the doorstep in the rain. Once inside the house, he'd fix a broken window latch or fetch in the coal if the scuttle was empty, those little tasks that Julia these days did not seem to have time for. Suzanne's death and Marius's absence from work had made Julia's already busy life a great deal busier. She found herself, almost without noticing it, starting to rely on Rick Hunter. For his strength, and for the way his company took her mind off some of the difficulties and exhaustion that these days threatened to overwhelm her.

He told her a little about himself; she guessed more. Every now and then his accent would slip, betraying a birthplace somewhere in the East End of London. She wondered whether he was ashamed of his origins and considered pointing out to him that she had always admired those who made their own way in life. She did not do so, partly because she guessed that he would prefer to hide his vulnerability, partly because such a conversation might imply an intimacy she was reluctant to encourage. But it was as if she had discovered something raw and soft, at variance with the strength he chose to project, an unexpected side to him that made her like him better.

He had a quick, sharp mind and his hunger for information — and for self-improvement — was vast. She loved his strange, seaswept house, loved seeing it slowly come to life as an army of decorators and seamstresses papered walls and hung curtains. He treated her like a princess, taking her, on the rare occasions that she had the time, to smart restaurants, solicitous always of her comfort and welfare, hanging on to her every word. It was nice to be worshipped, so different from the rest of her life. So different from motherhood, so different from Temperley's, where she was treated at best as an honorary male, one of the boys, at worst with the sort of sly sexual diminishment which Raymond Bell specialized in.

Yet once or twice she glimpsed another side to Rick Hunter, a side that unsettled her, reminding her of the unease she had felt meeting him that first time in Will's office. One day she was at his house, scribbling down suggestions for colour schemes, when the telephone rang. Rick's voice, answering it, broke through the dreamy quiet of the late Sunday afternoon. Clipped and cold and emotionless, he might have been a different person from the affable, easy-going Rick Hunter with whom she had become familiar. 'Get rid of him,' she heard him say. And then, impatiently, 'Don't give me any of that sob stuff. Just get rid of him.'

Only once did he let her see him angry. He had been refused membership of the golf club at Hernscombe; pounding his fist against the flat of his palm, the words spat out like cannon fire. 'Not good enough for them. Think I come from the wrong side of the tracks. Don't want my sort in their club room.' The smack of his fist punctuated the short phrases.

'What will you do?' she asked him.

There was a cold anger in his eyes that unnerved her. 'Find out who blackballed me. Fix them.'

That evening, she had considered severing her

connection with Rick Hunter. But two days later Suzanne had died and Julia had forgotten the incident. Remembering it in the aftermath of all that had happened, it seemed to her unimportant, and that his anger had been understandable.

He had never again spoken about Will. Sometimes it disturbed Julia that Rick had remembered her, yet she had forgotten him. Disturbed her that her first impression of him had been unfavourable, that she had seen in him something predatory, almost vulpine. Yet when she remembered her younger self — so proud and quick to judge — she found herself doubting her earlier verdict.

★　★　★

Since her mother's death Tara had become quiet and withdrawn, reverting to the habits of babyhood. She sucked her thumb, clung to Adele at the school gates, and once or twice she wet the bed. There was a bewildered look in her eyes that seared Topaz's heart.

As the weeks passed, Topaz noticed that Marius now largely ignored his daughter. If, when he was sitting on the sofa, Tara clambered on to his lap, he would endure her for a minute or two and then he would lift her down and leave the room. If Tara clamoured for a bedtime story, he would pass her on to someone else: Adele, Julia, whoever was to hand. As though, Topaz thought, Tara was an irritation, an interruption to the dark paths of his thoughts. As though she was nothing to do with him.

She said nothing for a while and then, three weeks after Suzanne's death, Tara arrived home from school one day carrying a large piece of blue sugar paper. 'It's a painting for Daddy,' she explained to Topaz. 'It's where they make the radios.'

Topaz admired Tara's painting. The old stone chapel, with its ornate wooden doors and arched windows was carefully drawn. A bright yellow sun, rays sprouting from its circumference, shone in a royal blue sky.

They found Marius in the drawing room. There was a glass of Scotch in his hand. When Tara, beaming, gave him the painting, Marius didn't even glance at it, but put it on the table and left the room. There was in Tara's eyes such a mixture of confusion and hurt that Topaz wanted to shake Marius. Leaving Tara with Adele, she went to find him.

He was in his study. The door was closed; she gave a quick knock and went in. He didn't look up. She said, 'That was unforgivable. What you just did to Tara was unforgivable.'

His face, pale already, whitened. 'This is my study', he said softly, 'and I didn't invite you in. I'd like you to go, actually.'

'No.' She shook her head. 'Not till you've heard what I've come to say.'

'Please go, Topaz.' His voice was dangerously quiet.

'You hurt Tara. You made her cry.'

Picking up his glass, he went to the window, his back to her, waiting for her to go. But instead she said, 'You shouldn't *ever* treat your daughter like that. Whatever's happened to you, however awful you feel, you just shouldn't.'

He swung round. 'And what on earth do you think gives you the right to barge in here and tell me how to bring up my daughter?'

'Tara needs you, Marius.'

He unstoppered the whisky bottle. 'Predictable, Topaz. Everyone's tried that.'

'But she does. She doesn't understand what's happened — she's lost her mother — '

'Now', he said, 'you're sinking into banality.'

389

She could see the fury in his eyes, yet she persevered. 'Have you talked to her at all? Have you tried to help her understand?'

His lip curled. 'Help her understand? How can I possibly do that? You make Suzanne's — Suzanne's death — ' he stumbled over the phrase, forcing it out ' — sound like some sort of mathematical problem. Just a question of putting things in the right order and they'll make sense.'

'You know I didn't mean that — '

'Didn't you?' His eyes were hard, pale blue stones. 'Go away, Topaz. Leave me alone.'

He had become unfamiliar to her, she thought. All the admiration — all the hero-worship — she had once reserved for Marius Temperley he was quickly stripping away.

She said again, 'Tara needs you.'

'She has my mother. You. Julia.' There was a note of finality in his voice, as though that settled things.

She could feel herself losing her self-control. 'She needs *you*.' Her voice trembled. 'Not just her aunts and her grandmother. She needs her *father*.'

He sloshed more whisky into the glass. Watching him, for the first time in her life she found herself almost disliking him. She said coldly, 'Or is that the trouble? That you're not really Tara's father. Is that why you're neglecting her, Marius? Because you don't really care about her?'

When he looked at her, it was an effort of will to remain in the room. Never in her whole life had Marius Temperley looked at her like that. She wanted to end this dreadful conversation here and now, and to run away, preferably all the way back to London.

He said softly, 'How dare you?' Then he crossed the room to her, still with that same expression in his eyes. For a moment she thought he was going to hit her.

But he said only, 'I *love* Tara. Now, for God's sake

390

go, before I do something I'll regret for the rest of my life.'

She had stepped back. But, opening the door, she paused.

'You asked me what gave me the right to tell you how to bring up Tara. Well, I'll tell you, Marius. I may not have any children yet, but I am a daughter, aren't I? And *my* father died when I was six. The same age Tara is now. And my mother's always made it obvious to me that she thinks I'm a nuisance rather than a blessing. You're right, of course, I don't know anything about being a parent, but I do know what it's like to be someone that no one much wants. And I don't want it to be like that for Tara.' She stumbled out of the room.

In her bedroom she pulled her suitcase out from under the bed and began to fling clothes into it. She had emptied the first drawer when she sat down on the edge of the bed, her head in her hands, and wept. She couldn't stop crying. She knew that she wept for Charlie, whom she had loved, as well as for Suzanne and for Marius.

She remained at Missencourt, she supposed, because she was too headachy and red-eyed to cope with timetables or trains or the difficult business of explaining things to the Temperleys. And because Adele hugged her, and Tara sat on her knee, and Julia, briefly dropping in on the way home from work, kissed her and gave her a box of chocolates. 'Someone keeps giving me them,' Julia explained. A roll of the eyes. 'And there's a limit to how many chocolates you can eat, isn't there?' After Julia had driven on to collect William from Prudence Chancellor, Topaz was left feeling exhausted and shaky, and wondering how on earth anyone could think there was a limit to the number of chocolates you could eat.

The following morning she woke early, once again. As she watched Marius leave the house, she stood irresolute, wondering what to do. Giving it one last chance, she went downstairs and made toast and tea.

In the boot room, he glanced at her. His gaze drifted to the cup and plate.

'Wouldn't you rather throw them at me?'

Mutely, she shook her head. Then he took the crockery from her hands and put them on the windowsill. And then he wrapped his arms round her and muttered, 'Sorry. I'm so sorry, Topaz.'

Which made her weep again, of course. Letting her go, he sat down on one of the old wicker chairs and hunched forward. He said softly, 'I keep going over it. Either it was my fault, for not driving Suzanne home that day — '

'Marius,' she said, shocked, 'you can't possibly believe that.'

When he looked up at her, she saw that his eyes were full of horror. 'But if it was just an accident, perhaps that makes it even worse. Because, if death is so random, then I could lose *her* too, couldn't I? I could lose Tara. And I couldn't bear that. Not after Suzanne. Not after the baby.' He looked away. He said quietly, 'It would be easier not to love her, you see.'

'But you can't *choose* who you love.' She thought of Charlie and felt that sharp, familiar pang. She hadn't chosen to fall in love with Charlie, had she? Or if she had, then it had been a foolish choice. It would have been far more sensible, wouldn't it, to have fallen for a more run-of-the-mill sort of man.

Now, she reached out a hand, and touched Marius's bowed head. 'Tara will keep loving you', she said, 'no matter what happens. But if you aren't kind to her, she'll begin to think she doesn't *deserve* to be loved. That there is something wrong with her.'

He looked exhausted, tired beyond endurance. After a while, he said, 'I know everyone's waiting for me to — what's the cliché? — to pick up the pieces. But I don't know how to, Topaz. I honestly don't know how.'

She sat down beside him. Her own life seemed scattered in fragments around her. She was not the person, she thought, to ask about picking up pieces. 'I don't know,' she said. 'People say you do a little bit at a time, don't they?'

It was a long while before he spoke. 'The only thing I feel at the moment is missing *her*. All the time. I can't stop thinking about it. Thinking about what happened. The evening before — when we were in London — we quarrelled, you see. I keep wondering — I keep wondering if that's why she went. Because she was fed up. Because of the quarrel. Maybe she was fed up with *me*.' He turned to her. 'That's why I drink. It stops me thinking. And as for work — ' he looked despairing ' — I know that everyone thinks that I should get back into the routine, take a day at a time, all that. But how can I go back to work when I can't face driving a car? Just the thought of that bloody Rolls makes me feel sick. Getting behind a wheel — making those sorts of decisions — now that I know what can happen — ' He closed his eyes tightly. He whispered, 'The car was hardly damaged, Topaz. She hit the verge, that's all. But it broke her neck. It broke her neck!'

She couldn't think of a single thing to say. It was not as though she had a cure for grief. So she took his hand in hers and sat for a long time, just keeping him company.

★　★　★

When the decoration of the ground floor of his house was almost complete, Rick invited Julia to dinner.

The dining room was one of the loveliest rooms in the house. Wide French windows looked out over the back lawn, through the thicket of shrubs to the sea. Julia had chosen a pale blue and cream stripe for the walls of the room, and the curtains were swathes of pale blue silk, lined and trimmed with cream. In the distance, she could hear the sound of the sea. She found herself for the first time in ages relaxing, letting some of the stresses and strains of the last few weeks fall away. There was something about the house, she decided. Something dreamy and restful and soothing. She rather envied Rick Hunter his beautiful house.

After dinner, there were Swiss chocolates, Turkish cigarettes and French brandy, with real coffee. 'Such luxury,' said Julia, giving a sigh of pleasure. 'Where do you find such marvellous things?'

He smiled. 'Here and there.'

'You're spoiling me, Rick. I can hardly move. I feel hideously fat.'

'You look beautiful. Perfect.'

There was something in his eyes that discomfited her, so she changed the subject. 'There's one thing you haven't thought about, Rick.'

'What's that?'

'A name. A house like this should have a name.'

'It was named after the family who built it,' he explained. 'I won't have that, of course, now that it's mine.'

'I wonder whether it's bad luck to change the name of a house? Like it is with a boat.'

'You don't believe that sort of rubbish, do you?'

'Probably not.'

'*Probably* . . . ?'

'Everyone's a little bit superstitious, aren't they? We like to think we're not, but we all are.'

'I'm not,' he said.

'Everyone touches wood — or crosses their fingers — '

'I don't. People make their own luck.'

'Some of the time, perhaps. But not always. Things happen by chance.' Julia's eyes darkened. 'Think of

Suzanne. Perhaps she forgot to touch wood that day.'

'Perhaps she skidded on black ice,' said Rick. 'Or perhaps there was mud on the road. Or she was tired, and lost concentration, and didn't brake soon enough for the corner.'

There was a silence. He said, 'You're thinking of your husband, aren't you?' and she looked up, startled that he had read her mind so easily.

'Will didn't exactly make his own luck, did he?'

Rick made a dismissive gesture. 'You don't really understand what happened that night, Julia. You said so yourself. You don't know why Will chose to go to the pub, or why he stayed out late, or why the three men went sailing. There must have been reasons for each one of those things.'

Julia remembered the account books, with their scrawled, blotted explanations of Will's anxiety. She remembered returning to Hidcote Cottage a few days after Will's death and finding it ransacked. She said slowly, 'There are so many things I'd like to understand. I never thought Will was the secretive sort. Yet there was so much he didn't tell me.'

He glanced at her sharply. 'What sort of thing?'

Julia shrugged. 'Nothing that matters now.' She stood up. 'I should go home.'

'So soon?'

'Early start tomorrow.' She gave a rueful smile. 'Early start every day, these days.'

He fetched her coat. In the courtyard Julia looked up. It was a clear, cold night, and in the black velvet of the sky there glittered a multitude of stars.

Rick said, 'My nan used to show me the stars. She taught me how to find the Plough. I can still remember. She was a great old girl, my nan. Worth the rest of them put together.' He squinted. 'Always seem to be more stars here than in London.'

'That's because of the lights,' she said. 'You can't see

the stars so well in London because of all the lights.' She pulled the collar of her coat around her, shivering in the chilly spring weather. 'Will you settle here, Rick? Or have you bought this house as a weekend place?'

'I'd like to settle,' he said. 'If things work out.'

Then he kissed her. She hadn't kissed a man since Jack, since Will. She had forgotten how much she had missed both the reassurance of being desired and the comfort of being held. To begin with, his lips were cool and speculative, as though he half expected her to push him away. Then his kisses became more urgent. His breathing thickened and his hands pressed against the contours of her body, kneading the flesh at the back of her neck, following the bones of her spine. Her own response shocked her in its speed, its intensity. Caught up in motherhood and in the business of survival, she had put aside her own needs. Now, as his mouth caressed her neck and her throat, she found herself wanting him. His palms cupped her buttocks, pressing him against her. She could feel his insistence, his strength. There was something seductive about it, something that made her almost want to give in to him, to let him take her here, in the moonlight, the sea pounding such a short distance away.

She heard him murmur her name over and over again. *Julia, Julia, Julia.* The repetition was almost a groan, almost a cry of pain. She pulled away from him. 'Rick. Please — '

'Sorry.' The word was a gasp. 'I'm sorry.'

As she tucked her hair back behind her ears and straightened her clothing, she saw him turn aside, and walk a few yards away, and stand, his back to her.

On the journey back to Longridge he seemed to snap back into the familiar Rick Hunter, talking to her about the house, light, easy conversation that distracted and did not demand. She found herself wondering how many Rick Hunters there were. And which one was the real one.

They were driving along a narrow country lane when they caught sight of a car's headlights, coming towards them. Because the road was wide enough to permit only one vehicle, Rick tucked into the entrance to a field, giving way to the other car.

As it passed them, Julia gave a small gasp.

'What is it?' he asked.

She whispered, 'I thought I saw — '

'What?'

'Someone I once knew.' She took a deep breath. 'It's nothing. I'm sure I must be mistaken.' She knew that was not true.

They drove on. In her mind's eye she saw clearly the face of the other car's driver. *Jack*, she thought, as the night and the trees crouched over them. Jack.

★ ★ ★

Still, she kept an eye on Marius. From a tactful distance, Topaz watched him go through the motions of living again: playing with Tara, talking to his mother, writing replies to the many letters of condolence. There was something hesitant and mechanical about his attempts to gather up the threads that made Topaz's heart ache. It was like watching someone trying to remember lines from a forgotten play.

She joined him on his early morning walks. The dogs ran ahead, scurrying in the leaf mould. Their breath clouded the crisp spring air and sunlight tumbled between the branches. Sometimes they talked. Once, he spoke about the loss of his unborn child. All that unrealized potential, all those hopes that had come to nothing. They sat on a fallen log as his fingers clawed at the bark, tearing it from the wood. The futility, he said, of a story ended before it had even begun. He had pictured, as all prospective parents do, the child they might have. If it had been a boy, they would have called him Francis, after Marius's father. Elizabeth for a girl, for no other reason than that they both liked the name. Suzanne's black eyes or Marius's blue. Her nimble fingers, his strength. Now even those images were fading and the fantasy children were faltering shadows, slipping fast back into the twilight. He had no photographs, no memories. Nothing to tie that child to him. One day he'd have forgotten even what might have been. One day, he said savagely, there would be nothing left, nothing at all.

On a rainswept morning, he talked to her about Suzanne. They were climbing the hill behind Missencourt. The words came out fast, tumbling, as though he was afraid that if he stopped he'd never start again.

'We met in a pub,' he said. 'A little grey stone pub in a village in Northumberland. The Bird in Hand or the Woolpack or something. The locals resented us because we took their seats by the fire. It was all there was — that, or the Officers' Mess, and you found yourself going stir crazy if you stayed at the camp all the time. I looked across the room and there she was. You couldn't not notice her, somehow. It wasn't that she was the prettiest. There were some real glamour girls.'

She said, 'You fell in love with her.'

'Yes. It took me a long time to realize. *Years.*' He threw her a smile. 'Though we weren't a marriage made in heaven, were we?'

'It was rather a shock.' Topaz recalled that hot August day in 1946 when Marius had announced his marriage to Suzanne. 'So unexpected. Everyone was in such a flap.'

She and her mother had gone back to London early. She remembered sitting in the train and feeling miserable for no easily definable reason.

'I didn't want to marry her,' Marius said. 'Not then. I

knew I had to because of the baby, but I didn't want to. I felt trapped, forced into something I hadn't chosen. That's why I made sure we did it quickly, so I didn't have time to change my mind.' He threw a stick for the dogs and they hurtled off into the mist. 'Suzanne shook me up. Made me think about things. Challenged my assumptions. Maybe I'll forget all that. Maybe I'll go back to being what I was before I met her.'

She thought about Charlie, what she had been before Charlie. 'No,' she said. 'It doesn't work like that.'

He dug his hands into the pockets of his coat and continued fast up the hill. 'I'd led such a narrow life,' he said. 'Home and school and the army. I did everything I was told to do. Until I was in my mid-twenties, every step I took was chosen for me — by my parents or my school or my country. Falling in love with Suzanne was the first time I managed to break away from that. She wasn't who my family would have chosen for me. She wasn't the sort of woman I was *expected* to marry. And it was difficult sometimes. We didn't always fit together. And I was never sure, God help me, that she loved me. But you can never be sure, can you? I thought', he said, and she had to look away, unable to bear the pain in his eyes, 'that if we had another child, then I'd be sure. That she'd never leave me. But I was wrong, wasn't I?'

He turned away, pressing on to the summit. She hurried to keep up with him, her wellingtons slipping on the wet chalk. Her breath came in short, ragged puffs, as she called out after him, 'I always admired you for what you did.'

'Admired me?' He paused, startled. 'For what?'

'For standing by Suzanne. A lot of men wouldn't have done. I used to read such awful things in the paper.' She drew level with him. She remembered, just after the war had ended, those bleak little paragraphs tucked away at the foot of newspaper columns. The soldier who, returning to England after three years abroad, had strangled his wife after finding her with newborn twins. The prison camp survivor who, unable to accept the presence of another man's child, had locked the infant in a back room and given him rags to wear and scraps to eat.

He said, 'Your instructions, Topaz, I seem to remember.'

They were almost at the top of the hill; he stared out through the rain over fields and woodland. 'Can't see the sea,' he said. 'She always loved the sea.' She wasn't sure whether it was the rain, or whether there were tears in his eyes.

'Do you regret it?' she said. 'Do you regret marrying Suzanne?' She needed to know. Whether it was better to have loved and lost . . .

He said, 'It was never dull. It was always exciting. Exhilarating. She made me feel alive.' He frowned. The rain had thickened, hammering on to his head, plastering his hair to his scalp.

Then he said slowly, 'I chose to walk Suzanne home from the pub that first night. I chose to look for her after I came back from France. And I chose, as you said, to stand by her after she told me about Neil Finlay. These past weeks, I've sometimes wished I hadn't. Then I couldn't have lost her. Then I wouldn't feel like this. But that's nonsense, isn't it? There's the time we had together and there's Tara. You can't unthread your life, just keeping the best bits.' He looked up at the grey, heavy sky. 'I keep thinking', he said softly, 'that she's just gone out for a while. Whenever someone comes into the room, I think that it's her. When I turn over in bed, I reach out for her. Every morning, when I wake up, I remember it all over again. And it's as though I've been told for the first time. If I could just get used to it, Topaz. At the moment, that's all I ask. Just to get used to it. So that I don't have to find it out again day after day after day.'

* * *

She sat beside him when he drove a car for the first time
since Suzanne's death. The Rolls in which Suzanne had
died had been sold, replaced by a two-year-old Wolseley.
She watched him go through the familiar sequence of
ignition, clutch, gears and handbrake as if for the first
time. She saw how his hands shook and the colour
drained from his face. They had intended to drive to
Hernscombe, but after the short run from Missencourt
to the Temperley's workshop at Great Missen they
looped back to the house. Parking on the gravel, Marius
climbed out of the car, slamming the door behind him,
and walked to the edge of the copse. He leaned forward,
his fists clenched. She thought he was going to be sick.
Instead, he fumbled for his cigarettes: they spilled from
the packet, flecks of white on the grass. Then the click
of the lighter, and the small plume of blue-grey smoke.

He came back to the car. 'Sorry. An undignified
exhibition.' She saw the desperation in his eyes. 'Things
to do — ' he said, and turned quickly away, heading
back to the house.

A few days later he tried again. This time she talked
to him. Did not make the mistake of thinking she must
be quiet, so that he could concentrate. She talked about
anything that came into her head. Her flat, her work at
Angelique's, the dinner parties. By the time she told
him about the disastrous dinner party where the cat had
got at the salmon, they were halfway to the coast. She
felt triumphant.

The next day they drove to Lyme Regis. Parking in
the town, a little of Marius's tension seemed to drain
away. He braked, reaching for his cigarettes. 'Must stop
smoking so much,' he muttered. 'Tomorrow. I'll stop
smoking tomorrow.' He glanced at her. 'Do you drive,
Topaz?'

'Not yet. Though Charlie once showed me how to

start and stop the car.'

'How is he, your chap? Won't he be missing you?'

She knew that he was talking to fill the gap, talking so that he did not have to think. She said, 'I shouldn't think so. He's gone to America.'

'For how long?'

'I don't know.' She wound down the window, tapped ash on to the pavement. 'We're finished, actually.'

She climbed out of the car and headed down the narrow street towards Cobb Harbour. She hugged her arms around herself, thinking of Charlie, her Charlie. She knew that Marius was behind her, his footsteps matching hers. The knowledge comforted her. And it seemed to her that Charlie had slipped a little further away, becoming less clear, as though someone had drawn a curtain.

★ ★ ★

Jack came to see her, of course, at the worst possible time; after a tiresome day's work (a late consignment of valves: Julia had to make a dozen phone calls to discover that they were stranded somewhere near Ludgershall because the van that was transporting them had broken down). Then, driving home that evening, the car began to make a peculiar noise. Coming into the village, she saw Rick Hunter's Morgan parked outside her front door and her heart sank at the effort of having to be civilized when all she wanted was to settle William and sink into a hot bath.

But Rick heard the Aston Martin's clunking and stood in the intermittent showers and fading light, fiddling beneath the bonnet. So when he knocked on the door, it was the least she could do to invite him indoors to wash his hands and offer him a drink. He followed her into the kitchen, where she was heating up stew for William's supper; at first, while she was mashing the potatoes and straining the carrots, he just *watched* her, which she found rather irritating. Then he began to talk, and, after a few moments, forcing herself to pay attention, she realized that he was inviting her to a dinner-dance. She was racking her brains for an excuse when the doorbell rang.

She went back to the hall and opened the door, and there was Jack. After the initial shock, she felt an unanticipated and almost overwhelming fury. That he should, after two years' absence, just *turn up*. When he said, 'Do you mind if I come in?' a part of her wanted to tell him to go away, but instead she made a humphing noise and beckoned him indoors. Her heart was pounding so hard she felt dizzy, and she held William tightly, as if to draw comfort from him.

Then she had to introduce the two men to each other. She thought how different they were: the bullish, powerful Rick and the darkly handsome Jack. Though they shook hands, it seemed to Julia that they circled each other like dogs, wary and possessive, their movements informed by a scarcely restrained aggression.

Then Rick, picking up his coat, said, 'Next Friday, then, Julia?' and she found herself agreeing. Because she wanted him out of the house. And because she was too tired to think of an excuse.

Jack's first question, when they were alone, was, 'You're dating him, then?'

'Rick's just a friend,' she snapped. She could not have said why his assumption made her feel so cross.

Jack said, 'He's in love with you.'

'Don't be ridiculous.'

'He is.' His tone was cool, matter of fact. He came to stand beside her. 'Is this my nephew?'

Something about the softening of his voice made Julia, too, soften. 'This is William. He seems to be falling asleep, I'm afraid — and he hasn't had his supper yet — ' She sniffed, noticing a burnt, acrid smell. 'The *stew!*' she cried. 'Oh God, I've forgotten the stew!'

Jack went into the kitchen. She heard him turning off the gas, running the tap.

'It's burnt, I'm afraid,' he said, when he came back, 'but I've saved some of it.'

'It doesn't matter,' she muttered. 'William's asleep, so there's only me, and I'm not really — '

He sat down beside her. 'Julia . . . ?'

'Turning up like that!' she hissed. '*Again*, Jack!'

'I know. I'm sorry.' He looked apologetic. 'I thought if I phoned you might tell me to push off. But it's a bad time, isn't it? Shall I go?'

She let out a sigh. 'It's not *you*, Jack.' She made an effort. 'It's lovely to see you again, honestly.' Which was true. One of the brothers she had loved had come home. 'It's just that things have been so *awful*. Suzanne — and poor Marius — '

He held her as she wept. There was such comfort in his familiarity. It was the first time, she realized, that she had cried since Suzanne's death. She had been too busy for grief.

When she could speak, she said, 'Why have you come home, Jack?'

'Mum wrote to me about Suzanne. I thought — I don't know — I thought I should be here. Poor old Marius. Doesn't know what's hit him, does he, the poor bugger.' His gaze shifted to her. 'You look worn out.'

Julia sat back, and closed her eyes. 'I'm exhausted,' she admitted. 'Absolutely bloody exhausted.' It was true; she didn't know how she would even get off the sofa. She asked, 'Could you do something for me? Could you unbuckle William's shoes?'

He knelt on the floor in front of her and slid William's shoes from his feet. Very carefully, so as not to wake him, Julia carried William upstairs and tucked him up in his cot.

Back in the sitting room, she asked Jack whether he had eaten. Jack shook his head.

'Do you fancy some burnt stew?'

He smiled. 'I can't think of anything nicer.'

They ate in the kitchen. Jack talked about Canada. 'So vast,' he said. 'And that feeling of being up against the elements.'

'You always liked a challenge, Jack.' Idly, she pushed food around her plate. 'I imagine you driving a sledge through the snow. With those dogs — what are they called — '

'Huskies,' he said. 'It wasn't quite like that. Though it had its moments. Blizzards and ice storms and freezing bloody cold.' He had finished his supper; he went to the sink and began to hack the layer of blackened vegetables out of the bottom of the saucepan. She heard him say, 'It gave me time to think.'

Julia put down her knife and fork. She really wasn't hungry anyway. 'What did you think about?'

'Will. Me. Us.'

He was silhouetted against the window, his back to her. She found herself looking at his broad shoulders and the small, black curls in the nape of his neck. And wondering whether, after all this time, after everything that had happened, she still wanted him.

'And did you come to any conclusions?'

'That, at the very least, I'd been a stupid, jealous idiot. That I had wrecked quite a few lives.'

'Oh,' she said lightly, 'I think you overestimate your importance, Jack. I think Will and I managed to do that quite well ourselves.' She gathered the plates and cutlery together. 'And you don't have to clean that saucepan. Leave the beastly thing to soak.'

But he continued to chip at the charred layer with a knife. 'I've never had a forgiving nature,' he admitted.

405

'Always was one to bear a grudge. And when you married Will, I couldn't forgive either of you. The way I saw it, Will had taken what belonged to me. And everything went from there, didn't it?'

Julia felt weary and bedraggled and beyond any sort of effort, but two years was a long enough exile and she knew that there were things that needed to be said.

'The truth is', she said firmly, 'that I should never have married Will. We were good friends, but we weren't right as man and wife. I knew that the day I married him. I probably knew it before I married him, but I was too proud to admit I'd made a mistake. Will realized it too, I suspect. Oh, he thought he loved me — and he did love me in his way. And I loved him, too. But I didn't love him enough to be married to him.' She looked at him appraisingly. 'But I don't know that you and I would have managed much better, Jack. Both of us like to have our own way too much. We'd have fought like cat and dog, wouldn't we?'

He grinned. 'Argued as we headed down the aisle.'

She said softly, 'It's so nice to see you again. I thought you might have met someone in Canada.'

He said, 'There is someone,' and her heart gave a little squeeze. She wondered whether she was relieved or jealous.

'Tell me.'

'She's called Esther. She runs a lodging house in a town called McKenna. She was married, but her husband died in the war.'

'Children?' He shook his head.

'What does she look like?'

'Brown hair . . . brown eyes . . . '

She said impatiently, 'Is she beautiful, Jack? Are you going to marry her?'

'Yes, to your first question. I don't know, to the second.'

She put the plates in the sink. 'Time you did,' she

said firmly. 'You'd be happier. Marriage would suit you.' She looked him in the eye. 'It didn't suit me. I don't think I'll marry again. But you mustn't think I've been unhappy since you went away. Quite the opposite, in fact. Oh, it was very hard at first and these last weeks have been dreadful, of course. But I've been so lucky to have William. He's the best thing that ever happened to me, truly the best.' She paused and then she said curiously, 'Why *did* you come back?'

'I'm not sure.' He put the saucepan on the draining board. 'Loose ends, I suppose. Debts to pay. To my mother. To Will. And to you and William. You shouldn't hitch your life to someone else's when you've debts to pay, should you?'

★ ★ ★

Jack's homecoming seemed to return some optimism to their lives. He reminded them of better times, Topaz thought, and, in his company, Marius brightened a little.

He went back to work. At first just for a few hours, then for half a day. Topaz felt herself relax a little, as though she had been holding her breath for a very long time. Some mornings she overslept and did not wake until eight o'clock. When she tested herself, thinking of Charlie, it seemed to her that the stab to the heart did not now go quite so deep. She must be fickle, she thought, to have recovered quite so quickly. Or was it because, like Marius, she had lost some of her capacity to feel?

In future, she promised herself, *I shall have brief, meaningless affairs*. She imagined herself sitting on a tall stool in a sophisticated cafe, a more glamorous version of the one in Leicester Square where she and Francesca had met Charlie. She would be dressed in richly coloured silks and velvets; she would wear at her neck and throat ancient, mysterious jewels. She would smoke a cigarette in a holder, and she would drink cocktails and laugh a deep, low, throaty laugh. Men would cluster around her and, cold-hearted, she would favour them for a night or two.

What she would most definitely *not* do, she resolved, was fall in love again.

15

It was strange the way that, now Jack had come home, she started to notice things about Rick. As if, Julia thought with some exasperation, she was *comparing* the two men. As if she was making a list of pros and cons and discovering that Rick fell resoundingly on the debit side.

There was the dinner-dance, for instance. It was a grand affair, held at Bournemouth's Winter Gardens. Julia wore a black dress she had bought in Selfridge's. She was in London one day, and she saw it in the shop window and fell in love with it. It had a tiny waist and a wide, full skirt that fell to the calf, and panels of black embroidery on the bodice and skirt. The sales assistant persuaded her to buy elbow-length gloves and a pair of narrow, high-heeled black shoes to go with it. She managed to find time to visit the hairdresser, who swept up her unruly hair into an elegant knot, glueing it into place with setting lotion. Her own looking glass, and the expression in Rick's eyes when he called for her, told her the effort had been worthwhile.

The dinner was passable and, as always, she enjoyed the dancing. Rick was courteous, attentive, admiring. Yet, as the evening wore on, his company began to grate. Just little things, at first. He listed for her his latest acquisitions for his new house. The furniture, the paintings, the carpets and china and glassware. She noticed that he always told her the price of things. *Cost me a hundred and fifty quid, that rug. Didn't know you could pay a hundred and fifty quid for a rug.* It took her a while to work out who he reminded her of. Then she realized: Maurice Chancellor. Rick sounded like a more successful, wealthier version of Maurice Chancellor.

She was being a snob, she told herself. It was easy for her, who had been born in a lovely house, and who had always been surrounded by beautiful objects, to look down on someone who talked about money. And what a ridiculous convention, after all, to pretend that cost didn't matter. As if she herself did not, like everyone else, have to work out her household accounts.

Then she noticed that, throughout the evening, Rick made disparaging remarks about the other guests. *Looks like a battleship*, he murmured, of a very buxom woman wearing a grey satin dress and rather too many diamonds. *All lit up and about to put out to sea.* Julia giggled because the comparison was apt, but after a while she couldn't help realizing that he never said anything nice about anyone. That he never admired, never praised. Though her fellow guests were, as Rick pointed out to her, an uninspiring lot, whose conversation seemed limited to hunting and to listing the faults of the government, there was something rather wearing about the stream of softly voiced criticisms. Amusing enough at first, but ultimately dispiriting. As though he couldn't find anything much to like in anyone. As though he shored up his own ego by belittling others. And as though there was true worth only in the beautiful objects with which he filled his house, value only in that which could be bought.

Julia wondered whether she had always been aware of this less attractive side of Rick and had disregarded it. And, if so, why? None of the answers to that question was especially flattering. Either she had been weak enough to put up with his faults because she had needed her self-confidence fed by his admiration, or — an even more uncomfortable thought — her loneliness had been such that she had accepted the company of a man she did not always, in the end, much like.

Or had she begun to view Rick in a colder light since

410

that comment of Jack's, made on his first visit to her? *He's in love with you, Julia.* Though she had dismissed his remark at the time, believing it to be ridiculous, she had not forgotten it. Now she struggled to convince herself that Rick saw their relationship as she did: unimportant, just for fun. After a while, thinking back, she found herself wondering whether, for him, it had ever been so. She recalled his persistence after their first meeting at Maurice's party. His refusal to take no for an answer. His gifts, his eagerness after Suzanne's death to help her with all those little tasks. If he had been a different person, a nicer person, then she could have passed that off as a natural, selfless sympathy for the bereaved. But with Rick, that just didn't quite fit.

With growing disquiet, she remembered her first visit to his house, when he had torn up the interior designer's plans and asked for her advice instead. She had assumed he lacked confidence in his own good taste, but there was another interpretation, wasn't there? That he wanted to please her. That he wanted to flatter her, charm her, court her. She had chosen the shade of every wall, curtain and carpet in that house. The realization discomfited her, as though she had without noticing it slipped into an intimacy she would have preferred to avoid, an intimacy that seemed to bind her closer to him than the kisses they exchanged at the end of a date. Her stamp had been put on his bricks and mortar: when they parted, would he wash over those walls with a different colour? Or would they remain there for years, those dove greys and sea greens and azure blues, evidence of his infatuation?

She knew that she must put an end to the relationship, but she found herself putting off the moment. She must be tactful, she thought, she must choose the right time. It disturbed her that her caution stemmed not so much from a desire to avoid hurting his feelings as from a fear of provoking Rick Hunter's other

side, the cold, ruthless side. *He's in love with you, Julia.*
Jack's remark had opened a Pandora's box of possibility,
one she would have preferred not to see, but could not
now ignore.

And oh, *Jack* . . . Sometimes she wished he had
stayed in Canada. An ignoble thought because anyone
could see how much happier his mother was since he
had come home. He had been a good friend to Marius,
too, calling frequently at Missencourt, refusing to give
up even during the days when Marius had been at his
most uncommunicative. Yet his homecoming had
unsettled her, recalling to her feelings she had believed
were finished with and best forgotten. When Jack was in
Canada, she had been able to put him out of her mind.
Welcoming him to her house once or twice a week,
seeing him with William — the dark head and the fair
side by side — recalled the past to her in all its vivid
colour.

Something stirred inside her, something restless and
dissatisfied. She had become aware of the shortcomings
of the life she thought herself content with and she
sensed change, sniffing it on the wind in much the same
way as, nearing the coast, you sensed the salt of the sea.

★ ★ ★

During the weeks immediately following Suzanne's
death, while Julia ran Temperley's single-handed,
Raymond Bell made his resentment of her clear. He
usurped her position when the opportunity arose,
making decisions that should have been hers alone to
take. When she challenged him, he said, with the
smooth smile she had come to loathe, 'But I was only
trying to help you out, Mrs Chancellor.' When she made
mistakes, he pointed out to her her shortcomings
— preferably in public, in front of an audience of
technicians and assembly workers.

Marius went back to work full-time at the end of April. Afterwards, Julia found herself sidelined. Though she had intended to ease Marius's return to work by continuing to come into the office daily, she found herself sitting in her office twiddling her thumbs. Every problem was passed on to Marius, every suggestion she herself made ignored. 'So good to see Mr Marius back,' Raymond Bell said pointedly. Though she could have discussed her difficulties with Marius, she did not. She would not whine and neither would she lose her temper. She had grown out of that and, besides, to give in to her anger would be to play into Raymond Bell's hands. It would confirm his opinion of her as over-emotional, unreliable, hysterical.

As she put on her coat to leave work that evening, she told herself that she should be relieved, should be glad to hand back the reins. Which she was in a way, of course, because it meant that Marius was surviving, was getting through this awful time. Yet a part of her did not feel glad, but felt instead flat and weary. In spite of the long hours, in spite of Raymond Bell and his like, she had enjoyed running Temperley's. It might have been tiring, demanding and sometimes frustrating, but it had never been *boring*. Whilst grieving for Suzanne, she had nevertheless relished the opportunity to put her own stamp on the company. Now, once again, she must step back. She must remember once more the limits of her aspirations and authority. Whatever she did, however good she was, the mere fact of her sex was a barrier to both ambition and success. Tonight the thought depressed her and, parking outside her house, she sat for a moment, tears pricking at the corners of her eyes, her head aching.

Indoors she took William upstairs with her so that she could keep an eye on him while she was changing. While she sat at the dressing table, yanking the knots from her hair, he opened her jewellery box, which he

413

knew was forbidden. When she scolded him, he edged away for a few moments and then went back to the box when he thought she wasn't looking, fiddling with the little compartments and drawers, tangling up the bracelets and pendants. So she told him off again and pushed the box to the back of the table, and turned aside for a moment, searching for a hairgrip that had fallen to the floor. When she glanced back, he was holding her little pearl engagement ring. 'Oh, William!' she said, exasperated, and tapped his hand. It was just a little tap, not a smack at all really, but his face crumpled and he toddled away, retreating, she assumed, to a corner of the room.

She was quickly plaiting her hair when she heard the sound. A stumble, a cry, and the awful thump, thump, thump of William tumbling the length of the stairs. Her stomach lurched and her heart pounded so hard it hurt as she ran, trailing hairpins and elastic bands, out of the room.

William was lying at the bottom of the stairs. As she hurried down to him, she heard herself moan with terror. When he moved, she felt weak with relief. Then she saw the blood. The entire side of his face was covered in blood. It trailed down the curve of his cheek, and dripped on to the floorboards. He began to scream, a high-pitched, frightened yell. When she picked him up, making frantic efforts to find out where the blood was coming from, he yelled louder. She was aware while she was kneeling on the floor, sweeping aside William's wet, scarlet hair, that there was someone at the door. The bell was ringing, her name was being called. She tugged at the handle and saw Jack.

He took in the situation immediately, lifting William out of her arms, carrying him into the sitting room. When she stood up, she realized she had been kneeling on the metal toy truck on which William must have fallen. There was a small, bloody imprint on her knee.

Jack was pressing his handkerchief against William's forehead. 'He's cut his head just below the hairline. I think he's going to need a few stitches.'

'Oh God — ' She was shaking.

'Look at me, Julia. William's going to be fine, he really is. Every kid falls over.' Jack's voice steadied her. 'We'll take him to the doctor, patch him up.'

At the surgery in Hernscombe Julia sat with William in her lap while the doctor put six stitches into his forehead and checked to see whether there was any concussion. William's howls had diminished to tremulous, intermittent moans and he curled his body into hers, as if to hide from the pain. On the journey home, he sucked his thumb with fierce concentration and his eyelids drooped.

In his bedroom Julia peeled off his clothes and dressed him in his pyjamas. He hardly stirred as she put him into his cot and tucked the blankets around him. She knelt by the cot, watching him as he slept, feeling outrage at the sight of the white bandage against the golden hair.

Downstairs, Jack put a cup of tea into her hands. Gripping the cup hard, she said, 'I smacked him. I smacked him just before he fell downstairs.'

He shot her a glance. 'Beat him black and blue and threatened to lock him in a cupboard?'

'Of course not!'

'Thought not. A little tap on the hand, then? It wasn't your fault, Julia.'

She said flatly, 'I'm his mother. He hasn't got a father. If it isn't my fault, whose is it?'

'You might just as well blame me for running off to Canada and not staying here to help you out. Or you could blame Will for getting himself killed in a bloody stupid accident. But there's no point in thinking like that, is there? No point in trying to apportion blame.'

'He'll have a scar, Dr Frobisher said so.' Julia twisted

her hands together. 'When they're born, they're perfect. I wanted him to stay like that. I wanted nothing bad ever to happen to him.'

'It doesn't work like that. You know it doesn't. And, anyway, his hair will cover the scar. I bet he'll be proud of it, show it off to the other little boys.'

She said bitterly, 'Everything has a silver lining, does it, Jack?'

He flushed. 'Of course not. I didn't mean that. But these things happen, don't they, and you have to make the best of them.'

'Always look on the bright side?' She wasn't sure why she was taunting him.

'No. Just that you shouldn't dwell on things. You have to move on.'

'Is that what you think? That I *brood*? That I *mope*?' She was furious. 'That I'm stuck in a rut?'

'I didn't say that — '

'It's what you meant, though, isn't it? That I've stayed here while you've travelled the world — '

'Julia — '

'Let me tell you, Jack — ' and she thumped her teacup on to the saucer ' — that it's not so easy when you've got a child. You're not free just to cut and run.'

She saw his eyes spark and she knew she had hit a nerve. 'Staying at home may seem dull to you, but it was what I had to do. And I have my job — ' she said defensively, 'and I meet lots of people — '

'That character I met the other week?'

'I told you,' she said coldly, 'Rick's just a friend. An acquaintance.'

There was a silence. Outside, a blustery wind beat at the lilacs in the back garden. Her anger died as suddenly as it had been born. She closed her eyes and sank back on the sofa.

'I don't know why I'm behaving like this,' she said wearily. 'And after you've been so marvellous. I'm sorry

— it's been a rotten day, that's all.'

He said, 'You're right, of course, I did run away.'

'Jack — '

'It's true. After Will died I had to get away. I couldn't live with myself.'

She went to him. He was standing at the window. She rested her head against his shoulder. 'I thought you were very brave,' she said. 'Going to a new country, making a new start.'

'Did you?' He sounded sceptical.

She shivered. 'Sometimes I feel that I'm surrounded by ghosts. Will . . . Suzanne . . . my father . . . '

He put his arm around her. 'You should come to Canada. Bring William. Great country to bring up a kid.'

She wasn't sure what he was saying to her. He was stroking her hair; now his hand paused and he frowned.

'What is it?'

He drew out a hairpin. She laughed unsteadily. 'I was doing my hair when William fell downstairs. I must look a fright.'

'No. Never.' He turned to her, his eyes blue and intent. 'You look beautiful, Julia. But then, you always did.'

'Tangles in my hair and bloodstains on my jumper — '

When he kissed her forehead, she gave a little gasp, but did not draw back. 'Jack — '

He said, 'I'll go, if you like.'

She saw, and understood, the question in his eyes. 'No,' she said, quite calmly. 'Please stay. I want you to stay.'

Then she tilted up her face, and touched her lips against his. When he kissed her, she closed her eyes and the events of the day seemed at last to begin to slip away. Her fingertips traced the hollow of his spine, and his hands threaded through her hair. Gently his mouth brushed against her neck, her throat, her face. There was a familiarity about him that she found both exciting and reassuring. She peeled her jersey over her head and he bent and kissed her breasts. Then he knelt in front of her, pressing his mouth against her flat stomach with its feathering of tiny white stretch marks, while he unzipped her skirt.

Always in the past, desire had been tainted by fear or by guilt. But now she wasn't afraid and she didn't feel guilty. She was twenty-six years old and for the first time in her life making love to a man was an uncomplicated pleasure and an unmixed joy.

★ ★ ★

It was less than twenty-four hours later that Rick Hunter called. Since she had parted from Jack that morning, the hours had passed in a dreamy haze, all the little irritations and humiliations of work unnoticed. She couldn't concentrate; several times she caught herself staring into nothingness, thinking about Jack. She wondered whether her colleagues could tell, whether they could read the joy on her face just by looking at her. If they could, she decided, then she didn't particularly care.

She took the afternoon off to look after William and was relieved to see that his natural boisterousness was already returning. She had just put him to bed when the doorbell rang. As she showed Rick Hunter into the front room, he said, 'There's something I wanted to ask you.' He looked edgy, ill at ease. *There's something I have to say to you too*, she thought, as she offered him a drink.

Silent at first, he paced around the room. Then he thumped his fist into the palm of his hand, and said, 'I've come here to ask you — ' he ran the tip of his tongue over his teeth ' — I've come here to ask you to marry me, Julia.'

Her mind went blank. She sat down on the sofa, gripping her glass hard. She felt a mixture of shock and embarrassment.

'I've been trying to say something to you for weeks.' He was flushed, his brow beaded with sweat. 'Couldn't seem to find the right time.'

She said weakly, 'Rick, I had no idea.' She was angry with herself for having let the situation drift on too long. For having, however inadvertently, given him hope.

'You don't have to give me an answer now. Think about it.'

She put down her glass and pressed her fingertips together, choosing her words carefully. 'I'm sorry, Rick. I'm very flattered to be asked, but I can't marry you.' She searched for an excuse that would not hurt his pride. 'It's too soon after Will.'

'I can wait,' he said brusquely. 'I don't mind. As long as it takes.'

She shook her head. 'I don't want you to wait, Rick. You see, there simply isn't room in my life for marriage. Not with William, not with my work. Marriage takes hard work and energy and commitment — I found that out with Will. I wasn't up to it then and I'm certainly not up to it now. I'm so sorry.'

He sat down beside her. 'If you married me, Julia, you wouldn't have to work. And I'd get you help with William. You could have a nanny, a nursemaid, whatever you need. You wouldn't have to struggle on like this. You wouldn't have to live in a poky little house, or drive a rundown old car. You could have everything you want.'

'I have William and I have my work,' she said firmly. 'I don't want anything else.'

He made a dismissive sound. 'I don't believe that. Everyone wants to get on. Everyone wants to better themselves.'

She felt a flicker of impatience. How much plainer could she be? 'It depends what you mean by *get on*, doesn't it? It depends what you value. And I don't think you and I value the same things. So I'm sorry, Rick, but I can't marry you. I really can't.'

'But I love you, Julia.'

She stilled. Then she shook her head. 'No, you don't. You like me because of the way I look. And because I represent something you aspire to.'

He said slowly, 'I loved you the first time I saw you. Years ago, at Will's garage. I can remember what you were wearing — grey shorts and a red and white top. And you had combs in your hair.'

Her cotton shorts, her gingham top. She still wore them in the summer. Her tortoiseshell combs, long since mislaid. For the first time, she felt frightened. She looked away. 'That's not *love*, Rick, that's desire. You might have wanted me. But you didn't *love* me.'

'I bought the house for you. What more proof do you want?'

She spun round, horrified. 'The house . . . ?'

'My house. You like it, don't you? It's there, waiting for you. Done up just how you like it, just how you told me.'

She thought of that beautiful house by the sea and felt cold inside. 'Rick, the house is *yours*,' she said desperately. 'It's for *you*.'

He shook his head. 'It's yours. I always meant to be for you. For us.'

She was aware of a growing sense of horror. She said crisply, 'Then I'm sorry that you've wasted your money. Because I can't marry you, Rick. Not now. Not ever.'

First there was disbelief in his eyes and then pain. Seizing her hands in his, he said, 'Is it because of who I am? What I am? I'll better myself for you, Julia. Once a barrow boy doesn't mean you always have to be a barrow boy. I may have come from nothing, but I've made something of myself, haven't I?'

'Please, Rick — '

'Took elocution lessons — did you know that? Paid some woman in Highgate to teach me how to sound my aitches. Only took me a couple of weeks. I'm a quick learner, Julia. I'll read books, if that's what you want. Talk fancy, brush up my manners. Learn a foreign language, if that's what it takes — I can speak a bit of French already. I wouldn't let you down.'

She pulled away from him, wrapping her arms around herself. 'It isn't that, Rick.'

'What is it, then?'

'I don't love you,' she said quietly. 'I'm sorry.'

She saw him blink, look away. Then he said, 'Even that . . . I can manage without that.'

'*I* can't.'

'In time — '

'*No*. We're too different. We have nothing in common.'

'I can change.' As they rested on her, his eyes were avid and hungry.

She said softly, 'You see, I'm not even sure whether I *like* you, Rick.'

He leaned forward, hands gripping his knees. 'I see.' There was a long silence. When next he looked at her, she saw that his expression had altered. He said, 'Is this to do with Will's brother?'

Her stomach gave a little squeeze. *Jack*, she thought. But she said, 'It's nothing to do with Jack. Nothing at all.'

'I just wondered. I saw the way he looked at you.'

She was sitting on the edge of the seat, pressing her nails into her palms. In Rick Hunter's eyes she had glimpsed something flicker, something venomous and reptilian.

He said, 'Nothing like keeping it in the family, is there?'

She had to quell a shiver. Hiding her fear, she said

firmly, proudly, 'I think you should go, Rick. I'd like you to go.'

But he did not move. 'And *what* a family. All nice and proper on the outside, but underneath — *well*. I mean — ' and he sat back, his dark eyes still focused on her, never letting her go ' — some of my dealings may not be whiter than white. But the Chancellors — fingers in some pretty murky pies, haven't they?'

She said angrily, 'You're talking about Maurice. You mustn't judge the rest of the family by him.'

He said, 'I'm talking about your husband, Julia.'

She stared at him. 'Will? Don't be ridiculous.'

He gave a small smile. 'It's true. Will's dealings weren't exactly above board, you know.'

'Nonsense. That's nonsense.'

He stood up and lit a cigarette, cupping his hands around the flame. She had to force herself to sit still, not to squirm beneath that cold, dark, relentless gaze.

He said, 'Didn't you know, Julia? Will was selling forged petrol coupons. I always wondered whether you knew. But you didn't, did you? How — *forgetful* of Will, not to tell you.'

She whispered, 'You're lying — '

'No.' His voice was sharp. 'Your perfect, sainted and rather conveniently deceased husband was selling forged petrol coupons. He was also handling stolen goods. I don't suppose you knew that either. *I* know, you see, because Will was working for me. Good old Cousin Maurice put us in touch when Will needed to earn a bit of extra cash. But he was willing enough, Julia, willing enough.'

Now the room was stifling and airless. She went to the window, resting her hands on the sill. She could hear the shudder of her indrawn breath. Outside the light was draining away and shadows patched the lawn and shrubs. Into her disbelief had nudged a kernel of doubt. *Will needed to earn a bit of extra cash.* She remembered the account books.

She whispered, 'He was in debt. Will was in debt.'

'Course he was. I helped him out.'

'Helped him out . . . ' She stared at him, beginning to see how it had happened. Will, you *idiot*, she thought. She said, 'You got Will involved in the black market?'

'Oh, he got himself involved. All I did was to smooth the way for him. Usual story, I suppose. He'd started up the garage without enough capital to cover his initial costs. And, besides, Maurice had sold him a pig in a poke.'

Everything Rick was saying rang true. It made appalling sense. Will had invested in a business that had never really got off the ground. When he had run into trouble — because of bad debtors, because of the severe winter weather — he must have flailed around, looking for a way out. First, he had taken out the bank loan, which he had struggled to repay. Then, Julia realized, he would have gone to Maurice. And Maurice had introduced him to Rick Hunter.

Rick said coldly, 'What I'm trying to point out to you, Julia, is that your disdain is a little misplaced. You and I, we're just the same. Nothing in common, have we? Not true. Simply not true. How do you think Will paid the rent? Paid for *you*?'

With deepening horror, she remembered the gifts. The flowers, the perfume, the cigarettes. Had they, too, been courtesy of Rick Hunter?

'The black market . . . ' She stared at him. 'So you're a criminal,' she said scornfully. 'Just a common criminal.'

In the depths of Rick Hunter's pupils, something dark moved. 'You shouldn't say things like that, Julia. You should be grateful to me. For keeping Will afloat.'

'*Grateful?*' She could hardly bear to look at him, her loathing was so intense. 'Grateful for mixing him up in something he couldn't cope with? Grateful for frightening him?'

'He went into it with his eyes open. No one forced him.'

An even more terrible realization had begun to dawn. In her mind's eye she saw Will, bruised and beaten, the night before he died.

'He was hurt. Someone had hurt him. Just before the accident. Was it *you*?'

'Not *me*.' His lips stretched over his long, feral teeth. 'Not *personally*.'

'*Why*? *Why* did you do that to him?'

Rick shrugged. 'He wanted out. Couldn't have that, not after all the trouble I'd gone to. Business doesn't work like that. You understand, don't you, Julia? You're in business, after all, like me.'

'I'm not like you,' she whispered. 'I'm not like you at all. You're disgusting. You revolt me.' She backed away, unable to bear his proximity. 'How I could ever have let you near me . . . ? You *hounded* Will.'

'I *helped* him.' His gaze was black, lightless. 'I helped him out when he was in trouble.'

'No. You hounded him. To his death.'

A flick of the eyelids. The hurt and anger dropped away, and was replaced by something calculating and cruel. The corners of his mouth curled. 'Hounded him . . . yes, I suppose so. But to his death? Well, maybe.'

'*Maybe*?' She heard her voice rise. 'What do you mean, *maybe*?'

'You see', he said calmly, 'I've never been completely convinced that Will *is* dead.'

'Of course he's dead. The boat — '

'Yes, yes. The boat that sank. If Will was on that boat then he's dead. *If* he was on it.'

She went to the door and opened it, and said, 'Go, please go,' in a voice that shook more than she had intended. But he remained in the room, watching her with those scavenger's eyes.

'To tell the truth, I don't give a damn whether Will Chancellor's alive or dead. I was willing to take the chance that he won't come back, won't ever have the guts to face up to things. But if I can't have you, Julia, then no one else shall.'

'I don't see — ' She was trembling; she could no longer disguise it.

'Don't you? Think, Julia.' He gripped her arms, gave her a little shake. 'Will's alive. I *know* he is.'

'You're wrong — '

He was still holding her; his fingers bit into her flesh. 'Oh, I can't *prove* it. But it was all a bit of a coincidence, wasn't it? Will wants out, and a couple of days later he manages to get himself blown up by a mine. I've never liked coincidences. And besides, there's the little matter of a piece of my property that's gone missing.' His grip relaxed; he gave her a little push. 'You look a bit pale, Julia. You should sit down.'

Her legs seemed to give way and she sat down heavily on the sofa. She felt him press a glass into her hands. She drank two large, throat-scorching gulps of Scotch. Then she rested the glass on her knees, and watched it jiggle up and down in time to her shaking legs. When she was able to speak, she said, 'Property . . . ?'

'A painting. Little thing.' His hands sketched a small square. 'Angels. Woman in a blue dress. Picked it up in France. You could find a lot of nice things a few years back. Will was looking after it for me.' He saw her incomprehension. 'Oh, come *on*, Julia. You're supposed to be smart. It wasn't exactly *kosher*.'

'It was stolen?'

'Several times over, I should think. First by the Nazis, I'd guess, from some rich old Jew at the beginning of the war. Or from a gallery, perhaps. Then, a few years later, when things started going sour for Hitler, it would have been sold on. God knows how many times or what for. A sack of coal, perhaps. Or a passport. I bought it in Paris in nineteen-forty-eight from some old crook who'd collaborated during the war. He wanted cash. He wanted to get out.'

She swallowed. There was a sour taste in her mouth. 'I still don't see — '

'Can't just bring that sort of thing into the country, can you? Can't just show it at Customs. That's where Will's garage came in handy. That's why I helped him out. You didn't think I got to know him for the pleasure of his company, did you? The garage was nice and secluded. Near the coast, so we could bring things in by boat. Somewhere to keep my property till I'd found a buyer.' He made a quick, impatient gesture. 'I had an arrangement going with a Yank at the Embassy. Plenty of money in the States. Plenty of buyers for a nice little painting like that and no questions asked.' His expression changed, momentarily he looked bewildered. 'And then the bloody thing went missing. And at just the same time your husband disappeared.'

She closed her eyes, trying to think clearly. 'I still don't understand — '

'Will took the painting with him, didn't he? He must have opened the package, realized what it was worth. I didn't think he had it in him, to take off with something like that. Didn't think he had the *nerve*.'

She said obstinately, 'Will's dead. He died when the boat sank.'

'No. If he's dead, then why couldn't I find my painting? Why wasn't it at the garage? Or at your house?'

Her mind seemed to be working very slowly. Into it came an image of Hidcote Cottage. The cupboards emptied, their contents strewn haphazardly across the floor. Writing paper, packs of cards, Will's model aeroplanes . . .

She said, disbelieving, 'You searched my house?'

'Of course.'

'I thought — vandals — ' She broke off. 'And you found . . . ?'

'Nothing. Not a damned thing.' His eyes narrowed. 'I wondered whether you were in on it. Whether you knew what he'd done, whether you'd worked it out together. But he left you just as much in the dark as me, didn't he?'

'You're wrong,' she muttered. 'Will's dead.' But it was as though she was repeating a prayer to a god she no longer believed in. Scrabbling desperately for explanations, she seized on one. 'He must have taken the painting with him on the boat. Yes, that must be it. That's why you can't find it.'

'Why should he do that?'

'I don't know.' Her head was pounding; she pressed her fists against her temples. 'Perhaps he didn't want to leave it at the garage. Perhaps he was worried because he knew it was stolen — '

'Perhaps. But I don't think so. Because Will wanted out, remember. He wanted out.' At last, he went to the door. He paused, glancing back at her. 'But just bear it in mind, won't you, Julia, next time you're giving some other poor bastard the glad eye, that you might not be available. And don't go signing any marriage lines, will you? Because it might be rather awkward, mightn't it, if Will decides to come home.'

He left the house. After he had gone Julia remained where she was for a long time as the room darkened around her. In the back garden a barn owl shrieked, swooping like a white ghost through the inky sky; on the road cars passed, rushing to unknown destinations.

Grabbing a torch from the kitchen, she ran upstairs. Climbing the stepladder into the attic, her movements were clumsy and she stumbled on the rungs, skinned her hand on the trapdoor. Kneeling on the rafters, she swung the torch around, shining it on boxes and cases.

She remembered packing those boxes before leaving Hidcote Cottage. In them were unused wedding presents and Will's belongings, things she had not wanted in the house but could not bear to throw away. It was possible, wasn't it, that in the miserable task of sorting through her dead husband's belongings, she had overlooked something. Overlooked a painting, less than a foot square, of a madonna and angels.

She scrabbled feverishly through the boxes, hurling the contents aside as she delved deeper. Will's scarf, which she had knitted for him one Christmas, his school reports, and an old pair of spectacles, the hinges held together with Elastoplast, now lay on the rafters. But there was no painting.

After she had emptied out the last box, she began to tidy everything away, neatly folding the scarf, replacing the spectacles in their case. But there seemed something futile about her attempt to impose order, and after a while she gave up, and sat back against the water tank, exhausted.

She tried to recall his face. Fair hair, blue eyes, and that expression that seemed to say that the world continually took him by surprise. *Where are you, Will?* she whispered out loud. *Where are you, damn you?* But it was as though she was putting together a jigsaw with half the pieces missing, and she wondered whether in spite of their long friendship and their short marriage, she had ever really known him at all.

Was it possible, she thought bitterly, really to know anyone? Now, her mind drifted to Jack. The bliss of the previous night and the elation of the day that had followed it seemed a distant dream. She thought dully that though she had always loved him, they would not be lovers again. Not only because of Rick Hunter's revelations, but because they were too alike, they knew each other too well. And because their shared history encompassed both passion and betrayal, and edged uncomfortably around the dangerous boundaries of too close an affinity.

When she looked back, it seemed to her that she had allowed herself to become locked into the past, that she had chosen her lovers from too small a pool. As a young girl, her father's possessive love had both guarded her and kept her ignorant of the world. His death, and her reaction to it, had increased her isolation. Because Marius had been away from home, and because her relationship with her mother had then been difficult, she had turned to Will. When Jack had come home in 1946, she had known nothing of sex and little of love. Several people, including herself, had paid a price for her ignorance. Cornered by loneliness and by the loss of her job and her identity, she had floundered, entering into a marriage she had neither truly wanted nor been ready for. In twenty-six years she had moved only a few miles from the place where she had been born. She was surrounded by the family and friends among whom she had grown up. She worked for the family business. She had not, like Topaz and Jack, travelled. Neither had she, like Marius, married out of her class.

She knew that she must break away. She knew that if she did not do so, she would never know what she might have become, and that she would dwindle, diminish. It was just that, at this moment, sitting in the darkened attic, the pathetic mementos of her marriage scattered around her, she did not know how she would find the courage. The courage to tell Jack to go back to Canada, to his brown-eyed widow.

★ ★ ★

Topaz walked to Great Missen on Friday evening and sat on a fallen log, waiting for Marius. From the hilltop she could see the old grey-stone chapel that housed the radio workshop nestling in the bowl of the valley. A fitful sunlight gleamed on the leathery leaves of the rhododendrons that lined the narrow lane and flickered between the high branches of the conifers.

She caught sight of him leaving the chapel building. She pressed her hands together and chewed a loose strand of hair with intent concentration. There was a particular pleasure in watching him unobserved. He dipped out of sight for a few moments, hidden by the steep swell of the hill, and she leaned forward, waiting. When she saw him again, she stood up and ran to him.

'Topaz.' He kissed her cheek.

'I thought I'd come to meet you.'

'What a lovely idea.'

'Shall I carry your briefcase?'

He looked startled. 'Certainly not.'

'When I was little and you'd just started work at Temperley's and I came here on holiday I used to meet you sometimes and you used to let me carry your briefcase. I felt terribly important. Do you remember?'

'Of course I do.' He smiled. 'You used to hide behind a tree to surprise me. I always saw you, though.'

They walked for a while, and then she said, 'I've decided to go home. Tomorrow, I think.'

He stopped, and turned to her. 'I won't try to persuade you to stay because you've given us so much of your time already. But we'll miss you, we'll all miss you.'

She said lightly, 'I'll come and visit. Lots and lots.'

'You will. That's an order.'

She had been putting off the decision for some time. *When Tara goes back to school after the Easter holidays,* she had said to herself, *then I'll go back to London. When Marius goes back to work full-time.*

'My mother phoned,' she explained.

'Ah,' he said. 'She's missing you?'

'*Marius.* Mummy's bridge partner is ill and her most recent admirer has just married his secretary.' *And she's drinking too much*, thought Topaz, recalling her mother's slurred, querulous voice, but did not, of course, mention *that*.

He said, 'Will you be all right?' Which was an odd thing to say: surely *she* should have been asking that of *him*.

'Of course I will. I'll find another job.'

'I meant', he said gently, 'Charlie.'

'Oh. I've got used to that, I suppose. And he's a long way away just now — no chance of bumping into him by mistake.'

'That doesn't mean', he said, 'that it doesn't hurt.'

The narrow road wound through the woods. From the perspective that time and tragedy had given her, she could see that there had been something glib, something second-rate about their love affair. That she had sold herself too cheaply, allowing herself to make do with something that had only passed for love.

So she said, 'I've decided to give up men for a while. They are far too much trouble. I'm going to become famous instead.'

The corners of his mouth twitched. 'How will you do that?'

'I don't know yet.' She threaded her hand through his arm. 'I wondered — '

'Yes?'

'I thought I'd start doing my dinner parties again — I did enjoy them. And I wondered whether you'd help me with all the money sort of things, Marius. I really should keep accounts, shouldn't I?'

'It would', he said, 'be preferable. Keeps the tax people happy. Of course I'll help. I'd like to and, besides, it's the least I can do.'

They walked for a while in silence. Then he said, 'I don't know whether you remember, but a couple of months ago there was something you said to me. It was when you were telling me off about Tara.'

431

She shifted uncomfortably. 'I expect I said all sorts of things. It might be better if you forgot them, Marius.'

'You said that you didn't think you deserved to be loved. Is that what you really believe?'

She looked away. 'I was talking about Tara.'

'Were you? You told me that you knew what it was like to be someone no one much wants. I just wanted you to know that you're wrong, Topaz. So completely, utterly wrong. I just wanted you to be sure before you leave that you know you are wanted and needed — and very much loved — by Tara and by my mother and by Julia. And by me, of course.'

★ ★ ★

The following morning Marius dropped Topaz off in Longridge so that she could say goodbye to Julia before catching the train to London.

Sitting in the back garden, Topaz thought that Julia looked unwell, pale and strained, with dark shadows around her eyes. Julia told her about William's accident; a white bandage now encircled William's forehead, like a Red Indian's headband. Topaz said sympathetically, 'Poor you. How awful. No wonder you look shattered.'

Julia gave a small, unconvincing smile. Topaz explained that she was going back to London. Julia looked startled. 'Of course. Selfish of us to keep you here so long. We'll miss you, though.'

'Marius will be all right, I think.'

'Marius?' Again, that look of surprise, as though Julia's thoughts had been travelling along an utterly different path.

'Well, not *all right*, of course. Not for a long time — years and years, if ever. He's quite good at pretending, but you can see sometimes, can't you, how hard he has to try. But he'll manage, I think. He's good at managing. Just like you were after Will died.'

'*Will*,' said Julia. The remains of the colour bleached from her face. She stood up, twisting her hands together. 'Something's happened,' she said suddenly. She pressed her knuckles against her teeth. 'Do you think it's possible — ' She broke off. Her gaze darted towards Topaz. Then she said, quite calmly, 'You'll think I'm crazy, but do you that Will could still be alive?'

Topaz stared at her. William was playing in the sandpit; in the adjacent garden Julia's next door neighbour was pegging out her washing. White sheets flapped against a blue sky.

She shook her head. 'No. No, I don't think so. I'm sorry.'

Julia's eyes were haunted and she was biting her nails. She said, 'What if he wasn't on the boat?'

After Will's death Topaz had thought she had seen him in the street, on the Tube. It had taken her months to accept the finality of his leaving. 'People *saw* him.'

'They didn't see him *on the boat*.' Julia's voice was rising in pitch. 'No one saw the boat leave the harbour. They *assumed* he was on it because he was seen leaving the pub with the Gambles. And because his car was parked at the harbour.'

'But if he wasn't on the boat', said Topaz gently, 'then he would have come home, wouldn't he?'

Julia sat down on the deckchair, her hands folded in her lap. She shook her head. 'No. That's the thing. He might not have. He was in trouble, you see. Will might not have come home because he was in trouble.'

Topaz's heart seemed to miss a beat. She remembered Will at Hernscombe Bay: the sea rushing against the shore, and despair in his eyes.

'Will was selling black market petrol coupons,' said Julia flatly. 'And there was something to do with a stolen painting . . . I know, I know — it doesn't sound like Will, does it?' She grimaced. 'He used to quake in his boots if he'd forgotten his homework.'

I'm in a bit of a mess, Topaz. She stared at Julia. 'How do you know all this? Are you sure?'

Julia made a quick gesture. 'I can't be certain, that's the thing. Someone told me, you see, but I don't know whether I can trust him. Well — ' she gave a hollow laugh ' — actually, I'm sure I *can't* trust him. But I have a feeling that he just might be telling the truth about this. And when Will died I went through the garage's books. He owed quite a lot of money. He'd begun to pay some of it back. I looked at the books again last night and during Will's last year of business there was money coming into the garage that wasn't accounted for.' She sighed. 'And I remembered that he wouldn't let me help him with the bookkeeping. Well, now I know why, don't I?'

Julia was very pale; the skin around her fingernails was torn and raw. Topaz said, 'Shall I make some tea?' and Julia nodded.

She noticed, as she filled the kettle and struck the match to light the gas, that her own hands were shaking. If she was Julia, she thought, then she too would be tearing the skin from her fingers.

She went back into the garden. Julia was sitting in the deckchair, elbows on her knees, fists against her face. 'Perhaps he's making it up,' she muttered. 'That's what I keep thinking. Perhaps he's making it up to punish me.'

Topaz took a deep breath. 'I saw Will a couple of days before he died. I was in Hernscombe with the theatre. Will and I spent the afternoon together. And there were things that he said. He told me he'd done something wrong, but he wouldn't say what it was. I tried to persuade him to tell me more, but he wouldn't.' She made herself meet Julia's wide, alarmed eyes. 'And he told me that he wanted to run away. That he wanted to start again. To become someone different.'

In the silence they could hear the skylark rising from

434

the field and William chattering to himself in the sandpit. Topaz said lamely, 'I didn't tell anyone because he made me promise not to.'

'Secrets,' said Julia viciously. 'I never imagined Will had so many secrets.' Her clenched knuckles were white. 'I've been trying to work it out. Whether Will was capable of doing such a terrible thing. Whether he was capable of deceiving us all like that. Deceiving his mother. Deceiving *me*. And I think that perhaps he was. I mean he didn't tell me about the money, did he? Didn't tell me he was in debt. And you know what he was like . . . never had his feet on the ground . . . always thought things would work out for the best. Always thought you got a second chance.' Once more Julia tore at her nails, leaving them bloody and ragged.

Then her angry, troubled eyes focused on Topaz. 'You said he told you he wanted to start again. Well, maybe that's what he did. Maybe he's got a new life. Maybe he's happy now. Maybe he couldn't give a damn about the people he's left behind, couldn't give a damn about how they might feel — ' She shut her eyes, clamping her hand over her mouth.

After a while, she whispered, 'What should I do? Should I tell Jack? Should I tell Prudence?' She looked across to William, playing in the sandpit. 'Should I tell William? Tell me, Topaz, what should I do?'

★ ★ ★

From her window seat in the railway carriage, Topaz stared out at the familiar passing countryside. The high chalk escarpment, the valley that enfolded Missencourt, and the bulky, irregular shape of Sixfields farm flitted past, fleeting and transient. Only the changeable, unpredictable sea was constant, a band of glittering blue-grey across the horizon.

There was only one other person in the carriage, a

435

very young clergyman with a pinkish, friendly face, who, given the least encouragement would, Topaz suspected, welcome a conversation. Later, perhaps. Just now she needed to think. About her conversation with Julia, and about the glorious, shocking, tantalizing possibility that Will might still be alive.

And she needed to think about Marius. *I wanted you to know you are very much loved.* She treasured his words, wrapping them away in a corner of her mind much as, years before, she had folded the note he had written to her (*So you don't have to kiss any more colonels. Love, Marius*) and hid it in a corner of a drawer.

Leaning across, she breathed gently on the window. Then she wrote a name on the misted glass. A different name from the one she had written years ago on that first visit to Dorset after the war.

She wrote Will's name. And did not, this time, rub it away, but let it remain, a token of her hope and faith that, one day, he would come home.

* * *

A lorry carrying sugar beet disgorged Will Chancellor on to the Lincolnshire Fens, and he walked for several miles, surrounded by flat black fields and vast skies. After a while it began to rain, a steady, determined downpour that seeped around the collar of his coat and through the soles of his shoes.

He had travelled south that morning. The lorry in which he had hitched a lift had chosen his destination for him. It seemed to Will that was what his existence had become: random, directed by some external, dispassionate hand.

The landscape was uncompromising, the few small patches of trees offering little shelter from the rain. It was getting late and he hadn't eaten for hours. In the distance a clutter of buildings lay low and black against the heavy sky. Will headed in their direction. At a five-barred gate he paused, weighing up the prospects of shelter. Beside the farmhouse there was a barn and a scattering of smaller buildings. Beyond, more outbuildings and, in the distance, hidden among a clump of birch and poplar, a long, low structure that looked — Will wiped raindrops from his glasses — suspiciously like a railway carriage. A name was painted on the gate: Coldharbour Farm.

The barn door was ajar; through the gloom Will made out bales of straw. The windows of the house were dark and there were no vehicles in the courtyard. Making for a break in the fence, he darted across fields and yard. In the barn, breathing in the obscurely comforting smell of rotting hay, he slipped off his wet coat, took a dry jersey from his rucksack, curled up in the straw and fell asleep almost immediately.

When he woke a few hours later, it was almost dark. Hungry and thirsty, Will broke off a few squares of chocolate and ate the remains of a loaf. The dry bread magnified his thirst. He glanced through the open barn door. There was sure to be a tap or a well in the yard. Brushing straw from his clothes, he went quietly to the door and looked out.

Then something hit him hard on the head and he saw the cobbles of the courtyard, slick with rain, rushing up to meet him.

★ ★ ★

A girl's voice said, 'You'll have to help me. You're too heavy to carry.'

He was being dragged, as if he was a sack of potatoes, across the courtyard. His head, which hurt, bumped — bang, bang, bang — on the cobbles. He managed to say, 'Just give me a minute,' and the dragging and the banging stopped.

'Your spectacles,' she muttered and placed them in his hands.

'Thanks.' He put them on. They weren't broken, thank goodness.

'If I help you,' she said, 'do you think you could stand up?'

His rescuer — attacker? — was very young; the torch she carried illuminated her fair curls, which dripped with rain, and the worried look in her eyes. When Will put his hand up to his head, it came away scarlet.

'Please try.' Her voice wobbled. 'You are bleeding rather a lot.'

He hauled himself to his feet. The ground swayed and he felt nauseous.

'I expect you're concussed,' she said.

She took his arm and they shuffled across the courtyard. As she opened the door, he leaned against the wall of the house, his eyes closed, fighting dizziness. 'Come on,' she said encouragingly. She took his arm again. 'Almost there.'

The door led into a narrow corridor paved with red tiles. Mackintoshes and sou'westers hung from pegs on the walls; shoes and wellingtons were scattered on the floor. There was a stand from which spilled walking sticks and umbrellas.

A door at the end of the corridor gave into a large kitchen. The light and warmth struck Will and he swayed.

'Sit down,' she said, and pushed him into a chair. 'Here.' She thrust a tea towel into his hands. 'Hold this on your head while I get the bandages.'

While he was alone, he looked around the room. Pots and pans hung from racks slung from the ceiling and logs crackled in the wide mouth of the fireplace. There was a stove, a huge affair of brass knobs and little doors, and a large table and a dresser covered with crockery. And books. There were books everywhere. On the table, the dresser, the window sill. Books towered beside the wing-backed chair in which Will was sitting. He glanced at the top copy: *Romany Rye* by George Borrow.

The girl came back into the room. In her arms she carried lint, bandages, disinfectant. 'You mustn't worry.' She beamed at him. 'I'm going to be a doctor.'

'What happened?'

'I hit you.' She looked embarrassed. 'I thought you were a fox. One's been after our hens. I was trying to scare it a way. I am most terribly sorry. Although — ' she sounded slightly exasperated ' — I wasn't to know, was I? What on earth were you doing in the barn? Are you a tramp? My Dad was a tramp once.' She looked suddenly stricken. 'You're not one of Dad's waifs and strays, are you?'

A beam of light moved across the window; Will heard the sound of a car engine. Footsteps approached the kitchen. Will braced himself, anticipating suspicion, anger, outrage.

The man who came into the room was in his late forties, Will guessed. He was short and stocky, with fine, straight, grey hair, blue-grey eyes and strong features. Catching sight of Will, he said, 'What on earth have you been up to, Philly?' He sounded more amused than outraged. 'I go out for a couple of hours, and when I get home there's a wounded man in my kitchen.'

'I hit him with the cricket bat, Dad.'

'Did you, now? Your aim was good, by the look of him.'

'It might need stitches,' said Philippa optimistically. 'Shall I get a needle and thread?'

Fingers gently parted Will's hair. 'That won't be necessary, child. Go and make the poor man a cup of tea while I repair your handiwork.'

'Dad — '

'Tea, Philippa. For myself as well. It's raining cats and dogs out there.'

Will said, 'I'm terribly sorry, sir, but — '

'I think it should be I who should be apologizing, for having such a combative daughter.'

Will had a sudden, irrational urge to protect Philippa. 'It's my fault. I was in the barn and she thought I was a fox.'

'An easy mistake. Let's see . . . I think this looks worse than it is. Now, I could drive you to the doctor in Lincoln, but if you'd rather not bother, then I can make a reasonable job of patching you up myself. And I promise I'll spare you the needle and thread my bloodthirsty daughter is so keen to use. What do you say?'

'Go ahead,' said Will.

'Very well. Doctors' waiting rooms are such dispiriting places, aren't they? My name's Harold Bellchamber, by the way. And you've met my daughter Philippa.'

'Will Brown,' said Will, giving the alias he usually adopted. They shook hands.

'The disinfectant stings a bit, I'm afraid. I assume Philippa's explained her medical ambitions to you, Will? The girl's set on becoming a doctor. Her dolls were always covered in bandages and splints, and any kitten or rabbit unfortunate enough to scratch itself had to put up with her attentions. Still, I have to say that I'm proud of her. I'd be proud of her whatever she does, mind you. Just now, she's struggling with her Latin. Hard for an eighteen-year-old girl, Latin, but you have to have it, apparently, to become a doctor.'

Philippa came back into the room, carrying a tray. 'I was telling our guest about your fondness for Latin, child,' said Harold.

'Yuck.' Philippa made a face. 'Latin is just the end.'

'I thought so too,' said Will. 'Especially when I had to teach it.'

'You taught *Latin?*' Philippa's eyes widened. 'Poor you.'

Will fell silent, horrified at himself. He never spoke about his past. Never spoke about Will *Chancellor's* past. Will Chancellor, after all, no longer existed. The blow to the head, or the pleasant, dozy atmosphere of the comfortable room must have loosened his tongue.

'What an awful job,' said Philippa sympathetically. 'Why did you teach *Latin?* Why not something nice, like chemistry or art? Why didn't you — '

'Philippa, my love,' Harold interrupted. 'Leave the poor man be. You'll tire him out with your questions. My daughter has an enquiring mind, I'm afraid, Will. An asset in many situations, no doubt, but it can be rather wearing.' He stood back. 'There, that's you patched up. Some dinner inside you and you'll feel right as rain.'

'I couldn't possibly — '

'Of course you could. I always cook extra in case of visitors. You'd be helping us out.'

Will found himself sitting at the wooden table with Harold and Philippa. The conversation rambled, easy and entertaining, and the radio played quietly in the background. And after dinner, when Harold said, 'There's a spare bed made up, isn't there, Philly?', Will, unable to face the wind and the rain and a night in a ditch, made only a token protest. Soaking in a hot bath, putting on the pyjamas that had magically materialized on top of the spare bed, he curled up between clean sheets and drifted off to sleep, and dreamed that he had come home.

★ ★ ★

Home. Will had lost count of the places in which he had lived since he had run away from Dorset. Bedsits in London, lodging houses in the north of England, caravans and barns and farmhouses and ditches. Not one had been *home.*

Three years ago, sitting in a dingy cafe in Paddington, Will had opened a discarded newspaper, and had caught sight of the article that had informed him of his death. The newspaper had described the sinking of the *Katie Rose,* and the assumed loss of her passengers. '*All three men are missing, presumed dead. John Gamble and William Chancellor have each left a wife, Michael Gamble was unmarried. A number of townspeople commented on a spate of recent tragedies involving fishing boats and mines. Maurice Chancellor, cousin of William, said, 'This accident is a shocking tragedy. The young men will be greatly missed.'*

Back then, sitting in the cafe, Will had believed himself to be free. He, who had longed to start again, had by an extraordinary stroke of fate been allowed to do so. Clutching the newspaper, his heart had pounded with exhilaration and relief. A few days later, in a seedy little pub in Baker Street, he had bought a forged ration book made out in an assumed name. You couldn't eat without a ration book and, naturally, Will Chancellor — the *deceased* Will Chancellor — wasn't eligible for one.

He found work and somewhere to live. Those first few weeks he had felt strangely unburdened. He'd catch himself wondering whether he'd forgotten something, lost something — his jacket, or his wallet, perhaps. It took him a while to realize that his lightheadedness was caused by lack of worry. The bliss of knowing he would not wake in the night, cold sweat trickling down his spine at the thought of what the next day might bring.

At first he seemed incapable of any emotion apart from relief. He kept his distance from other people, and avoided involvement. Only the thought of his parents sometimes jolted him. But then, he told himself, there was Rick. Hadn't he spared them shame, this way? Given the choice, mightn't his parents prefer a son of good character tragically dead to a son who was a criminal?

That first winter he had lived from hand to mouth, taking what work he could. A few days labouring, a one-off job driving a van to Dover. His employers were the sort who asked no questions, demanded to see no papers. He was often hungry, always cold. The characters who peopled those months were fleeting and shadowy, the flotsam and jetsam of the lodging houses: ex-servicemen who had not been able to fit back into civilian life, widows eking out constrained existences on tiny pensions, young lads who, whey-faced and undergrown, had spent their short lives ricocheting from children's home to Borstal to lodging house.

Inevitably, though, the numbness that had at first protected him dissolved. Slowly, something cracked apart, forcing him to feel again. He was short of money and he felt ill most of the time. London had begun to seem like a prison, so he travelled north and found work in Leeds, helping out in a grocer's shop. He rented a room in a stone villa owned by a woman who had lost her fiancé in the Great War. He left the city in the summer because his landlady had become fond of him, and had taken to inviting him into the parlour and asking him questions about his home, his family, his background. In the Trough of Bowland, with its tall, glittering beech trees and fast-running streams, he took casual work on a farm, supplementing his income by doing odd jobs in the village. When the farmer's daughter made eyes at him, he moved on. After all, he was a married man.

The pattern continued. Starting afresh, settling down, moving on. By then he knew that certain things were not permitted him: to use his own name, to travel abroad, to be close to anyone. Real intimacy demanded truth. His loneliness gnawed at him, bringing him close to despair. He drank too much and slept badly. When he thought of his family it was with a mixture of grief and intense regret. He knew that he had squandered something precious, something irreplaceable. No longer able to deny the enormity of what he had done, it seemed to him that behind the exterior he presented to the world, nothing much existed. He was a shell, without name, without history, without connection to the rest of humanity. In faking his own death, Will Chancellor had truly ceased to exist.

So it was a logical, easy step to come to the conclusion that because he no longer existed he might as well be dead. After all, no one would miss him, no one would mourn him.

He was renting a caravan near Bamburgh beach; he bought aspirins and a bottle of Scotch to wash them down. But the aspirins stuck in his throat, making him retch, and he found himself staggering outdoors, the whisky bottle in one hand, a rope in the other, in search of a tree branch with which to hang himself. But the dunes were empty and treeless, and eventually he lay down and fell asleep, cushioned by sea pink and marram grass, the rope slipping from his fingers, the last dribbles of whisky staining the sand.

Waking in the morning, his head pounding and his clothes smelling of alcohol and vomit, he scrambled over the dunes. Heading out across the beach, he walked into the sea. When he was waist deep, he paused, knowing that he had a decision to make. He could walk on, or he could go back. Will closed his eyes, feeling the shock of the cold water against his skin and the cleansing scour of salt and wave. After a while, he went back to the shore.

It had been, literally, a turning point. After that day

444

he had stopped drinking and had taken to five-mile walks along the beach so that he was tired enough to sleep at night. Pacing the white, impacted sand, he had thought through the events of the last few years. He had faced up to certain truths: that it was he, and he alone, who had knocked his life off course; that he had repaid his parents' love and trust with dishonesty and desertion; that his own misjudgements had led to his involvement with Rick.

And as for Julia, he acknowledged that he had wanted Julia, at least in part, because Jack had wanted her. In taking her from Jack he had hoped to assume some of Jack's strength, Jack's confidence. Marrying Julia had made him Jack's equal. Only it hadn't, of course, and the nagging suspicion that Julia preferred Jack had persisted throughout their marriage. His fears had made him insecure and morose, afraid to confide in Julia when the business ran into difficulties, uninterested in anyone's problems but his own. When she had offered to help him, he had rejected her. His worst suspicions had been confirmed in that terrible moment when he had looked through the window of Sixfields cottage and had seen Julia and Jack embracing. Now he found himself wondering whether he had driven her to that.

Slowly he began to acquire a perspective; slowly he began to forgive himself. He slept well, felt stronger, and was once or twice aware of a sort of contentment. Not the numb lack of feeling that had followed his flight to London, but something else: the beginnings, perhaps, of a recovery of equilibrium and self-respect. Through his peripatetic existence, he acquired new skills, and with them a new confidence in himself. He rarely felt afraid now, he who had once been dogged by fear. Sometimes it seemed to Will that he had truly become a different person from the one who in the summer of 1948 had stumbled blindly away from a sea of troubles.

445

At Coldharbour Farm Will gave a hand with the household tasks and with Harold's market garden; in the evenings he helped Philippa with the detested Latin. It amused him to see them together, the father and daughter. Philippa was busy, enquiring, energetic; Harold was serene and unruffled. Their arguments were frequent and lacking in acrimony, and were not about the sorts of thing you might have expected a father and his teenage daughter to argue about — bedtimes and boyfriends and the wearing of lipstick. Harold seemed to give his daughter absolute freedom; Philippa herself wore not a scrap of make-up, generally dressed in corduroy slacks and jerseys, and was contemptuous of boys. Instead, they quarrelled about whether people should eat meat, or whether eighteen-year-olds should have the vote, or whether motor-cars would lead to the ruin of the countryside.

After a fortnight Will packed his knapsack. It surprised him how miserable he felt. He thought he had become used to it, this drifter's life. He found Harold in the kitchen. Will gave his carefully prepared speech about not outstaying his welcome and his appreciation of the Bellchambers' kindness. Harold listened patiently and then said, 'You don't have to leave, you know.'

Taken by surprise, Will mumbled something incoherent.

Harold was coaxing strands of tobacco from a leather pouch. 'Where do you intend to go, Will?'

'I haven't decided yet.'

'What have you been doing with yourself this past little while?'

Which was two more questions than Harold had asked him the entire length of his stay. 'This and that,' Will said vaguely. 'I've moved around a lot.'

'I was like that when I was younger. Had some

romantic notion of taking to the open road. Thought I'd feel free.'

Will remembered sitting in the cafe in Paddington and reading about the explosion that had sunk the *Katie Rose*. In his naivety, he had believed himself to be free.

Harold's next words voiced his thoughts. 'That sort of freedom begins to pall after a while, don't you think? You begin to want a place. A home. After a year on the road I know I did.'

'Was that when you moved here?'

Harold shook his head. 'After I married, I lived in Manchester. My Philippa was born in nineteen-thirty-three. I went to Spain in 'thirty-six, to fight the Fascists. Another of my romantic notions.' He tucked tobacco into the bowl of the pipe. 'I bought the farm after I came back from Spain. I'd volunteered for the army, but they wouldn't take me.'

'Your health?' asked Will sympathetically.

'My politics,' said Harold. He held a match to his pipe. 'They didn't want me because I'd fought in Spain. I was a member of the Communist party for a short while and I suppose they thought I'd be a troublemaker.' He drew on the pipe. 'I've lived here ever since. My wife left me when Philly was ten — women can have enough of romance, you know, Will. Then it was just me and the girl.'

'Philippa accused me of being one of your waifs and strays.'

'Did she now? Cheeky monkey.' Harold slid the tobacco pouch into the pocket of his jacket. 'We've had a lot of visitors over the years. She's used to it. Likes the company.'

Will shifted from one foot to the other. 'I have to leave, Harold.'

'Do you?' Harold's eyes focused on him. 'Are you sure?'

'I've trespassed on your kindness long enough.'

447

'You're not trespassing. We've enjoyed you being here.' Harold frowned. 'I've fought in one war and wasn't thought good enough for another. Things like that, they make you think. You're not the same person afterwards. Things aren't so black and white.' He drew on the pipe. Then he said, 'You've nowhere to go, have you, Will? If you had, you'd have gone by now.'

Will's heart began to hammer. Harold said gently, 'There's no need to be afraid. I've no wish to pry. Whatever you've done — whoever you are — is your business, Will, not mine. Never mine.'

He began, 'I've nothing to hide — ' but he broke off, red-faced, hating himself.

There was a silence. Then Harold said, 'I told you that we've had a lot of people to stay over the past few years. Some of them I met in my days on the road. Some were poor souls who'd lost their homes in the Blitz and couldn't settle anywhere else. One was a deserter. Another young chap couldn't face National Service.'

Harold paused, and struck another match. Will watched him. He felt as though he was teetering on a tightrope.

'Not everyone can take army life,' said Harold. 'Don't blame 'em, myself. After Spain, I knew it wasn't the mark of a man, to fight. Fighting's the worst part of a man, not the best.'

Will stared at Harold. He whispered, 'What are you saying?'

'That I'll ask no questions and you'll tell me no lies. And that you can have the old railway carriage, if you want. It's out of the way, might suit you. And that I could do with someone who knows a bit of Latin.'

'Latin?' Will felt dazed.

'I run some evening classes in Lincoln. People ask for Latin every now and then. You'd be surprised.'

Will was speechless. Harold said, 'Well, what about it? Shall I show you round the carriage so you can make up your mind? I'll get a torch, so you can see the damp and rust in their full glory. What do you say, Will?'

He found his voice at last. 'Yes,' he said.

Part Four

The Long Way Home

1952–1953

16

Topaz's catering business grew steadily. She cooked for dinner parties, buffets and receptions, hiring waitresses and extra kitchen staff through an agency when necessary. The wealthy people she had met through Charlie proved a useful source of clients. She loved the work, loved the theatrical sense of occasion that each evening engendered, loved that she could fit her work easily around the people she wanted to see, the things she wanted to do.

Helena, who had returned to London, began to work for her at the beginning of 1952. No more theatres, Helena had said firmly, the life no longer suited her. She needed something steady and, besides, she had always enjoyed cooking. Topaz could not have managed without Helena, nor without Jerry, who often drove them to the houses where the dinner parties were to be held.

In the spring Helena and Jerry married. It was best to settle for what you could get, Helena explained to Topaz one evening, as they sat in the quiet little garden behind Topaz's flat sharing a bottle of wine. And Jerry was a sweet, kind man, and it was such a nice change to be the object of devotion.

Topaz was the only one of the old circle of friends from the Leicester Square cafe to attend the small register office wedding. They had lost touch with Claudette and Mischa, and Francesca was unable to travel because she had just given birth to her second child. As for Charlie, he remained in America. Charlie, too, had married. The ceremony had taken place at the beginning of the year, after Jennifer's divorce to Brian had come through. On hearing the news, Topaz had felt a mixture of bitterness and resentment. *Marriage,* she remembered Charlie saying. *All that red tape. Takes the fun out of it.*

Well, she thought, *you didn't take long to change your tune, did you, Charlie Finch?*

In the summer she went abroad again to stay with a cousin of Angelique's in the south of France. She fell in love with the Provençal countryside, with the lazy heat and the air perfumed with thyme and lavender. In September she visited Italy for the first time, pausing for a few days in Florence before travelling to Umbria, where she stayed in a villa near Assisi, learning how to cook boar pâté and pasta filled with sage and butter. The owner of the villa knew Mary Hetherington's husband, who had been on the staff of the British Embassy in Rome.

She kept in touch with the Temperleys. Marius had gone back to managing the workshop in Great Missen full-time, while Julia had moved to London, where she ran the sales office and the cabinet-making workshop. The arrangement had allowed Marius to spend more time with Tara and Julia to make a new start in the city. Temperley's Radios continued to prosper, but it seemed to Topaz that Marius himself survived, rather than prospered. Once a month or so she and Marius spent an evening together. Though they maintained a mutual, unspoken pretence that his visits were to help her with the accounts, Topaz had discovered quite quickly that keeping the books of a small business like hers wasn't really all that difficult. She supposed they needed an excuse to see each other; she wasn't sure why. The evenings allowed her to continue to keep an eye on Marius, to make sure that he was all right. She assumed that he visited her largely out of habit and because, since Will's disappearance and Suzanne's death and Jack's emigration and Julia's removal to London, there was that unsettling sense of all the old friends and family dispersing, fragmenting, falling apart.

Sometimes Topaz remembered how she had felt when she was seventeen: her longing to be part of something — a family, a clique of friends, a couple, anything. Now her address book bulged; now, if she chose to, she could go out every night of the week. Now there were pubs and clubs and restaurants in which, when she visited them, someone would call out to her, demand she sit with them. That those friends remained just that, *friends*, was, she told herself, because she was too busy to fall in love with anyone. That sometimes still, especially at night, she found herself wondering whether the thickness of her address book wasn't much more than a charm to ward off the old, lingering sense that she didn't quite belong anywhere was, she thought with some exasperation, quite ridiculous.

★ ★ ★

Tara said, 'Can I do the shells, Auntie Topaz? I like doing the shells.'

Topaz slipped the hard-boiled eggs into a colander and placed them under the cold tap. 'Like this.' She tapped a shell with the back of a spoon.

Marius warned her, 'They'll be scrambled.'

'Then I'll mix them with mayonnaise and spread them on finger rolls. I'm never sure about hard-boiled eggs anyway, are you? Especially for a buffet. Rather *bouncy*. But Lydia asked for them.'

It was the end of November; that evening Topaz was catering for a friend of Mary Hetherington's called Lydia Prescott. Lydia lived in Bloomsbury and, as Jerry had flu and Marius was in London on business, he had offered to drive Topaz there.

She gave a quick glance around the kitchen. 'I think we're almost ready. So good of you, Marius, to help out.' She tucked greaseproof paper around the smoked

455

turkey and checked that the lids on the salad boxes were secure. She frowned. 'What time is it?'

'Almost six.'

'*Heavens*. I'm not changed yet — '

'You go and get ready. I'll load this lot into the car.'

'Thank you, dear Marius.' She kissed his cheek and dashed into the bedroom, where she looked through her wardrobe. She always wore something lovely when she was catering for a party. It would be all too easy, she had decided a long time ago, to slump drearily into slacks and shirt and spattered apron, so instead she had acquired a small collection of cocktail dresses, bought from a little shop on the Brompton Road.

She chose a red velvet, the colour of holly berries, and swept up her hair into a pleat. She took care over her face, drawing a narrow black line along her upper lids, and painting her lips the same red as the dress. She felt, as she always did, a mixture of apprehension and excitement. As though it was *her* party — which it was in a way, she supposed. After she had put on her gold earrings and a quick spray of perfume, she glanced in the mirror once more. 'You'll do,' she said to her reflection, and left the room.

Marius looked up as she came back into the kitchen. She saw his eyes widen slightly. She held out her skirt, gave a little twirl. 'Like it?'

'You look stunning. Are you ready?'

She looked at her list. 'Turkey . . . veal . . . salads . . . pickles . . . I think so.'

At the Bloomsbury house, Marius unloaded the boxes of food and carried them to the kitchen. 'I think that's everything. When will you finish?'

'Nineish, I hope.'

'Give me a ring, if you like. We could go for a drink.'

Topaz spent the next half-hour slicing the smoked turkey and dressing the salads. At half-past six the waitresses arrived and at seven o'clock the guests.

456

Because she had got to know most of the guests over the last couple of years, and because Lydia Prescott insisted, she left the kitchen once the buffet had been served and joined the party. Lydia's husband placed a drink in her hands and Mary Hetherington waved to her from the far side of the room. A young man offered to fetch her a plate of food, but she shook her head emphatically, and said, 'Sweet of you, but I'm afraid I'm sick of the sight of the stuff.'

'You cooked it, didn't you? Lydia told me. That's why I knew I had to introduce myself to you. Well, one of the reasons. Such lovely food. I can't boil the proverbial egg, myself.'

'Actually, boiled eggs aren't easy. People think they are, but they're not.' She studied him covertly as she drank her gin and tonic. He was in his mid-twenties, she estimated, tall, fair-haired, blue-eyed.

He said, 'I always admire people who do practical things. I'm hopeless at anything practical.'

'What do you do?'

'Oh, I just fiddle about with numbers.' He offered her his hand. 'My name's Christopher Catchpole. And you're Topaz Brooke, aren't you? Mary told me.' He smiled. 'Are you sure I can't get you anything?'

'Another drink would be lovely.'

She watched him disappear into the crowd. Mary Hetherington came to stand beside her. '*Frightfully* rich,' she whispered. 'He's a stockbroker. Terribly successful. And he's only twenty-seven. Mad keen to get to know you.' She looked meaningfully at Topaz. 'What do you think?'

'Perfect,' she said lightly. 'Handsome, rich . . . doesn't seem to be an axe-murderer or to have any noticeably repulsive habits.'

Yet at the end of the evening, when she was clearing up the kitchen and Mary said, '*Well?*', Topaz shrugged.

'He asked me if I wanted to go on to a nightclub, but I said no.'

'Oh, *Topaz*.' Mary sighed. She leant against the edge of the table. 'I suppose you saw the article in *Picturegoer*?'

Helena had shown her the magazine a few days ago. Charlie and Jennifer had given a party in their Beverly Hills home. The photographs accompanying the article had seemed slightly blurred so that Charlie's familiar, attractive face had lacked clarity and sharpness.

'A hundred guests,' said Topaz. 'Imagine the catering. All those vol-au-vents.'

'Did you notice', said Mary cattily, 'that there were more photos of the guests than there were of Charlie and Jen? The perils, my dear, of inviting guests who are more famous than you are.'

Topaz nestled boxes one inside the other, like Russian dolls. 'Anyway, it's not because of that. It's not because of Charlie.'

'Why is it, then? I know simply dozens of men who are madly in love with you and you won't even look at them.'

'That's not true. I go out with them.'

'For a date or two. And then you terribly tactfully get rid of them as soon as they start to get serious. I *know*, darling, because they weep on my shoulder. I've begun to believe you've a secret admirer you're keeping to yourself. Mean of you, Topaz.'

'There's no one,' she said. It was true; there hadn't really been anyone since Charlie.

Mary said sternly, 'You have to try. You have to make an effort.'

'I do try.' She packed utensils into a carrier bag. 'I don't know why it doesn't work. It's not that they're not nice. It's just . . . ' She fell silent. She really didn't know why it was that the young men who were interested in her didn't interest her a bit, and why she hadn't fallen in love with anyone since Charlie. It wasn't that she didn't want to. It would be nice to fall in love; she hadn't forgotten that falling in love made you feel rather wonderful.

She said vaguely, 'I suppose I've been rather busy. With the parties and my mother.'

Mary looked sympathetic. 'How is she?'

Topaz had confided to only two people, Mary and Helena, about the problem of her mother's drinking. She hadn't told anyone else: not Julia, certainly not Marius. Again, she didn't really know why. Because she couldn't quite rid herself of the suspicion that it reflected in some way on her that her mother had fallen into the habit of taking her first drink of the day around mid-morning and the last around midnight, sometimes without much of a break between. And because she wanted as few people as possible to know that something — drink or bitterness or just the passing of time — had worn away at Veronica Brooke, robbing her of the beauty she had always taken for granted, and leaving her, in the absence of friends and occupation, without much to fall back on. There was an emptiness about her mother's life that troubled Topaz, that made it hard to resist the slurred late-night demands for company.

'Mummy's not too good,' she said. 'She hates the winter. Hates the cold and the fog. She was brought up in India, you know.'

'There's a marvellous man in Harley Street,' said Mary kindly. 'Owns a clinic in the depths of the countryside.'

'Perhaps I'll mention it.' She knew that she wouldn't. She could hear her mother's voice. *You're not shutting me away in some loony bin, Topaz.*

She took her leave of Mary and hurried home. She would have a quick bath, she decided, and then she would phone Marius. She had just stepped into the bath when the telephone rang. Wrapping a towel around herself she answered it, expecting to hear Marius. But the voice on the other end of the line announced herself as Mrs Foley, a neighbour of Veronica's. Mrs Foley explained to Topaz that her mother had lost her front-door key. Then there was a tactful pause before Mrs Foley said, 'And she's a bit under the weather, dear.'

Topaz dried herself hastily, pulled on a skirt and jersey and caught a bus to Bayswater. In Mrs Foley's drawing room she found her mother sitting on the sofa, the contents of her handbag strewn around her as she searched for her key. Lipsticks rolled to the floor, tablets escaped from pillboxes. Veronica's jaunty, feather-trimmed hat was slightly askew.

Topaz scooped everything back into the handbag and escorted her mother downstairs.

'But I can't *walk*,' Veronica complained, rubbing her ankle. 'I tripped. That rug on the landing.' Her weight pressed against Topaz's shoulder and her fingers dug into her arm. As Topaz unlocked the door, Veronica said irritably, 'Basil *promised* to see me home.'

'Basil?'

'You know. The major.'

There had been a great many majors — and colonels — in Veronica's life. They fused together in Topaz's mind, identically dressed in houndstooth jackets and maroon cravats.

She helped her mother into a chair. Veronica said, 'Of course, he isn't really a major.' She gave a scornful laugh. 'NCO in some tinpot little regiment, no doubt. I can always tell. Hasn't the deportment. Or the *manners*.'

Topaz slid Veronica's shoe from her foot. 'Why do you see him, then?'

'There doesn't seem to be the *choice*, these days. There are so few *gentlemen* left.'

'Your foot looks all right — '

'It hurts.' Veronica's lips stretched in an attempt at a smile. 'You must make me a drink, Topaz. One of your lovely martinis.'

'I'll get some cold water so you can bathe your ankle.'

As she came back into the room with a bowl, Veronica said glumly, 'Perhaps I should have married again.' Lines of bitterness and disappointment channelled her face.

Curious, Topaz asked, 'Why didn't you?'

Veronica's sapphire blue eyes were blank, bewildered. 'None of them were really up to scratch, I suppose. And besides, I couldn't face going through all *that* again.'

'All what, Mummy?'

'Bed. Sex.' Her mouth curled in distaste. 'Of course, it might have been different — '

'What might have been different?'

'I was almost engaged before, you know.'

'Before Daddy?'

'Mmm.' Veronica lit a cigarette. 'I had ten proposals of marriage, my first season. Half the regiment was in love with me. And there was someone . . . But it didn't work out. His family didn't have the breeding. Box-wallahs, my father called them. You must have breeding as well as money, mustn't you?' She drew on the cigarette, her eyes narrowed. 'Still, I've always wondered . . . '

'Wondered what, Mummy?'

'Whether I would have been happy.'

There was a silence. Then Veronica muttered, 'Perhaps not. It probably wouldn't have been any different.' She gave a sour laugh. 'All cats are the same in the dark, they say, don't they?'

Topaz said, 'I'll make you something to eat and then I must go. I'm having a drink with Marius.'

'The Temperley boy?' Topaz nodded.

'Has he married again?'

461

'Of course not.'

'People *do*. Just because *I* didn't. Just because I was loyal to Thomas.'

'I'll make you a sandwich,' said Topaz and went into the adjacent kitchen. The clock on the wall told her that it was almost ten o'clock. She hurried, cutting bread, spreading butter.

Then she heard her mother say thoughtfully, 'You could do worse, you know.'

'Pardon, Mummy?'

'Marius Temperley. You could do worse. Plenty of money in that family.'

She went back into the drawing room. 'I don't know what you mean.'

'Don't be naive, Topaz.' Veronica's lighter snapped. 'I wouldn't blame you for throwing your cap at Marius Temperley. If I was a few years younger . . .'

Throwing your cap . . . She said stiffly, 'Marius and I are just friends.'

Veronica exhaled a narrow stream of smoke. 'If that's what you think then you're more stupid that I thought. Men and women are never *just friends*. He's older than you, of course, but that doesn't matter. And as I said, the family's well off.' Veronica's calculating eyes focused on her daughter. 'Don't imagine you won't have to think about money, my girl. That wretched Socialist government put paid to most of my savings, so you needn't expect much when I go. Of course, the Temperleys are in trade, but one can't be too fussy these days, can one?' She gave a little laugh. 'Don't look so outraged. And don't tell me you haven't thought about it because, if you do, I shan't believe you.'

Veronica rose and went to the sideboard, and poured herself a drink. 'I shouldn't leave it too long, if I were you. Plenty more fish in the sea. I know you think he's the grieving widower, but he won't put up with an empty bed for long. Men never do.' Again, she laughed.

'Of course, you could always do the same as that cheap little tart he married. Get him into bed and make sure there's a baby on the way. He's the honourable type, isn't he? He'd marry you like a shot.'

Topaz could not, just then, bear being in the same room as her mother. In the kitchen she furiously grated cheese and sliced tomatoes. Then she slammed the plate on to a side table in the drawing room, and muttered, 'I have to go now,' and grabbed her coat and left the flat. Travelling home, her mother's voice echoed. *I wouldn't blame you for throwing your cap at Marius Temperley . . . Don't tell me you haven't thought of it . . .*

She hadn't, though, not really. For a long, long time, she hadn't thought of Marius as anything more than her oldest and dearest friend. She had had a crush on him years ago, of course, when she was seventeen. Returning to Dorset for the first time after the war, she had been almost an adult herself, and had for the first time seen Marius as an equal. She still remembered the intense and painful pendulum lurches of her emotions during that bittersweet week. Talking to him in his study in Missencourt, her blurred childhood memories had been replaced by his proximity. It had been as though she had met him for the first time. How could she not have noticed before the blueness of his eyes, the generosity of his smile, the strength and presence of him?

He had been kind to her after she had dropped the bottle of gin at Jack's homecoming party. She remembered their conversation in the garden of the school when he had offered to take her to the cinema. Something had changed in her then: she had begun to see herself as a different person, entitled to both respect and liking — worthy, even, of love. If Marius liked her, if Marius believed her to be — she could still remember the word he had used — *serene*, then she must be all right, mustn't she?

She remembered how her happiness had lingered

after that conversation, enabling her both to put up with her mother's habitual criticism and to weather an unsettling visit to Carrie Chancellor's house. And she remembered how her mood had altered, darkened, after Marius had phoned to tell her that he must remain in London, that they could not go to the cinema after all. A few days later there had been the announcement of his unexpected marriage and the discovery of a daughter whose existence none of them had suspected. She had cried herself to sleep that night. Some of her tears had been tears of anger, an anger directed at herself, for her foolishness in thinking, even for the smallest of moments, that Marius Temperley might be interested in her.

Leaving Dorset at the end of the week, she had waited for him outside the railway station. The thought of going home without saying goodbye to him had been intolerable. Her heart had lifted when she had glimpsed his car, heading through the rain. She remembered how, at a time when his life and emotions must surely have been in chaos, Marius had taken the trouble to search through a London still blighted by rationing to find her chocolate. So that she would not have to kiss any more colonels.

It had been his name she had written on the misted train window, his note she had treasured. She still had that scrap of paper, tucked into a corner of her writing case. Why had she kept it all these years? Out of sentimentality, a memento of a not particularly happy holiday, or for some other reason, one she had not dared to face?

She noticed, almost too late, that the train had reached her station and had to rush and squeeze through the doors before they closed. Travelling up the escalator, she dug her hands in her pockets, staring at the posters on the wall. But the advertisements for theatres and cold cures failed to distract her. Of all the

Temperleys and Chancellors, Marius had been the one who had kept in touch with her. They had quarrelled over Peter de Courcy; she had counselled him when Suzanne had told him the truth about Tara's parentage. Theirs had been, she now saw, a relationship whose balance had altered through the years. His protectiveness towards her had, by the time of Suzanne's death, been equalled by her need to give him comfort. She might have felt angry with Charlie for marrying Jennifer, for having betrayed his own principles, but she hadn't *minded*, not really, honestly *minded*, because Marius had long since taken Charlie's place in her heart. And tonight she had not wanted to go out with perfectly nice, perfectly eligible Christopher Catchpole because Marius had been in London, waiting for her to phone.

And did she desire him? That was the difference, wasn't it, between friendship and love. Did she long, as her mother so tastefully put it, to get him into bed?

Unlocking the door to the block of flats, Topaz paused for a while in the hall, leaning against the wall. The light illuminated the objects around her: a pram, a child's tricycle, and a clutter of small wellington boots.

Of course she wanted him. Of course she wanted to share a bed with him. But she wanted even more than that. Her gaze rested bleakly on the pram. She wanted, some day in the future, to have children of her own. But to have the family she had always longed for with Marius Temperley was, she knew, an impossible dream.

She climbed the stairs and let herself into her flat. By the telephone, she paused, her fingertips brushing against the receiver. Her hand fell away to her side and she sat motionless, still wearing her coat and hat, staring into the darkness.

★   ★   ★

It had been Rick Hunter who had pointed out to Julia that she was in limbo, neither a wife nor a widow. To begin with, the ambiguity of her position had angered her. But she had become used to it and had largely accepted it; mostly because, she supposed, the idea of remarriage did not hold much appeal for her. She had tried marriage and had found herself not to be all that good at it. Just as she had tried being a housewife, tried being how women were supposed to be: satellites circling around the twin suns of home and family. That she was an adequate mother to William was, she knew, the product of her fierce, protective love for him. Yet William had recently started nursery school and there was still that small sigh of relief as she handed him into the care of his teachers each morning. She had concluded that it was something to do with her need to keep herself all in one piece. That was how she described it to herself; it wasn't something she spoke about to anyone else for fear that they might think that she was slightly mad. But she had recognized that other peoples' needs ate away at her and that in some unfathomable way they threatened to diminish her. Except for William, who was, of course, a part of her.

She had come to London because she had needed to escape both the Chancellors and her own family. In retrospect there seemed to have been something claustrophobic about the first twenty-seven years of her life. Away from all that was familiar, she felt that she had more room to breathe. She found herself discovering her own tastes and character, almost as though she was getting to know a stranger. Some of what she found out about herself surprised her: that she preferred jazz to the classical music her father had always loved, that she decorated her new flat in bright colours and the new, fashionably abstract designs of crystals and atoms instead of the swagged satins and chintzes and traditional muted shades of Missencourt.

Other self-discoveries only confirmed what she already knew about herself: that she was a private person, who needed space, time and the freedom to decide the direction of her own life. That she was ill at ease with her own beauty; that beauty had always seemed to her a double-edged sword, something that made men want to control her and own her. That she might have found it easier, in some ways, to be merely pleasant or striking or even plain because beauty took privacy from her, making men stare at her whenever she walked into a room, prompting strangers to speak to her just to be close to the symmetry of her features and the unconscious grace of her body.

Often, these past eighteen months, she had thought about Will. At first, after that appalling interview with Rick, she had felt a mixture of shock and anger. No, worse than anger: *rage*, an incandescent, blinding rage at the possibility that Will might have intentionally deserted her, that he might have meant to cause so much pain. Rage had fuelled her to return to Hidcote Cottage and the garage (both now empty and forlorn), where she had searched every nook and cranny for Rick Hunter's lost painting. She had found nothing. Rage had forced her to confront Rick one last time. In the drawing room of his house by the sea (the shifting light playing on the soft blues and greens of the decor that *she* had chosen) he had stuck to his version of events, had not altered it one bit. Will had been working for him; Will, he believed, was still alive.

The longing and desire which Julia had recognized once more in Rick Hunter's eyes had momentarily unnerved her. Then, as she had turned to leave, he had spoken to her. Once more he had told her that he loved her. *Just think what I can give you, Julia*. She had realized then, for the first time, that her beauty was also a weapon and her dismissal of him had been short, brutal, wounding. Watching him, she had known that he suffered, and she had said to herself triumphantly, *That was for you, Will. Wherever you are. To even things up a little.*

Shortly afterwards she had left Dorset for London. She had needed to be a long way away from Rick Hunter and his house by the sea; she had needed to start again. At first the city was shocking, exhausting, exhilarating. Quickly, though, she came to love it. Sometimes at night she would wake and go to the bedroom window and look out, staring at the streetlamps and headlights, watching the trail of cars and lorries that, even in the small hours of the morning, headed down the road. She loved the busyness, the constantly changing scene, the realization that, living here, she would never, ever be bored. She loved her Fulham flat, with its deep sash windows and polished wooden floors. She found a cleaner, who kept the half-dozen rooms in a state of order that Julia knew she herself could never have achieved and she found a girl, Mitzi, to look after William in the afternoons. Mitzi was a German Jew who had been shipped to England just before war broke out; the rest of her family had remained on the Continent to die in ghettos and concentration camps. Mitzi adored William; Julia wondered whether he made up, just a little bit, for the family that Mitzi had lost.

Away from her birthplace, her optimism lurched and swerved, driven by mood, circumstance, even the weather. Sometimes it seemed to her foolish even to consider the possibility that Will might still be alive. Rick Hunter had lied to her because he had wanted to hurt her for her rejection of him.

Or Rick himself had been mistaken, and Will, along with Rick's stolen painting, had been blown to atoms when the Gambles' boat had struck the mine. Will had died in 1948, a belated casualty of the war. And even if Will was alive, then what if he should decide never to come home? It was four years since his disappearance. She might never know for certain whether he was alive or dead.

Sometimes the possibilities reeled endlessly in her head, exhausting her. She did what she could to discover the truth, engaging a private detective to search for Will, placing advertisements in *The Times* that Will, and only Will, would know were addressed to him. There was no reply to the advertisements and every avenue the detective explored came to a dead end. If Will had survived the sinking of the *Katie Rose*, then he had since hidden himself well. If Will was alive — *if, if* — then he would come home when he chose to come home, and not before.

Sometimes it made her bitter, not knowing. Sometimes she caught herself thinking that it had been easier when she had been certain that Will was dead. Then she remembered her father and Suzanne, and Mitzi's lost family, and she knew that anything was preferable to that utter absence of hope. She was fortunate to have hope, even if it sometimes seemed to her a ridiculously fragile, frayed sort of hope. She knew that Prudence, too, hoped, cherishing a quiet, persistent belief that one day Will would come home. Julia found herself wondering whether Will might be here, in London, a small speck hidden in all the milling crowds. Walking through the busy streets, she looked out for him, her quick gaze flicking towards a fair head, or a tall, slightly stooping figure.

As for Jack, he had gone back to Canada, where he had married Esther. A year later they had had a daughter, Louise. Jack had sent Julia photographs: a white, weatherboarded house, a pretty, brown-eyed woman, and a baby sleeping in a crib. Looking at the pictures of the woman and the child, Julia had remembered her parting gift to Jack, and his parting gift to her. She had given herself to him for one long, glorious night; he, in turn, had shown her that physical love could be one of the great pleasures of life.

Moving to London, one of her first visits had been to a hairdresser, where she had had her long, troublesome hair cut into a short, feathery crop. As the locks of hair fell away, her head seemed to feel lighter, her spirits too. She had made a second appointment, at a clinic in Harley Street, where she had been fitted with a Dutch cap. Though she had originally viewed the extraordinary object with a mixture of laughter and revulsion, it allowed her both freedom and independence. Her affairs were discreet, pleasurable, and on the whole short-lived. If the men she met threatened to fall in love with her, she ended the liaison. After all, one could not possibly say: *I could never marry you, darling, because I don't know whether my husband is alive or dead*. It was altogether too melodramatic and much too tedious to explain.

She kept to her own self-imposed rules. She never dated Temperley's employees, never went out with happily married men. She never slept with men who disliked women (there were quite a few of those, she had discovered, on her belated voyage of discovery around the opposite sex). She never let her lovers stay the night and never introduced them to William. She kept the compartments of her life — work, child, sex — separate.

As the months passed, she found herself settling into a sort of contentment. She enjoyed her work, enjoyed the relative independence that running the London branch of Temperley's gave her. She learned to handle the Raymond Bells of this world with quiet authority, never losing her temper, never letting them see that they hurt her. Sometimes it seemed to her that she had her unruly spirit under control at last. And that she neither felt so much nor expected so much. For the first time she could remember, she was beginning to feel at peace with herself.

★ ★ ★

Will had been living at Coldharbour Farm for almost eighteen months. The disused railway carriage in which he had made his home was shadowed by poplars and stood some distance from the road. As Harold Bellchamber had pointed out to him, it was both quiet and private. Will had repaired the leaks in the roof and had sealed around the windows and doors to keep out the wind, which, even in summer, lashed the isolated farm. Inside the carriage was divided into a kitchen and living area, a bedroom, and a rudimentary bathroom. He had a camp bed and a small table and chairs, and he had filled the shelves with second-hand books. His ornaments were the shells and pebbles and driftwood he had collected on the beach when he lived in Northumberland. Behind the carriage he had dug a small garden, where he grew vegetables. Though the carriage was cramped and in winter often quite cold, he had become fond of it. Perched on the edge of a field, the railway carriage seemed to have been washed up on a distant shore, a twentieth-century Noah's Ark, and Coldharbour Farm the Mount Ararat on which its endless journeying had come to rest. Rather like himself, Will sometimes thought.

During the day Will helped Harold in the market garden and ran a peripatetic car repair business, driving around the Lincolnshire countryside in a second-hand van to isolated farms and houses, where he mended punctures and plugged leaky radiators. His admiration for Harold, and for Harold's patience, altruism and unfailing sense of humour, was unlimited. That Harold and Philippa believed in him — believed in lost, homeless Will Chancellor — often seemed to Will

471

miraculous. In the evenings he was a tutor at the Workers' Educational Association in Lincoln, where Harold was a tutor-organizer. He had initially agreed to teach as a favour to Harold, to whom he owed so much, but as time passed he had found to his surprise that he enjoyed the work. He lectured at summer schools as well as giving evening classes. They were so different, those miners and railway workers and navvies, from the bored teenage boys he had endured during the war. They saw learning as a privilege rather than an imposition, and their keenness and willingness to learn humbled him.

Many of the men he and Harold taught had had false starts in life; some of them had failed marriages behind them, a few had served a stretch or two in prison. And yet, almost without exception, they seemed to Will to be good, well-meaning people. If other people's mistakes could be forgiven, he found himself thinking, then so might his own. Looking back, he could now see that many of his misdeeds had been the consequence of youth and inexperience.

He knew that when, on that rainswept afternoon, he had ended up at Coldharbour Farm, he had had a stroke of rare good fortune. It had been another turning point, that day he had first sat by the fire in the Bellchambers' kitchen. It had allowed him to rediscover so much that he thought he had lost to him for ever: warmth and hope and family life.

And he had rediscovered love. His love for Philippa hadn't been a sudden blow, like the clout with the the cricket bat that had marked his entrance into the Bellchambers' lives. It had grown steadily, nurtured by her proximity. He loved her kindness and her spirit, he loved her utter lack of vanity and calculation. He loved the warm, demonstrative nature that she had inherited from her father; he loved her intellectual curiosity and strong sense of social justice. He loved it that she laughed at his silly jokes; he loved her gentle teasing, which, even on his darker days, always lifted his black mood. He would, if he had let himself, have loved her fine, freckled skin, her softly voluptuous body. But he was scrupulous in keeping his feelings to himself and in keeping his distance from her.

He believed that Philippa herself looked upon him as an elder brother. They went to concerts in Lincoln and for cycle rides in the countryside; in the summer he taught her to drive. He helped her with her Latin, he mended her punctures and made a hen coop for her Rhode Island Reds. He would, if things had been different, have kissed the ground on which she walked.

When, in October 1952, he waved her goodbye as she left home to study medicine at Cambridge, he smiled cheerfully and promised to write. Privately he felt bereft. Without Philippa, Coldharbour Farm seemed emptier, shabbier, drearier. He wrote her letters, cheerful, conversational missives about the farm, the weather and the hens. Rather to his surprise, she wrote back. He had assumed that, given the distractions and company of Cambridge, she would forget him, that he would receive perhaps a letter or two and then their correspondence would tail quickly to a halt.

But letters continued to arrive regularly throughout her absence. Writing back to her, he did not tell her how, without her, he and Harold rattled around the farm like pebbles in a shoe, as if they had lost purpose, as if they didn't quite fit. Nor did he tell her how greatly he dreaded the day that she would write to him: *I've met this boy.*

★   ★   ★

Late one evening in mid-December Will drove back from Lincoln to Coldharbour Farm. It was a blowy night and a sharp wind scythed across the flat, black

473

fields and shook the branches of the stunted willows that marked the entrance to the farm. As he parked the van in the yard, Philippa came out of the house. In the pale light of the coach lamp, her fair curls gleamed silver. '*Will!*' she called out, as she ran across the yard to him. When she said, 'Give me a hug, darling Will,' and flung her arms around him, happiness welled up inside him.

Disentangling himself, he said, 'I wasn't expecting you till tomorrow, Philly.'

'Our anatomy lecture was cancelled — my lecturer has flu. And anyway, I wanted to go home. I've missed it *so much.*'

'I don't believe you,' he teased her. 'I bet you forgot us as soon as you got to Cambridge.'

'*Silly.*' She tucked her arm in his. 'Where's Dad?'

'In Lincoln. He shouldn't be long. Some of the students and tutors are having a Christmas do at the pub.'

She looked at him. 'As antisocial as ever, Will?'

He shrugged. 'Would you like a drink?'

She walked with him across the meadow to the railway carriage. Inside, he poured her a glass of beer, and she sat down and gave a great sigh.

'So lovely to be home again!'

He was suddenly concerned. Perhaps she had been homesick. Perhaps the work was too hard, or her room at Girton College was small and uncomfortable. He said anxiously, 'You do like Cambridge, don't you?'

'Immensely. But home's best. It always is, isn't it?'

He let that one pass. 'And medicine — you are enjoying it, aren't you?'

'Very much. Though it'll be nice when it's real people instead of dead bodies.' She looked stern. 'Why didn't you visit me, Will?'

His back to her, he was lighting the bottled gas fire.

He said lightly, 'I thought you'd have plenty of new friends.'

'I do. But that doesn't mean I don't need my old ones.' She grinned. 'I always think that, meeting the way we did, there's a special bond between us, don't you?'

He gave a mock grimace and rubbed his head. 'I've still got the scar.'

'I've missed you, Will.'

'I've missed you too. It hasn't been the same here at all. No arguments. Far too quiet.'

'I mean', she said seriously, 'I've *really* missed you.' She looked troubled.

'Philly?' Again, that fear that she was keeping something from him. Perhaps she had met someone. Perhaps she meant to confide in him. Perhaps she meant to ask his elder-brotherly advice about whichever spotty, fumbling youth had fallen in love with her.

She was looking down at the floor. 'Will,' she said, 'there's something I wanted to say to you. I haven't said anything before because — '

There was the sound of a car turning up the driveway. Headlamps arced through the darkness. Will jumped up, glad of the interruption, and moved aside the curtain.

'It's your father.'

Her expression altered, and she smiled. '*Dad,*' she said, and ran outside.

★   ★   ★

Topaz hadn't seen Marius since the conversation with her mother. She avoided their end-of-year drinks and balancing the books evening by telling him that she was too busy, which was true, at least in part. She couldn't quite face him, not yet. For what might she see, glancing at him and knowing now what was lodged in

475

her own heart? Obligation, she feared, and responsibility, and the sense of duty that was central to Marius Temperley's character.

Though she cooked for a dozen parties in the fortnight before Christmas, her work failed to distract her. She was aware of a sort of weary disbelief that she had fallen for yet another unattainable man. After the unfaithfully married Peter de Courcy, after ambitious, uncommitted Charlie, she had completed the triumvirate by falling in love with Marius Temperley. Not that she classed Marius with either of his predecessors. But he was, in his entirely different way, every bit as beyond her grasp. It was obvious to her that Marius still loved Suzanne, and the possibility that he might realize how she, Topaz, felt about him, that she might read in his eyes embarrassment, or worse, pity, was not to be contemplated.

Two days before Christmas she threw a party. Sixty people crammed into her small flat. She kept the food simple: bread and cheese and quiche, served with plenty of beer and cider. She dimmed the lamps with tissue paper, hung paper streamers, and borrowed a gramophone and records from Jerry. In the soft pink light, the sensuous notes of a saxophone coiled and uncoiled. Guests crowded into the kitchen, shouting to make themselves heard. In the sitting room they danced, their movements limited by the confined space. New friendships were made, new love affairs begun. It seemed to Topaz, weaving through the crowd, that it was in every way a successful party and that everyone was having a good time.

Everyone, that was, except for her. Why was *she* not enjoying herself? Why did a part of her long for everyone to go home so that she could be alone again? She felt exasperated with herself. She wasn't trying hard enough, she decided. So she had another drink and then another, and danced with a succession of partners

476

until one persisted, and she found herself in a corner of the room, being kissed.

Even the kissing didn't quite take her mind off things, and she was about to dredge around for a polite way of disentangling herself, when, though the hubbub of music and conversation, she caught a fragment of conversation.

'She's here somewhere, darling — '

'Thanks,' a familiar voice said. 'I'll have a look round.'

When she looked up, he was only a few feet away. '*Marius.*'

'I thought I'd drop by,' he said. 'Give you this.' He placed a parcel on a side table. 'But you seem to be busy.' Any lingering hope that he might not have seen her, locked in an embrace, was dismissed by the chill in his eyes.

Topaz tugged at her clothing and hoped her lipstick hadn't smeared. 'Won't you have a drink?'

He shook his head. 'I don't think so.' He turned away.

'*Marius!*'

Fleetingly, he glanced back. 'Yes?'

'You can't just *go*!'

He didn't reply. She heard the front door slam behind him. Topaz stood for a moment, her hands clenched in impotent rage. Her gaze skimmed across the sitting room. Couples were draped around each other on the sofa and on the rug in front of the fire. Cigarette ends overflowed from saucers and there were pools of beer on the coffee table. Torn paper chains were turning to papier mâché in the spilt beer.

She ran out of the flat. Catching up with Marius just before he turned the corner of the street, she yelled at him, 'You always do that! *Always!*'

He spun round, taken by surprise. 'Always do what?'

'*Disapprove.*' The words hurled from her like missiles. 'Peter de Courcy. Charlie. Anyone I'm ever

477

with. As if it's anything to do with you. As if you have the *right*. Well, you don't, Marius. You don't have the right to tell me what to do, and you don't have the right to lecture me about my friends! You just don't. I'm not your — your — your *sister* — or your *cousin* — anything like that! It simply isn't your business!'

In the pale light of the street lamps, his features seemed cold and unmoving, as if they were carved of stone. He said calmly, 'You're perfectly correct, of course. What you do is none of my business. I apologize.' He glanced at her. 'You should go home. You'll catch a chill.'

She followed the direction of his gaze. The three top buttons of her dress had come undone, revealing, she thought, mortified, an *acre* of plump white flesh.

By the time her fingers, clumsy with cold and anger, had done up the buttons, he had gone. She went back to the flat. Her guests had begun to drift away. She found the Christmas present he had left her, and threw it in the broom cupboard and kicked the door shut.

★   ★   ★

Christmas was always busy at Coldharbour Farm. The first of Harold's guests arrived in mid-December and the last left with a shake of the hand or a clenched fist salute after the New Year. They were an anarchic mixture of old comrades from the International Brigades, ex-WEA tutees, and, turning up in patched coats and holed boots, a tramp or two to leaven the mixture. They slept in spare bedrooms and attics and barns. A one-armed Spanish comrade spent the night on a bench in the railway carriage's kitchen; a burly miner dozed in the back of Will's van. Harold and Philippa cooked enormous meals, while Will chopped wood to stoke the fire, ran errands and washed up. On Christmas Day they played charades and chess and argued and sang carols and Socialist anthems and then argued some more. At midnight, tramping across the field to the railway carriage, Will found that he couldn't remember a Christmas he had enjoyed more.

When, after New Year, the guests dispersed, Will and Philippa cleared up. Stripping camp beds in the attic, Philippa said, 'It always surprises me that the comrades are untidier than the tramps.'

'It's because everything has to go into a knapsack. There's a limit to how untidy you can be if everything you own has to fit into one bag.'

When she shook out a pillow, feathers escaped through holes in the striped cover. 'I read a book of Dad's about being a tramp. It sounded lovely, sleeping under the stars.'

Will was rolling up a mattress. 'Actually, it's cold and wet and miserable and you can't see the stars because there's frost on your eyelashes.'

'Real frost?'

'Once,' he said.

'You must have looked like a polar explorer.'

He looped the mattress over his shoulders and extended a shivering hand. 'Captain Oates, heading out into the blizzard — '

Philippa giggled. Feathers danced in the attic's gloomy light. 'Lost in the snow — '

'Miles from civilization — '

'Eating whale blubber and polar bears — '

'Not *polar bears*. Wrong continent.'

'So *precise*, Will. So *picky*.' When she struck him with the pillow, it split, gouting white fluff. Laughing, she sat down on the edge of the bed. A feather wafted down, landing on her nose.

'Oh dear.' She sneezed. There were feathers on her head and on her shoulders. 'Buried beneath the snow. You'll have to rescue me, Will.' He held out his hand. She said, 'Not like that.'

'How?'

'With a kiss, of course.'

His breath caught in his throat. He gave her a quick peck on the cheek, and she murmured, '*Properly*.'

'Philly — '

'Haven't you read your fairy stories, Will?' She stood up. Though her voice was gently mocking, he glimpsed uncertainty in her eyes. 'The prince has to kiss the princess, doesn't he?'

Just one little kiss, he thought. Couldn't do any harm. He let his lips touch hers.

Only it wasn't one little kiss, of course. Not when she responded to him, her fingers looping around his neck, drawing him towards her. Not when, in the dusty silence of the attic, surrounded by a sea of feathers, he sensed in her a delight that equalled his own. He could hear the blood rushing through his veins. He could feel the beating of her heart.

Then there were footsteps in the corridor below and Harold called up, 'I'm just about to head off to Lincoln. You're coming with me, aren't you, Philly?' and they sprang apart.

Will went back to the railway carriage. The memory of that kiss transformed the remainder of the grey January afternoon. Yet gradually, in synchronicity with the fading of day into night, reason crept back, sobering him, draining away his elation. Nothing momentous had occurred, he told himself, but he knew that was not true. The kiss had changed everything. Though he longed to let events take their course, to let himself love her, he knew that to do so was unthinkable, the worst sort of betrayal.

He stared out of the window in the railway carriage. It was a clear, frosty night. Every branch, each blade of grass was coated with a thin film of ice. Will groaned aloud. To protect Philippa, he must nip any feelings she might have for him in the bud before they had time to take root. The thought dragged at him, dreary and burdensome, erasing the magic of the night.

★ ★ ★

He meant to do it kindly, not to hurt her. So much for good intentions. When she tapped on the window of the carriage the following day, he opened the door to her.

'Philly,' he said. 'About yesterday — '

'Dear Will.' She took his hand, threading her fingers through his.

He made himself say, 'Philly, don't fool around.'

Her fingers stiffened, as though she had been stung. She looked confused. 'I'm not fooling around, Will. I promise I'm not.'

He moved away from her. 'It's just that — well, I thought we were *friends*.'

'We are. Of course we are.' She frowned. 'Is that all you want, Will? It's not all *I* want.'

He steeled himself. 'What I want doesn't matter. You and I can never be anything more than friends.'

'*Never?*' she whispered. He could hardly bear to see the hurt in her eyes. 'I don't understand. Why not?'

'Because — oh, a dozen good reasons. For a start, I'm a lot older than you, Philly.'

'Oh *that*.' She looked relieved. 'That doesn't matter at all. It's hardly *decades*. You're hardly *senile*.'

'And I've barely two pennies to rub together. I've only got a home because your father's been kind enough to give me one.'

Now she looked haughty. 'You don't think I care about *money*, do you?'

'And anyway — ' he was floundering ' — what would your father think?'

'Dad likes you. You know that he does.'

481

He was running out of options. She looked so young, so vulnerable. It was like crushing a butterfly underfoot.

For her sake, he hardened his heart. 'Philippa, you might think you're keen on me . . . that you have a crush on me . . . but believe me, you'll meet someone else. Soon, I'm sure.'

'I do *not* have crushes.' Her eyes flared. 'I have never in my life had a crush. I'm not some lovesick schoolgirl.'

He took off his glasses, polishing the lenses. Without them, her features were blurred and inexact. Which made it easier. 'I meant', he said, 'that you'll meet someone. At college, I expect.' The thought made him feel utterly bleak, but he ploughed on. 'Someone who deserves you. Then you'll know that whatever you think you feel about me is unimportant. Just a nine days wonder. Nothing more.'

She sat down on the wooden bench. After a while, she said quietly, 'But I've always liked you, Will. I don't believe in love at first sight, so I won't use *that* word. But the first time we met, when I hit you with the cricket bat and you were unconscious, I felt so *awful*. Not just embarrassed or worried I'd hit you too hard, but — ' she frowned ' — I thought you had such a nice face. Such a friendly face. And I wouldn't have felt like that about just anyone, I know I wouldn't.' She paused. When she began to speak again, her voice shook slightly. 'I remember that it was raining and there you were, at my feet, and your head was bleeding, and I was afraid I'd broken your glasses. I knelt down beside you and I dipped my hanky in a puddle — I hoped the cold water might wake you up. But it didn't, so I thought I'd better get you into the house. It was a cold day and I was afraid you'd get pneumonia if you stayed out in the yard any longer.' She looked up at him. 'It's not a nine-day wonder, Will. I haven't said anything before because I knew you'd say I was too young for you.

That I was just a girl and you were grown up. And I was afraid — '

She broke off. He whispered, 'Afraid of what?'

She looked up at him. 'That you might not feel the same way about me. That there might be someone else. In your other life. The one that you never talk about, Will.'

His heart began to hammer. He went to the window and looked out, resting the palms of his hands on the sill. The frost from the previous day lingered, greying the countryside.

She said, 'Don't you like me, Will?'

He did not turn round. 'Of course I like you.'

'But you don't love me.'

All he had to do was to remain silent. After a few moments, he heard her whisper, 'I seem to have made rather an idiot of myself. I'm so sorry.'

She left the carriage. He heard the door close behind her. He remained at the window, hating himself, his gaze focusing on the path her feet had made through the frost.

* * *

After a night without sleep, he rose early the following morning and drove to Market Rasen, where he repaired the brakes of an old Vauxhall. The work took longer than expected and he did not return to Coldharbour Farm until mid-afternoon.

As he parked the van, Harold came out to meet him. 'Good day?'

'Fine.' Though a heaviness had hung over him, matching the gloominess of the weather. 'Where's Philippa?'

'She's gone back to Cambridge.'

Harold's words jolted Will as he lifted his tools from the van. 'I thought she was at home for another week.'

'So did I. She said she had an essay to write.' Harold looked at Will. 'You haven't fallen out, you and Philly?'

He shook his head. In spite of the cold weather, his face felt hot.

'Good,' said Harold. 'I'm pleased to hear that.'

Will went back to the railway carriage. Dumping his tools on the table, he stood for a moment, looking round the small room. It looked shabby and cold, and his few belongings seemed, in their paucity, to sum up his overriding sense of failure, and to mock him.

★　★　★

Topaz spent Christmas Day day with her mother. The Bayswater flat was airless and stifling; Veronica, perpetually cold, had turned every heater to its highest setting. In the afternoon two of Veronica's friends called round for a rubber of bridge. It was hard to concentrate on cards, what with the heat and the persistent memory of Marius Temperley's cold, pale blue eyes. And his voice saying, *What you do is none of my business*. Which admission should have pleased her, she supposed, but somehow didn't. Instead of triumph that he had conceded her point, she was aware of a persistent sick, empty feeling, coupled with rage that he should have just walked out on her like that, rage that he should have judged her so harshly, so easily.

Well, she resolved, she wasn't going to let Marius Temperley stop her enjoying herself. In the succession of parties between Christmas and New Year, she took Mary Hetherington's advice once more and *tried*. She dressed in her nicest frocks, swept back her hair in the way that Sylvia Ryder had shown her, dabbed on French perfume and wore the gold jewellery she had inherited from her paternal grandmother. Catching sight of herself in the looking glass, her reflection sometimes took her by surprise. If she was never quite

484

beautiful, then some time ago she had ceased to be plain, fat Topaz Brooke. It was amazing, she said rather cynically to herself, what you could do if you made the effort.

She made an effort at the parties, too. She laughed, she sparkled, she was witty and charming. If she tried hard enough, then she would forget to be in love with Marius Temperley. Surrounded by friends, she told herself that this was what she had always wanted: to be part of something, to be in the centre of the circle.

The trouble was that the circle no longer seemed to her complete. As the days passed, her anger lessened and was replaced by misery. On New Year's Eve she drank a lot and danced with a friend of Mary Hetherington's called Stephen Page. Stephen had dark hair and thick, black, bullet-shaped eyebrows and a smooth, pale skin. He was an antiques dealer. When she told him about her catering business, he raised his heavy eyebrows and said, 'How extraordinary.' When the bells rang, announcing the beginning of 1953, he kissed her, small darting kisses that made her think of a pigeon pecking at grain.

They went back to his Belgravia flat for a nightcap. Objects — huge Chinese vases, curving Queen Anne cabinets — lurched out of the dim light. When he caressed her breasts, he looked at them with an assessing eye, as though he was placing a valuation on them. Tip-top condition or slightly foxed. When she tried to sit down on a nearby sofa, he said sharply, 'Not there. It's antique, you know. Eighteenth century.'

In a French *bateau-lit*, he stripped her of her clothes and made love to her. She found that she welcomed the fleeting blankness of sexual pleasure. But afterwards, realizing that she did not want to stay the night, did not want to wake in the morning beside this stranger, she hurried back into her clothes. He made only perfunctory noises of protest.

Walking home, her head ached and her silk dress felt crushed and grubby. At the flat, glancing in the bathroom mirror, she saw a different reflection from the one she had glimpsed earlier in the evening. Her mascara and eyeliner had smudged, forming black circles around her eyes. Shadows dragged at her nose and mouth, and her narrowed lips were pressed together tightly. She looked, she realized with a shock, like her mother. Younger and fuller-faced, but there was, nevertheless, a similarity in the expression in her eyes and in the downward turn of her mouth.

She sat on the sofa, still wrapped up in her winter coat. She remembered the night of her party, let herself see it for the first time through Marius's eyes. The couples entwined on the sofa, the smell of beer and cigarettes. Herself, falling out of her dress, and yelling at him incoherently in the street. He'd probably thought she was drunk.

She opened the door of the broom cupboard. Scrabbling through the muddle of dustpans and furniture polish and Windolene, she could not at first find Marius's present. Then, beneath a heap of yellow dusters, she glimpsed tissue paper and ribbon. Sitting in the doorway of the cupboard, she tore open the wrappings.

He had bought her a scarf, a beautiful Chanel scarf. The silk was patterned in rich, swirling blue-greens. How surprising, she thought, that he had known her favourite colours.

Cradling the scarf in her hands, she knew that she had a choice. She could follow in her mother's footsteps, drifting from man to man, never quite finding the right one. Or she could settle for what she had, for friendship instead of love.

If, that was, he ever spoke to her again.

17

One night he dreamed of the dancing angels. So oddly suspended in the blue air, their bare, narrow feet in balletic poses, their feathered, surprisingly substantial wings unfurled. They held in their hands some sort of banner; he was unable to read the words written on it. Their heads tilted to one side, and their expressions were benevolent but uninvolved, as though they were slightly amused by the world they looked down on.

That morning Will made phone calls, rearranged appointments. Then he drove to Cambridge. The recollection of his quarrel with Philippa lingered too vividly, bruising the weeks since she had left home. Himself, defending his honour like some elderly maiden aunt. The hurt in her eyes. He must find a way to patch it up, he told himself. Find a way to save her pride while putting paid to any possibility of a relationship between them. He had to. All the alternatives were appalling.

It was a grey, drizzly January day. Water puddled at the sides of the road and dripped from the branches of the trees. In Cambridge the tiles on the roofs gleamed, slick and wet, and black-gowned students scurried through the streets, umbrellas jostling. Will drove to Girton in the hope of catching Philippa during her lunch hour. He was in luck and a message was sent up to her study-bedroom. Then he waited, edgy with nerves and expectation.

Hearing footsteps, he turned and saw her. She said, 'What are you doing here?'

'I came to see you. To see that you're all right.'

'Well, you've seen.' She hugged her arms around herself. 'I'm fine. Apart from this blessed cold.'

She didn't look fine. She was heavy-eyed, red-nosed,

bundled up in a thick jersey with a scarf round her neck.

He said, 'I wondered whether you'd like to have lunch.'

'I don't think so.' Her voice was toneless, heavy with cold.

'About the other week — before you left — '

'Yes?'

'I wanted to explain.'

She looked at him properly for the first time. 'Is there any point?'

'I think so, yes.' Other students were crossing the hallway; curious gazes flicked towards them. 'Just lunch,' he coaxed. 'In a pub or something. Then I'll bring you back here, I promise. *Please.*'

She paused, irresolute. Then she said, 'I'll get my coat.'

During the short journey they hardly spoke. Will parked the car in the centre of Cambridge, and they walked to the Eagle in Bene't Street. There was a handful of other medical students at the bar when they arrived. Philippa flirted with them, a snuffling, half-hearted sort of flirting, as though she couldn't really summon up the enthusiasm even to hurt him. After a while the medical students left and they sat down at a table in the adjacent room. In the grate, a log fire spat orange sparks.

'About what I said to you — '

'It doesn't matter.' She was pulling the crust from her sandwich.

'I didn't mean to hurt your feelings.'

'You didn't,' she said disdainfully. 'I told you, it doesn't matter. I made a mistake, that's all.'

He had never before encountered this cold, contemptuous Philippa. He tried again. 'It's not that I don't care about you.'

'Mealy-mouthed, Will.' She had given up any

pretence of eating; she looked away to where drops of rain crawled down the windowpane.

'It's just that I can't get involved with anyone. It wouldn't be right.'

Her lip curled. 'You came all the way here to tell me *that*?'

He said softly, 'I never meant this to happen,' and she hissed, '*Feeble*, Will! So feeble and pathetic!'

Because she had turned away again, it took him a while to realize that she was crying; there was just the glitter of a tear on her cheek. He said, 'Oh, *Philly*,' and put his arm around her, pulling her half-resisting towards him.

It seemed to him that he teetered on the edge of something frightening, something liberating. He wondered whether he could let go of the fictions he had created, whether he could face again the person he had once been. During his years of exile he had discovered that secrets imprisoned you, that they cut you off from other people. The thought of escaping from that prison made the blood rush through his veins. He wasn't sure whether what he felt was fear, or excitement.

He said, 'Your father believes that I'm on the run because I couldn't face National Service.'

Her pale face was blotched pink. 'I know. He told me. I don't mind that. You know I'm a pacifist.'

'Harold's wrong. I'm not eligible for National Service.' Will touched his ribcage, gave a fleeting smile. 'Sub-standard issue. Dodgy ticker. I had rheumatic fever when I was five. There's something wrong with one of the valves.'

'Oh.' She looked first confused, then anxious. 'But you're all right now?'

'Fine. Never better. But not good enough to fight for my country.'

'But you let my father think — '

'Yes. I'm sorry. It was . . . convenient.'

The expression in her eyes made him flinch, but he went on, 'I didn't want Harold to know the truth. I was ashamed of the truth. Still am.'

There were dark shadows around her eyes; he thought she looked very young, very fragile. He said, 'When I told you I wasn't worthy of you, I meant it, Philly. It's true. I'm not.'

'Isn't that up to me to decide?'

'I would give *anything* for things to be different. Anything at all.'

'Then *make* them different,' she said fiercely. 'Whatever it is that you're ashamed of, put it right.'

'It's not that easy.'

'The best things aren't always *easy*.' She frowned. Then she said, 'Do you love me, Will?'

'Philly,' he said, 'dear Philly. I'm married, you see.'

He only knew she was crying by the trembling of her shoulders. This time he did not touch her. His heart felt like a dead weight. He said, 'If I was free to love you I would, Philly. But *you* shouldn't love *me*. You don't know anything about me. You don't know what I've done. You don't know who I am.'

She stood up. At the door she paused. Her reddened eyes focused on him. 'Then perhaps', she said, before she walked away from him, 'it's time that you told me.'

★   ★   ★

In the middle of January Topaz received a letter from Prudence Chancellor. Prudence's fast, untidy hand scolded her for not having visited over the Christmas season. Topaz glanced at her diary. There was always a lull at the beginning of the year when no one wanted to give dinner parties. And it would be nice to escape London: a dreary, post-festive gloom seemed to hang over the city, so that people jostled for seats bad-temperedly on the Tube and rushed through their daily business, their faces pinched and impatient.

That she was visiting Dorset because the School House was near Missencourt, and that this allowed the possibility of running into Marius and making up their quarrel, was something she hardly admitted to herself. Since the evening of her party he had neither phoned nor written. She had had a thank-you note from Tara for her Christmas present, but nothing from Marius. She veered between optimism and despair. Optimism because old friends surely didn't stop speaking to each other just because one came across the other slightly tipsy and with half her buttons undone. Despair because it had occurred to her that if she had wondered whether she might turn out like her mother, then so might Marius. Perhaps he had decided it was better to break off their friendship now, rather than in twenty-five years time have to put up with her far too fond of gin and batting her eyelids at anything in a military uniform.

But all her worries were pointless because on her first evening at the School House, Prudence mentioned over dinner that Marius was away from home on business in the north of England. Topaz had to hide her disappointment so that Prudence didn't notice.

For the first few days she pottered around, helping Prudence and reading books and magazines, and falling asleep in front of the fire. She hadn't realized how tired she was. And how nice it was not to have to worry about whether the mushroom soufflé would rise or whether she'd put enough salt in the vichyssoise. When the weather cleared a little, she took to going for long walks in the countryside, tramping mile after mile along narrow lanes that had been familiar to her since childhood. Ice cracked as her shoe caught the frozen edge of a puddle and her breath made smoke signals in the cold air.

One of her walks took her to Sixfields. As she headed up the long, slow incline of the hill, the house loomed out of the mist, dark and massive. She paused, slightly out of breath. In the distance, she heard boys' voices, punctuated with shrieks of laughter. Nearing the house, she remembered the last time she had visited Sixfields, on the day after Jack's homecoming party: teetering on a chair to put the plates on top of the dresser, while Carrie Chancellor's sharp blue eyes snapped at her, angry and impatient.

She stood at the gate, ready to walk quickly away if she heard the tap of Carrie's stick or the growl of dogs. It seemed to her that the great house was crumbling away, that it was losing the battle against time and the elements. There were cracks in the brickwork and roof tiles were missing. Guttering yawned from the eaves and one of the tall, ornate chimneypots lay in shards in the orchard.

The voices were coming from behind the house. Topaz opened the gate and walked down the path. Ivy scrambled over the front door, binding it shut, and several of the small, mullioned windowpanes were chipped or missing. Lichen clung to the walls, making green and gold blisters on the weathered brickwork. The voices became louder. 'Break the glass!' someone shouted. 'Break the glass!' She stood still for a moment, peering into the back yard. Half a dozen boys were hurling stones at the upstairs windows of the house. Their calls, ecstatic with the pleasure of wrongdoing, sliced through the frozen air.

'Get the glass!'

'Come on!'

'Hit the bugger!'

There was a loud impact, followed by whoops of delight. Fragments of glass jangled as they fell to the cobbled courtyard.

One of the boys said, 'I'm scared, Gary.'

'Soppy git. She's a cripple, ain't she? Fancy being afraid of a cripple.'

Topaz said loudly, 'I've telephoned the police from the cottage. They'll be here any moment.'

Several of the smaller boys turned tail and ran. One of the older youths, who had insolent eyes and a scattering of whiskers on his chin, sauntered up to her and said, 'What's it to you, you silly bitch? Friend of yours, is she?' Then he walked away with deliberate slowness, pebbles spilling from one hand to the other, his friends straggling after him. When he reached the corner of the house, he swung round and hurled the pebbles. They struck Topaz's back, stinging like hailstones. There was the sound of running feet as they darted round the corner.

She brushed down her coat, opened the back door and called out Carrie's name. There was no reply. Inside the lobby, cobwebs festooned the glass bottles that lined the shelves. The small window was curtained with dust.

An inner door gave into a corridor. 'Miss Chancellor?' Topaz called, her voice smothered by the gloom and vastness of the house. Passages branched off at odd angles and, taking one at random, she had to duck to avoid hitting her head on the low ceiling. Through open doorways she glimpsed rooms filled with bulky, old-fashioned furniture. Tables and sideboards, each with its clutter of books and ornaments, were blurred by a grey felting of dust. She wondered whether anyone ever entered those rooms. She wondered who had cast the spell that had frozen them in time.

A sudden sound made her jump. From above her, an insistent drumming interrupted the silence. She climbed the stairs. Heading towards the source of the noise, she saw a shape sprawled on the floor. Carrie lay next to the narrow attic steps, her body curled against the stairwell. She was rapping her stick on the floorboards. She called out to Topaz.

493

'Here, girl. Quickly.'

Topaz ran to her. Papers were scattered around Carrie, pale diamonds against the dark oak floor.

'Give me your hand.' Carrie's imperious voice barked orders. 'Help me up.'

'You might have hurt something. Perhaps I should phone the doctor — '

'Don't answer me back, girl, just help me up. Can't get my breath lying here.' Carrie's icy hand grabbed at Topaz's. Her lips were blue.

'How long have you been lying here, Miss Chancellor?'

Momentarily, Carrie looked confused. 'Morning . . . I went up to the attic this morning . . . '

It was midday. Topaz said, 'If I put my arm around you, perhaps you can sit up.'

Carrie struggled into a sitting permission. 'Hurt my ankle,' she muttered. Her foot was badly swollen. She was leaning against the wall, taking gulping, noisy breaths.

She focused on Topaz. 'Who are you?'

'Topaz Brooke. Prudence's — '

'I know, I know. Prudence's brother's daughter. I remember. Help me to the bedroom.'

'I really think I should get a doctor — '

'I don't hold with doctors,' said Carrie brusquely. 'Not one of 'em ever did me any good. And anyway, I'm dying, so what's the use of a doctor? A waste of money.'

'I'm sure you'll feel much better soon, Miss Chancellor,' said Topaz politely.

'I'm dying, I say.' The anger faded, and Carrie mumbled, 'That's why I had to get these. Have to burn them. Mustn't let him know.'

The pieces of paper strewn across the passageway were letters, Topaz realized, the paper yellowed and flimsy, the clear script brown and faded. *My dearest Caroline*, one of the pages began. As she helped Carrie stand up, the square of paper beside her foot trembled. She caught a glimpse of the signature. *Your loving Francis*.

Carrie said, 'You must help me to my bedroom. Just there — the door's open — '

They walked slowly down the corridor. Her arm supporting the older woman, Topaz sensed the effort that every step demanded of her. Carrie's lungs rattled with every inward breath and her frame seemed too fragile to bear even her slight weight.

In the bedroom Carrie sank on to the bed and lay still, her eyes closed. Her face was as white as the pillow. When Topaz shook out a moth-eaten rug and tucked it over her, Carrie muttered, 'You can go now. Please go.'

She went downstairs. In the kitchen, she made tea. A quick exploration of the ground floor of the house revealed a dusty bottle of sherry. She had to pull hard at the stopper to free it from its encrustation of sugar crystals.

She carried the tray upstairs. Halfway along the corridor she paused. A weak winter sunshine gleamed through the mullioned windows. Pale lozenges of light illuminated the letters scattered on the floorboards. *I have to burn them*, Carrie had said.

Topaz put the tray on the window sill. Then she gathered up the letters and shuffled them into a tidy stack. Leaning against the sill, the papers clutched in her hand, she reminded herself sternly that it was one of the worst things one could do, to look at someone else's letters. Sneaky and underhand, altogether inexcusable.

She began to read.

★ ★ ★

In Carrie's bedroom she poured tea and put the cup and the glass of sherry on the bedside table. Carrie did not seem to have moved since she had left her, but a little colour had returned to her cheeks.

Topaz said, 'I've got Francis Temperley's letters. Do you want me to put them on the fire?'

Carrie's eyes jerked open. 'You've read them — '

'I saw the signature. I was curious.'

Carrie gave a tight little smile. 'Curiosity killed the cat.'

Topaz sat down on the edge of the bed. 'You were engaged to him? To Marius and Julia's father?'

A small shake of the head. 'Not *engaged*. Never *engaged*. He promised me, though.' Her voice was bitter.

'Where did you meet him?'

'None of your business, missy.' Carrie's fingers clawed the edge of the sheet. Then she seemed to relent, because she said, 'At church, of course. Where else would a nicely brought-up girl meet a young man?' She smiled. 'I was pretty then. Not *beautiful*. Never *beautiful*. But presentable, personable. Not *ugly*. Not *repulsive*.' She threw a glance at Topaz and gave a cackle of amusement. 'You can't imagine it, can you? Carrie Chancellor, *pretty*. Well, I was. In the spring, I wore a white lawn dress with a blue sash and a straw hat with flowers in the brim. Violets,' she said softly. 'I always loved violets.'

Her voice faded away. Topaz put the teacup in her hands. Carrie was still for a while, staring at it, and then words began to pour out of her, as if pent up far too long. As if, silenced by her own reclusiveness for years, she welcomed the release of confession.

She said, 'Francis walked me home from church one day. My father was unwell, so I'd gone by myself. I was seventeen, Francis was a few years older. We'd seen each other since we were children, of course. Here and there — at church, on the beach, at the shops. He was a handsome man, Francis Temperley. Tall and fair. He had light blue eyes, the colour of the sky. Never thought he'd take notice of me, mousy little Carrie Chancellor. That first time I thought he was just being polite. But the next Sunday, he passed me a note in church, asking me to meet him that afternoon.'

'Your father — '

'Would never have let me have anything to do with Francis Temperley. Didn't think he was good enough for me.' There was a flicker of fear in Carrie's eyes. 'He wasn't an easy man, my father. You didn't cross him. He shut me in the cellar once when I talked back to him. I didn't do it again. And, besides, a young woman couldn't be alone with a young man. It wasn't done in those days. You'd lose your reputation. Of course — ' Carrie coughed ' — everything's different now. The war — the second war — changed everything. Even children — those boys in the farmyard. The eldest lad, Gary Prior. His father used to work for me before the war. A good man. Then he was sent away to Burma. His children went wild, of course — boys need their fathers, don't they?' Carrie paused, gathering her breath. 'He was three years in a Japanese prison camp, Michael Prior. Not the same man when he came home. Hardly speaks. Can't hold down a job.'

In the silence there was only the tick of the clock, and the creaks and moans of the old house settling on its foundations. Carrie took a few sips of tea. 'He loved me,' she said suddenly. 'Francis Temperley loved me.'

It was almost forty years since Carrie Chancellor, unimaginably young and comely in her straw hat with the violets, had loved Francis Temperley. What had happened? Why had they parted? Why had Francis married Adele, rather than Carrie? Absorbed in this old, unexpected story of lost love, Topaz no longer noticed the chilly damp of the bedroom.

'Did your father find out you were seeing him?'

Carrie gave a quick shake of the head. 'It was nineteen-sixteen. Francis had failed the medical when

497

he'd volunteered for the army two years before, but they were less fussy by the middle of the war. It was the time of the Somme — they were mowing young men down like corn. Cannon fodder, poor souls.' Her eyes had darkened. 'Francis was sent to the Front. We wrote letters . . . I wrote to him every day. He came back a year later for a fortnight's leave. He was different, then. Quieter. He'd seen some terrible things, they all had. He wouldn't talk about it to me. He'd only talk about happy things. He said that when the war was over, we'd get married. As soon as I turned twenty-one.'

Carrie's knuckles were white where she gripped the cup. 'He went back to the Front. And I fell ill that winter. Polio. I was in the fever hospital for six months. It was January nineteen-eighteen when I went in, June before I came home. The only thing I thought of — the only thing that stopped me giving up — was Francis.' She glared at Topaz. 'The war seemed to have gone on for ever. So many had died. I was always afraid for him.'

'But he survived, didn't he?'

'He survived. Yes.' Carrie's features were still and frozen. There was a long silence. Then she said bitterly, 'When he came home in November he came to see me. I had a caliper on my leg. I'd taught myself to walk with a crutch. When he looked at me, I could see that I disgusted him. That I *revolted* him. That afternoon — ' she gave an odd little laugh ' — he didn't mention getting engaged any more. And neither did I, of course. Never could believe my luck, anyway, and after my illness . . . ' She looked away. Her ribcage rose and fell, matching the struggle for breath in her waterlogged lungs. 'Six months later, I heard he'd married. Some yellow-haired beauty. It took me a while — I was never an especially *clever* girl, you understand, cloth-eared Carrie, my father called me — but I realized that I'd reminded him of what he'd seen in France. All those wounded men, all those crippled bodies. He didn't want *that*, did he? He was a fastidious man, Francis Temperley. Liked things just so. He wanted a wife who was whole and perfect, who would bear him perfect children. He didn't want a *cripple*.'

Topaz couldn't think of a single word of comfort. Couldn't think of a phrase that might soften a pain that still seared after forty years. She imagined how a much younger Carrie, rejected by the man she loved, must have begun to hide away from the world. How she must have become defensive, unable to trust another human being. How the shy young girl had developed a hard outward shell, taking pleasure in the only things that seemed to her dependable: money and land.

Carrie whispered, '*He* was my chance. My only chance. Of a family. Of a child. A child for Sixfields. He took all that away from me.' The cup slammed down on to the saucer. 'Not that I *moped*. Father was dead by then and I had the farm to run.' Her narrowed eyes glittered. Topaz only just caught the next muttered words. 'But then, when I found out Jack was seeing his daughter — '

'Jack?' Topaz stared at her.

'Best of the bunch.' Carrie's mouth curled. 'A feeble lot, the Chancellors. It happens to old families — the good blood runs out. Money-grabbing and workshy, the lot of 'em. Except Jack.' Carrie's tone softened. 'Jack was never afraid of me. Took me as he found me. Got that from your Aunt Prudence. A good thing John Chancellor married out of the family, took a sensible wife.' She looked down. 'He's a good boy, Jack. And I couldn't have *that*, could I?' Suddenly, Carrie's voice was venomous. 'Couldn't have *his* daughter having my Jack. Having Sixfields. Not after what he'd done to me.'

Topaz's heart was pounding. It was hard to take in what Carrie was saying. Now she felt cold. Now she clutched her coat around her, but the chill remained.

She said slowly, 'You didn't want Jack to marry Julia — '

'Francis left me. He *betrayed* me. I wasn't going to lose Jack as well. I wasn't going to lose him to *her*.' The proud, snapping glare rested on Topaz. 'So I made him choose. Made him choose between the land and the girl.' She smiled to herself. 'I knew what choice he'd make. I could read my Jack. They're a greedy lot, the Chancellors, they know what side their bread's buttered on. I knew he'd not waste time mooning over a silly girl.'

'But Jack *loved* Julia! And she loved him!'

Carrie looked unmoved. Her eyes were blue slits. She said, 'I wanted her to know what it felt like. *His* daughter.'

Such hatred. Topaz had to look away. Her eyes latched on to the faded phrases of the letters she still clutched in her hand. *My only love . . . till we next meet . . . I think of you all the time . . .*

She said disbelievingly, 'You couldn't hurt Francis Temperley, so you hurt Julia. You couldn't hurt the father, so you hurt the child.'

'An eye for an eye . . . ' whispered Carrie. Once more, she smiled. '*You* told me. Do you remember? *You* told me.'

Standing on a stool, putting the plates on the dresser. *Jack's like me, he doesn't like parties.* Malice had danced in Carrie Chancellor's eyes. And she, Topaz, had said, *Aunt Prudence thinks Julia and Jack might get married. They're awfully fond of each other.*

She looked away from the bed. Outside, the mist had lifted, showing a landscape of shades of grey and brown. She said harshly, 'But you have lost Jack, haven't you? He left you, didn't he?'

Carrie herself had sent Jack away. Carrie's inability to show love had driven Jack from Sixfields. Had it been worth it, Topaz wondered? Had the pleasure of vengeance made up for what Carrie had lost?

There was a whisper from behind her. 'I always thought he'd come back to me.' Carrie sounded bewildered.

Topaz wondered whether Carrie was thinking of Francis Temperley, or of Jack Chancellor. Of the lover, or of the man she had come to think of as a son.

Suddenly, she was desperate to leave. Old griefs and old enmities seemed to bleed from the fabric of the house. She heard Carrie say, 'You won't tell him, will you? You won't tell Jack?'

She thought of all the events that had stemmed from Carrie's inability to forgive. Jack's rejection of Julia, Julia's marriage to Will. Even Will's disappearance had roots in that single act of revenge.

And yet they had survived, hadn't they? Jack was happily married with a baby daughter; Julia — restless, unconventional Julia — had found contentment through her son and through her work. And it was possible, wasn't it, that in some far-off place even Will had found happiness. Who knew whether, had Carrie Chancellor not given her own little twist to the wheel of fate, the outcome would have been any better?

Topaz made her promise. 'I won't tell Jack.' She held out the letters. 'What shall I do with these?'

'Burn them.' Carrie fell back on the pillows, grey with exhaustion. 'Burn them.'

★ ★ ★

Fleetingly, Will thought of leaving Coldharbour Farm. It was what he had always done when people came too close to him. He only got as far as taking his knapsack down from the peg before he abandoned the idea.

Through the next couple of weeks he was glad of the distraction of work. Midwinter was always a busy time for any car-repair business: radiators froze, engines

501

failed to start, and cars skidded on icy patches on the road, breaking windscreens and denting bumpers. Several times he dreamed of the dancing angels. He would wake at four in the morning, the dream lingering, haunted by an awareness of tasks left incomplete, obligations undischarged. In his dreams the air of expectancy that had hung over Rick's painting seemed intended for him. Perhaps those angels, with their kind, amused eyes, were waiting for him to make restitution, to put things right.

In the library in Lincoln he sat at a desk for hours, leafing through weighty books on the history of art. He was surrounded by angels: stern angels, kindly angels, bored-looking angels. Angels reading books, angels playing musical instruments. Angels balancing improbably on cotton-wool clouds, angels in shadowed interiors, complaisant and mundane, looking for all the world as though they had been invited to Sunday tea. None of the paintings of angels were quite the same as his dancing angels.

In another room in the library he confronted darker images. Studying newspaper reports of the Nuremberg Trials, he thought about Rick. Rick had been an insignificant parasite compared to the Martin Bormanns and Hermann Goerings of whom he now read, those men who had let loose the evils of war and displacement. Rick had merely fed off the scraps that fell from their tables. War had given Rick opportunity, creating the conditions in which he and his kind had flourished. He wondered whether Rick himself continued to profit from the changing conditions of peacetime, or whether he, too, was struggling.

When he thought of his family, it was with an intense and painful longing. He knew that, separated from them these past few years, a part of him had indeed died. He found himself remembering the illnesses he had suffered as a child. Throughout those weeks and months his mother had sat at his bedside, nursing him back to health. He had often been cantankerous or tearful, but he could not remember Prudence ever being anything less than patient and encouraging. He knew what his absence must mean to her. He remembered what she had suffered when Jack had gone away to war and her joy when he had returned. And with a deep regret he remembered the specious, self-serving rationale that had accompanied his decision to pretend he was dead. He had told himself that his parents would prefer a dead son to a disgraced son. What nonsense, what calumny. His years of exile had taught him about love. He knew now that he would love Philippa sick, disfigured or disgraced. If he were to lose her, he would mourn her for ever. He had run away because he had been unable to face the consequences of his own actions; he had run away because he had not wanted to endure the pain of witnessing his family's disappointment in him, the favoured son. Self-protection had been his guiding light; his family's suffering had hardly figured in his reasoning.

Returning to the farm, he found Harold in the barn, knocking mud off bunches of turnips. He said, 'I have to go away. I'm not sure how long for.'

Harold turned to him. 'But you will be coming back?'

'I hope so.'

There was a silence. Harold laid the turnips on a wooden rack. 'You and Philippa . . . have you made things right between you?'

Will could see in the distance, beneath the poplars, the railway carriage that had been his home and his refuge. 'I intend to,' he said, 'but I did some bad things, Harold, before I came here. Things that were very wrong. I intend to put them right. If I can, then I'll be back.'

Harold straightened. 'Philippa means everything to me. She's all I've got. I'll not see her hurt, Will.'

He made himself meet Harold's gaze. 'You never asked me questions,' he said. 'You trusted me. I can never thank you enough for that. I'm asking you to trust me just a little bit longer.' He gave Harold a folder. 'I've prepared some notes for my classes. Some work for them to get on with while I'm away.'

When Harold glanced at the folder, he frowned. The name *Will Chancellor* was written in bold letters across the front cover. It had shocked Will how exhilarating it had felt, to reclaim his own name.

★ ★ ★

It rained at Carrie Chancellor's funeral, a grey, incessant downpour that draped the churchyard and the surrounding countryside in a shimmering veil. The hymn was 'Lord of all Hopefulness, Lord of all Joy', which seemed to Topaz utterly inappropriate for Carrie, who had nursed her unhappiness for more than half a lifetime. Carrie's God had surely been the God of the Old Testament, patient and vengeful, a God who visited the sins of the fathers on to the children.

It was three weeks since she had seen Carrie Chancellor; three weeks since she had learned of Carrie's love for Francis Temperley. A fortnight after her visit Carrie had died, her stubborn spirit vanquished at last by pneumonia. Topaz had kept her promise to Carrie, confiding her secret to no one. Yet Carrie's story haunted her.

After the service and burial the great tribe of Chancellors trooped back to Sixfields, where they devoured the food which Prudence and Topaz had prepared. Prudence and Mrs Sykes had spent the previous week scrubbing and dusting, so that half a dozen of Sixfields' downstairs rooms were presentable. When the funeral breakfast was cleared away, Carrie's solicitor read out the will. Topaz remained in the kitchen. At first there was silence and then the entire family seemed to erupt simultaneously from the parlour, grumbling or shouting or spoiling for a fight, according to their different natures. Returning to the kitchen, Prudence filled kettles and put them on the stove. 'A cup of tea will calm them down,' she said. She looked dazed.

Topaz escaped from the melee and went upstairs. Here the rooms and passageways were still choked with clutter and dust, and there was hardboard pinned over the broken windowpanes. Opening the door to Carrie's bedroom, she saw that ash lay grey and cold in the grate. She wondered whether, if she stirred that ash, she would glimpse the last fragments of Francis Temperley's youthful passion. Carrie had destroyed his letters only when she had known that her own death was imminent. She had destroyed them to prevent Jack finding them, so that he would never know why she had tried to divide him from Julia. Bitterness and fear had twisted Carrie's soul more profoundly than disease had deformed her body. Fear had made her avoid love, fear of rejection, fear of pain.

She would not make the same mistake, Topaz thought. You had to take risks; sometimes you had to put yourself on the line. Letting the door swing shut, she muttered to herself sternly, *Nothing ventured nothing gained*, and ran downstairs. Outside in the yard, she chose a bicycle from the half-dozen leaning against the wall and set off.

★ ★ ★

When he came out of the old chapel, she called out to him. In his sudden smile, she saw not a scrap of disapproval or duty or politeness, but only surprise and pleasure.

She said, 'I thought I'd come and meet you.'

'*I* was about to try to find *you*.' Marius crossed the road to her. 'I knew you'd be here for the funeral. I thought you might need rescuing from the Chancellors.' He frowned. 'No, that's not true. I wanted to apologize to you.'

'To me?'

'For that evening. When I turned up at your party.'

'It wasn't as bad as it looked,' she said quickly. 'You know what it's like at Christmas — you end up kissing people you wouldn't otherwise kiss in a thousand years.'

'You were right, though. It was none of my business.' He grimaced. 'How appalling — and how pompous — you must think me, barging into your life every now and then and telling you off. It's a thoroughly bad habit and I promise I won't do it again.'

She felt an upsurge of joy. He wasn't cross with her. He had forgiven her. She said lightly, 'We could go on apologizing to each other for a while, if you like, but it is raining, and I really should get this — ' she tapped the bicycle's handlebars ' — back to Sixfields before anyone notices that it's missing.'

'Isn't it yours?'

'I borrowed it.'

'*Borrowed?*'

'Well, stole.' She made a face. 'The *noise*, Marius. At Sixfields. I had to get away. They're arguing. All the Chancellors. I thought they were going to start *fighting*. They've just heard the will, you see. Carrie left everything to Jack. The house, the money — and there seems to be rather a lot of it — the land and all Carrie's belongings. Maurice wants to contest the will.'

'Does he now?' Marius looked amused.

'Jack and Carrie had quarrelled, of course. He thought she'd disinherited him.'

'But she hadn't?'

She felt suddenly sad, remembering the lonely woman trapped in the decaying house. 'I think she'd always meant Sixfields to go to Jack. She loved him, you see.'

He said, 'I've missed you, Topaz.'

'Honestly?'

'I was afraid you were avoiding me. Or I thought you might have grown away from me. It happens. I'd understand if that was how you felt.'

She said simply, 'I'll never grow away from you, Marius. Never.'

Something flickered in his eyes. Her heart fluttered, seeing it.

He said, 'You can't be sure.'

'Oh, I can. And I've just been busy. I've had things to work out.'

'And have you? Have you worked them out?'

She smiled. 'I think so.'

He said suddenly, 'There's a concert at Tara's school tonight, which I really must attend — but will you still be here tomorrow night? We could have dinner. Or a film, if you'd prefer it.'

'A film,' she said. 'A film would be lovely.'

'Good.' There was still that light in his eyes. 'Sevenish, then.'

She cycled back to Sixfields. Clearing up, helping Prudence transport plates and utensils back to the School House, she no longer noticed the cold, wet weather, or the grumbles of the Chancellors as they left Sixfields for their various homes.

In the peace and privacy of her room at the School House her emotions teetered between confidence and uncertainty. Marius had asked her for a date. Surely it was a real date this time, rather than the consolation prize he had offered her at seventeen? Don't be silly, the doubting half of her said sternly: he was only trying to make up the quarrel, nothing more.

But she could not quite convince herself of that. *I've missed you, Topaz*, he had said. And there had been

507

that look in his eyes. She hardly dared consider that it might have been hope.

Downstairs the telephone rang, interrupting her thoughts. Opening the wardrobe, she began to search through the handful of clothes she had brought with her. There was the black wool she had worn for the funeral — rather *severe*, she thought — or her tartan skirt and rust-coloured jersey. Or her jade silk blouse; she could wear the scarf Marius had given her with it.

There was a knock at the door. Topaz opened it.

Prudence said, 'That was your mother on the phone. She's had a little accident, I'm afraid, dear.'

★ ★ ★

The news of Carrie's death had prompted in Jack a mixture of emotions, disbelief and regret being uppermost. Disbelief because he had somehow assumed the old harridan would live till she was a hundred, regret because at the back of his mind he had always intended to attempt, if not a reconciliation, then at least a truce.

Leaving Esther and Louise in Canada, Jack sailed back to England for the funeral. During the voyage, he thought about Carrie. In spite of their differences, he had retained for her both respect and a sneaking affection. His respect was for her tenacity and her courage. He recalled Carrie at harvest time, pitchforking hay into the cart, working longer hours than any of them, refusing to let herself be dictated to by the feebleness of her body. She must often have been in pain, yet she had never complained. Looking back, it seemed possible to Jack that Carrie's shrewishness had in some way fuelled her, giving her the strength to keep going when a sweeter nature might have given up.

He paid his last respects to her at the funeral. Then they read out the will. His disbelief returned, coupled this time with amusement. How typical of the old witch to keep them guessing to the end. He imagined her looking down on them, cackling with malevolent laughter at the hornet's nest she had stirred up. She hadn't even bothered to divide her wealth. No bequests to faithful servants, no trinkets left to those relatives who had endured uncomfortable visits for years in the hope of being remembered in her will. She had left everything, lock, stock and barrel, to him, Jack Chancellor. From the heaps of old newspapers and rusting farm implements at Sixfields to the bonds, stocks and shares in Coutts Bank in London.

The day after the funeral he drove to Sixfields. Approaching the house, he parked the car at the top of the hill. From this vantage point he could see the entire estate. In the distance the sea shifted through the mist. It was hard, he thought, to imagine Sixfields without Carrie. Her stubborn, recalcitrant spirit seemed as much a part of the estate as the house's crooked roofs and twisting corridors. He wondered what Sixfields had really meant to her. Had it been a refuge or a prison? Had she truly loved it or had her ownership allowed her no freedom of movement, no chance of escape? He himself had nearly allowed his own longing for Sixfields to dictate the course of his life.

Inside the house Jack began the mammoth task of sorting through the contents. A methodical man, he worked through room after room, dividing Carrie's possessions into three categories: to keep, jumble sale and bonfire. Clouds of dust rose into the air and Sixfields' damp cold was somehow chillier than Saskatchewan's much lower, drier temperatures. Impatient to complete the task, he camped out in the house, making sandwiches, opening tins, and sleeping on one of the less dilapidated sofas. He couldn't quite face the bedrooms with their frayed curtains and greying linen. If ghosts walked anywhere, it was among those low-ceilinged, small-windowed rooms. Soon the rubbish intended for the bonfire was a mountain in the middle of the courtyard. An armless doll, a rolling pin without its handles, and an assortment of books without spines, their words blotted out with mould, protruded pathetically from the pyre.

And yet the house yielded up treasures, too. Though much of the furniture was fit only for kindling, Jack unearthed dark Jacobean chests and cabinets, and delicate Regency desks and chairs. Hidden among the cracked earthenware in the kitchen were lovely old plates and bowls, some of them dating back, he guessed, to the seventeenth century. He would give the plates to Prudence, Jack decided. In the library he found first editions of the complete works of Dickens and a collection of paintings, seascapes mostly, whose light and colour seemed to capture all the changeable beauty of the Dorset coast. He decided to ship the paintings back to Canada so that Esther could understand why he had so loved this place.

After two days he had completed the ground floor; on the third he moved upstairs. By late evening he had worked through half a dozen rooms. Breaking for something to eat, he wondered whether to return to the School House that night. He was tired of tinned soup and sandwiches and, besides, there was something unnerving about the empty house. It played tricks with you, made you turn your head at the creaks and groans of the ancient timber. Shadows pooled in hidden corners, doors slammed suddenly shut in the middle of the night. Driven by an ancient, temperamental generator, Sixfields' electricity supply had an alarming habit of giving out and suddenly extinguishing all the lights, plunging the house into darkness.

One more room, Jack decided. One more room, and he'd go back to the School House. He needed the company. It would drive you insane, being here too long on your own.

He chose a little boxroom at the end of a corridor. The door was stiff to open, as though no one had been inside for years. Moths, trapped decades ago in the dusty, airless little cage, lay on the window sill, their fragile bronze wings turning to dust. A spider's web as thick as a rope was slung from one corner to the other. When Jack brushed it away the grey filaments clung to him.

Inside, there were half a dozen cabinets, shunted side to side, taking up most of the floor space. Jack began to fling open drawers, to prise apart locks in dusty glass doors. Women's magazines dating from the previous century were yellowing in cardboard boxes. Balls of knitting wool, dark maroons and gloomy bottle greens, were bundled in a shoebag. A baby's ivory rattle rubbed shoulders with a decaying surgical support.

Jack put the rattle in his pocket and hurled the truss quickly out into the corridor. At the bottom of the drawer there was something wrapped in sacking. Something small and square and solid-seeming. Like a floor tile or a block of wood.

He unpeeled the sacking. When he saw what was inside it he leaned back against the door jamb, his breath catching in his throat.

★   ★   ★

Sitting in the car, Will waited. Thick clouds meant that the night was moonless; drops of rain trailed down the windscreen. Every now and then he ran the engine to take off the chill. Then he waited some more.

It was hard to keep his nerves in check. It crossed his mind that he could just drive away and start again somewhere new. Yet he did not do so, and instead forced himself to concentrate on practicalities. He hoped that

511

his memory of Sixfields' layout was true. He hoped that on this night, as on that other night, the dogs would remember him, and would not bark. He hoped that everything was as it had been, and that Cousin Carrie had not, through some piece of ill fortune, discovered the treasure he had hidden in her house.

At ten o'clock he climbed out of the car. From the boot he unearthed a raincoat and a bag of chocolate drops. The chocolate drops were for the dogs.

But there weren't any dogs, he discovered on reaching Sixfields. The courtyard was silent. Carrie's Bentley was parked beside the makings of an enormous bonfire. *She must be having a clear-out*, he thought. About time, too.

The house was in darkness, so he assumed that she had gone to bed. He hoped that she was sleeping soundly. The walk had soothed his nerves and he felt unexpectedly calm as he tried the handle of the back door. It was open and his torch made circles of light on the walls of the lobby. He stood for a moment, raindrops dripping from his clothes on to the tiled floor. The room was empty, the familiar clutter of bottles and jars swept from the shelves. Opening the inner door, the branching passageways confused him and he paused. Then he saw the stairs that led off to the right. They creaked as he climbed them, the small sounds like gunfire in the silent house. Left, he said to himself as he reached the landing; at the top he turned left. Doors gave off to either side of him and, failing to duck for a low ceiling, he hit his head and had to stifle a curse. Then he couldn't remember which room it was. Opening first one door and then another, he was afraid that he'd open the wrong door and find Carrie in her nightgown, spouting fury and with a shotgun in her hand.

But all the rooms were empty, their furniture tidily rearranged, the clutter that he recalled as characteristic of Sixfields noticeably absent. At last, rounding a corner, he saw the door with its peeling pea-green paint. He turned the handle.

A voice from behind him said, 'Will? Will, is that you? Is this what you're looking for?'

18

When he was able to speak, Will said, 'What the hell are you doing here?'

Jack came towards him. 'I'm packing up.'

'Packing up?'

'Carrie's things.' He glanced at Will. 'You all right?'

'Fine.' He was leaning against the wall as his heart rushed and gulped. 'You gave me a hell of a shock. I thought you were — I thought you were — ' He was staring at Jack, had not been able to stop staring at Jack. As though he might ebb, bodiless, back into the plasterwork.

'A ghost?' said Jack sharply. 'What do you think it was like for me, waking up and hearing you clattering about?'

Will rubbed his forehead. 'Packing up . . . ' he said again.

'Carrie died a month ago. She left the house to me.' Jack shot a glance around the gloom. 'I'm trying to get the place sorted out so I can get back to Canada.'

'Canada?' He seemed to have been reduced to an echo, repeating phrases in the darkness.

'Esther's Canadian. Esther', said Jack, catching Will's blank stare, 'is my wife.'

'*Oh.*' An avalanche of thoughts rushed through Will's head. Julia. Jack. *Esther.* He looked at Jack. 'Have you any cigarettes?'

Jack tossed him a packet of cigarettes and a lighter. Struggling to steady his trembling hands, Will lit up and inhaled. He heard Jack say, 'You came back for this, didn't you?' Jack was holding up the picture of the dancing angels. They still turned and smiled, their strong, feathered wings outstretched as

514

they poised, waiting for him.

Will said, 'It's stolen, you see.'

'You don't say,' said Jack, rather sarcastically.

'I wanted to give it back to whoever it belongs to. I wanted to — to make restitution.'

It all sounded rather pompous and ridiculous, put like that, in the prosaic gloom of the corridor, with Jack, as so often in the past, his judge and jury. And it seemed that Jack thought so too, because he snorted and said, 'For God's sake, Will. Always so bloody melodramatic.'

Will felt irritated. 'Well, I had to start somewhere. Had to put things right.'

'How about just coming home and opening the door and saying, 'I'm back'?'

So utterly typical of Jack to greet his homecoming with such characteristically elder-brotherly scorn. He had never been able to do anything right for Jack. He said angrily, 'Have you any idea how hard that would be? To *just come home and open the door?*'

Jack gave him a withering look. 'Seems a reasonable solution to me.'

'When I don't know what they think about me — when I don't know *whether* they think about me — or whether they *hate* me?'

Jack's lip curled. 'Do stop dramatizing, Will.'

'*Dramatizing?*' His voice rose. 'Have you any idea how hard this is?'

'Do you think it's been easy for us?' The curl had become a sneer. 'Letting us go on thinking you were dead — when all you had to do was pick up a phone?'

'Don't you see — ' now, he was furious ' — don't you see why that was so impossible?'

Jack's response was short, blistering, crude. Will said disgustedly, 'You've never had much of an imagination, have you, Jack? Just because things have always been easy for you.'

'Oh, for God's sake — '

Will was pleased to see that he had ruffled Jack's customary composure. 'I didn't know whether you wanted me home, did I? I thought you'd forgotten me. I thought you were probably managing quite nicely without me.'

'Convenient for you, was it, to tell yourself that *we'd* forgotten *you*?' Jack's tone was contemptuous. 'Made it all right, did it?'

'Course it didn't make it all right — '

'Made it more comfortable, did it, Will, to blame everything on us?'

Will was almost incoherent with rage. 'You always have to think the worst of me, don't you? Coming home — ' Memories of his years of exile flashed through Will's mind: the grim boarding houses, the nights spent sleeping in ditches, the *loneliness*. 'I've been trying to pluck up courage for *years* — '

Jack's dark blue eyes betrayed an equal fury. 'Not trying *that* hard — '

'How would you know?' Will's fists clenched, aching to hit him. 'You've never been afraid of anything, have you? How would you have any idea what I'm talking about?'

Jack's hand chopped through the air, a quick, dismissive movement. 'Don't try that one. Poor old Will, no one understands him. It was just the same for me, wasn't it, after the war?'

'No, Jack, it wasn't.' Will's voice shook. '*I'm* not a bloody *hero*. *You* were.'

There was a silence. Will turned away. That Jack should see that he was weeping would be unendurable.

But eventually he heard Jack say, 'Yes. Of course. I see that.' Another silence. 'It *was* difficult, though, coming home.'

Will blinked, forcing the tears back. 'You don't have to say that. You don't have to *lie*. I don't want your *pity*.'

'I'm not lying. It *was* hard. Didn't you realize?' Jack's tone had altered, stripped of its customary pride and bravado. 'I thought it would be marvellous. I'd looked forward to it for years. I was so damnably homesick when I was away. And then, when I came back, I didn't seem to fit in any more.'

Will said, 'But everyone was waiting for you. There was a *party.*'

Jack gave a short laugh. 'Well, don't think you'll get away without that.' He sighed. 'And they don't hate you, Will. Quite the contrary. They'll be slaughtering the fatted calf.'

Will wanted to believe him, but could not. 'No. It's not the same. What I've done — '

'Come and have a drink,' interrupted Jack impatiently. 'You look like you could do with one. Me, too, to tell you the truth.'

Momentarily he hesitated, and then, too drained to argue any more, he followed Jack downstairs. In the parlour Jack poured two glasses of whisky and gave one to Will. 'The generator's packed up', Jack explained, 'which is why the house is dark. I can light a fire, though. The heating in this place is archaic, but I've had quite a blaze going with old bits of furniture and sump oil.'

When the fire was lit, Will, who had been thinking, said, 'You knew about the painting.'

'I didn't know it was *here*. Julia looked for it at Hidcote Cottage and at the garage, but neither of us thought of looking *here*.'

'*Julia,*' he whispered.

'She's living in London. She's doing well.' Jack topped up their glasses. Then he said smoothly, 'Your old partner in crime, Rick Hunter, told her about the painting.'

It crossed Will's mind, horribly, that Jack knew everything. From the black market petrol coupons to the illegal currency. He put his head in his hands and groaned.

'You are an idiot, Will,' said Jack, quite pleasantly. 'Why didn't you come to me if you were in a mess?'

He slid his parted fingers down his face. 'I was going to. But I saw you with Julia. The evening before the accident. I saw you at the cottage.'

Jack looked away, but not before Will had glimpsed the shame in his eyes. Will said, 'You were having an affair, weren't you?'

'No.'

'I told you, you don't have to lie. It doesn't matter now.'

'Julia was breaking it off that night. We had been seeing each other, that's true. But she hadn't been unfaithful to you.'

Will looked disbelieving. Jack said bitterly, 'Not that I wasn't trying my damnedest to persuade her to go to bed with me.' He made an impatient gesture. 'I don't know what the hell I was thinking of.'

'You loved her.'

Jack's blue gaze flicked towards him. 'And that makes it all right?'

'Perhaps it makes it . . . understandable.'

In the silence the fire crackled and sparked. Jack said, 'Anyway, that was why I left Sixfields, why I went to Canada. I couldn't seem to stand the sight of myself any more.'

'You, Jack?'

Jack's eyes, focused on Will, narrowed. 'You've always thought of me as the perfect — and perfectly galling — elder brother, haven't you? *Your* opinion, Will. Not mine.'

'You always seemed to find things so *easy* — '

'What you said up there — ' Jack nodded towards the upstairs of the house ' — such *drivel*. Such *rot*. About not being afraid of anything. *Jesus*. If only you knew. I mean, that was one of the things that was *nice* about coming home. Not having to watch your back all the time in case a sniper put a hole in it. Not having to worry about every step you took in case you trod on a mine. God, I was wound up like a *spring* for four bloody years.'

'Then why didn't you say?'

'Couldn't.' Jack gave a quick shake of the head. 'Don't know why. I mean — you don't talk about things like that, do you? And if you did, who would there be to talk to? Blokes who'd been through worse hell than you? Or the ones who'd stayed at home and hadn't a clue what you were talking about?'

'You could have talked to *me*. I may not have been much use, but I'd have *tried*.'

Jack did not reply. Will said, 'The reason I came home — '

'Yes?'

'I've met someone.'

'*Ah*.'

'Only I'm still married to Julia.'

Jack drained his glass. 'Tricky.'

'Do you think', Will said hesitantly, 'that she might agree to divorce me?'

'Well — ' Jack snorted ' — I hardly think she'll want to take up where the two of you left off, will she?'

'She's all right, then? Really all right?'

'As I said, she's fine. She's been working for Temperley's since Suzanne died.'

Will said, 'Suzanne?' and Jack frowned.

'You don't know. How could you? Suzanne died a couple of years ago. A car crash.'

Will felt very shaken. Odd how, in spite of all reason, you expected everything to be just the same.

Jack was still talking. 'Marius went to pieces, the poor bastard. Julia was terrific — stepped in, kept things going.'

Will said suddenly, anxiously, 'How's Mum?'

'Fine. Just fine. And Dad.' He paused. 'Will?'

'It's just that — ' suddenly he felt frightened ' — I don't *belong* any more, do I?'

'You've a bit of catching up to do, that's all.'

He looked away. It had been a long way home. Such a long way. He clenched his fists. 'I'm not sure I can face it. I thought I could, but now I can't.'

'Nonsense,' said Jack briskly. 'Course you can. I'll come back to the School House with you. Keep the conversation going.' There was a silence. Then Jack said quickly, awkwardly, 'It's good to see you, Will. Really.' He poured out more Scotch. 'Drink up. Dutch courage.'

He began, 'What if — ', but Jack placed his hand on his shoulder.

'It'll be all right. I promise you it will be all right.' Then he gave a quick frown, and said, 'There's something else you ought to know.'

Jack took some snapshots out of his jacket pocket and passed one to Will. 'That's my wife. That's Esther.' He handed Will a second photograph, of a plump baby. Then he said, rather gently, 'And I have a daughter, Louise. And you, Will — you have a son.'

★ ★ ★

John, Prudence always said to herself, would sleep through a typhoon, so when at midnight the doorbell rang, it was she who got up to answer it. Swathed in a thick plaid dressing-gown because the School House was always so cold at night, she hurried downstairs. She was aware of a feeling of apprehension: late-night visitors were too often, she knew from experience, associated with bad news.

Snapping back bolts, turning catches, she opened the door. She saw Jack first. Then she noticed that he was not alone, that there was a second figure, slighter and fairer than Jack, standing further back, his features shadowed by the darkness.

Recognizing her younger son, she began to weep.

★ ★ ★

Veronica had slipped stepping off an escalator in Selfridge's, and had broken her wrist. Returning to London, Topaz moved back into her old bedroom in the Bayswater flat. In pain, confined to the flat and denied her usual distractions, Veronica was tetchy and more than usually complaining. The food that Topaz cooked was too fiddly to eat left-handed, Topaz didn't brush her hair properly, the laundry seemed to have mislaid Veronica's silk blouse, and it was quite ridiculous of Topaz to refuse to make cocktails before six o'clock. Veronica *needed* a drink, it was the only thing that helped with the pain.

Topaz veered between a longing to escape the stuffy, cluttered flat and sympathy for her mother. Veronica's attempts to apply her make-up left-handed before her visitors began to arrive at midday were clumsily pitiful. In the morning the business of shoehorning her mother into the barricade of foundation garments she insisted on wearing was a mutually embarrassing ordeal that left both of them exhausted and tearful.

Topaz distracted herself by thinking about Marius. *I've missed you,* he had said. And when he had looked at her, it had been with something like longing.

Three days after her return to London, she was cooking lunch when the telephone rang. She answered it. A voice said, 'Topaz?'

'*Marius.*' Her heart gave a little bounce. 'How are you?'

'I'm very well. Topaz, I'm phoning to tell you — I wanted to be the person to tell you — '

'What?'

521

He said, 'That Will has come home.'

She stood in the hallway, clutching the phone. From the other end of the line, she heard his disembodied voice say, 'Topaz? Topaz, are you there?'

'*Will.* Are you sure?'

'I've seen him. Had to — I couldn't believe it either. He came home last night. He turned up at Sixfields. Jack was there.' There was a pause, and then he said, 'I'm sorry. I've given you a shock, haven't I? Are you all right?'

'Yes,' she whispered. But her legs seemed to have turned to jelly and she had to sit down on the Indian rug, the telephone receiver shaking in her hand. 'Tell me,' she said. 'Tell me everything.'

'I don't know much. I only saw him for a few minutes. Prudence won't let him out of her sight, needless to say. But he's alive and well, which is what's important. Changed, I thought, but then you would be, wouldn't you?'

'But . . . the *boat* — the *Katie Rose* — '

'He was never on it. He left the pub with the Gamble brothers, but was too drunk to drive and had to get out of the car to be sick. Mick and Johnnie drove on to the harbour without him. Apparently he fell asleep in a field. Then he hitched a lift to London *after* he'd hidden Rick Hunter's painting at Sixfields.'

'But where has he *been*?'

'At a farm in Lincolnshire for the past year or so. Before that — all over the place. It sounded . . . hard. I think he's had rather a bad time.'

'Did he say *why*?'

'Oh, it was what we thought.' Momentarily, Marius sounded exasperated. 'Got himself into a mess and couldn't think of a way out of it. Poor old Will. That bastard he got himself involved with — sorry, Topaz — but I'd like to kill him. Passes himself off as a respectable member of society now, did you know that?

In the bloody trade association. Rotary club, next, I should think.'

'People don't always get what they deserve, do they?'

'No,' he said. He sounded sad. 'No, they don't.' Then he said, 'There's a girl, apparently. Philippa something.'

From the adjacent room, her mother called out to her. Topaz said quickly, 'The only thing that matters is that Will is home. Which is just too wonderful. Like a dream.'

'You have this fear that you might wake up, don't you?'

'Does Julia know?'

'Jack went to London first thing this morning to tell her in person. He thought it best. Will didn't know about William, remember.' There was a silence, and then Marius said, 'I wonder how he'll cope with *that*. Such an enormous thing, to suddenly find out that you're a father. I suppose I should be able to give him advice, but I don't think I shall. I seem to remember making rather a mess of all that. Will must find his own way.'

Veronica called again, '*Topaz!*'

'Marius, I'm going to have to go — '

'Must you?'

'*Will,*' she said. She couldn't stop smiling. 'When shall I see him?'

'I have a feeling that Prudence is planning a party. This weekend.'

'Oh Lord.' Sitting on the floor, she wondered whether she would ever believe it, let alone get used to it. Whether it would ever seem ordinary, mundane, that Will had come home.

Veronica called out, 'The cushions need plumping up, Topaz! And my arm's hurting!'

'In a minute, Mummy!'

She heard Marius ask, 'Are you managing? How's your mother?'

'Better. Much better. The hospital put a proper plaster on her arm yesterday.' She smiled. 'My high point of each day is when I escape to the shops. The greengrocer's and the baker's . . . such bliss. *Will*,' she said again. Tears were rolling down her cheeks. 'I can't believe it. Oh dear, I mustn't cry. Not when I'm so happy.' She sniffed hugely, and then she said, 'I'm sorry about not managing the cinema, Marius. I hope it won't be another seven years before you ask me again.'

From miles away in Dorset, she heard him chuckle. He said, 'I was thinking — '

'Yes?'

'Of coming to London this Friday. After work, so it would be lateish. Would you be free for an hour or two?'

'Yes,' she said. Such a perfect day. 'Oh yes.'

* * *

Opening her front door to Will, seeing him for the first time in four years, Julia felt little more than exhaustion and a longing for this difficult interview to be over. There was an awkward moment in which neither of them seemed able to think of what to say, and then she blurted out, 'William's at nursery school. I have to pick him up in an hour.'

'Mum showed me photos. He has your eyes.'

'I think he looks like you.' She added drily, 'But he has my temper, I'm afraid.' She showed Will into the drawing room. 'Tea? Or coffee?' she offered, in a desperate attempt to inject some normality into the situation.

'No thanks. Mum's been feeding me up. She thinks I look thin.'

She considered him. 'I think you look . . . different.' Older, she thought. Stronger and more sure of himself. And somehow terribly remote. It was strange to consider that he was still legally her husband when she didn't seem to know him any more.

He said suddenly, 'I like your hair. It suits you,' and she found herself recalling the diffident, eager-to-please boy she had once known. Then his smile died and he said, 'There are things we have to talk about, Julia. I was going to ask you for a divorce. After all, I deserted you. But that was before I knew about William. When Jack told me — well, I thought you might need me.'

'No, Will.' She looked away. 'I don't need you. Not any more. I thought I needed you once, but I was mistaken.' Her words echoed in the silence. She gave a small sigh. 'I'm sorry. I don't mean to be so — so brutal.'

'I think *brutal* is the least I deserve.' He was standing at the window; he gave a small shake of the head. 'What I did — the hurt I caused — apologizing doesn't seem enough, does it? Not nearly enough.'

She pressed her hands together. 'When Rick first told me you might still be alive, I was so angry. I ought to have been happy, I suppose, knowing that you might be alive. But I wasn't. I was just furious to think you could choose to hurt us so much. But now — well — ' she looked up at him ' — I don't seem to feel anything much at all. Not angry or glad or anything. It's odd — I should feel *something*, shouldn't I? But I don't. I suppose I shall eventually.'

Her gaze drifted around the room, from the photographs of William on the sideboard to the work she had taken home the previous night. She had made a new life for herself, a life which, though unconventional, suited her. She would not let Will's homecoming disrupt her precarious contentment. She knew that he had no place in her new life.

She said firmly, 'I'd like a divorce. And I'd prefer you to take the blame. It's hard enough sometimes, working at Temperley's — plenty of the men think I should go back to the kitchen. And the newspapers painting me as a scarlet woman really wouldn't help.'

'Yes,' he said. 'Of course. I'll set the wheels in motion.'

She said, 'The painting — '

'Jack said Rick told you about it.'

'Why did you hide it at Sixfields? Of all places — why Sixfields?'

'I couldn't think what else to do with it. And Sixfields is so big, so untidy, I thought no one would find it there.' He ran his fingers through his hair. 'I didn't want to leave it at the cottage because I was afraid you might find it, Julia. I knew you'd wonder what the hell I was doing with something like that.'

'Why didn't you take it with you?'

'Because I knew it was valuable. Because I didn't know where I was going. Because I didn't want the responsibility of lugging *that* around with me.' He frowned. 'I wanted it to be safe. And I didn't want Rick to have it, you see. It was too beautiful for Rick.' He had perched on the window sill, his long legs flung out before him. 'Marius knows someone who works at Christie's. He's going to show it to him. Try to find out who's the artist, and who it belongs to.' He made a quick gesture with his hands. 'Rick's not going to lay claim to it, is he?'

Julia said wryly, 'Not now he's become a respectable citizen.'

'It's funny, but I'm not afraid of Rick any more. I was, for a long time.'

'Did you know that he proposed to me?' Julia saw Will's eyes widen. She said savagely, 'I'd like to think that he'll pine away and die of a broken heart — that would be a suitable punishment for everything that he's done, wouldn't it? But people like Rick always recover, don't they? I've no doubt he'll find someone else — some deb who's gone down in the world, perhaps, and needs the cash.' She gave a bitter smile. 'The odd thing is that Rick despises people like that. And yet he longs to be accepted by them.'

Will shrugged. 'Rick isn't important, is he? Never was. The important thing is for the dancing angels to go back where they belong. The important thing is for them to go home.'

There was a silence. Then he said, 'Dad and Jack think it's best for me to pass off what happened as some sort of a breakdown. Mental instability being marginally more acceptable than criminal activity.'

She looked at him closely. 'Did you have a breakdown, Will? Did you?'

'Maybe.' His eyes were troubled. 'I know that I couldn't think straight. Couldn't sleep, couldn't eat. And I did once try to kill myself. Rather incompetently, I'm afraid. Do you think attempted suicide constitutes a breakdown? And I do remember that I had to get away. I didn't know what to do or where to go, but I had to get away.'

She, too, had needed to get away. After Jack, after Rick. For the first time, she felt sorry for him. She whispered, 'Poor Will.'

He gave a little shrug. 'But in the end, there's only so far you can run, isn't there? You can't run away from yourself, can you?'

She was looking down, pleating the folds of her skirt. 'I'm sorry I didn't make things better for us,' she said slowly. 'I did try, but I couldn't seem to get it right.'

'Oh,' he said, with his familiar, easy smile, 'we both tried, didn't we? But it would never have worked, would it? We would never have worked.'

Which fair and logical judgement stabbed her, for some reason she could not fathom, to the heart. Breaking into a silence which had gone on too long, she said, 'Are you sure you won't have that coffee?'

He smiled. 'Actually, I'm parched. All this talking.'

She went into the kitchen. Spooning coffee, she had

to pause, grains spilling on to the table as she squeezed her eyes shut to stem the tears. *I don't seem to feel anything*, she had said. *Julia, you are a fool*, an utter fool, she thought, as she was overwhelmed by her sense of loss.

She put down the spoon and coffee, and went to the window and breathed in great, gulping breaths of cold city air. London, in all its chaos and excitement, spread out before her, but just now the sight did not offer any comfort. Once, not so long ago, she had believed Will dead. Though he had now come back to them, she knew that she had nevertheless lost him. The quiet, serious man sitting in her drawing room was a stranger to her. Just as Jack, who had visited her two days ago to tell her of Will's return, had also been a stranger. The prodigal son and the family man. Jack and Will: she had loved and lost them both. *There'll be others*, she muttered to herself. *One day they won't matter at all*. But just now, knowing that love would never be so sharp nor so sweet as it had been then, that seemed no consolation, merely an extra turn of the knife.

Then she straightened herself, and scrubbed her eyes with the back of her hand, and went back to the kettle and the coffee. And forced the semblance of a smile on to her face as she walked into the drawing room, and said brightly, 'It's nearly time for me to go and collect William. Would you like to come with me, Will? Would you like to meet your son?'

★ ★ ★

Friday came. Lateish, Marius had said. Which meant eight or nine o'clock, Topaz guessed. Somehow she had to fill the intervening hours. So she cooked and cleaned and washed her hair and played interminable games of German whist with her mother and then, in the afternoon, escaped to the shops.

Walking back to the flat, turning the corner into Cleveland Close, her basket full (only meat still rationed now: so much easier, she thought, for Prudence, cooking for Will's party) someone called out her name.

Mist swirled around railings and streetlamps. She turned and saw him. 'Charlie,' she said.

★　★　★

She invited him into the flat. Her mother was having a rest. He had changed, of course; he was fuller-faced, suntanned, heavier. And his features seemed to have blurred, rather like the photographs in *Picturegoer*.

'How's Jennifer?' she asked.

'Jen? I don't know. I haven't seen her for weeks.'

He had followed her into the kitchen; she was putting the shopping away. He said, 'We've split up. Jennifer wants a divorce.'

Topaz opened the fridge. 'That seems . . . rather sudden.'

'Not really. It'd been going wrong for some time.' He looked sad. 'I'm not sure it ever really went right.'

She unpacked the last of the bags. 'So you're back in England, Charlie?'

'The work seems to have dried up, rather.' He gave a little smile. 'In Hollywood it's who you know. And though I knew an awful lot of people when I was married to Jennifer, I don't seem to know all that many without her. Jen's on a seven-year contract, so she's staying out there. I thought I'd come back. I'm buying a house. Got my eye on a little place in Cheyne Walk.'

She remembered dancing along the Embankment with Charlie: primroses in her buttonhole and kisses in the dark.

She smiled. 'A little mews house where you'll have lovely parties?'

'I hope so. Though I'm rather sick of parties.' He

grimaced. 'Never thought I'd say that. It was what I always wanted, wasn't it? A bit of glitter.' His face darkened. 'Well, I've had enough glitter to last me a lifetime.'

She rinsed apples under the tap and dried them carefully. She heard him say, 'I suppose you always want what you haven't had, don't you? I wanted foreign travel and parties and fun and the high life because that was what I didn't get when I was a kid.'

'That was why you wanted me. Because I wasn't what you were used to.'

'No.' He shook his head. His eyes were serious. 'You were different.'

'Oh, come on, Charlie,' she said lightly. 'You liked me because you thought I was a little bit out of your league. A little bit *posh*. You said so yourself.'

'Did I? Then I was an idiot. But I know *that*. Letting you go — not one of my better moves.' A quick smile. 'On my wedding day, I was the least famous person there. I was the person no one could be fagged talking to. It's a funny thing, fame. It's as though there are layers and each one's harder to get through than the one before. I thought I was doing rather well before I got to Los Angeles. Then I realized that I was *nothing*. A very small minnow in a horribly deep pool. And then — well, you think it's going to change you. You think it's going to make you interesting and beautiful and fascinating and the sort of person everyone wants to know. But it doesn't. You're just the same. You're still *you*.'

There was a bitterness in his voice that she could not remember having heard before. And, as he moved into the brighter light from the window, she glimpsed a few grey hairs, clustering among the black curls.

She said gently, 'Charlie, you always were interesting and beautiful and fascinating. It was only you who didn't think so.'

'I thought *I* was ambitious till I met Jennifer. *God*. Talk about vaulting ambition o'erleaping itself.'

'Has she?' Topaz thought of fair, slender Jennifer Audley. 'Has she overleaped herself?'

'Not yet.' He offered her cigarettes; she shook her head. He lit one himself. 'But she will do. She never stops, you see. It's one thing after another — shows, parties, dinners. Then she can't sleep because she's so wound up, so she has to take pills to make her sleep, and then she has to take different pills in the morning to wake herself up so that she can cope with filming.' He shuddered. 'I couldn't stand it after a while. She'd get so angry. Screaming at me. Throwing things at me.' He looked down at his hands. The tips of his fingers were yellow with nicotine. 'And I got so bloody homesick. Never thought I'd miss England. Never thought I'd miss the drizzle and the fog and the *drabness* of it all. But I did. You can get sick of the sun, you know.'

She looked at him. 'Why did you come to see me, Charlie?'

He smiled his easy, charming smile. 'Old times, I suppose. I tried your flat first, but you weren't there. Your neighbour told me you were staying with your mother. How are they all, the old crowd? Helena and Donald and everyone.'

'Helena and Jerry have married.'

'*God*.' Charlie's eyes widened.

'They're very happy. Jerry's teaching at a grammar school in Harrow. And Francesca has two daughters now. The others — I don't know. You lose touch, don't you?'

He said, 'And you, Topaz? How are you?'

'Oh, I'm just the same,' she said cheerfully. 'Still cooking. But just the same.' She thought of telling him about Will, thought of pointing out to Charlie that when, years ago, she had looked for Will in every street, train and cinema, she had not been foolish to do so. But she did not. He would have forgotten, she thought. Or he would not really be interested.

Instead, she said, 'My mother will be up soon, Charlie.' It was half-past five.

'Of course. I should go.' He crushed the cigarette stub into the ashtray. 'It's been marvellous to see you, Topaz.'

She went downstairs to the front door with him. Outside, on the steps, he paused for a moment.

'I'd love to see you again.'

She hugged her arms around herself. 'I've rather a lot on.'

'I'd like you to see my new place. Don't you remember? We always said I'd invite you to dinner when I had a nice house and we'd eat olives and things.'

Just for a moment, she thought about it. Being with Charlie again, a different Charlie who would love her and need her. And then she said, 'Dear Charlie. I don't think that would be a good idea.'

He had dug his hands into the pockets of his coat. 'You've met someone else, haven't you?'

'Yes,' she said.

'Ah.' He smiled. 'Worth a shot, though.' Then he took her hands in his and kissed her. 'I wish you every happiness, Topaz. You deserve it. Every happiness.'

He walked away into the mist.

★ ★ ★

At midday, surrounded by paperwork and with the phone ringing non-stop, Marius put on his jacket, told his secretary he was going out for the afternoon and left the office.

On the train, heading towards London, he still felt surprised at himself. It wasn't the sort of thing he usually did, to take an afternoon off on the spur of the moment. But there was a glorious sense of freedom; he must, he thought with a smile, play hookey more often.

He simply hadn't been able to wait. He needed to see her. He'd get to London early, surprise her. Thinking of her that morning, he had found himself making stupid mistakes, losing his train of thought halfway through a meeting. He needed to see Topaz and tell her at last how he felt about her, he thought, before Temperley's Radios folded in a morass of miscalculated figures and ill-placed orders.

He couldn't pinpoint the moment when he had fallen in love with her. Love had grown slowly, twisting around his heart like ivy. His earliest memories of her were of a plump little girl, all pigtails and two left feet, forever running to keep up with the rest of them. Then there had been the war and afterwards he had kept in touch with her, he supposed, because he had felt sorry for her. Because of her appalling mother and because of her lack of a father.

Years later, when Suzanne had died, it had been Topaz who had protected him, Topaz who had cajoled, coaxed and bullied him into beginning to live again. In the months following Suzanne's death he had often felt as though he was fighting his way out of a dark cave. If it hadn't been for Topaz, he might still be trapped there.

Everything had changed on that evening two months ago, when he had gone to her flat to give her her Christmas present. She had been holding a party; he had guessed, dazed, that there were a hundred people squashed into the small flat. He had found himself wondering — a cold flicker of doubt — whether he himself could have scraped up half that number of friends. Then, in a corner of the room, he had seen her. He had watched for a moment the hand that pawed her body, the fingers that threaded through her hair. He had felt a rage so overwhelming that he had been almost unable to breathe. Mixed with the rage had been jealousy, sexual jealousy. He had taken away with him that evening a memory of white breasts spilling from russet-brown velvet, and someone else's lips pressing against soft flesh that, against all reason, he thought of as *his*.

And he had taken away a memory of her standing in the street, shouting at him. *What I do is none of your business.* And she had been right, hadn't she? Sitting in the buffet car on the train home, grimly drinking a whisky, he had been oppressed by an awful image of himself, the meddling old friend who hadn't the wit to notice that their relationship was long out of date, burnt out. It had occurred to him that she only continued to see him because she was sorry for him. The rather dull widower, ten years her senior, an encumbrance from a stage in her life she had grown out of years ago. Because she wasn't clumsy, lonely little Topaz any more. She was a beautiful woman who was running her own successful business, who had created, out of her Kensington flat, an attractive home, and who was surrounded by friends and admirers. How arrogant he had been to believe that *she* needed *him*. She didn't. It seemed to him all too possible that she merely put up with him.

He had known for a long time that he respected and admired her. He hadn't known until then just how much he loved her. After that evening he had stood back, had not contacted her, suspecting that she might feel only relief at his absence. Over Christmas he had struggled, for Tara's sake and his mother's, to conceal his gloominess. He was thirty-three, after all, hardly a candidate for lovesick moping. Yet mope he had, in his few private moments, in the chill quiet of midwinter.

Then Carrie Chancellor had died and, coming out of Temperley's on the day of the funeral, he had caught sight of Topaz on the other side of the road. She had cycled five miles on a stolen bicycle to see him. She had said, *I'll never grow away from you, Marius.* And he had begun to hope.

At Paddington Marius hired a taxi to take him to Bayswater. It was five o'clock and they stopped and started through the rushhour traffic. At Cleveland Close, the taxi parked as Marius hunted in his pocket for change. Something made him glance across the road to the entrance to the block of flats. The front door was open; a lamp framed the couple standing on the steps.

He recognized Topaz immediately. It took him a fraction of a second longer to realize through the swirls of mist that the man kissing her was Charlie Finch.

★ ★ ★

She didn't give up hope till midnight. She sat beside the drawing-room window for hours, her face pressed against the glass, watching the pavement below. When she stood up, her limbs were stiff, hard to unfold. She drew the curtains, blotting out the empty street. In the hall, the telephone, which had not rung all evening, crouched, a black toad. She could have phoned Missencourt, she supposed, but she did not.

In the morning she rose early and put on her green wool frock and a warm coat. She was travelling to Dorset for Will's welcome home party. If it hadn't been for Will, she would have made some excuse, feigned illness, invented an appointment to avoid the occasion. She imagined meeting Marius at the party and making polite small talk. She imagined pretending not to mind that he had forgotten their date. Hiding from him just how brutally his forgetfulness had brought home her limited importance to him.

The train was late and, arriving at Longridge Halt, there wasn't a taxi in sight, so she walked the mile to the School House. Snowdrops and aconites clustered beneath the trees, the first signs of spring. Spots of rain fell from an unforgiving sky. When she reached the School House the party was already in full swing,

535

Chancellors bursting out from rooms into corridors, arguments and conversations bawled over the music of a gramophone.

Prudence was in the kitchen, hurling sandwiches on to plates. So nice of Dorothy Blanchard, Prudence said, hugging Topaz, to sit with Veronica so that she could come. So kind of Topaz to travel all this way. So glorious — and Prudence's eyes shone; she looked, Topaz thought, ten years younger — that Will had come home. And, no, she didn't think the Temperleys were here yet. Julia wasn't coming — Prudence quite understood that Julia would find the occasion awkward — but Marius and Adele and Tara should be here any moment. And — a smell of burning — she had forgotten the cheese straws . . .

Leaving the kitchen, Topaz walked through the crowded rooms. Jack and Will's cousins, aunts and uncles jostled against each other, reminiscing, or bawling with laughter at anecdotes many times told, or raking up forgotten quarrels and restarting old rivalries. Threading through the clumps of people, she realized that she didn't feel a part of them any more. No one called out to her, no one grabbed her arm and insisted she have a drink with them. No one muttered confidences to her, no one spilled secrets, exchanged gossip, upbraided her for imagined slights.

She had never, she thought dully, really belonged to them. She had existed only on the periphery, always an outsider, looking enviously on at the warmth and busyness and lack of loneliness that large families took for granted. She had been tolerated rather than eagerly accepted. She was never first, always an afterthought. *And we must ask Topaz*, she imagined the Chancellors saying, as they planned their parties, as they scribbled names on a list.

A child, she had thought of them as her family. Her little bit of paradise. Something to plug the gap, to fill the vacuum. The need had all been on her side, she concluded. Without her, they had been complete.

She found Will by himself in the little bit of garden at the side of the garage. When she had finished hugging him, when she had said *Oh Will* several times, and had wept into his shoulder, she stood back and looked at him.

'Are you hiding?'

'Yes. Are you?' She nodded.

He had a plate of food; he offered it to her. 'I'd forgotten what it was like,' he said. 'All these people. I've been living on my own for ages.'

'A farm, Marius said.'

He threw her a grin. 'I live in a railway carriage at the edge of a field. Suitable, don't you think, for a travelling man?'

'Will you go back there?'

'As soon as all the fuss has died down.' He took off his glasses and polished the lenses in a gesture that sharply recalled to her the boy he had once been. 'It's funny,' he said, 'but this doesn't seem to be home any more. I mean,' he added hastily, 'it's so marvellous to see everyone, and they've all been so good to me when, really, I half-expected them to show me the door, but . . .'

'You've moved on.'

'I suppose.' He leaned back against the garage wall. She had forgotten how tall he was; she saw that he had filled out across the shoulders, that he looked stronger, fitter.

She said, 'Tell me about Philippa.'

He told her, at length, while she ate two sausage rolls and three macaroons (full of starch, she supposed, but didn't particularly care). She thought Philippa sounded a sensible, practical sort, a suitable counterweight, perhaps, for a dreamer like Will. When he had finished, he scowled, and said, 'Anyway, I've no idea whether she

537

wants anything to do with me any more, but I have to try, don't I?'

'Yes,' she said. 'You do.' She, too, had tried. But there was a moment, she thought, when you gave up, admitted defeat.

'I'll come back, though,' he said. 'Come back and see everyone.' He looked out at the dripping garden. He said slowly, 'Sometimes I think I've got off so lightly. I mean, when you think of what I did. I could have ended up in prison. *Should* have. But then, there's William. He's a smashing little boy. *My* little boy, he should have been. But he isn't really, is he? Because of what I did, I missed out on all that. Whatever happens now — however hard I try to get to know him — I can never get back the years I wasn't there, can I?'

She was peeling the icing from a fairy cake; she stared at the little ball she had rolled it into and then flicked it into a flower bed. She said, 'Prudence told me that Jack's going back to Canada next week.'

'He's decided to sell Sixfields.'

She thought of the ramshackle old building. 'Everything?'

'The house and the land. He's given the cottage to Tom Crabtree. And he's given some of the money to Dad, and he's insisting that I have some too. When I tried to refuse, I thought he was going to hit me. You know what Jack's like — he can be so bloody bossy. And it's decent of him, of course. I can't say it won't be useful. I've decided to train to be a teacher, you see. So the money will be handy.'

He offered her the plate again. She ate another fairy cake and felt slightly sick. He went on, 'I said I'd go and visit Jack in Canada when things settle down a bit. Meet the family.' He glanced at her. 'What about you? How are you, Topaz?'

She told him about the dinner parties and the buffets. And about her flat and her friends and her mother. She sensed that though he listened attentively there was now a distance between them, that his allegiances had altered.

Then he said, 'And what about — I can't remember his name — you were with him that day we met in Hernscombe — '

'Charlie?' Strange to think that she had seen Charlie only yesterday; strange to think how completely he had slipped out of her mind. 'Oh,' she said, 'we split up ages ago.'

There was a silence. Then she said, 'I was always looking for you. Every fair-haired young man. I could never quite believe you were dead, you see.' She folded her hand in his.

'You're frozen,' he said, and rubbed her cold fingers between his own. 'It's hardly the time of year for standing around in gardens, is it? Shall we go back in, face the music?'

She was shivering in her thin wool dress. 'I think I might just slip away, actually, Will.' There was that persistent sense of dislocation. She seemed to be in the wrong place, at the wrong time. She wanted to go home, even though she wasn't completely sure where home was any more.

He looked concerned. 'Are you all right?'

'Course I am.' She made herself smile. 'It's just . . . parties. And such a long journey.'

'So good of you to come.' He kissed her. 'You'd better say goodbye to Mum.'

'She won't notice.' Suddenly, it seemed urgent to be away. 'So many people. I'd rather just go.' She imagined going back inside the house, bumping into Marius in the hallway, perhaps. 'Will,' she said, 'would you do me a favour?'

She slipped out of the little side door to the front courtyard. A few moments later, Will appeared with her coat. All the way along the narrow, winding road she was afraid that she might meet Marius, driving to the School House. But she did not; only a grocer's van splashed through the puddled lane and, though she stood outside the station for a while, looking through the rain, this time he did not appear.

On the train she managed to find a compartment to herself. Time for a new start, she said to herself briskly, as she settled down with a magazine and a bar of chocolate. Like Will, she must move on. Time, perhaps, to bring to fruition the ambition that had for some time now hovered at the back of her mind. And she could manage on her own, couldn't she? After all, she had managed on her own for years.

But she couldn't seem to concentrate on the magazine, which was all about brides and babies, and she didn't want to eat the chocolate. So she put them away in her bag and sat back, watching the world rush by. And after a while she breathed on the window and wrote his name on the glass. And sat watching the letters ebb away, until there was nothing left.

★　★　★

He was late for Will's party just as, years ago, he had been late for Jack's. Tara, always fussy about her clothes, decided at the last moment that her tartan wool dress looked babyish, and insisted on changing into her pink organdie. He tried to coax her out of it — the day was chilly and damp and he didn't want her to catch cold — but saw that she was about to sink into an enormous huff, and conceded, provided she wore a cardigan. Then, of course, she wasn't able to find the right cardigan, only her bottle-green school one, which she hated and didn't go with the dress. Marius eventually unearthed the correctly pink cardigan. Then they went downstairs and the moment he saw his mother he knew, though she at first denied it, that she had one of the headaches she nowadays suffered from frequently, headaches which the doctor didn't seem to be able to do anything about, and which reduced poor Adele to immobile, white-faced nausea. So he made her a cup of tea and found her some aspirins and waited while she gathered her breath and was able to face the journey. Then he drove them slowly and carefully (these days he always drove slowly and carefully) to the School House.

Only to discover that Topaz had been and gone. Stayed just half an hour and then slipped away while no one was looking. Couldn't wait to get back to that bloody actor, he thought savagely.

★ ★ ★

He brooded. He wasn't normally a brooder, but now the same dark thoughts pounded repetitively through his head. How could she? How could she throw herself away on a man who didn't in the least deserve her? A man who had never properly appreciated her, who had never been there for her when she needed him, who had dumped her for some empty-headed film star. Who had hurt her; and who, returning to England, seemed to have snapped his fingers, expecting her to come running. Just the thought of it made his blood boil.

At the office on Monday he was short with his secretary for sending a couple of letters late, and he bit his foreman's head off for some other minor error. He noticed, after a while, that his secretary's eyes were red-rimmed and that all the technicians fell silent when he came into the workshop. Disliking himself, he went to the cloakroom, where he splashed cold water on his face. Back in the office he sat for a while, drumming his fingers on the desk. Then he grabbed his coat and went outside.

He'd put up a fight, he decided, as he drove to the railway station. He didn't have to stand aside and watch her throw herself away. He'd point out to her that there were, at least, choices.

It was six o'clock by the time he reached Cleveland Close. Veronica answered the doorbell. He followed her up to the drawing room.

'My arm's a little bit better now,' she said. 'Such a wretched nuisance — and one feels so *useless*.'

He muttered sympathy and apologies for disturbing her. 'Is Topaz in?'

Veronica shook her head. 'You must have a drink with me, Marius. I insist. So miserable for me, here on my own.'

It seemed impolite to refuse. At the sideboard Veronica struggled with the stopper on the gin bottle, so he said, 'Let me,' and took it from her, and poured out two measures.

'A teensy bit more,' she said. 'I like a man who mixes a decent drink.' She was, he knew, rather drunk.

'Topaz — ' he said, but Veronica was peering into the ice bucket.

'All gone. Fetch some more, would you, darling? It's in the fridge.'

He fetched the ice cubes from the kitchen. '*Lovely*.' She beamed at him. He noticed that her lipstick did not quite match her mouth. 'Such a treat,' she said. 'A nice drink and a handsome man to chat to.'

'I can't stay long,' he said quickly.

'You're not going to dash off and leave me on my own, are you, Marius?' She looked up at him through her eyelashes. She patted the sofa beside her. 'You must tell me all the news.'

Sitting down, he said again, 'I was hoping to see Topaz.'

'She's not here. She's gone back to her flat. So I'm on my own again. Well, Dorothy Blanchard visited, but one can hardly call her *company*.' Veronica looked peevish. 'Young girls can be so *moody*, can't they? Topaz was so cross yesterday. Cross with *me*. With her *mother*. So I told her I could manage perfectly well without her.' She finished her drink and set down the glass heavily on a side table. 'Anyway,' she said with a bright smile, 'let's not talk about *her*. How are *you*, Marius, that's what I want to know. How are *you*?' She put her hand on his knee and leaned forward, her blurred blue gaze struggling to focus on him.

'I'm very well.'

'*Good*. Because I thought you might be lonely. I know what it's like, of course, to lose your better half.'

He said, 'I really must go.' And, taking her hand, gently but firmly moved it away.

She pouted. 'Always in such a rush. Just like Topaz. I told her I didn't want her here if she was going to be bad-tempered. *So* ungracious. I said that if she couldn't be good-humoured, then she might as well go. A sweet temper is so important in a woman, isn't it? I said — '

The monologue continued, but Marius was no longer listening. He stood up.

'You're not going, are you?' She looked both surprised and put out.

At the door, he paused. 'The trouble with you, Veronica,' he said calmly, 'is that you don't know how lucky you are. You have a lovely daughter who has always been loyal to you. God knows why, because you're the most vain and selfish person I have ever had the misfortune to meet. In all the time I've known you, I can't remember you once putting Topaz's needs before your own. I don't expect you have ever listened to her when she was unhappy or rejoiced with her when things went well for her. You don't know the meaning of the word *love*. And if Topaz ends up throwing herself away on a man who doesn't deserve her, then it's you who must take the bulk of the blame.'

Veronica's mouth was a round O of astonishment. Marius left the flat.

Topaz sat at the kitchen table, her notebooks, pens and a copy of the *Evening Standard* spread out around her. She had spent the previous day cleaning her kitchen, scrubbing the floor, polishing the copper pans until they shone. In her absence a film of dust seemed to have settled on the room. That morning she had gone to Soho, where she had bought garlic, herbs, lemons and spices. Their scents perfumed the air, reminding her of warmer countries. Perhaps this year, she thought, she would visit North Africa. She would learn to make kebabs and pilaffs. She wrote it on her list and underlined it. *Travel.* And tried not to think how much nicer it would be to visit places with someone you liked, someone who wanted to see the world with you.

The doorbell rang. When she opened the door, there he was, Marius Temperley, as if she had conjured him up with her imaginings of deserts and souks.

She said lightly, 'You're three days late.'

'Can I come in?'

'I'm rather busy, Marius.'

'Just a few minutes.' There was a steely, determined look in his eye that made her realize it was probably pointless arguing.

He followed her into the kitchen. He glanced at the things on the table. 'What are you doing?'

'I'm thinking', she said, 'of running a restaurant. My own restaurant, I mean, not someone else's. I was trying to work out how much money I would need.'

He nodded. Then he said, 'I didn't *forget* about Friday. I came to London. I was earlier than I expected. I saw you with Charlie.'

'*Oh.*' She remembered Charlie, kissing her on the doorstep. She felt herself go pink and said quickly, 'It wasn't — '

He interrupted her. 'He's not good enough for you,

544

Topaz. He'll let you down again.'

'Marius — '

He silenced her with an impatient gesture. 'I know what you're thinking — here I am again, telling you what to do. Well, I suppose I am, but not because I think it's somehow my God-given right to order you around. It's because I care about you. And it's because I don't want to see you hurt again.'

She said, 'I told Charlie I didn't want to see him any more.' It was Marius's turn to look confused. 'I told him it was over between us. It was over years ago, of course.'

He was leaning against the dresser, looking at her. He said slowly, 'I thought that was why you left the Chancellors' party early. Because you wanted to get back to Charlie.'

She shook her head. 'I left the party because I didn't feel I belonged there any more.' The bleak, sad feeling of her afternoon at the School House lingered. 'It's all changed, hasn't it? Julia's living in London and Jack's going back to Canada. Even Will means to go away again, he told me so. I felt so alone. And I've been thinking what an idiot I am, always hoping things will stay the same, always hoping we'll all be together again — but those days are over, aren't they?'

He said, gently, 'Topaz — ' but she went on, 'And as for you — you have Tara. And you'll always love Suzanne, won't you, Marius? I do understand that. I do understand completely.'

She stared down at her list, blinking back the tears. The words blurred. *Restaurant*, she had written. *Travel. Decorate bedroom. Darn stockings.* There seemed something empty and pathetic about this scribbled summing up of the rest of her life.

He began to speak, but she said quickly, 'You and Julia — ' her voice shook slightly ' — you were always Jack and Will's friends, weren't you? I just *borrowed* you, didn't I? And I'm tired of that. I'd like something to belong to *me*. I'm tired of borrowing what belongs to other people.'

He frowned. Then he said, 'Then how about something a little more permanent? If you're sick of borrowing other people's families.'

She sniffed, trying to focus on him. 'What do you mean?'

He sat down beside her. 'Where were you hoping to open your restaurant?'

Dear, kind Marius, she thought. *He is going to offer to do the bookkeeping, or to help choose the premises.*

'London, I thought.'

He took her hand in his. 'Does it have to be London?'

'Perhaps not. Why?'

'Could it be in Dorset, for instance?'

'Marius,' she said, 'I don't know what on *earth* you're talking about.'

He took her hand to his mouth and pressed his lips against her palm. He said, 'You're not alone, Topaz. There's Tara and Adele. And there's me.'

She tried to smile. 'We're friends again, then?'

'Not *friends*,' he said.

'Oh.' The dull, heavy feeling returned.

'I wondered', he said, and she noticed that he sounded untypically hesitant, 'whether you'd think of marrying me, Topaz.'

Her heart seemed to pause. Before she could speak, he added, 'I'd quite understand if you weren't keen. What you said about Suzanne is true — I shall always love her. But that doesn't stop me loving you, Topaz. But then I've a child, of course. And there's Adele. If you married me, then you'd be taking on a ready-made family. You may not want that.'

The world seemed to have turned, shifting from misery to joy in a spectacular instant. She whispered, '*Marry* you? You'd like me to *marry* you?'

'Yes, I would. Very much. In fact, I can't think of

anything I want more.' He kissed the pale skin on the inside of her wrist. 'I've taken you by surprise, haven't I? I suppose it's a bit sudden — falling out with you one day and proposing the next. And I haven't even kissed you properly yet. Though that would be easy to put right.' He glanced at the newspapers and notebooks on the table, and grinned. 'Hernscombe could do with a decent restaurant, you know. You'd be up against the Copper Kettle, of course. But I'd think you'd win hands down.'

Her heart was battering against her ribs. But she said, 'I'm not planning to serve corned beef sandwiches or gristly stew.'

'The Copper Kettle's speciality.' Looping back her hair carefully with his hand, he kissed the hollow of her throat.

'Something more sophisticated — quiches and *coq au vin* — '

'Hernscombe won't know what's hit it.' Another kiss. 'There'll be riots.'

His lips touched hers. She closed her eyes. Odd, she thought, how everything could suddenly seem all right — well, not just all right, *perfect* — just because Marius Temperley was holding her.

'So what do you think?' he said.

'Yes,' she whispered, and kissed him. 'Oh yes.'

'*Oh,*' he said suddenly.

She opened her eyes. 'What is it?'

'I've thought of another problem.'

'What's that?'

'I've just been extremely rude to your mother. She may not forgive me.'

'Oh, *Marius.*'

'Oh, *Topaz,*' in a rather different tone of voice from the one in which people usually said, *Oh, Topaz.*

And then he began to kiss her again.

We do hope that you have enjoyed reading
this large print book.

Did you know that all of our titles
are available for purchase?

We publish a wide range of high quality
large print books including:
Romances, Mysteries, Classics
General Fiction
Non Fiction and Westerns

Special interest titles available in
large print are:
The Little Oxford Dictionary
Music Book
Song Book
Hymn Book
Service Book

Also available from us courtesy of Oxford
University Press:
Young Readers' Dictionary
(large print edition)
Young Readers' Thesaurus
(large print edition)

For further information or a free
brochure, please contact us at:
Ulverscroft Large Print Books Ltd.,
The Green, Bradgate Road, Anstey,
Leicester, LE7 7FU, England.
Tel: (00 44) 0116 236 4325
Fax: (00 44) 0116 234 0205

COLDITZ: THE GERMAN STORY

Reinhold Eggers

This is the story of the famous German prison camp Colditz — as the German guards saw it. It was a place where every man felt that in spite of the personal tragedy of imprisonment, it was his duty to overcome. The book vividly describes the constant battle of wits between guards and prisoners, the tunnelling, bribery, impersonations, forgery and trickery of all kinds by which brave men sought to return to the war.

CHARLOTTE GRAY

Sebastian Faulks

It is 1942. London is blacked out, but France is under a greater darkness, as the Vichy regime clings ever closer to the Nazi occupier. From Edinburgh, Charlotte Gray, a volatile but determined young woman, travels south. In London she conceives a dangerous passion for an English airman. Charlotte goes to France on an errand for a British organisation helping the Resistance, and for her own private purposes. Unknown to her, she is also being manipulated by people with no regard for her safety. As the weeks go by, Charlotte finds that the struggle for France's soul is intimately linked to her battle to take control of her own life.

AS TIME GOES BY

Michael Walsh

The World's most romantic film ends on the tarmac of Casablanca, but it is where this novel begins . . . What happens to Ilsa Lund and Victor Laszlo? Did they make it to America? Do Rick Blaine and Louis join the Free French garrison in Brazzaville? How did Louis end up in Casablanca? What secrets prevent Rick from returning to the States? And most of all, will Rick and Ilsa ever see each other again? Here, filled with wartime adventure and intrigue, daring courage and timeless romance, the story of the men and women who made CASA-BLANCA so unforgettable is continued.